T0028926

DANGEROUS PURSUITS

LEAH NASH MYSTERIES BOOK 7

SUSAN HUNTER

SEVERN 🜛 RIVER

PUBLISHING

Severn River Publishing
www.SevernRiverBooks.com

ISBN: 978-1-64875-459-3 (Paperback)

ALSO BY SUSAN HUNTER

Leah Nash Mysteries

Dangerous Habits

Dangerous Mistakes

Dangerous Places

Dangerous Secrets

Dangerous Flaws

Dangerous Ground

Dangerous Pursuits

Dangerous Waters

Dangerous Deception

Dangerous Choices

To find out more about Susan Hunter and her books, visit

severnriverbooks.com/authors/susan-hunter

In memory of Mary Ellen Hunter McKinney
A woman of heart and mind

PROLOGUE

Jancee smiles flirtatiously at the man as she flips her long hair over one shoulder and settles back in the seat. She doesn't bother with the seatbelt; she never does. It just messes up her clothes, and her short dress is already riding up her thighs. Of course, she probably should give him a little more to look at. After all, it's their last time together.

Jancee is young, and blonde, and pretty. She has a little talent for dancing, and a big talent for attracting men. So far, it's been enough to get her by. But she has plans. Big plans that she's ready to make happen.

She smiles at him again as she repositions herself. He doesn't return the smile. Inwardly she shrugs. Oh well, maybe in his situation, she wouldn't either. Fine, then, she'll just sit back and think about her future, which looks very bright tonight.

No more dancing at Tanner's. Krystal, the owner, can call it a "Gentlemen's Club," but it's really just a dive for hick-town regulars, half-drunk hunters, and grabby old men. They're mostly so cheap that some shifts she barely makes enough to pay the house fee for her time on stage, let alone the tip-out fees to the DJ, the bartender, the wait staff, the bouncer.

She could get better shifts if she kissed up to Krystal like some of the girls do. But Jancee doesn't kiss up to anybody; that's what her mother taught her. She's got her own thing going, scores her own private party jobs like the one tonight. If

Krystal knew, she'd ban her from the club. But who cares now? Her side hustle is about to pay off big.

"It's cold," she says, shivering in her red halter-top dress. "Can I turn up the heater?"

He doesn't answer, but he takes his hand off the wheel long enough to move the temperature higher.

She tries again. "Today's my mom's birthday. 10/13. Thirteen's my lucky number."

He doesn't respond.

She smiles to herself and touches the small fairy tattoo on her left shoulder. Her mother is looking out for her tonight all right. She wants to say to him, "Get over yourself. This time, I win, that's all."

Jancee's hard, but she's not mean. She's just taking care of herself, like she'd promised her mom she would.

"Jancee, you got to be tough. When I'm gone, you got nobody but you."

Jancee had cried then, the last time she ever did. Her mother had taken Jancee's face in her hands.

"You're my little Aquarius baby. My airy-fairy girl. I don't want to die, honey, but I got no choice. It's a tough world, Jancee. You got to fight. You got to take care of yourself. I know you can. Promise me you will."

Through all the foster homes, the runaway shelters, the survival sex, that's what Jancee had tried to do. That's what she's doing right now. Tonight, she's done with Tanner's. Tomorrow, she'll be in Chicago.

"You gotta come down, Jancee, you got the looks, you got the moves. They got a whole different class of guys here. Rich guys. Big spenders, not like at Tanner's. I cleared twelve hundred dollars one night." That's what her girl Fauna had said.

But Jancee wasn't ready, not then. She had learned the hard way what happens if you don't have the money to set yourself up. Nope. She wouldn't leave Tanner's without a nice stash of ready cash. But this is the last time she'll have to go home to the run-down cabin she rents at Tanner's. When she gets to Chicago, she'll find a real nice place to live, maybe even with a doorman—in uniform! She'll have the money. She can class herself up, get a makeover, some new clothes. Then, look out, Chicago.

Thinking about it, she laughs out loud—a clear, frothy sound, like a brook splashing lightly over stones.

"What's so funny?" he asks.

"Nothing," she says. Happiness is making her feel generous. Maybe she'll give him something extra as a going away present, a bonus. She leans forward to turn on the radio. As she does, she brushes her hand suggestively on his leg.

"No." His voice is harsh as he pushes her hand roughly away.

She looks at him in surprise.

"What's wrong?"

A small flutter of apprehension radiates through her body as she sits back against the seat. In Jancee's line of work, you always have to be careful. You have to pay attention. You can't trust anybody. She's not afraid—yet. He's a little uptight, a little tense, but relieving tension is her specialty.

"Hey, we're good, right? It's not personal, okay?" She makes her tone playful and light.

He turns and stares at her with hard eyes and lips set in a straight line. Her flutter of alarm ramps up to full-on fear. She tries to keep it out of her voice.

She picks up her phone, says casually, "You know what? Maybe this isn't such a good idea right now. We're both tired. I'm just going to call for a ride. You go home, I'll go home, and we'll meet up tomorrow."

In one swift move he tears the phone from her grip so forcefully her hand flies back and hits the dashboard. Hard. For a second her anger outpaces her fear. Recklessly, she retaliates and strikes him sharply across the face.

He recoils and howls in pain. She reaches for the door handle behind her and tumbles out. Without a plan she takes off running. The moon and the stars show her a way, across a field of cornstalks to the woods on the other side. If she can reach it, she can hide until she's safe. She has a head start, and fear fuels her run. But soon her advantage is undone by the uneven ground and the stiletto heels she wears. She can sense him closing in on her. She turns to look over her shoulder.

As she does, her foot catches in a hole. She's thrown to the ground. Pain shoots through her ankle, but it's no match for the panic racing through her whole body. With frenzied fingers she tears off her shoes, flinging them aside. She scrambles up and hurtles forward, ignoring the rocky ground lacerating her feet. Her breath comes in short, ragged bursts from her burning lungs. Tears born of terror stream down her face. Every cell in her body is focused on reaching the safety of the dark forest ahead.

"Stop!" *His voice is only yards behind her.* "Jancee, I'm sorry. I just want to talk to you!"

She doesn't heed his words, her fear pulsating in time to the heavy thud, thud, thud of his fast approaching feet. Closer and closer. But the line of trees is coming closer, too. She's going to make it. With a final burst of speed, her bare feet skim the ground as she sprints toward the woods. Once inside that shadowy shelter, she'll be safe. Just a few more yards, a few feet, another step—

Abruptly, her body is lifted from the ground as he grabs her from behind. She twists and struggles, flailing out, but his grip on her waist is strong. He moves his other arm in, catching her neck in the crook of his elbow. Desperate, she writhes and twists like a feral cat caught. Then like a feral cat, she bites. Her teeth clamp down fiercely on the tender part of his hand, between the forefinger and thumb. She can taste blood in her mouth as he roars and flings her away.

She dashes toward the woods once again. But his rage is too great, his need to stop her too strong. He lunges forward, clutching at, then grasping the leather strap of her cross-body bag. He yanks her back toward himself. Again she struggles. The strap of the purse bites into her neck as he pulls it tighter. She claws at it. She can't breathe. She hears his shuddering gasps as he chokes the life out of her. Please, please, please, she prays to a God she doesn't believe in.

Her eyelids flutter. A voice from long ago whispers softly in her heart. You're my airy-fairy girl, Jancee. *Her muscles relax. Her fear is gone. She's a little girl, sitting on her mother's lap, looking up at the stars.* That's your sign, *her mother says, pointing to a constellation high overhead. Jancee's eyes open to the night sky. It's there now. Aquarius. Her eyes close, and life leaves her body with one last breath, as soft and light as a cloud passing over the moon.*

1

The afternoon was perfect for a drive in the country—blue sky, bright sun, crisp fall air, gorgeous colors on the trees, little roadside stands selling pumpkins for Halloween. It was the quintessential Wisconsin October day. Which is why I'd offered to drive Miguel Santos to his interview with a local farmer. Miguel is both my friend and my favorite reporter at the *Himmel Times Weekly*. I co-own the paper in our small town with my business partner, Miller Caldwell.

I waited by the car while Miguel got some pictures in the farmer's field to run with his story. As soon as he finished, we would be headed to the Eldorado Grill in Madison for dinner.

I shivered a little as a breeze raised goosebumps on my arms, and my stomach began to growl.

"Good grief, Miguel, how long does it take to get a picture of corn? I'm starving!"

"Chill, *chica*," he called back, breaking through a row of cornstalks with the slow-mo walk of an action movie hero. But instead of a gun, his hands held something red that sparkled in the sun.

Miguel is a mother's dream match for her child, if said child happens to be an adult gay male. He's tall and lean, with dark brown eyes that look out on the world with joyful anticipation. His hair is dark and shiny, expertly cut and styled, and his clothes are always on point. At the moment he looked like the cover of a men's fashion magazine in olive green chinos, an oat-colored Henley T-shirt, and well-polished brown lace-up boots. Just FYI, I was wearing jeans, trainers, and a red Badgers T-shirt. But it was a new one.

"Look what I found in Mr. Pearson's cornfield!"

As he approached he thrust his right hand out toward me. Dangling from his fingers by the straps was a pair of glittery red high-heeled shoes.

I shook my head.

"If you're an envoy from Prince Charming, let me save you some time. I'm not Cinderella. Don't even bother to ask me to try them on. I can tell just by looking that those are not going to fit on my size nine feet. How did you find them?"

"I wanted to frame a 'harvest end' shot to go with the story. I backed up to get the right angle, and then, boom! I tripped right over one shoe. Then I saw the other one just a little way off. What do you think they were doing in the middle of a cornfield?"

"They don't look like they've been there that long." I took them from his hand and turned them over for a close-up examination. "They're dry and they're not all that dirty. Maybe King Harvest was dancing in the moonlight, and things got a little crazy."

His look told me that my reference to King Harvest had missed its mark. I wouldn't know it either, if my mother hadn't indoctrinated me with her 70s music immersion program when I was a kid.

"Be nice to me, or I'll tell my mother that you don't know who King Harvest is, and that you never heard of 'Dancing in the Moonlight.' Then, watch out. She'll probably make a mix tape for you."

"I would love that."

I laughed, because that was no doubt true.

"Yes, I'm sure you would. But now, can we please move on from the Queen of the Cornfield mystery? There's a plate of grilled enchiladas stuffed with lobster and crab waiting for me at the Eldorado."

I got into the driver's seat and tossed the shoes in the back.

"What are you going to do with them?" he asked, buckling his seatbelt.

"I'll run them over to St. Vinny's. They're not Manolo Blahnik, but I'm sure someone would like them. They're basically new." I had tossed off the designer shoe name casually, as though I were an expert on fine footwear.

Miguel gave me some side-eye. "I would like to think that you are learning, but I know you don't listen when I talk fashion shoes to you. Don't toy with me."

"I do so listen. I remembered the name, didn't I? You know, you could get a few fashion shopping tips from me, too. Tell me this, are you a DSW VIP member?" I asked, referring to the ubiquitous discount shoe store. "Do you get those sweet, sweet perks? Do you get a five-dollar reward on your birthday? I think not. We just move in different fashion worlds, that's all, but you have to admit, mine has its own rewards."

"Someday, *chica*, someday I'll lure you to mine. Meanwhile, it's good for you to take the shoes to St. Vinny's. Everybody should be able to get some sparkle in their life."

It was Miguel's turn to choose the playlist as we drove to Madison. Lady Gaga, Daddy Yankee, Dolly Parton, and Prince accompanied us on this trip.

"So, how are you doing with Maggie out for a couple weeks?" I asked after a while.

No answer. I glanced over and saw that he was lost in his car dance moves to the insistent beat of "Shaky Shaky."

"Hey! Can you turn that music down?" I raised my voice to be heard, feeling a little like somebody's grandma. Miguel is twenty-three, only about ten years younger than me, but sometimes it feels like ten *long* years.

"Sorry. I just got to move, move, move when Daddy Yankee's on." He grinned and did a quick demonstration.

"Okay, okay, never mind. You dance, I'll think, and we'll talk over dinner. Just put in your ear thingies, please," I added.

As he did, I turned my mind back to the question I'd just asked him. Maggie McConnell is the managing editor at the *Himmel Times*. Neither I nor my business partner Miller is supposed to have much to do with day-to-day operations. Miller is a lawyer, not a journalist, and he has no problem staying out of things. But it's harder for me. I spent years as a reporter, and even now I'm still a journalist. However, my focus is writing true crime books, not daily copy.

At the moment, it was legit for me to mix in newsroom business, because Maggie was out of the office, recovering from minor surgery. Miguel had to take care of her work, plus cover his regular beats. He hadn't complained. He never does. But he only had Troy Patterson, a pretty inexperienced reporter, and a handful of not-always-available stringers to put out the paper. It worried me a little. As always, *GO News*, our digital-only competition, was breathing down our necks.

Wait. I probably should back up just a bit. My name is Leah Nash, and why I own a struggling newspaper is a long story. I'll make it short.

The *Himmel Times Weekly,* in my hometown of Himmel, Wisconsin, is where I started as a reporter more than a decade ago. It's also where I landed after my career with a paper in Miami took a nosedive. Although I'd expected my stopgap gig in Himmel to be pretty routine, it turned out to be anything but. I uncovered a story that went national and wrote a book about it. The book did pretty well, and I left the paper to write more books. Then, when the *Himmel Times* was on the verge of closing last year, I took all the money I had in the bank, and convinced Miller Caldwell, a local attorney with a lot more cash than me, that he should invest with me in saving the paper. Lots of things had happened in the intervening months— my second book tanked, my publisher ditched me, the paper began losing ground to *GO News*, my book agent found me a new publisher, things began looking up, my best friend Coop quit his job, then decided to run for sheriff. You know, life stuff.

At the moment, I was trying to support Coop in his campaign for sheriff, complete the manuscript I owed my new publisher, and keep *GO News* from gaining on us. I wasn't doing super-great at any of those things.

2

"I love the Eldorado, but why did you use your gift card on me instead of Gabe?" Miguel asked. The waiter at one of the best restaurants in Madison had just delivered our drinks—a Honey Ginger Margarita for me, a Pineapple Basil Mojito for Miguel—and taken our entree orders.

The Eldorado manages to be spacious and cozy at the same time, with lots of wood and leather, exposed brick, polished wood floors, and whimsical cowboy and bucking bronco silhouettes.

"Hey, nothing but the best for you, my friend. Did you notice that I sprang for the extra $2.99 for chips and salsa? When you're with me, it's class all the way," I said, dipping a chip into the perfectly seasoned salsa. "Also, my gift card runs out tomorrow and Gabe texted last night that he won't be back until Saturday."

Gabe Hoffman is an attorney in town who is my partner in romance and occasionally crime. For me, the crime part is easier to handle than the romance.

"What's he doing?"

"He went to see a friend who needs help. Someone back in New York. It must be some kind of legal tangle, because he couldn't tell me much. And then he plans to see some people he used to work with when he was with the district attorney's office. I've got Barnacle at my place for a few days, by the way, so if you want to get in some quality time with him, feel free to come upstairs and get him for a walk."

My loft apartment is on the top floor of a renovated downtown Himmel building. The *Himmel Times* office is on the ground floor, which makes it pretty convenient—at times, too convenient.

"Who's covering the League of Women Voters candidate night tomorrow?" I asked.

"Me. Troy has the school board meeting."

"Is anyone doing a follow-up on that fatality on Roosevelt Road last night?"

"Troy is."

"Do you have anyone on the zoning meeting in Omico? The fight over a variance to build condos in a single-family neighborhood is really heating up."

"No stringers available, so I'll do a follow-up phone call with the committee chair."

I shook my head.

"Someone really should be there if we want to stay on top of things. I can pick it up for you."

He looked at me, surprised.

"But don't you want to be at the candidate night, *chica*? It's going to be a big one. Coop and Sheriff Lamey on stage together, the first time. I could do the zoning and you could cover the candidates."

"*Acting* Sheriff Lamey, you mean. Sure, I'd like to watch Coop decimate Lamey, but I couldn't report on it. It's one thing for the editorial board of the *Times* to endorse Coop's run for county sheriff. It's another for me to do the write-up of candidate night."

David Cooper, Coop to everyone but his mother, has been my best friend for more than twenty years. He was also the smartest cop in the Himmel Police Department, until he quit in disgust a few months ago. I was a thousand percent behind his run to defeat the incompetent and quite possibly corrupt acting sheriff, Art Lamey.

"Oh. *GO News*," Miguel said, picking up on my point immediately.

"Right. Spencer would have a field day with that." Spencer Karr is the publisher of *GO News*. He, Coop, and I went to high school together. We weren't friends.

"I feel bad—"

"Don't. You're doing a great job balancing things with Maggie out. We just don't have a very deep bench for you to pull from. Not enough stringers, for one thing. And then there's Troy."

"He picked up the fatality last night and he did fine. Yes, he did mix up the name of the Hailwell Homecoming King, but that's not so very bad."

"It's not the only thing he didn't get right, Miguel. What about the cutline that identified Gloria Busboom as chair of the county Democratic Party, only, oh-oh, she's the Republican chair. I had to spend twenty minutes convincing her not to cancel her half-page ad for Busboom Heating and Plumbing."

"Okay, yes, that wasn't good. But Troy is trying hard. You can make mistakes when you try too hard," Miguel said.

"I guess you could be right."

"I am right. Also, you scare him a little."

"I scare him? How do I do that?"

Miguel laughed.

"*Chica,* you scare *me,* sometimes. You are so sure, and you say it so strong. Sometimes it can be ..." He paused for a moment, cocking his head and holding his thumb and forefinger a quarter inch apart. "Just a *little* intimidating."

It always surprises me a bit when someone thinks I'm sure of things, although I try hard to project that image. The truth is, most of the time I feel like I'm working over my head. I just don't let very many people know it. I feel safer that way.

"You're making me sound kind of obnoxious, Miguel. If I'm so bad, why do you hang with me?"

"You're not obnoxious. Obstinate, yes. But not obnoxious. I hang with you because you're funny, and smart, and I love you, *chica.*"

"Thanks, I love you, too. And maybe you're just a tiny bit right. I'll try to lighten up around Troy. I guess he can't help it if he's not you. But I need him to kick it into gear. We can't afford to lose regular advertisers like Gloria Busboom. *Ask Miguel* is picking up steam—and subscribers—but we still need those ads."

Miguel's *Ask Miguel* column in the *Himmel Times* started a few months ago. It's his take on an old-school advice column. He happily dispenses fashion tips, dating advice, and general life coaching—all areas in which he feels extremely at ease. We started the column as counterprogramming to *Tea to GO,* a collection of mostly blind, often vicious items featured in *GO News.* Unfortunately that kind of "news" appeals to the *schadenfreude* in all of us, and it's still very popular.

The waiter brought our entrees then, and we settled down to more general conversation. Miguel told a long and very funny story about one of his million cousins, most of whom live in Milwaukee. Laughing as he finished, I looked up and locked eyes with someone at the table across the room. I stopped laughing.

"What?" Miguel asked, and then turned, his gaze following mine. There, sipping on a cocktail, was Andrea Novak, one-time *Himmel Times* employee, currently the lead viper at *GO News.* As I gave a slight nod, she smiled and quickly withdrew the hand that had been resting on the arm of the current acting sheriff of Grantland County, Art Lamey.

Miguel reached out to restrain me, but I had already jumped up. I strode across the crowded restaurant, a wide and fake smile on my face. This was going to be good.

"Acting Sheriff Lamey, hello!"

He hates it when I call him that, so I make it a point to do it whenever I can.

"And Andrea! So nice to run into you."

I turned back to Lamey.

"Is your wife here, too? I want to thank her for that wonderful letter to the editor last week. We may not agree, but I always appreciate subscriber engagement." My voice was honeyed and my eyes bright as I looked around the table, which was quite obviously set up for two, not three.

Lamey's toad-like small head flushed an unbecoming red from his neck to the tips of his ears, more from anger than embarrassment, I was sure. Unperturbed, Andrea resumed a more upright sitting position than the one that had given Lamey an unobstructed view down the front of her scoop-neck black sweater. She answered instead of him.

"Hello, Leah. I'd invite you to join us, but I'm doing an in-depth interview with the sheriff for a profile in *GO News* this week."

"A profile, oh, I see. Nice. I'll look forward to reading it." I turned to Lamey. "Acting Sheriff, I'm so glad to see that your calendar has opened up. I hope that means you'll have time to sit down with our reporter soon. So far, you've turned down every request we've made to you."

"Why would I sit down with you? Your paper is supporting David Cooper."

His anger had slightly increased the high pitch of his odd, rather whistling voice, so that his answer sounded like the trailing notes of a badly played flute.

"Well, maybe if you had come in for a candidate interview like he did, you could have answered for your abysmal record. Who knows, maybe your explanation would have won us over," I said.

"Ha! That's rich. As though I'd ever get a fair hearing from your fake news outfit."

"Just because you don't like what we report doesn't make it fake. Though I can see how actual journalism might be confusing to you, given the kiss-up coverage you get from *GO News*."

I had chosen the phrase "kiss-up coverage" deliberately, but Lamey was too furious at my interruption of his tête-à-tête to do more than sputter, and Andrea was too cool to be baited.

She gave a slight toss of her head, brushing a lock of long red hair over her shoulder.

"At *GO News*, we think the media should support law enforcement, not tear it down."

She gave Lamey a sweet smile, and he returned it with one of his own. Sickening.

"Yeah? Well, at the *Himmel Times* we don't think it's our job to be law enforcement's lap dog—or lap dancer, as the case may be. I'll let you two get back to your 'interview.' " I turned on my heel and left the table before she could respond.

"What did you say to them? When you were talking to him, Sheriff Lamey got as red as this hot sauce," Miguel said.

I shared the conversation with him.

"Oh, that was so savage! But Andrea, she is not going to forget that."

"Good. She's a backstabbing, unethical imitation of a journalist who uses her sexuality to get stories. I do not approve. Besides, what can she do to me, write a bad review of one of my books? She won't be the first."

He shook his head. "I don't know what she'll do, but if I know Andrea, it won't be good."

Gabe's dog Barnacle treated me to such a frantic dance when I walked in the door that I knew Courtnee had not remembered to let him out as she had promised. Courtnee Fensterman is the *Times* receptionist. I grabbed his leash, clipped it on his collar, picked up a bag for his deposits, and we zipped down the back stairs. Usually, Barnacle enjoys a leisurely circular walk as he searches for the perfect spot to relieve himself. This time, he barely contained himself until we got outside.

"Hey, buddy, I'm sorry," I said. "I should have double-checked on Courtnee and made sure you were okay. Don't worry, I'll have a word with her tomorrow."

Barnacle is a small mixed-breed dog that Gabe adopted a few months ago when his eccentric owner, who wasn't much into grooming for dogs— or people—had died. Now that he was regularly cleaned up and trimmed, it was easy to see that he had some cocker spaniel, maybe a little terrier, and an assortment of other breeds in his ancestry. He's normally quite placid, and he doesn't talk much. However, the sharp bark and disgusted look he gave my apology told me I wasn't getting off that easy.

"Look, I know, I shouldn't have asked her. And you did great, holding on that long. Next time, I promise, if I can't get Coop, I'll get my mother to do it. I suppose you're going to tattle-tale to Gabe, aren't you? How about this, we'll go for a nice long walk, and we can work things out, all right?"

I took the little body shimmy he gave me as assent, and we started off toward Coop's house. The long walk would be good for both me and Barnacle.

3

"You're out kind of late, aren't you?" Coop asked as he turned off the sander he was using in his workshop and smiled at Barnacle and me, in that order.

"Hey. Yeah, I'm trying to make up with Barnacle. He got stuck inside while Miguel and I were in Madison. Courtnee forgot about him. I told him you might have a treat here for him."

"I think that might be true," he said, bending down to give Barnacle's head a rub.

"Is that the coffee table you're building for Miguel?" I asked, pointing to an oval piece of wood that was taking shape.

He nodded.

"You know if this whole sheriff thing doesn't work out, you could seriously turn pro."

"This is how I relax. If I had to do it for a living, I don't think I'd enjoy it as much."

He'd started putting his tools away as he talked. Coop's a lot tidier than I am.

"Let's go inside. I've got a Diet Coke with your name on it."

Coop's kitchen is compact but well laid out. I pulled a chair up to the table while he got out glasses with ice and a Diet Coke for me, a regular for himself. He grabbed a doggie treat and tossed it to Barnacle before sitting down across from me.

"How was dinner?" he asked.

"The food? Great. The company? Greater. Catching Sheriff Lameass in a very cozy dinner with Andrea Novak? The greatest."

"Andrea and Art? Was anyone else there?"

"Nope. Mrs. Acting Sheriff Lamey must be out of town. Or else Lamey killed her and buried her in the basement. Coop, this just proves what I've been telling you. Andrea's got Lamey eating out of her hand. Wait, the visual I just gave myself is truly disgusting. Scratch that. But I hate that *GO News* is basically erasing you from the race. It's all-Lamey, all the time."

"I kinda prefer that to the stuff they were writing when I left the police department. They made it seem like I was fired for incompetence—without ever coming right out and saying so."

"Yeah, well, I told you, your ex-friend Captain Rob Porter is a snake. I'm sure he was the 'highly placed source in the Himmel Police Department' they quoted. He hated you being better at the job than him, and he hates that you might become sheriff now. Face it, he just hates you."

"No. He's just an insecure guy who puts his career ambitions ahead of his friendships. I didn't know that for a while. Now I do. People that know me know I was a good cop, and I can be a good sheriff."

"Well, sure, that's true. The trouble is, not enough people outside of Himmel know you. And you've got to reach voters across the whole county. As far as *GO News* is concerned, Lamey is the only viable candidate running, and you're just a wannabe after-thought. You can't ignore that they're ignoring you. You need to push back. Why don't you start talking about Lamey giving his buddy Bruce Dengler a pass when he resigned to 'spend more time with his family?' "

"I could, if I had any more than rumor to go on."

"Jen saw the report. The one the county administrator hired the fraud consultant to do on Dengler's department."

"How did Jen get hold of it?"

Jennifer Pilarski is the administrative assistant to the acting sheriff. She was also my co-conspirator in classroom shenanigans starting in kindergarten and all through school.

"When Bruce Dengler resigned, the county administrator gave the report from the fraud guy to Lamey to review it for criminal investigation. Jen got a peek at it. There was stuff in there about Dengler taking county equipment for personal use, hitting up vendors for tickets to Bucks games, directing county business to his buddies. But Lamey basically said nothing to see here, and that it didn't need a criminal investigation."

"I can't accuse Art of covering up for his buddy without seeing the evidence myself. And I can't get hold of evidence when I have no standing. I'm just an ex-cop running for office. Why don't *you* run a story in the paper?"

"Touché. Same reason you have. I haven't seen the report either. I can't use Jennifer as a source, she'd lose her job. No one in the Forestry Management department will talk on the record. Though off the record, they'd all like to see their ex-boss Dengler face some consequences." I slumped back in my chair.

"Can't you hit the county with an Open Records Act request for the report?"

"Sure. We already did. But guess who the records custodian is? Don't bother. It's Lamey's cousin. Eventually she'll have to release it. But she can drag her feet until after the election. And even then she'll redact the heck out of it. And once Lamey's elected there's no way to get rid of him without a recall."

"I know Art's a problem. That's why I'm running. I want to focus on the issues: transparency, community policing, accountability. I've got no taste for politics. I want to talk about the good I can do, not the bad that he may have done."

"I get that. But I just think you could draw a stronger contrast between the two of you. Try it at the League of Women Voters tomorrow. You don't have to accuse him of corruption—although he's definitely corrupt. But ask him where he stands on the public's right to know. Ask him what happened to the Dengler case, and why he chose to close it.

"You've got to hit him and hit him hard on candidates night. You already have the edge against him in a visual side-by-side. You're a half-foot taller and your voice doesn't sound like a reed instrument gone rogue. I'd keep Kristin in the background until you're elected, though. If they don't know you have a girlfriend, the ladies can still dream—and vote."

Kristin Norcross is an assistant district attorney Coop has been dating for a few months. I like her.

He shook his head, but I was on a roll.

"Talk more about the things you've done. The work you did on the drug task force. The Top Cop award you got. The citation for valor when you were with the Madison PD. The murder cases you've wrapped up—no need to acknowledge me as your mentor and guide," I added. He gave me some side-eye on that.

"You've got the track record, you look the part, plus you're smart, and you're ethical. I don't know why you're not running away with this race, to be honest. Even with *GO News* in Lamey's corner. You need to own your excellence," I said, borrowing a favorite phrase of Miguel's.

I was really getting wound up, thinking of all the things Coop could fire at Lamey, all the ways he could challenge the job he was doing, what a missed opportunity it would be if he stayed with his strong-silent-type lawman persona. Then I noticed the glint of laughter in his gray eyes.

"What?"

"Nothing. I'm just listening to my mentor and guide. Just listening and learning."

"All right, all right. You already thought of all those things. You already have a plan. You could have just said that."

"It seemed better to let you run down than to throw myself in front of your speeding thoughts."

"It's just that you're the best one for the job, Coop. I'm trying to have your back here."

"I know you are, and I appreciate it," he said. "But I can do this. You've got enough going on without worrying about my campaign. Besides, that's what my dad's for."

"Hey, where is Dan, anyway? It's eleven o'clock, don't you give him a curfew?"

"Usually he's in by ten, but you know him. He likes to talk. Said he was going to Omico to do some campaigning. He's been trying to get Lester to endorse me. It'd be nice, but it's a long shot. Early on, he wished me luck but said he was going to stay neutral. Kristin thinks it's because Art Lamey has something on Lester."

"Yeah? I like the way that girl thinks. Still, I doubt Sheriff Dillingham has a dark secret. I'm sure Rebecca would have uncovered it when she was digging around to discredit him last year."

As soon as I said it, I regretted it. Rebecca had been the publisher at the *Himmel Times,* my boss, and my nemesis until she was killed the year before. She had also been Coop's wife for a few months, and his obsession for longer than that. It wasn't until after she died that he'd discovered the enormity of her deceit and the lengths to which she would go in pursuit of her goals. She was still a fraught topic. I moved on quickly.

"You couldn't ask for a more connected campaign manager than your dad. And I mean connected in a good way, not a sleazy old-boys-network way. Sometimes when I'm with him, it's like he knows all sixty-five thousand people in the county. On a first-name basis."

"He pretty much does," he said as he began ticking off Dan Cooper's networks on the fingers of one hand.

"He's done construction and finish carpentry work all over the county. He volunteered at every local high school with a building trades program, so he knows kids, parents, teachers, and administrators. He was on the County Board of Supervisors for eight years. And he was chair of the Winterfest Weekend for five years running. That's a lot of networks." I like the pride in his voice when he talks about his dad.

Just as he finished, the kitchen door opened, Barnacle's tail began a happy thumping against the kitchen floor, and Coop's double walked into the room.

When I say double, I might be exaggerating a little, but not much. It's easy to mistake a photo of Dan from years ago for one of Coop today. Both he and his son are lean and fit, just over six feet. Now in his late sixties, Dan's hair is all silver now, but it used to be a brown so dark it was almost black, like Coop's. Dan's eyes are a brilliant blue, usually with a hint of laughter in them, in contrast to Coop's dark gray, steady gaze, but they both have the same strong nose. Their smiles are wide and generous, though Dan's are more frequent. Where Dan is outgoing, Coop, though friendly enough, is quieter and calmer.

"Leah, hello! You haven't been around much lately, good to see you."

Dan came over and wrapped his arm around my shoulder for a quick side hug.

"Hi yourself," I said, leaning a little into him. "I'm glad to see you, too. Things have been a little crazy lately."

I settled back in my chair as he pulled out the one next to me for himself. Coop was already at the refrigerator, getting his dad's favorite drink, a Sprecher Root Beer.

"Seems like they always are with you, young lady. How's that book coming? Last time I saw you, you said you were almost finished."

"You sound like Clinton."

Clinton Barnes is my agent, my cheerleader, and my taskmaster. He took a chance on me when no one else would, and that's something I won't forget.

"I'm working on it, but it's not quite there yet. I've been filling in here and there at the paper, because we're short-handed. Maggie McConnell is off for a few weeks."

"I heard that. She's quite a gal. We got in a serious conversation down at the Elite Café a few weeks ago. She's got some strong opinions. I like that. I got the impression she wasn't one for sitting still."

"Go with that. She was barely out of the recovery room before she was trying to convince the doctor that she could come into the office in a couple of days. Every time I drop in to see if she needs anything, she starts grilling me about what's going on at work. It's killing her not to be in the middle of everything."

"Huh. Sounds a little like someone else I know," Dan said, looking over at Coop for a corroborating smile.

"Oh, quit it, you guys. I can back off, I can delegate, I don't need to control everything," I said, listing three of my besetting sins before they did. "At the moment, I'm needed. There's only Miguel and a few stringers to carry the load. And Troy."

Dan didn't miss the after-thought quality of my Troy mention.

"Doesn't sound like you have much faith in Troy. He seems like a nice young fella. He did a good job on the candidate interview with Coop," Dan said.

"Yes, he did. It's not that I don't have faith in him, exactly. He wants to do a good job, I know. He's just pretty inexperienced. Sometimes he hangs back when he shouldn't. I'm worried he's going to miss something that really matters. Miguel says I scare him," I added in the spirit of full disclosure.

To his credit, Coop didn't say anything. But I could see it was taking a lot for him not to.

"Oh, now, I doubt that," Dan said. "It's probably more that he doesn't have the confidence he needs yet. Troy might be a little starstruck, and that makes him nervous. After all, you've got those two books behind you, and those awards you won before you came back to Himmel. I'm pretty proud to say I knew you when."

Dan has the gift of making people feel good about themselves, because it's so obvious that he feels good about them. But if I'm not great at giving compliments—and I'm definitely not—I'm even worse at receiving them.

"Thanks, but, uh, it's not as great as you make it sound. I'm a one-book wonder unless my second book takes off after republishing it. Right now I'm just putting one finger in front of the other on the keyboard and hoping I can pull off the draft for the third."

He laughed, but he was shaking his head. "You need to have as much faith in yourself as I do, isn't that right, Coop?"

"Absolutely."

"Having faith in people is your specialty, Dan. What else explains those harrowing hours you spent trying to teach me how to drive a stick shift without grinding the gears? My own mother gave up in despair. And you never yelled at me once. Unlike my mother. And your son."

"I was okay, until you tried to downshift to first at forty miles an hour," Coop said.

"True story," I said.

"Well there it is, then, Leah. You give Troy some room to maneuver, let him relax, and you just might be surprised."

"All right, I surrender, Dan. I'll try to channel you and try harder with Troy." I changed the subject then.

"Coop said you were trying to wrestle an endorsement out of Lester Dillingham tonight. How'd you do?"

"Couldn't get Lester to commit. After all, Art was his deputy. I think he figures it says enough that he's not endorsing him," Dan said. "But that's all right because I picked up a nice—a very nice—contribution to the campaign tonight. It's going to give a boost to our last few weeks."

"Yeah? From who, Dad?"

"Kent Morgan. He donated the maximum and so did his wife. Art Lamey's been flooding social media and TV with ads. Now we can get some traction there, too. And I want to see a lot more yard signs around the county. Art's only in the lead because he's got name recognition. And we're not that far behind."

"That's what I told Coop," I said. "Kent Morgan. Why is that name so familiar?"

"He's a pretty big deal in Omico. Has a financial services company, calls the football games on the radio for the high school, owns a lot of real estate. He was the Omico Citizen of the Year last year. And he's a nice guy. Real nice guy."

"Oh, yeah, yeah, that's right. I met him once when Miller and I were having dinner. They're on the hospital board or something like that together. That's great, Dan. Nicely done."

"Yes, thanks, Dad. That will help a lot."

"That's what I came down for, son. To help the best man get elected sheriff, and that's you."

4

"Smells great, Mom. What's the menu for Paul's birthday dinner?" I asked as I walked through my mother's kitchen door on Saturday night, carrying the cake I'd picked up for the celebration.

"Paul asked for Cranberry Crockpot Roast, redskin mashed potatoes, and oven-roasted green beans. It doesn't get much easier than that. One of the many reasons I keep him around," she said.

It doesn't sound that appetizing when you list the ingredients—dry onion soup mix, a can of jellied cranberry sauce, and a chuck roast, but after eight hours on low in a crockpot, the results are surprisingly good, and perfect for a cold October evening.

Paul Karr is our family dentist, my mother's long-time companion, and, unfortunately, the father of my nemesis, Spencer Karr, owner/publisher of *GO News*.

"You look nice," I said.

She was standing at the sink in her white and navy kitchen, the sleeves of the red sweater dress she wore pushed up to her elbows. My mother is small but fierce, with spiky black and silver hair, midnight blue eyes that can kill you—or comfort you—and a body kept at fighting weight through mostly daily runs.

"Thank you. I got the dress on sale at Nordstrom Rack in Milwaukee yesterday, half-off!" Her eyes were alight with triumph as she turned toward me to show it off. Shopping bargains are to my mother as scooping Spencer Karr is to me.

Her gaze took in the black leggings, ankle boots, and green tunic I was wearing. "Is that top new? I like it."

"I'll pass that on to Miguel. He picked it out for me. It's pretty sweet having the two of you as my personal shoppers. Though Miguel does sometimes go a little too fashion-forward for my comfort level."

"Leah, get real. Anything outside of jeans and hoodies pushes your comfort level. Without me and Miguel, you'd dress like an adolescent gamer all of the time, instead of just most of the time."

I considered trying to defend my fashion sense, but she was too on the mark to waste the effort.

"Can I help it if you kept the glam genes to yourself when I was conceived? But thanks for the eyelashes and the dimples. Admit it. You love me just the way I am."

At which point she broke out in song, as she is wont to do, and treated me to a stanza of "Just the Way You Are." She has a great voice, something else which I did not inherit.

She was just finishing up when the doorbell rang and the birthday boy came in to the opening bars of "Shake It Off." My mother has a wide-ranging taste in music, and a programmable digital doorbell to support it.

"Happy Birthday, Paul!" I said. His round, open face, topped by a receding hairline of sandy-colored curls, will never set a woman's pulse racing. But the kindness that shines in his brown eyes and the open affection he has for my mother are two things I find very attractive about him. He gives off a reassuring Paddington Bear aura. It was underscored at the moment by the dark brown crew-neck sweater he wore, which pulled just a bit over the little paunch he was developing, and his tan corduroys.

"Thank you, Leah—I think. It seems like I just turned fifty a couple of years ago. Now I'm sixty-three already!"

"Well, consider the alternative and it won't seem so bad," my mother said, reaching up to give him a quick kiss.

"Easy for you to say, Carol. You're ageless. And I love you. Will you marry me?"

My mother replied the same way she does to all of Paul's periodic proposals.

"Paul, I have a daughter I love, a job I enjoy, a man I cherish, and a house to myself. I don't want to jinx things. So, I'm honored to be asked, but the answer is no."

Paul smiled, like he always does, and said, "I'll keep swinging, Carol. One of these days, maybe I'll knock it out of the park. Now, what can I do to help?"

"Not a thing, it's your birthday. Give me your coat and have a seat. Would you like a drink?"

While she fussed over him and got him settled in the living room rocking chair with a bourbon on the rocks, I went back to the kitchen to finish the washing up my mother had started.

When she returned I asked, "Who all is coming?"

"Paul didn't want a big fuss. So it's you, me, Paul, Father Lindstrom, Gabe—he's still planning to come, right?"

"Yeah, his plane got in late. But he said he should still make it by six-thirty. I'm glad Father Lindstrom will be here. I haven't seen him for a while."

Father Lindstrom is the parish priest at St. Stephen's where my mother is a member, and I am not. I left organized religion a long time ago, but if every priest or minister was like him, I might be lured back. I pulled five plates out of the cupboard and set them on the counter. As I turned to the silverware drawer, I saw my mother reaching for another plate to put on the stack. I had a sinking feeling that I knew who it was for.

"Seriously?" I whispered into my mother's ear. "You invited *Spencer*?"

"Shhh. Keep your voice down, Paul will hear. Do not ruin his birthday," she whispered back in the same tone that used to precede *Leah Marie, go to your room!* when I was a kid.

I took a deep breath, nodded, and motioned her over to the far corner of the kitchen, out of sight of the living room.

"Mom, I'm sorry, I don't want to ruin Paul's birthday. But how could you invite Spencer? He's used every dirty trick in the book to thwart every positive move we've made at the *Times*. You know what an arrogant, nasty, unethical jerk he is. If he comes it will only be to make everyone—including Paul—miserable. He'll say or do something awful. He always does. If I'd known he was invited, I wouldn't have come."

I had kept my voice low and tried to inflect it with the normal rhythms of a casual conversation, not the righteous tones of a prosecutor's closing argument, so if Paul overheard the sounds, he wouldn't realize we were arguing.

My mother responded in kind, forcing a smile into her voice as she said, "That's why I didn't tell you. Spencer is Paul's son. I don't like him any more than you do, but it's Paul's birthday, we're having a party, and his son should be here. Just don't let him get under your skin, and we'll make it through the evening. Please. For Paul's sake."

Pleading is not my mother's style, but I could see in her eyes how much she wanted Paul to have a happy evening with no blow-ups between me and Spencer.

I sighed. It's always been hard for me to fathom how someone like Spencer could spring from a good man like Paul. Of course, there was his mother Marilyn in the mix. People really should be more careful about the gene pool they dip into when procreating.

Paul's ex-wife is a bitter, angry woman who spoiled her son, denigrated and derided her husband for years, and then blamed my mother for her failed marriage. The only thing Marilyn was generous with was her spite. She had blanketed me, too, with her petty meanness and vicious scorn. It was Marilyn who had bankrolled Spencer's start-up of *GO News* just as we were trying to get the *Himmel Times* back on its feet. Coincidence? I don't think so.

"All right. I promise to try. That's as far as I can go."

After all was in readiness for dinner, I poured myself a healthy shot of Jameson in preparation for the bumpy night ahead. When the doorbell rang, I answered it, glass in hand and an attempt at a cordial expression pasted on my face as I opened the door.

It soon changed to a genuine grin when I saw who was there.

"Gabe!" I gave him a quick hug and whispered, "Spencer is coming!" in his ear.

"Not exactly sweet nothings, but now I see why you're carrying such a big glass," he said with a quirk of his eyebrow.

I nodded grimly, then turned to the little man with a fluff of white hair and a sweet smile who stood next to him. "Father Lindstrom, I'm so glad to see you!"

"I'm very happy to see you, too," he said. The ankle boots I wore added a couple of inches and made me feel like I was towering over his small frame. I bent down and gave him a light kiss on the cheek.

I slipped my arm through his and led both of them to the living room, where my mother and Paul were standing in welcome.

While they exchanged greetings I set my glass down and said, "Let me take your coat, Father."

Gabe wasn't wearing one, but he helped Father Lindstrom off with his and came with me to deposit it on the bed in my old room.

"You look beautiful," Gabe said. "Did you do something different with your hair?"

"I'm far from beautiful," I said. "Maybe I look better than usual because you haven't seen me in a while. Hair is still the same, long, straight brown. Eyes, hazel but more brown than green. Features, average. However, I am styled to the max, thanks to Miguel."

"I think you look beautiful. Full stop. Take the compliment."

"All right, I will."

"So, where is he? Himmel's own William Randolph Hearst, I mean."

I immediately wrapped my arms around him and gave him my best full-focus kiss, which is pretty amazing, if I do say so myself.

"Wow. What was that for?" he asked as we drew apart.

"For being the world's best boyfriend. For knowing that reference to the original king of yellow journalism and news fabrication. Also, for understanding my deep and abiding loathing of Spencer Karr. And last but not least for looking very handsome tonight."

"Thank you. I'm trying to impress you."

"Well done, you."

Gabe has dark brown hair, a little long, and eyes such a deep brown they're almost black. He also has great eyebrows, an underrated feature in my opinion. His are straight and expressive. In a shawl-collared red sweater over gray chinos, he was way more than presentable.

"Maybe I should go away more often."

"No, you shouldn't. Barnacle doesn't like it."

"Oh. Barnacle doesn't?"

"Well, I might enjoy having you around a little myself."

"Stop, please. I can't take this over-the-top emotion," he said.

"Shut up. Come on, let's enjoy what little time we have before Spencer gets here."

As seven o'clock arrived and Spencer Karr hadn't, I began to relax and feel a little happier. Maybe he wouldn't show. But then I felt guilty as I saw Paul sneaking glances at his watch, no doubt feeling rising disappointment that corresponded to my rising hope. I forced myself to stop sending stay-away vibes to Spencer. I tried instead to think happy thoughts about Mom's pot roast and Paul's heavily frosted birthday cake.

When the doorbell finally rang at seven-fifteen, I was feeling Zen enough to go to the door myself, mouthing *I've got this* in response to the warning look my mother gave me as I passed her.

"Spencer! Hi, come in," I said, putting all the Mr. Rogers' good neighbor feeling I could into my voice. I found several true, nice sounding, but non-hypocritical things to say.

"I like your new glasses." Spencer had switched from blue plastic frames to Harry Potter-style round wire rims, which I did in fact like—on Harry Potter. On Spencer they looked like what they were, a pretentious attempt to be noticed.

"Thanks. Sorry I'm late. Had something interesting come up at the

office I had to look into." His light brown eyes fairly glittered with anticipa-
tory joy at forcing me to ask what. He would then be able to rub my nose in
another *GO News* scoop. I affected disinterest.

"Oh? Well, a publisher's work is never done, right? Go right on in," I
said, waving him ahead of me. I took a small amount of comfort in his
disappointed expression. As everyone greeted him, I veered off down the
hall to do a quick check of the *GO News* site on my phone. I scanned the
headlines but didn't see anything to worry about. Which of course made
me worry. I texted Troy, who was on for the weekend.

Anything come over on the scanner? I heard something might be breaking.

Weekend breaking news is typically a big fire, a major accident, or some
other catastrophe. We'd begun to emphasize more county-wide coverage at
the paper. That helped draw more readers in, but with our small staff we
sometimes got overwhelmed trying to keep up with several different cities
and a number of smaller villages and towns. Developing sources who
would give him a heads-up was something Troy hadn't done much of yet. I
considered my text to him mentoring, not micromanaging. The fact that
Troy didn't text me right back was a bit unsettling.

"Leah? We're about ready to sit down to dinner," my mother called from
the living room. I put my phone away and rejoined the group.

Dinner chatter centered mostly on how beautiful the fall weather had
been the past week, the success of the St. Stephen's Fall Carnival, the new
dentist who had joined Paul's practice, and my mother's failed attempt to
get Father Lindstrom to try out for a part in the play she was producing for
the Himmel Community Players. I was mostly quiet wondering what fresh
triumph Spencer was going to taunt me with.

When it was time for the cake, I felt my phone vibrate. Under cover of
everyone's hearty singing of the birthday song, I surreptitiously pulled it
out. I looked at the breaking news alert from the *GO News* site. Amid the
laughter and congratulations as Paul successfully blew out all his candles, I
stole a glance at Spencer. He was looking at me with a self-satisfied smirk.
GO News had beaten us to a story once again.

I excused myself, ostensibly to get the ice cream out of the freezer in the
garage. As soon as I closed the door I called Troy.

"What's going on? Why does *GO News* have a story about a dead body found outside of Hailwell, and all we have for weekend news is Miguel's photo spread on the biggest pumpkin in the county?"

5

"I don't know. I've got the scanner right here. I'm sorry. Nothing major came across all day," he said, misery evident in his voice. I remembered what Miguel had said about me scaring Troy. I paused a second before I spoke.

"Okay, well, the thing is, you weren't by the scanner all day, were you? With Miguel at his cousin's *Quinceañera*, you had to take photos at the girls swim meet in Omico. Plus, you covered the guest speaker at the library in Himmel in the afternoon."

"But I checked with all the departments when I got back to the office a little while ago. The sheriff's office didn't say anything about a dead body! And it's not really a story, just a paragraph," he said, belatedly trying to make a case for himself.

In answer I read the brief item aloud.

The body of a young woman was discovered late this afternoon in a wooded area in the southwest corner of Grantland County off Holmby Road, near the Rogers Road intersection. According to the Grantland County Sheriff's Office, two bow hunters tracking a wounded deer found the body. The death is under investigation, and no further details will be released at this time, pending notification of next of kin.

. . .

"It's short, but it's definitely a story, Troy. For the time being, you need to think of the sheriff's office as a hostile source. Lamey is royally pissed that we've endorsed Coop in the election. I'm sure he's issued orders not to give us anything they don't have to, and definitely nothing we don't specifically ask for. You can't just check in with them and ask, 'Anything going on today?' You have to be specific. 'Any motor vehicle accidents, burglaries, fires, DUIs?' Otherwise, they won't tell you. Though I can see why you wouldn't routinely ask if any dead bodies had turned up. But I guess you'd better add that to the list for now."

"I'm sorry," he repeated.

"Don't be sorry. Just follow up, get the info online, and keep on top of it, all right?"

"Well, Paul's birthday had sort of an awkward finish," Gabe said. We were sitting on the couch at his house, me leaning against him on one side, Barnacle on the other.

"That wasn't on me. I didn't say anything to Spencer. He's the one who needled me so much about the *Times* missing a story that his dad asked him to leave."

"Yeah, he's a piece of work all right. Why does he have it in for you so bad? Are you sure he's not nursing a grudge because you spurned him? Did you crush the candy valentine he gave you in third grade under your heel? Stab him with your sharp tongue when he carved *SK loves LN* on the oak tree at recess?"

"Hardly. Spencer's never had a crush on anyone except himself. I don't know why he doesn't like me. I think I'm very likable, don't you? But I don't want to talk about Spencer anymore."

I sat up, turned around to face him, and held my wine glass out.

"More, please, sir."

Barnacle grumbled mildly as Gabe stood and went to the kitchen to refill my glass and his own.

"Thanks," I said as I reached for my glass. I re-situated myself with one leg tucked under me and my back resting against the arm of the sofa. When Gabe had settled in facing me, I lifted my glass to him.

"To your safe return from the big city. I missed you. Tell me about your trip. Did you have fun? Fix your friend's problem? What was the problem, anyway? You didn't say."

"I didn't say, because I can't. And it's not fixed, no."

His voice was a little sharp and he seemed to realize it, because he smiled and put his usual light teasing tone in the next thing he said.

"I had dinner with my old boss and some friends from the office, and that part of the trip was great. You'll have to come with me sometime. I can show you all over the city."

I picked up on the "that part of the trip" phrase but decided not to push it at the moment.

"Yes, please. I'd love to do a *Law & Order* tour of New York. We could go to all the places where the bodies are found, take a trip to Alphabet City, Rikers, maybe stop by Hudson University."

"You do know Hudson University isn't real, right?"

"What? I suppose you're going to tell me that Jack McCoy isn't the real Manhattan District Attorney, either."

He lifted an expressive eyebrow and shrugged his shoulders. "Sorry for your loss."

"Well then, no. I don't want to go to any New York where *Law & Order* isn't real. You'll just have to stay in real world Himmel if you want to keep seeing me."

"Oh, I definitely do," he said, lifting my wine glass out of my hand and setting it down on the coffee table. Barnacle, sensing that we were about to engage in activity in which he had no part, jumped off the couch.

6
___

On Monday, I virtuously spent most of the day pounding out pages on my book, but around four o'clock, I got a surprise phone call from an old friend. I put everything away in favor of meeting her for a drink and dinner to catch up.

Linda Linkul is a tall, green-eyed blonde. I hadn't seen her in five years, but she looked just the same walking into McClain's Bar & Grill. Her long hair, parted on one side, waved softly to her shoulders. She could have been a suburban mom dressed for cheering on her seven-year-old at a soccer game—navy and white striped T-shirt, white and navy zip jacket, navy ankle pants, and white sneakers. But I knew she was actually a very tough reporter, who was a lot more at home shouting questions at a slippery politician than she would be shouting encouragement at a soccer game.

I slid out from the booth and stood to give her a hug.

"Linda! You look great."

"You, too."

As we sat down she said, "I like your watering hole. Something about duct tape on vinyl and scratched wooden tables speaks to me. This reminds me of the Tortoise and Hare. Remember how we used to go there after deadline?"

As she asked the question, a waiter came by with two glasses of Jameson on the rocks.

"Perfect timing, Brent, thanks," I said as he placed the whiskeys I'd ordered in front of us.

"You're welcome. Do you guys want a menu?"

"Mmm, it's a little early for eating. Maybe in a while. We've got a lot of catching up to do."

As he left I lifted my glass. "To old friends."

"To old friends," she said, clinking her glass against mine.

"Jameson!" she said with satisfaction after taking her first sip. "Even if you forget to stay in touch, at least you remember how I taught you to drink."

"Don't try to guilt trip me. I'm just the second-worst person in the world at keeping in touch. You're the first."

"Okay, you're right. It's great to see you now, though. What are you up to?"

"No, you first."

"Well, you probably read that the *Tampa Tribune* shut down a couple of months ago."

I had worked for a short while at the *Trib* before moving on to the *Miami Star Register*. Linda had been at the *Register* when I arrived but had moved to the *Tribune* shortly after that. Our careers had crisscrossed at several papers since we had first met in Green Bay.

"Yes, I heard about that. Things are getting scary out there."

"Yeah, they are. I've been doing some freelancing, but the constant hustle is wearing me down. I don't think I'm built for the gig economy. Lately I've been thinking I might follow in your footsteps."

"You mean you'd like to write a book, make some money, then throw it all into buying a newspaper that isn't making it? From personal experience, I have to say that's not the path to success it might sound like."

"I mean I'm thinking about trying to write a true crime book myself. I'm doing some research now. Do you remember a murder in Sherwood years ago? A young waitress was strangled and her killer was never found."

"Doesn't sound familiar."

"You were probably too busy being a college kid then. Or wait, no. God,

I'm old. You were probably still in high school. It was right after I started in Green Bay. It was my first murder."

"Is Sherwood that one-stoplight town southeast of Oshkosh?"

"You got it. It's just a post office, a grocery store, a second-hand shop, and Harvey's Wonder Bar. Harvey's is one of those out-of-the-way bars that people go to because the drinks are cheap, the burgers are good, and the staff doesn't look too hard at IDs. The murder was the biggest thing that ever happened there."

"So why do you think it will make a good book?"

"I'm not sure it will, but it's one of those stories I can't get out of my head. You must have a few of those."

"Yeah, sure," I said, thinking of the Mandy Cleveland murder, a story I'd been turning over in my mind and trying to write for years. "What makes this murder one of those for you?"

"Tessa Miles. The victim. She was nineteen. A foster kid who aged out of the system. No family to help her. She wanted to be a special ed teacher. So, when other kids were partying and living off their parents, Tessa got a job at Harvey's Wonder Bar at night and cleaned houses during the day. She lived alone in a rental about the size of a shipping container, but not as nice, and saved everything she made for college."

"She must have really wanted to be a teacher."

"According to the people she worked with, that was all she talked about. Though she didn't talk much. She was a cute girl, a little shy for waitress work. Everybody liked her, but nobody knew her very well. Tessa pretty much went to work, went home, walked her dog, and went to work again, according to her boss and her coworkers."

"So, how did she wind up dead?"

"It was the night Al Harris won it for the Packers against the Seattle Seahawks in overtime. One of the greatest games ever. January 2004. You have to remember it."

"Uh, no, but I'll take your word for it."

Even though I'm Wisconsin born and bred I have only the sketchiest knowledge of Packers—or any—football. Linda shook her head but continued.

"Harvey's was packed. Everybody celebrating, lots of happy drunks.

Even Tessa was a little looser that night. She told one of her co-workers she was making great tips, and she had a really cute guy at one of her tables.

"Tessa got off at eleven. A guy in the alley was taking a pee up against the wall. He saw her come out the back door and walk toward her car. He told the cops that a man wearing a Packers jacket caught up with her. The two of them got in the car and drove away. It was too dark for the wall pee-er guy—why do men insist on doing that?—to see what he looked like. That was the last time anyone saw Tessa alive."

"Did anyone in the bar see Tessa flirting with a guy?"

"No one noticed anything particular. She was a waitress. She had to flirt with a lot of people. I told you, it was a big game night. Harvey's was packed. People were drunk, or high, or just happy. They weren't watching the waitress to see who she talked to."

"Who found Tessa?"

"Harvey. She didn't show up for her shift the next day, didn't answer her phone. That wasn't like her. Things slowed down around nine, and Harvey went over to check on her. She was lying on her bed, naked and dead."

"What happened?"

"She was strangled with one of her own scarves. One of the cops told me it looked like a sex game gone wrong."

"You mean like a bondage fantasy?"

"Yeah. You can imagine that sparked a lot of interest. Tessa as a person kind of got lost in the coverage. It was the kinky way she died that people wanted to hear about."

"Did they get DNA, fingerprints?"

"Yeah, both. For all the good it did."

"Why?"

"They found three sets of prints in the house. One was from Tessa's old boyfriend. He swore he hadn't been there in a week, and then it was just to drop some things off for Tessa. His alibi was tight. He played in a band and that night they had a gig in Appleton. Afterwards they all crashed together at a friend's house.

"The other set belonged to a plumber who came in to fix the bathroom sink. He seemed like a possible, but his alibi was even better than the ex-boyfriend's. He got arrested for drunk driving and spent the night in jail."

"What about the third set of prints?"

"Couldn't be accounted for. They were on the nightstand, on the head-board of Tessa's bed, and the door of her bedroom. But they weren't in the database and no one else turned up."

"The DNA?"

"No match to the boyfriend or the plumber, and also nothing in the database."

"That was one lucky killer."

"Even luckier than you think. Tessa lived in the last house on the street. An empty lot on the left side, next to her on the right was a man who turned the lights out and went to bed every night at ten. He didn't see or hear anything. Next to him, the house belonged to a couple who wintered in Florida. Across the street was an abandoned house. Tessa's block couldn't have been any deader if she lived in a cemetery."

"What about the killer's car? If he went home with Tessa in hers, wouldn't his have been left in the parking lot after the bar closed? The owner didn't notice it?"

"Nope. He said the lot was empty except for his own car after closing. It's like she hooked up with a ghost."

"Or her killer rode to the bar with someone else who picked him up at Tessa's."

"The cops interviewed as many people as they could find who were at the bar that night. There were some regulars, but the place filled up with out-of-towners most weekends. They had a few leads that went nowhere. Tessa didn't have a family or close friends clamoring for answers. The cops went through the standard investigation process, came up dry, and moved on. Tessa Miles has been a cold case ever since."

"So why are you going back to it now?"

"Because I've never been able to forget her. Maybe because I wasn't that much older than her, maybe because I made a few stupid choices in my younger days, but I was lucky. Nothing bad happened to me. Why did it happen to Tessa?" She shrugged. "The eternal question, right? But I've got the time now to dig in and maybe I can find the answer."

"Well, if anyone can, it's you." I waved Brent over for another drink and a menu.

We spent the rest of the afternoon and on into the evening talking about old friends, crazy times, and current life events. It was pretty late when we went our separate ways, with a long hug but no promises to stay in regular touch. We knew we probably wouldn't, just like we knew we'd be able to pick back up where we were when we finally did connect.

I love my see-them-every-day friends, but I find it comforting to know that out in the world is another small group of people I belong to. We may fall out of touch, but never out of mind. And if we need each other, all we have to do is call.

7

On Tuesday I got up early, determined to make up for lost time from my fun but not very productive afternoon and evening with Linda. The sun was just rising on what promised to be another beautiful fall day. As its rays hit the leaves on the tree across the street, it created the most beautiful orange-gold colors. I really had no choice. I had to sit and stare for a while.

As I did, my worries about the paper and my own erratic career as an author lifted a little. I was really very lucky. I had the chance to fight for something I believe in—community journalism. And even though the specter of *GO News* gobbling up our subscribers gave me nightmares, they hadn't won yet.

My ego had been banged up a little when my second book didn't sell well and my publisher had dropped me, but I had a second chance with a new publisher. And even if I never made another dime as a writer, I had earned enough with the first book—and was still receiving royalties on it—to let me help my mother out with a few things, buy a new car, and set myself up in the nicest place I've ever lived.

I love the gas fireplace, which makes the grayest, rainiest, bleakest day feel warm and cozy. I love the window seat that looks out on the street below. I may never use the kitchen to its full potential, but its stainless-steel appliances, granite counters, and clean lines are beautiful. The wood floors and the exposed brick walls remind me of the building's start as a department store back in Himmel's boom time. I like being part of Miller's commitment to bringing back the feeling of hope and confidence the young town of Himmel once had. Seriously, how could I not feel happy all the time?

The jarring buzz of the intercom that announced visitors at the back entrance to my apartment brought the answer to that question.

"Yes?"

"Leah, you need to come down now. Nobody's here and I can't keep answering the phones."

Courtnee views her primary functions as receptionist at the *Times* to be talking, texting, and Tindering on the job. Answering calls and serving customers are merely inconvenient interruptions in her day.

"No, wait!" I said.

But she had already clicked off.

I raced downstairs and managed to catch Courtnee as she was buttoning her coat.

"Wait, wait, wait. Where are you going? It's only eight-fifteen. There's no one else here."

"My mom called. I have to go. Her stylist had a cancellation. He can do her balayage if she gets there right away. He needs to see mine, because she wants the same color."

"No, Courtnee. You can't go. Miguel is at a Chamber meeting. Troy has a dentist appointment, and my mother is helping Father Lindstrom at St. Stephen's. There's no one here. You can't leave the office empty this morning. You have to stay."

"Beh!" The sound she emitted conveyed both frustration at my unfairness and amazement at my stupidity.

"That's why I called you," she said slowly, as though to make sure I could follow along. "*You* can stay here, while I go. The office is covered then. See? I'll only be gone a half hour or so."

Courtnee doesn't have enough brains to be an arch enemy, but she has enough self-entitlement to be an arch irritant. She'd been fired by the former publisher, but returned, against my better judgment, after Miller and I bought the paper. Miguel had persuaded me. He has a soft spot for her. I do, too, apparently, but it's in my head not my heart.

"Do we really need this talk again, Courtnee? Your work hours are eight to five. You cannot take off on a whim. And you most especially cannot leave when you're the only one in the office, just to watch your mother get her hair done. Furthermore, I am not your personal backup. I'm your boss. Are we clear?"

She pouted for a second and blinked her large blue eyes rapidly to hold back tears of frustration at my meanness, but with a flip of her long blonde hair she began walking back to her desk.

"Fine. If that's how you want to be," she said as she unbuttoned her coat.

"It's exactly how I want to be, Courtnee."

As I left, the phone on her desk rang. I heard her pick it up and I felt relieved that the crisis had been averted for another day. I'd fire her if I had to, but my mother, who is our underpaid office manager, assures me she is working on her version of Kaizen with Courtnee. Kaizen being the Japanese practice of making small changes that lead to major improvements. To date, any changes have been so small as to be imperceptible.

However, even though there's no doubt there are better receptionists than Courtnee, there aren't many willing to work for as little as we can afford to pay. I was inclined to stick, as my mother advised, with the devil we knew for the present.

Before I went back up to my place, I stopped in the newsroom to grab a Diet Coke from the machine—my own supply had run out. While there, I used Miguel's computer to do a quick check of the general email account. Lots of people still call or stop in the office to drop off anniversary pictures, press releases, and special event information, but an even larger number now go the email route.

We use a catchall newsroom address that Maggie monitors. But Miguel, Troy, and I have the password, too, to make sure someone can always check it. That way we don't miss anything time-sensitive. As I scrolled through the routine stuff, I saw an email from the sheriff's office. A press release. It had come in the night before. When I finished reading, I texted Miguel immediately.

8

"*Chica,* why did you text me, 'The shoes! The shoes! Get to the paper now!?'
"

Miguel had come flying into the newsroom less than ten minutes after I had texted him.

"Because, Miguel, this!" I said, getting off his chair and directing him to the press release open on his monitor.

He scanned it quickly.

"The dead woman they found, she was murdered," he said, skimming through the paragraphs, reading some key points out loud. "Strangled ... no wallet, no identification with the body ... no phone ... they can't find next of kin ... no one reported her missing ... she was killed four to seven days before her body was found ... the sheriff's office wants help making the identification."

"Yes, yes, but you're skipping over the really important part. Here, let me," I said, turning the screen around. I read aloud the paragraph I wanted him to focus on.

"The victim is a female in her late teens to early twenties. Height, five feet, two inches, weight one hundred ten pounds, long blonde hair, blue eyes. She has a

*small tattoo of a fairy on her left shoulder. When discovered, she was wearing a short, red, sequined, halter-top cocktail dress, and **no shoes.**"*

The emphasis on the last two words was mine.

Our eyes met.

"The shoes, the red sparkly ones from the farmer's cornfield. You think they're hers?" he asked.

"I do. First of all, they're just the kind of shoes to go with that sort of outfit—glittery red high heels. Second, when you found them, they were dusty, but not stained or damp, like they would've been if they'd been lying out there for weeks. Those shoes had to have been left in the field after the ground finally dried up. That didn't happen until a week or so ago. That fits the time-of-death estimate. Those shoes belong to our murder victim. Trust me."

"But the body, they found it in the woods off Holmby Road. The red shoes, they were fifteen miles away on the other side of the county."

"I know, but seriously? How many women do you think there were roaming the countryside losing their fancy shoes last week? This woman, our woman, she might have been killed where you found the shoes, and then her body was taken away. Or, she could have been running from someone who caught her, lost her shoes, and the killer drove her elsewhere to murder her."

"Okay, but why was she even way out in the country, all dressed up for a party? How did she end up in a cornfield?"

"I don't know. But I think it's a question we should ask your farmer friend, Dwight Pearson."

"We? But the body, it's Troy's story. He caught the lead."

"Yes, he did. Barely. *GO News* had it first. And Troy doesn't seem to know what to do with it. He should be all over this. He—and the paper—shouldn't be waiting to be spoon-fed by Lamey with only what he wants us to know. I'll bet Andrea Novak hasn't been waiting. Oh, hell!"

"What?"

I didn't answer as I scanned the home page of the *GO News* site, which I'd pulled up as I talked. The headline *Police Seek Identity of Murdered*

Woman was followed by a story under Andrea Novak's byline. It included quotes from Lamey, and additional details from the medical examiner that weren't in the press release.

"Listen, Miguel, it says the soles of her feet were lacerated and bruised 'consistent with running over rough or rocky terrain.' That fits. The cornfield is full of rocks and stones. Beyond that is the woods. The ground there would be full of sticks and poky branches and pinecones just waiting to tear bare feet to pieces.

"Our Cinderella was there, all right, but she didn't lose her shoes running away from the prince at the end of the ball. She lost them running away from her killer at the end of the line—for her. Maybe Farmer Pearson had something to do with that. Maybe that's why he said he was 'too busy' to have you take his picture in the cornfield. He didn't want to return to the scene of the crime."

He looked at me dubiously. "*Chica,* I don't think so. He's very old. Seventy-one."

"Hey, Father Lindstrom is seventy-two, and look at all the stuff he still does. I'm not saying it's likely that your friendly farmer had anything to do with the red shoes—or the murdered woman. But it's possible. Damn! I hate that *GO News* beat us again. This story was posted last night, and now we're playing catch-up again."

"And now we have to tell the sheriff's office about the shoes. Do you still have them?"

"Yes. They're still on the backseat of my car. I forgot about them. And yes, absolutely we'll take them to the sheriff's office. Just not this very minute. We need to talk to Mr. Pearson first, and find out what he knows about what was going on in his cornfield last week."

Miguel shook his head as I finished. "No."

"No?"

"No. It shouldn't be me. You have to let Troy try. He's smart, he works hard, he has to learn, that's all. Take him with you."

"Okay, you're right on one count. It shouldn't be you following up, you've got your hands full. I'll do it and check in with the sheriff's office after to tell them about the shoes. But I think this is too big for Troy. He's not ready. We didn't even have this press release on our site this morning.

But *GO News* did. Plus they had extra information from the sheriff's office. Why didn't Troy get on this yesterday?"

"But look how late it came in. Six o'clock. No one was even here last night. You know that Sheriff Lamey would give Andrea a special alert that he won't give to us."

"That's my point. Troy knows it, too. He should have checked the mailbox from home. He should have called the sheriff's office to check on any developments. At the very least, he should have checked the *GO News* site."

"But so should I, or you, right?"

"No, Miguel, not right. You weren't on last night, neither was I. It was Troy's responsibility. He should take some initiative. We're all stretched thin. I don't have time to babysit him."

"I don't need a babysitter. I just need a chance."

We both turned to look in the direction of the voice. Troy stood in the doorway, his face flushed to the roots of his sandy hair, but his expression determined. How long had he been there? I ran a tape in my head of what I'd said and felt guilty. Less about what I'd said than that Troy had learned about it by overhearing me.

"I'm sorry, Troy. I should have spoken to you directly, and I was a little harsher than I had to be. But I'm frustrated because *GO News* seems to beat us at every turn. You've got to be on top of things. And it just doesn't seem like you've cultivated enough sources yet. It takes a while to build trust with cops, but that's what you need to get the story. I don't think you've done the work yet."

"Not like Andrea has, you mean?"

"Well, I wouldn't like you to build sources the way Andrea has, but she's got them, and you don't. I'll handle this for a little while, until we see where it's going. Maggie will be back soon and then maybe you can team up with Miguel to follow through."

"No."

"No?" That was the second time in less than five minutes a directive of mine had been contested. The firmness in Troy's voice surprised me, as did his willingness to push back. I respect a person who can stand his ground, so I waited for him to continue.

"I know I haven't done a good job on the story so far. I missed the scanner information and I don't have the sheriff as a source, like Andrea does. But I know that I can do better. I want to do this story. I'll get it right, I promise." He pushed his glasses up his nose and looked at me directly, his gaze steady.

I was quiet for a moment, assessing what he'd said. As I did, I looked at him more closely than I had in a while. I noticed then that he'd grown his hair a little longer, and he was wearing his shirt untucked. That had to be either Miguel's influence, or a new girl in his life. He looked a little less like an earnest Boy Scout.

As it happens, I also had some pretty big screw-ups when I was starting out, and Max, my first boss, had given me more than one second chance. Also, we didn't have a very deep bench, and I had a book to write. Maybe, with a little patience—and as everyone knows, patience is my middle name—I could bring Troy along. And when Maggie got back, and please God, make that soon, she could take over that job.

"All right. I won't take you off the story. But I'm taking the lead, until I'm sure that you're ready to fly solo. Got that?"

The smile he gave me was so wide it almost fell off the edge of his face.

"Got it. No problem."

"Get your notebook, Troy, we're going for a ride."

9

On the way to the Pearson farm, I filled Troy in on the red shoes and their significance, and why we were going to see Dwight Pearson.

"I'll start things out, but you ask any follow-up questions you have. Don't antagonize the man, though. We're looking for information, not accusing him of anything, okay?"

Troy nodded and neither of us spoke again until my knock on the front door of the Pearsons' stone farmhouse was answered.

I'd expected the door to be opened by Dwight Pearson himself. Instead, a short, gray-haired woman wearing a long-sleeved T-shirt and jeans stood in front of us.

"Yes?" The smile she gave us extended to the warm brown eyes behind her glasses, so I plunged straight ahead.

"Mrs. Pearson? My name is Leah Nash. I'm from the *Himmel Times Weekly*, and this is my colleague Troy Patterson."

"What? No, no. I'm not Mrs. Pearson." The idea seemed to amuse her. "I wouldn't have the patience! My sister Juanita is married to Dwight. I'm Kristi McGinness."

"Oh, I see. Is Mr. Pearson in?" As I asked, the unmistakable smell of warm cinnamon rolls drifted through the half-open door. My stomach growled loudly, reminding me that all I'd had so far that morning was a cup of coffee.

"Someone's hungry," she said, smiling again. "I'm afraid Dwight's not here. He and my sister drove in to Omico this morning. But I just pulled some cinnamon rolls out of the oven and frosted them. Come on in and join me."

A flash of disappointment had run through me at the news that Dwight Pearson wasn't available. But the offer of cinnamon rolls was a definite mood-lifter. She led the way through a pleasantly cluttered living room filled with family photographs on every available shelf. An oval braided rug in shades of brown and gold covered the wooden floor. The most recent edition of the *Himmel Times Weekly*—always nice to see—rested on the arm of a cracked leather chair. Across the back of a comfortable-looking sofa was a beautiful quilt in autumn shades of rust, gold, and green.

"That's gorgeous," I said, stopping to look at it.

"Thank you! I made that for Juanita for her birthday. Quilting is something I've always done. I got Juanita into it too, recently. In fact, we're working together on a Quilt of Valor while I'm here."

"Quilt of Valor?"

"Yes, the Quilts of Valor Foundation distributes the quilts volunteers make to service members who've been touched by war. We make them to say thank you, to wrap them in warmth if they're far from home, to comfort them wherever they are, really. It's just a small thing we can do. Our nephew, our brother Joe's boy, was badly wounded in Iraq. That's why I got started. I've been doing it for years."

"My brother Drew has one," Troy said. "A Quilt of Valor. He was a medic in Afghanistan. He had a pretty bad time when he came home."

I looked at Troy in surprise. I hadn't even known that he had a brother.

"I'm so sorry," Kristi said, touching him lightly on the arm. "Your family must be very proud of him."

He nodded but didn't answer. I noticed that he was swallowing hard and his eyes looked a little bright. To give him cover I said with unusual heartiness, "Those rolls smell great. I don't want to be pushy, but you did ask, and I'd definitely like to try one."

"Yes, of course, follow me."

Seated at the long, scrubbed-wood table in the large kitchen, with a plate of cinnamon rolls in front of me and a cup of coffee beside me, I felt the visit was already worthwhile, even without Dwight.

I took a bite and let the cream cheese frosting meld with the spicy warmth of cinnamon and the soft roll itself. Heaven ... I forced myself to refocus.

"You said Dwight and your sister are in Omico. Do you know if they'll be back this morning?"

"I don't expect them until supper time. Dwight has a doctor appointment at ten-thirty, and then they're going to go to a movie and do some shopping."

"Oh, is Dwight ill?"

"No, no. Juanita just finally got him to agree to a hip replacement. It took long enough. He's the most stubborn man! Our mother used to say, 'You can always tell a Pearson, but you can't tell him much.' It's getting so Dwight can barely walk across the living room without wincing."

As she spoke, my mental image of the seventy-something Dwight chasing a girl across a cornfield with murderous intent faded away. A candidate for a hip replacement certainly wouldn't have been running in the dark on uneven ground. As I regrouped, Troy spoke.

"Mrs. McGinness—"

"Just Kristi, please."

"Okay, Kristi. Can I ask how long you've been here?"

She frowned slightly, obviously puzzled by the question, but I wasn't. If Troy wanted to show me that he knew the right questions to ask, this was a good start.

"Three weeks, more or less. The first week was that terrible rain. The wet weather really bothered Dwight's hip. He was cross as a bear until the sun came out and things dried up a week or so ago. Why?"

He answered with another question. "Did he feel well enough to host a party recently? The drinks and dinner kind that you'd dress up for?"

She laughed, a warm and cheerful sound, and then said, "Dwight is a good man, but he is not a—what did you call it? A 'drinks and dinner' man.

If he did host a party, it would be hot dish potluck with euchre afterwards, and no one would be dressed up. But we haven't had any parties of either kind since I've been here."

"How about the neighbors? Did you notice a lot of cars parked at anyone's house the weekend before last?"

"There aren't any neighbors to speak of on this road. It's pretty much farmland and woods all around. Well, wait, now, that's not exactly right. Dwight sold a hundred acres a while back. The parcel starts right where his cornfield ends. The man who bought it built a hunting cabin back in the woods. He's in and out some, but he doesn't live there."

Troy sat back, looking deflated. I picked up the questioning.

"Do you know the man's name?"

"Kent Morgan. Nice man. He's a financial advisor. Lives in Omico. Now, why all the questions?"

I hesitated. Kristi had a right to be curious. And she had given me an awesome cinnamon roll. But I couldn't risk word about the shoes spreading before I gave the information to the sheriff's office, or before we ran our story. Both would be equally bad.

"Can't say right at the moment but look for a story on the *Himmel Times* online site, or in the paper later this week when the print edition comes out. Thanks, for the cinnamon roll and the conversation. You've been great."

"That was pretty much a bust," Troy said as we returned to the car and buckled ourselves in. "Are we going to the sheriff's office so you can turn in the shoes now?"

"It wasn't a bust, Troy. Your question about the neighbors got us the information that someone owns a hunting cabin right next to the cornfield where Miguel found the shoes."

"But Kristi said no one lives there, so ..."

"She did indeed. But she also said that Kent Morgan is 'in and out some.' So, as long as we're out here, we'll make a stop and see for ourselves just how close that cabin is to the cornfield, and who knows, we might even find Kent Morgan there."

"It's a workday."

"Ah, but if you're in the right line of work, you just might be able to spend a Tuesday morning puttering around your hunting cabin, especially with deer season coming up soon. Kent Morgan is a friend of Miller's. That's how I know who he is. He owns his own business, Kent Morgan Financial Services in Omico. If he wants to take a lazy day in the middle of the week, he can. If he's there, great. If he isn't, at least we can get the lay of the land."

10

If Kristi hadn't told us that there was a hunting cabin on the land adjacent to the Pearson cornfield, I wouldn't have suspected it. A narrow track ran from the road and up through a heavily wooded area. About two hundred yards in, it curved and disappeared from sight into the trees.

"What do you say? Shall we just try it and see how far we can get?"

"That's kind of what you do, isn't it?"

I shot Troy a look, and he gave me a shy smile. He was joking with me. Maybe I wasn't so scary after all.

"Yes, Troy, it kind of is. Now watch and learn."

The deep ruts in the road wreaked havoc with my car's suspension, or whatever it is that's supposed to keep you from bone-shattering bumps in a car. I slowed down after a pothole bounced us almost to the car roof, but it didn't help much. Just before another curve there was a turnaround on one side of the track. Just past that, a metal gate stopped our progress. I put the car in park and turned it off.

"Come on, Troy. Let's see what's on the other side."

Troy joined me at the gate, but hesitated after I scaled it to the other side.

"What's the matter?" I asked.

"Well, I don't think we should trespass."

"I like to think of it more as exploring. It's not posted. Do you see any 'No Trespassing' signs? The gate is to keep vandals or thieves from getting in. We're not vandals or thieves. Besides, I'm a friend of Miller's and so is Kent, so he's basically a friend of mine, too."

The expression on his freckled face was still reluctant.

"Troy, we're just looking, we're not going to hurt anything. I really don't think Kent Morgan would mind."

He didn't look convinced, but he did climb over the fence and begin walking with me.

I enjoyed the crunch of leaves under my feet and the pleasure of kicking them out in front of us as we moved up the trail.

Troy was silent, but I could tell he wanted to say something.

"All right, what's on your mind?"

"I just think maybe we should go back. The gate *was* locked. Maybe we shouldn't be here without permission."

"Troy, don't be the fish."

He gave me a puzzled look.

"You know. The fish in *The Cat in the Hat.* The Cat comes to visit the two kids, their mom is out. He starts setting up all kinds of fun things for them to do. Then the kids' fish keeps warning them not to break any rules, not to take any chances, to play it safe. Life is about taking chances. You can't always play it safe. In life or in reporting. I loved that Cat. Hated the fish. Don't be the fish, Troy."

"I take chances, sometimes," he said, a trifle stiffly.

"I'm sure you do, but—Oh, look over there!"

I broke off and pointed to a thin plume of smoke rising to the east of us. "That's the cabin I bet, and you know what they say, if there's smoke, there's somebody home. Come on!"

I thought I heard Troy mutter, "That's not what they say." But I ignored it.

The phrase "hunting cabin" conjures up in my mind a small, rustic structure built of reclaimed lumber and weathered boards, with a tin roof, and a wooden porch if it's deluxe. That was not what we saw as Troy and I rounded the curve and got our first glimpse of Kent Morgan's little house in the big woods.

Built of logs, the two-story "cabin" featured a wrap-around porch, a fieldstone foundation, a big picture window, and solar panels on the roof. A white Escalade was parked in front of a three-car garage that was set off to the side and connected to the "cabin" by a covered breezeway. The roar of a chainsaw came from somewhere behind it. I followed the sound, and Troy followed me.

Rounding the corner of the garage, I saw Kent Morgan. At least I assumed he was the man wearing safety glasses, ear protectors, and gloves. When he cut the motor to chuck a newly cut log onto a growing pile, I shouted to him.

"Kent! Kent!"

He looked up in surprise. As he pulled off his head gear, I walked toward him with a broad smile. I find that when you're someplace you really shouldn't be, it's best to approach with confidence.

"Hi, Kent. I'm Leah Nash. I don't know if you remember me. We met one night when I was having dinner with Miller Caldwell. You stopped by the table to say hello. Miller is my business partner at the *Himmel Times*. This is my colleague, Troy Patterson."

As I'd hoped, his good manners overruled any annoyance he might feel. He took his gloves and safety glasses off and returned my smile as he held out his hand to shake mine.

"Leah, of course I remember you." He smiled and was clearly waiting for me to explain our uninvited presence.

"I wanted to talk to you, but I didn't actually expect you to be here. I hope you don't mind that we climbed the gate and came on up."

"No, of course not, but I'm curious about why."

Troy, who had been looking around in admiration, spoke before I could answer.

"This is a great piece of property, Mr. Morgan. Do you have any marsh land?"

"We do," he said. "Please, call me Kent. Troy is it?"

Troy nodded.

"Are you a duck hunter?"

"No, I do a lot of bird watching. As close as we are to the Mississippi Flyway, you must see a big variety of migrating birds out here."

The day was turning into Meet Your Employee Tuesday for me. First an unknown brother, now a birding passion I hadn't heard about. I'd been slightly annoyed when Troy had interrupted with a non-work-related question, but I could see now that the conversation he'd initiated was putting Kent at ease.

"I like to hear them sing, but I can't identify any birds more exotic than cardinals or robins. But you're welcome to come out sometime with your binoculars, Troy."

"Really? That would be great. I'd like to add a Northern Pintail to my list," Troy said.

"Is that a rare species?"

"In Wisconsin, yes. My brother had a confirmed sighting the last time he was home."

"Well, like I said, come out and bird away—just not during hunting season."

"Right. Thank you."

Time to reap the rewards of Troy's diplomacy and get things back on track to our main objective.

"Kent, Troy and I are following up on a story. We hope you might be able to help."

"That sounds intriguing. I was just about to take a break. Why don't you and Troy come in for a minute and we can get something to drink and talk inside."

"That would be great, thanks," I said.

11

Kent removed his work boots in the small mudroom, and we followed suit before he led us into the impressive interior of the cabin. A massive stone fireplace with an oak mantel, over which hung a hunting rifle, dominated the main room. The polished oak floor was covered with wool area rugs in sage green and maroon. No wonder he had removed his shoes.

A dark red leather sofa faced the fireplace, as did a matching club chair. A bookcase along one wall held photographs and knickknacks as well as books. A staircase at the far end of the room led up to the second floor. The wall that ran perpendicular to the fireplace had a large window that offered a lovely view of the forest beyond.

"This is really beautiful, Mr. Morgan," Troy said.

"Yes. It's a little more sumptuous than I imagined a hunting cabin would be," I added.

"Troy, thank you, and please call me Kent. Leah, I can only say my wife got carried away with the building plans."

He gave a rueful shake of his head, his expression somewhere between exasperation and pride.

"I was thinking something a lot less luxurious, but Sydney, that's my wife, got together with my brother Wes. He's in construction and he was the builder for this place. She had other ideas. But she's got wonderful taste. To be honest, I'm really happy with what she did. Even though it wasn't what I'd been thinking of when the project started."

"Does your family spend a lot of time here? It's a beautiful spot."

"I'm here as much as I can be. That's why you caught me playing hooky today. Sydney is fine with the occasional day or weekend out here, but she prefers antiquing to tromping around in the woods. Our daughter Dinah loves it. But she's almost nine now and she's got more things on her calendar than I do—dance class, soccer practice, math tutor, swimming lessons. This has really become kind of a guy's retreat. I have a group of friends I hunt with. We're all at an age where the creature comforts here are kind of nice at the end of a cold day in the woods." He smiled and shrugged.

"Now, you two have a seat while I get some iced tea for us. Then you can tell me more about why you're here."

As Kent left the room, Troy sank down on the chair and proceeded to wriggle around a little. Then he said in a perfect Mike-Meyers-as-Linda-Richman voice, 'It's like butta.' "

"Troy! You just earned yourself some Leah points. How do you even know the Coffee Talk skit? I wouldn't, if it wasn't for Coop's dad and his *SNL* DVDs."

"My Uncle Steve and I watch *SNL* on YouTube. He's the one who got me into Mike Meyers."

"How do you feel about *Law & Order*?"

"My mom likes the one about the sex crimes unit. But I've never seen the other ones."

"Okay, you just forfeited your Leah points."

I moved over to the bookshelf to see what Kent was reading and to check out some of the photos. The books were mostly nonfiction, a few mysteries, a smattering of current best-sellers. An eight-by-ten family photo caught my eye. Kent, his wife Sydney, and their daughter Dinah posed in the faux casual way favored by family photographers. Kent and Sydney were back to back, half-turned and smiling at the camera. Dinah was centered in front of them but leaning back so she rested against her parents. She looked strikingly like her petite mother, with the same soft brown eyes, same rich brown hair color, same delicate features. I peered closer but couldn't see any resemblance to Kent with his blond-haired, blue-eyed Nordic looks.

On the shelf below the family portrait was a photo of Kent in racing gear next to a fancy bike. Troy had come over to join me, and it caught his eye immediately.

"Wow, that's a Kestrel Legend. What a sweet bike! It would take me a million years to save up for one of those."

But by then, my attention was focused on a framed picture of Kent and a grinning group of men seated around a poker table. Most appeared to be in their early forties, like Kent. Troy followed my gaze and to my surprise said, "That's Lewis!"

He pointed to the one man who looked quite a bit younger than the others and was dressed more business casual than hunting cabin casual. He wore a V-neck sweater over a white shirt. Everyone else in the picture had on flannel shirts with the sleeves rolled up, zip-up fleeces, or Henley T-shirts. I wasn't surprised that the dressed-up guy was someone Troy knew.

Kent returned just then carrying a tray with three glasses of iced tea and put it down on a coffee table. Troy turned to him.

"Lewis Webber, that's him in the picture, isn't it? It looks just like him."

"Yes, it is. How do you know Lewis?"

"He used to go out with my sister Erica. We still play World of War together sometimes. That's an online game," he said, a trifle condescendingly, I thought.

"We know what it is, Troy."

"Speak for yourself, Leah," Kent said. "*I* didn't know," he added, turning to Troy. "I'm an old guy, with an eight-year-old daughter. My expertise is Disney princesses, at the moment. Lewis is a very smart guy. He's about to make partner at Jennings and Holden accounting firm. It's quite an accomplishment for someone who just turned thirty. Lewis subs for Barton Jennings in our Monday night poker group when Bart can't play. I hope this isn't bad news for your sister, Troy, but Lewis is engaged to Bart's daughter."

"No, Erica's got a boyfriend," he said, then brought up the topic that really interested him. "I saw from your other photo that you have a Kestrel, Kent. What a great bike!"

"Yes, it is," Kent said. "I'm afraid I don't have as much time to ride as I'd like."

"If I had a bike like that, nothing would keep me off it," Troy said. "I've got a Cannondale. I do a lot of riding on the country roads here. I ride into work sometimes, too, but if I had a Kestrel, wow, you'd never get me off it."

"Cannondales are good, solid bikes, Troy. But you're right, a Kestrel is special. I'll tell you what, you ride your Cannondale out here sometime to do a little bird watching, and I'll let you take the Kestrel for a spin, too."

"Really? You'd let me ride it?" Troy was clearly thrilled.

"Absolutely."

While it's always good to establish rapport, I was afraid that next Troy was going to ask Kent to adopt him. Time to get down to business.

"That tea looks great," I said, grabbing a glass and plunking myself down on the sofa. Troy followed suit and Kent sat in the chair across from us.

"Kent, we don't want to take up too much of your time, so I'll get to the point. I'm sure you know the body of a young woman was found by some hunters this past weekend."

"Yes, that was the talk of the office yesterday, and at the Chamber meeting, too. She was found quite some distance from here, though, isn't that right? Over by Holmby Road?"

"Yes. Did you see the follow-up story this morning in *GO News*?" It pained me to spit out that last part.

"No, I didn't. Why?"

I started to answer, but Troy jumped in eagerly.

"You didn't have a party out here last week, did you? I mean like cocktails or a formal dinner?" he asked.

"The only parties we ever have here are family gatherings at Thanksgiving and Christmas. We all try to be presentable, but no one is formal. Well, I do have my weekly poker group, but as you can see from the photo, it's pretty casual dress. You've really got me curious now. What do formal dress parties and a murdered woman have to do with each other?"

"We're just trying to figure out why she was found in the woods, but dressed for a living room cocktail party," I said.

"But we're a good fifteen miles from where her body was found. Are you going down every road in the county trying to find anyone who hosted a dinner party? That's a pretty wide net you're casting."

"We're just following a lead," I said.

"I can't imagine what that is."

From the way he said it, I knew he was hoping for some inside information. People always like to feel they're in the know. I answered before Troy could give away more than I wanted to.

"You can read all about it in the *Times* soon." I smiled to take the sting out, because he'd been a pretty good guy about us barging onto his property. "We don't know if the lead will pan out or not. Lots of them don't. So it's best to keep it low key for now."

I nudged Troy, and we both stood up. We both handed him our cards, and he provided us with his.

"Thanks for the tea, Kent, and for letting us take up so much of your time."

Kent insisted on giving us a ride on his four-wheeler to the gate, even though it wasn't that far away. When he dropped us off, he also unlocked the gate for us. I thought that was a very nice gesture, given our uninvited visit.

"Troy, seriously, give me a call when you want to do some bird watching," he said.

"That would be great, thanks!"

Troy looked the happiest he had all day.

I waited until Kent had relocked the gate and started up his four-wheeler before I backed into the turn-around and pointed the car back toward the road.

"Now what?" Troy asked.

I turned my head to look at him. As I did, something flashed in the sunlight coming through the window. I threw the car in park and reached toward him. Surprise tinged with alarm crossed his face as I touched his hair.

"Relax, Troy, we don't have an HR situation here. Look at this."

I held my hand out toward him and showed him the tiny object resting in my palm. As he squinted down, I said, "It looks to me like a sparkly red sequin. The kind you might find on 'a short, red, sequined, halter-top cocktail dress,' " I added, quoting the news release from the sheriff's office.

When he looked up, the lenses of his glasses magnified the shock in his wide-open eyes. "Do you think this came from Kent Morgan's hunting cabin?"

"I do, Troy. Unless you were feeling particularly saucy when you fixed your hair this morning. It's an odd thing to find there, isn't it? Why would a hunting cabin, used almost exclusively by Kent and his merry band of poker players, where no fancy parties are ever hosted, be the resting spot of a red sequin?"

"Maybe a cleaning lady left it?"

"Really? A sequined cleaning lady, Troy? I'm beginning to think you have a secret life that bears some looking into. It looks like we need to dig a little deeper into Kent Morgan. What's your friend Lewis like?"

"He's smart, like Kent said. He doesn't talk a lot. Except when he gets nervous, like if someone's kind of intimidating to him. Why?"

"Would he get nervous around me?"

Troy hesitated, no doubt considering whether or not that was a trick question.

"Here's the thing, Troy. We know—or we're pretty sure we know—that the murder victim lost her red shoes in a cornfield right next to Kent Morgan's property. We also know that Kent Morgan has a poker party at his hunting cabin every Monday. The medical examiner said that the victim had been dead four to seven days before she was found. That means she could have been killed on Monday last week. I can verify that you were not wearing a red sequin in your hair before we went inside the hunting cabin.

"However, after sitting first on a chair and then on a couch, thanks to whatever styling product you use, you exited Kent Morgan's cabin with a red sequin stuck in your coiffure. I think it's possible that Kent and his friends had a special guest at their poker night last week. A young woman in a red-sequined dress.

"We could go back and confront Kent in the hope of taking him by surprise and forcing an admission out of him. But Kent strikes me as a very confident man not easily shaken. I don't think we could make him nervous enough to tell us how the red sequin got in his cabin. But based on what you said about Lewis, it sounds like he might respond to some pressure. What about it? Do you think that Lewis is the weakest link in the poker club?"

"He could be, I guess."

"Then I think it's time you reconnected with your gamer buddy. Why don't you give him a call and see if he can meet you for a quick lunch at that little coffee shop in Omico. We can be there in ten minutes. You don't need to mention that I'll be there."

"It's the Daily Grind, but I don't know if—"

I gave him a look that brooked no opposition. He had the lunch set up with Lewis before I got us back to the road.

12

Lewis Webber was waiting at a corner table when we walked into the coffee shop. He stood as Troy led the way toward him. If there was an American Boy line of dolls, Lewis would be the one wearing black-rimmed glasses and holding a calculator. He had on a well-cut gray suit, a crisp white shirt, and a confidence-inspiring red and gray striped tie, but his round face and rosy cheeks made him look more like a little boy playing dress-up than a thirty-year-old new partner at a prestigious accounting firm.

"Hi, Lewis. Glad you could come. This is my boss. Well, my boss's boss really. She owns the *Himmel Times*. Leah Nash, this is Lewis Webber. Lewis, this is Leah Nash."

Troy does have nice manners, I have to say.

"Nice to meet you, Leah," Lewis said as we shook hands. His confusion at my surprise guest appearance was evident.

"Same here, Lewis. What's good for lunch?"

He made a couple of recommendations, we placed our orders, and when we got back to the table, I got to the point of our lunch.

"So, Lewis, Troy and I were just talking about you with Kent Morgan. He said you're part of his poker group—the guys who play at his hunting cabin every Monday."

As he answered, Lewis began smoothing down a cowlick on one side of his short brown hair.

"Oh, well. I'm not a regular. I don't play every week. Just when my boss, Mr. Jennings—Bart, that is—when he can't play."

He said the name Bart the way a fourth grader says a teacher's first name, as though he was being a little daring and might get in trouble. Perhaps it hadn't been allowed until he made partner—or got engaged to the boss's daughter.

"Yes, that's what Kent said. He also said you're engaged to Bart's daughter. Congratulations. When's the wedding?"

Lewis stopped patting his cowlick.

"Thank you. Next month."

"So you haven't had your bachelor party yet?"

"No, we're going to have a couples party."

"Oh, really? I thought maybe the guys had a bachelor party for you at the poker game last week. There was a dancer there, right? Lots of booze, lots of fun, I imagine. But that wasn't a party for you?" I was taking a leap, but not too big of one, I thought, given the red-sequined, short cocktail dress, the sparkly stiletto heels, and Kent's denial of any knowledge. Looking at Lewis's face, I was pretty sure my leap had landed me on solid ground.

His cheeks had turned bright red. His eyes were downcast. His fingers carefully folded the paper his sandwich had been wrapped in as though he were making a paper fan.

"No, no. Nothing like that. No bachelor party."

"What kind of party was it, Lewis? Because there was a party at the poker game last week, wasn't there? Was it the kind of party a girl in a red-sequined dress would go to? Was it the kind of party your fiancée would like to attend?"

He cast a desperate look at Troy.

"Lewis. She knows. You might as well tell her," Troy said.

I pulled out my reporter's notebook then, and I noticed Troy did the same with his.

"We're working on the story about the dead woman found last weekend. She was wearing a dress with red sequins. Just like this one right here,"

I said, pulling it from my pocket. "We found this at Kent Morgan's cabin. We're going to be writing about this, Lewis. Now, what happened at your poker party last week?"

"It was Wes. It was all him. We didn't know anything about it."

The words came tumbling out of Lewis's mouth as though he couldn't wait to get rid of them.

"Kent's birthday was Friday, but since we were going to be together for poker on Monday, we thought we'd surprise him with a cake. Just a cake, nothing else. I bought it myself at Woodman's. But then Wes thought it would be funny to have a dancer there. He didn't tell any of us. He hired somebody from Tanner's."

Tanner's Gentlemen's Club is a strip club just inside the county line. Few locals admit to frequenting it. But it's been in business for more than twenty years, so at least *some* Grantland County citizens must be patrons.

"Nobody knew she was coming, not even Kent?"

"Especially not Kent. He's not like Wes at all. They may be brothers, but they're way different people. We sat down like always and started to play. After the first hand, Wes said he needed to get some ice. He went in the kitchen and started streaming music on the wireless speaker and then the girl—Jancee—she came out dancing."

"How did everyone react?"

"Kent had this stunned look on his face, like he couldn't believe Wes would do something so stupid. The girl must have noticed. She went right over to Kent and sort of danced up against him. She was leaning in and whispering in his ear and stuff. Wes almost fell off his chair laughing. Then she went around the whole table, dancing and, you know, doing all those stripper moves."

Troy, who I highly doubted knew "all those stripper moves," nodded sagely.

"How long was she there, Lewis?" I asked.

"An hour or so, maybe longer. Probably longer. She danced for quite a while. And she did lap dances with some of the guys and flirted with them and stuff. She asked if I wanted a lap dance, and when I said no thank you, Wes wouldn't let it go."

"How do you mean?"

"He just kept saying 'don't be shy, Lulu.' He knows I hate it when he calls me that. He's just such a pain when he drinks. Finally, she told him to let it go. Then she went over and danced for him. I think she did it to get him off my case, because she winked at me. I gave her a good tip. Not because she did anything," he hastened to add. "I just felt kind of sorry for her. For what she had to do for a living."

Lewis had stopped working on his fan. He looked back and forth between us. I gave a slight nod to Troy to take the lead.

"Lewis, the dancer—her name is Jancee?"

"Yes."

"You know Jancee was murdered, right?"

"I saw it online this morning."

"The police are looking for help identifying her. You have to tell them what you know."

"But I don't know anything, Troy. None of us does, except Wes. He's the one who hired her."

"Yes, you do, Lewis," I said. "You know what she looks like, what her name is, that Kent's brother hired her, where she worked. Who else was there that night?"

"Greg Vogel, Eric Tripp, Richard Pullman. I rode with them. Wes and Kent came alone. I'm not a regular, just a sub. Hannah's dad—Bart, that is —it's his poker group. He's been away for a month. I don't even like poker. How is this even happening? Hannah won't understand," he said, shaking his head.

"If Kent was unhappy with Wes hiring a dancer, why didn't he shut it down right away?"

"He puts up with a lot of dumb stuff from Wes. He—Wes, not Kent— he's one of those guys who wants everybody to like him, only hardly anyone does. Especially when he's drinking. He can get pretty belligerent. Maybe Kent didn't want to have it be a big thing. I think he paid her to leave early, though."

"Why's that?"

"Kent was standing in the kitchen talking to the dancer, not looking very happy. She was smiling, kind of flirting, you know, flipping her hair and stuff. Then he handed her something. I figured he told her she could leave, and he gave her some extra money to go."

"And she left?"

"Yeah. She stopped and said something to Wes, then she blew everybody a kiss and went out the back way. Her car must've been out there."

"Then what?"

"Wes went into the kitchen and started talking to Kent. They got kind of loud, so the rest of us left. We stopped for a beer in town and wound up closing down the place. It was sort of a crazy night. They didn't drop me off until after two o'clock."

"Do you know if anyone's gone to the cops yet?" Troy asked.

He shook his head. "We decided not to."

"What do you mean 'we' decided not to? Who decided? When?" I asked.

"This morning. I called Kent early, when I saw the story. I said maybe we should go to the police. Kent said first we should get the guys together so nobody was blindsided. We all met in the conference room at his office, before anybody came in to work."

"And you all agreed not to go to the police? Why, Lewis?" Troy asked.

He shook his head, his face suffused with misery.

"Well, after we started talking about it, it started to seem like not a good idea. Wes and Richard, they said we didn't know her. And like Wes said, she didn't have anything to do with us. She just came, she danced, and she left."

"A woman is dead, Lewis, *murdered,* and you're all going to ignore it? You know that's not right," I said.

"Richard said think about how this would look to everybody—our families, our friends, our business clients. Six guys have a party with a stripper and she gets murdered? That's not how it happened, but that's what people would say. Greg said we didn't need to get involved and mess up our lives. He's in a custody fight with his ex-wife, so he really didn't want this to get out. He said somebody else would identify her. Someone who actually knew her."

"Lewis, Wes is someone who actually knew her. He's the one who hired her."

"Yes, but he said he didn't know her that well. He just heard she did private parties, and he hired her. He said somebody at Tanner's would identify her after they saw the description in the news.

"Then Richard told Wes he could save us all a lot of trouble if he went to the cops himself, because he's the one who made this mess. Wes could keep us all out of it and just say he recognized her description because he'd seen her dance at Tanner's."

"And how did Wes respond?"

"He said no. He said we all liked it well enough when she was there. Either we all talked, or nobody talked. And if none of us talked, nobody would ever know about it. Finally, we all agreed to stay quiet. Only now everything is going to blow up in all our faces, right? You're going to do a story and we'll all be in it."

Lewis picked up his sandwich wrapper, smoothed out the fan he'd made, and began furiously folding it into ever-smaller triangles.

"The best thing you can do is get out ahead of this, Lewis. Go to the sheriff's office and make a statement. And then prepare yourself. There will be follow-up interviews. They will be talking to other people in your life. Get yourself straight with Hannah and her father if you can, and then hang on tight. If you truly don't know anything more than what you just said—"

"I don't. I don't!"

"All right. We're going to be reporting this story out, which means we'll be contacting other people, including the sheriff's office and your poker buddies, to get corroboration. You've got a little time before it hits the paper. It's up to you what you choose to do with it."

His hands were still now, resting on the table as he looked down at them. He nodded his head to show he'd heard me, and then we left.

13

"Your connection with Lewis really opened this story up," I said to Troy as we headed from Omico to Himmel.

"Now we've got something *GO News* doesn't have. This will be a big story, won't it? Do you think any of the poker guys had anything to do with the murder? I mean, we know Lewis didn't, for sure, and Kent Morgan. But those other four guys ..."

"No, Troy. We don't know that Lewis had nothing to do with Jancee's death, or Kent either. At this point, nobody gets a pass."

"But Lewis—"

"I know. Lewis is your friend. I admit, he doesn't strike me as a killer. Neither does Kent Morgan, but they both lied at least by omission about the dancer. I understand why, but still, there it is. Have you ever heard the saying 'If your mother says she loves you, check it out?' It's a reporter's job to be a skeptic. To verify, to check, and recheck. Because if it isn't true, you can't use it. And you can never use just one source, even when the source is a friend."

"I know that. I was a reporter on my college paper for three years. I understand about sourcing. I know you have to verify. But don't you ever trust people, people you know?"

"Sure I do, a few. But for a story, I'd still verify what they told me. And it isn't actually people I don't trust. It's life and the things it throws at every-one. Those slings and arrows can make people—even good people, people you like—do some pretty bad things. Do you see what I mean?"

"Yes, I get it. I know I can do the job, Leah. Just keep me on the story and I'll prove it."

"Well, I need you right now, so you'll have plenty of chances to show what you can do. When I drop you at the office, call Tanner's and speak to the owner, confirm that Jancee worked there. Ask him why no one reported her missing, too. I want to get this story up before *GO News* gets wind of it, so you don't have to dig too deep; we'll circle back and dig into the whole Tanner's thing later."

"Okay. I'll try to get hold of Kent and Wes Morgan and the other players to verify what Lewis said, too."

"Good. Write it up and have Miguel take a look at it. I'll add what I have when I get back from the sheriff's office."

When I walked into the sheriff's office, I stopped first to check in with my friend Jennifer Pilarski.

"Hey, Jen. Is Lamey in?"

"Yeah, but he's in a meeting. A real one this time, not one with himself," she said, taking a bite out of a cookie and opening her drawer to offer me one. "They're homemade, chocolate-chip coconut."

"I thought you just joined that weight loss club."

"I did. But then I saw this art history show on PBS and I found out that I'm not fat. I'm Rubenesque. Rubens was this great artist who painted 'well-rounded' ladies that everybody thought were beautiful back in the day. I was just born in the wrong century. And why should I punish myself for that?" She batted her eyelashes at me and flipped her wavy brown hair over her shoulder.

"Why indeed?" I agreed as I took the cookie she offered me. "How long do you think Lamey's going to be?"

"I don't know. Detective Fike, the new guy, was in there with him when I left for break, but the door was open. When I got back, there was a note on my desk not to disturb him. Do you want me to schedule an appointment for you?"

"No, I didn't come to see him. I'm looking for Ross, and I was actually hoping Lamey wasn't around. I'd rather not run into him just now. Or ever. Is Ross in?"

Charlie Ross is a detective in the sheriff's office. We used to be at odds all of the time. Now it's just some of the time. I'm not sure if he's the one who's changed, or me. Either way, I like it. And I like his fifteen-year-old daughter Allie, too. She works part-time at the paper.

"Yeah, he's in a cranky mood, though. Watch out. He came into the break room as I was leaving. He's probably still there. You can go back and look. If the sheriff comes out of his office, I'll text and you can go out the side door."

"Never. I'm not afraid of that toad, I just don't want to see him if I don't have to."

"I feel the same way. Unfortunately seeing him is part of my job description," she said. "Here, take a cookie for Charlie. He'll be nicer if he's fed."

Ross was the only one in the break room. He didn't hear me come in. I watched him for a minute as he stood with his back to me, scooping coffee into the industrial-size coffee maker. Ross is in his late forties, short and solid, a little overweight, though not as much as he used to be. His hair, a light brown, is rapidly receding into a fringe circling his head. His small, close-set eyes are an odd sort of mustardy brown color. They darken a little when he's thinking hard or interrogating a suspect. His mouth is small with plump lips that he often compresses into a thin line when he's talking to me and I'm irritating him. Which is a fair amount of the time.

"What are you doin' here, Nash?"

He asked the question before he even turned around.

"How did you know it was me, Ross?"

"Eyes in the back of my head. That's why I'm such a good detective."

"More like reflection in the break room window," I said.

He looked at me then and grinned. "Want some coffee?"

"Sure. And I've got something to go with it," I said, handing him one of the two cookies I held. "And better yet, I've got some information you might enjoy even more than the cookie."

"Yeah? What's that?" he asked, putting two cups of coffee down on the beaten-up wooden table that took up most of the break room floor space.

I pulled out a chair across from him and situated myself, my cookie, and my coffee. Then I slid off the canvas bag hanging over my shoulder. I reached inside, and with a flourish befitting the news I was about to give him, I pulled out the glittery red high heels.

"I think these belong to your body. I was with Miguel when he found them last week. Don't lecture me about fingerprints. It's way too late, we've both had our hands all over them. We had no idea they would figure into a murder when he stumbled over them in a cornfield."

"What cornfield? Where?"

"It's on Bannock Road. Belongs to a farmer named Dwight Pearson. Miguel was shooting photos out there when he found them. Your victim wasn't wearing shoes. I've got a pretty good reason to believe these were hers."

His clever little eyes narrowed. "Huh."

"Huh? That's all you have to say? Don't you want to know how I made my amazing deduction? Well, how about this then? I know the name of your victim. At least the first name. It's Jancee. She's a dancer at Tanner's Gentlemen's Club. And I know who can tell you a lot more: Wes Morgan. In fact, I can give you the names of five others, including Kent Morgan, who were all with your victim last Monday night. Which is probably the night she died."

"You're talkin' like this is my case."

"Isn't it?"

I was shocked. Ross is one of the better detectives in the sheriff's office, and he's the most experienced.

"Whose, then?"

"Owen Fike."

"Jen mentioned he was a new guy. What's his story?"

"Right now, he's Lamey's best boy. Lateral transfer in from Dorset

County. His aunt is Judge Cain. My 'amazing deduction' is that Lamey is kissing up to everybody he thinks can help him get elected. So, he gives the judge's nephew a nice murder case. I dunno, Fike might be good. I can't tell yet."

"If Lamey wants to get elected, it seems to me he should use his best detective. And that would be you, Ross."

His thick eyebrows lifted in surprise.

"No. I mean it," I said. Then I added, "Given the relatively small number of detectives he has on the force, that is."

He shook his head.

"That sounds more like it. Lamey doesn't see this as a major crime. Yeah, sure, it's a murder. But he figures the girl wasn't somebody that anyone important cares about. Maybe a druggie or a hooker, got dumped way out here by her pimp. He lets Fike cut his teeth on it. No harm no foul if he doesn't clear it. Nobody reported her missing. No family's gonna come forward and put up a fuss."

"What are you working on then?"

"I'm on paperwork patrol. Goin' through old case files from thirty, forty years ago. Nobody's gonna solve those now," he said, shaking his head in disgust. "When I'm through with that, I'm supposed to put together a crime statistics report for the last ten years. He's tryin' to force me into quitting. If your boy Coop doesn't win this election, I'm gonna have to bail. I can't work for that self-dealin' idiot Lamey much longer."

Lamey's only qualification to be sheriff, as far as I could see, was being in the right place at the right time when Sheriff Dillingham had stepped down.

"I hope that doesn't happen, Ross. Not that I'd miss you or anything. I'd just hate to have to break someone else in."

"Yeah, same here. I don't wanna have to start all over with some other pain-in-the-ass in another county. Though I gotta say, I think you're in a class by yourself."

"Thank you. You know, even though it's not your case, I'm going to give the information to you. Maybe it'll give you a little leverage with Lamey."

"No offense, Nash, but I don't need Lamey thinkin' you and me are a team, okay? But tell me anyway. I'll pass it along if it's worth passin'."

I proceeded to give him the details on the shoes, and why they had to belong to the murder victim, Jancee. I filled him in on Kent Morgan's poker club and checked my notes to be sure I gave him the correct names of the players as well.

"Where'd you get all this?"

"Troy had an in with Lewis Webber, one of the poker players. Lewis broke open like a *piñata* when I whacked him with a few good swings of my skillful questioning."

"You're real proud of that metaphor, aren't you?"

"Kind of. It's more of a simile, though. And where did you dig up the word metaphor? That doesn't sound like you."

"I got hidden depths, Nash."

"Whatever," I said, shaking my head before I went on. "Lewis isn't a regular player, just an unlucky sub who happened to be there the night Jancee was. Also, he's younger than the other guys by ten years or more, I'd say. I tried to convince him that he needs to get out ahead of things and tell what he knows to the cops. I think there's a fair chance he'll come in to give a statement on his own."

"Okay, that's some nice work, I'll give you that."

"Thanks. Anything else you can give me?"

"Not much. I know Wes Morgan a little. He did some work at my house when Allie moved in. I read where teenage girls, they like to spend a lotta time in their rooms, so I wanted to build hers out, give her more space. Wes did a good job. But he's one of those guys who wants to be a big shot, only he's not."

"How do you think Lamey's going to react to this information?"

"My guess is he's not gonna like it one bit."

"You mean because that poor little toady is going to be walking a tightrope trying not to upset an important guy like Kent Morgan? Lamey's a good kiss-up, but this situation is going to take the fine art of diplomacy, yeah? 'These things must be done delicately.'"

I did a very good impression of Margaret Hamilton, but it was lost on my audience.

"Oh, come on. *The Wizard of Oz*? The movie? Margaret Hamilton? The Wicked Witch of the West?"

"Never saw it."

I sighed and shook my head.

"Ross, your lack of knowledge about American film is shocking. You need to come to a remedial evening of classic movies with me sometime."

"Sorry, I'm busy that night."

As I stood up to leave a question popped into my head.

"Ross, Jancee was strangled, but it's not that common for a killer to use his bare hands to choke someone to death. Was anything found at the scene? I mean like a scarf, or a belt, or the strap of a purse?"

He didn't answer, but his expression had changed just slightly when I suggested a purse strap. Which was, of course, an answer.

"That's it, isn't it? The killer used the leather strap of her purse. The press release said there was no wallet and no identification, but there wasn't any purse either, was there? The killer had to take it away, in case of fingerprints or DNA. Am I right?"

"Off the record? Yes. But they're holdin' that back, so they can weed out the crazies. You know, the look-at-me guys who make up stuff just to get attention or be part of things. So don't use that."

"I know the drill. I'll keep a lid on what you told me—or didn't tell me —until it's released. Do what you will with the information I gave you. At least now they can identify the victim. I'm out of here. Got questions to ask, facts to confirm, stories to write."

As I was talking, Jen had come into the break room. She had a funny expression on her face.

"They already know who the victim is," she said. "That's what I came to tell you."

"Really? How?"

"Someone came in that knew her. He recognized the description in the press release we put out. That's who Lamey and Fike were meeting with. Leah, it's Dan. It's Coop's dad. He said that he's a friend of hers."

14

I did not see that coming.

"What? How is Coop's dad friends with a stripper?"

"I don't know. This could be bad for Coop, couldn't it?"

"Yes. It could."

I sank back in my chair. My mind ran through variations on a theme for future *GO News* headlines when Spencer Karr got hold of this. *Candidate's Father Close Friend of Murdered Stripper. Cooper's Campaign Manager Questioned in Stripper's Death.* The facts wouldn't matter. The simple, logical explanation wouldn't matter. And I was sure that with Dan involved, the truth would be both simple and logical. Misleading headlines are a *GO News* specialty. And way too many people don't bother to read anything more than a headline. I groaned.

"Maybe it won't be so bad," Jen said. "Dan has lots of friends; they're not going to believe anything sleazy about him."

"You have a very touching faith in human nature, Jen."

"Nash is right," Ross said. "Nothin' the public likes better than a scandal. A campaign manager, who is also your dad, mixed up with a stripper is bad enough. Add in murder, and Coop's gonna get plenty of name recognition. Just not the kind he needs."

"Is Dan still here? Does Coop know?" I asked as the ramifications of the news continued to hit me.

"I don't know. I—"

I jumped up and called over my shoulder as I ran past Jennifer, still standing in the doorway. "I'll talk to you guys later."

I dashed down the hall and into the open office where Jen sits. Dan Cooper wasn't there, but Art Lamey was. He stepped in front of me so abruptly that I almost plowed into him.

"Looking for someone?"

"Nope, just in a hurry. Got a deadline, sorry, can't chat."

I stepped around him and headed for the door, hoping I would find Dan in the parking lot.

"Oh? I thought you might be trying to catch up on our murder investigation," he called after me.

I stopped and turned back.

"Detective Fike and I were just talking to a person of interest in the case. Dan Cooper. My opponent's campaign manager. Who is also his father." He didn't even try to keep the satisfaction out of his thin, reedy voice.

"Dan Cooper? What does he have to do with the case?" I asked, putting as much nonchalance into my voice as I could muster. Which wasn't much.

"You're a little late to the party. I just talked to a reporter from *GO News*. I imagine the story's up already. It pays to play fair with the sheriff, Ms. Nash." He gave the "Ms." an exaggerated emphasis, stretching it out so it became Mizzzzz, to make sure I knew he had the upper hand.

The tiny ping from my phone just then alerted me to a *GO News* update and proved Lamey was correct. Our digital rival already had the story online. The *Times* had been scooped once again. I refocused as Lamey droned on.

"Now, I'm an impartial man. So, even though your paper doesn't play fair with me, I'm going to update you on where we are in this very interesting case."

"Okay, why is Dan Cooper a person of interest in your murder investigation?"

"Mr. Cooper came to see us, he said, after reading our news release asking for help identifying the victim. He told us that the victim's name is Jancee Reynolds. She was a dancer at Tanner's Gentlemen's Club. We have confirmed that with the owner, who also identified her from a photo we texted."

"How did Dan know the victim?"

"He indicated that he's a 'friend' of Ms. Reynolds." I hated the heavy quotes Lamey put around the word friend. It conveyed exactly what readers of *GO News* were going to say about Dan having a relationship with a girl young enough to be his granddaughter. This was going to be a mess.

"So, why are you calling him a 'person of interest' instead of a witness? Do you have any evidence that suggests Dan was involved with her in any way?"

"As you should know, a person of interest is exactly that. Someone we are interested in. He's not a suspect ... at this time. We are investigating his ties to the victim."

I could see Lamey's plan to smear Dan, and by extension, Coop's campaign pretty clearly. Lots of innuendo, hints, and constant references to Dan's friendship with the murdered dancer. All designed to portray Dan's relationship to Jancee as sleazy at best, and criminal at worst.

"Why do you think he has any ties? Maybe she used to work in a convenience store where he got his coffee. Or maybe they had the same dentist, or they were in a long line at the donut shop and he struck up a conversation with her. What did Dan say about it?"

"I am not going to reveal confidential information about the details of a murder investigation to the press. The only thing I'll say is that Mr. Cooper's story raised more questions than it answered. That's why, as I already stated, we are investigating his connection to the victim."

"Are you going to recuse yourself from oversight in this investigation?"

The question took him by surprise, though it shouldn't have. "Why would I do that?"

"Because the public could perceive that you're more interested in hurting your opponent's campaign than in finding a killer. How can you be objective when you're investigating your rival's father?"

His back stiffened and he drew himself up to his not very tall height.

"Are you questioning my ethics? This investigation will be completely impartial. The public knows that Sheriff Art Lamey is a man of integrity and competence. And this investigation will reflect those values, whether or not your fake news tries to smear it, and Art Lamey."

Referring to himself in the third person meant that I had gotten under his skin. Good. Even though that was a creepy-crawly place to be.

Jennifer, who was standing behind Lamey, signaled it was time for me to cut my losses and leave by drawing her index finger across her throat. But, as is my way, regrettably, I couldn't resist making things just a little bit worse by firing off one last parting shot.

"I wasn't questioning your ethics, Acting Sheriff Lamey. I think the way you handled the fraud investigation of your friend Bruce Dengler makes them pretty clear. You not only didn't recuse yourself, you killed that investigation. The *Times* will be following this one very closely. And there will be more questions, believe me."

15

I tried Dan's number as soon as I got to my car. When there was no answer, I called Coop.

"Where's your dad? Have you talked to him yet?"

"So we're just totally dispensing with hello, now?"

"I'm not playing, Coop. Did you know that your father gave the sheriff the identity of the murdered woman they found in the woods? And that Dan said he knows her because they're friends? Do you know how *GO News* is going to spin this?"

"Dad knows the woman who was killed? He didn't say anything to me. Are you sure you got that right? Wait, hold on a second, he's just pulling into my driveway."

"I'll be right there."

I called Troy on my way to Coop's to see how he was coming on the story.

"I talked to Kent Morgan. He was pretty surprised we made the Jancee connection, but once he knew that we knew, he confirmed who was there. He said that his brother did it for a joke. That she didn't stay very long. That he was embarrassed by the situation and he thought everyone else was, too."

"Did you reach any of the other players?"

"I got hold of Eric Tripp. He was pretty upfront. Basically confirmed what Lewis said about the poker game and Jancee and the reason they didn't come forward. I talked to Wes Morgan, too. First he tried to say he didn't know anything. I told him I had multiple sources, but I didn't name them, and I told him what Lewis and Eric had said. So then he tried to act nicer. He asked how he could talk me out of printing anything. When I said we were going with the story, he hung up on me. I tried the other guys and left voicemails, but no one's called me back."

"I doubt they will. Did you talk to the Tanner's owner, find out why he didn't report Jancee missing?"

"It's a she, not a he. Krystal Gerrard. She said that 'girls' at Tanner's come and go. She didn't consider her missing. She assumed Jancee took off with a man. She doesn't pay attention to the news. Then she hung up on me, too."

"I found out Jancee's full name at the sheriff's office. It's Jancee Reynolds. Now I'm on my way to see Dan Cooper to find out what he knows."

"Why would Coop's dad know anything about Jancee Reynolds?"

"While I was there being a good citizen and telling Ross what we'd found out, Dan was sitting in the sheriff's office giving him the murder victim's name. According to Lamey, Dan said that she was a friend of his."

"Whoa! Coop's dad was friends with a strip club dancer? That's not good."

"No, Troy, it's not. But it's news and we have to report it. I'm sure *GO News* will have it up soon, maybe before we do. But don't rush our story. They may beat us out of the gate, but we've got stuff they can't possibly have yet. And we'll have more after I talk to Dan."

"Okay. Oh, Kent Morgan might call you to see if you'll leave out the poker party and the stripper thing. He didn't ask me not to run it, but I think that's what he's hoping."

"That's not too surprising, I guess. Is Miguel there?"

"Yeah, do you want to talk to him?"

"No. Just tell him I'll be in shortly. Okay, I'm at Coop's now, I'm hanging up."

"Leah—"

"Yeah?"

"This is exciting, isn't it?"

"Yes, Troy, it is."

Coop and his dad were seated at the kitchen table as I walked in. Dan looked miserable and Coop didn't look much better.

"Dan, what's going on? Why did you tell the cops that you were friends with a murdered stripper?"

"I didn't say we were friends, but I told Art that I knew her. I only met her once," Dan said. "When I read that no one had reported her missing, no family came forward to identify her ... Well, I just felt awful that the poor kid was dead, and not one person cared enough to even wonder where she was. I had to speak up for her because there wasn't anyone else."

"That was a nice thought, Dan. But there *were* other people who knew who she was. Someone at Tanner's would have recognized the description. Heck, I turned up six guys at Kent Morgan's weekly poker game who recognized her. Now Lamey and *GO News* are going to make things as rough as they can for you and Coop."

"I know," he said, his shoulders slumping. "I realized that as I was talking to Art and Detective Fike. I blew it, didn't I?"

"Leah, lighten up. Dad was just trying to do the right thing," Coop said, frowning at me.

I took a breath.

"Coop's right, Dan. I shouldn't have come down so hard on you. It's not your fault that Lamey is a shady schemer who will do anything to win. You did the morally right thing. It's just our bad luck that Lamey and *GO News* always do the morally wrong thing."

"Dad, don't beat yourself up. Just tell us how you knew Jancee. When did you meet her?"

"Wait a sec," I said.

I pulled out my notebook and flipped it open.

"Dan, we're running with a story about Jancee being hired by Kent Morgan's brother Wes to 'entertain' at a poker party last Monday night. It

was Wes's birthday surprise for Kent. I need to have the facts on your relationship with Jancee to use in the story, too. So, this is on the record."

"Yeah, sure. There wasn't anything wrong about me knowing Jancee."

"Where did you meet her?" I asked, hoping it was, as I'd suggested to
Lamey, in a long line at the coffeeshop, but I was pretty sure that wasn't
going to be his answer.

"At Tanner's."

Coop shot me a warning look.

"Do you remember me telling you about Ricky Travers, Coop?"

"Doesn't sound familiar, Dad."

"He was a high school kid in my building trades class at Omico High a
couple of years ago. Big guy, real quiet, pretty shy. Didn't have a lot of
friends. He's slow—I don't mean mentally impaired, but he takes his time
processing things. He got a lot of teasing from the other kids. He fought
back a few times and got himself in a little trouble at school. But he did
great in my hands-on class, really came into his own. I helped him get
connected with a carpentry program. He's doing an apprenticeship right
now with Wes Morgan's construction company in Omico."

"You know Wes Morgan, too?" I asked.

"A little, both of us being in the trade. He's a good carpenter."

"What does Ricky Travers have to do with Jancee and Tanner's?" I
asked.

Instead of answering, Dan turned to Coop.

"You remember Wes, don't you, son? We played Packers Trivia with him
one night last spring. We stopped at Stan's Bar in Omico when I was down
to help you with that china cabinet?"

"He's kind of loud, talks a lot?"

"That's the one," Dan said. "Wes is all right. Kind of a big talker, is all.
Anyway I put in a good word for Ricky, and Wes took him on. I ran into
Ricky when I was in Omico in August for Bob's retirement party. We got to
talking and Ricky said he really liked carpentry, but he still worked some
weekends at Tanner's as a bouncer. His uncle's a bartender there."

At last we had a Tanner's connection. I was having a hard time not
urging Dan to get to the point. Coop could tell and took pity on me.

"So is Ricky linked to you knowing Jancee Reynolds?"

"He's how I met her. When I saw Ricky, he mentioned he was running into problems with a window replacement in one of the cabins that Tanner's rents out to dancers. They're up the road just a little from the club. I offered to help. I drove up there with him. It was tricky, but it wasn't a tough job with the two of us. When we finished, Ricky invited me into Tanner's for lunch."

"Tanner's has a restaurant?" I asked, surprised. "I didn't think people went there to eat."

"It's just bar food. But it wasn't bad. His uncle Jerry was working at the bar, and while we were eating and talking, Ricky left to pick up a tool he'd left back at the cabin. I stayed to finish up my lunch. A young lady came in to talk to Jerry."

"That was Jancee?" I asked.

He nodded. "Jerry introduced us and I chatted with her a little."

"What did you talk to her about?"

"Just this and that, you know, where was she from, did she have family in the area, that kind of thing."

"Do you remember anything specific?"

"She told me that she was from Eau Claire. She lived in foster homes mostly, then on her own. Someone told her she could make decent money at Tanner's. She told me she was saving up to move to Chicago. She was going to dance in a place 'with class,' she said, make a lot of money. She had kind of a tough-girl attitude, but it was easy to see how young she was. I almost told her that there were other ways to earn a living. Then I figured she didn't want the opinion of an old guy like me."

"So that's your only connection to Jancee?" I asked.

"That's it. I never saw her again."

"Then how could you be so sure that the dancer you met and the murder victim were the same person?" Coop asked.

"I wasn't sure, but it sounded like her. Right down to the blue fairy tattoo. That's why I went to the sheriff's office. I didn't like the thought of Jancee lying in a morgue, unclaimed, like a lost umbrella. I'm sorry, Coop. It never occurred to me it would make a problem for you."

"It's all right, Dad. We'll tough it out."

16

On my way back to the newsroom, I got the call Troy had told me to expect.

"This is Leah Nash."

"Leah. Kent Morgan here. Do you have a minute?"

His voice was hesitant, not angry as I'd expected.

"Just about. I'm in the car, on my way to the office."

"This won't take long. I'm calling to apologize, and also to ask if you'd consider doing me a favor."

"Oh?"

"Yes. I spoke earlier with Troy. It was stupid and wrong of me to lie to you—I admit that's what I did."

"Okay, so why did you?"

"For selfish, not criminal, reasons. I was trying to save myself—and my wife and daughter—from embarrassment. Caused, as usual, by my brother Wes. Everyone who was there that night felt the same. We all wanted to protect our families. I know it doesn't make us sound very good. But that's the reason. Now we can all see that we should have gone to the police."

"Yes. You should have. Have you spoken to them yet?"

"I'm due at the sheriff's office to talk to Art Lamey and the detective in charge of the investigation in about an hour."

"You said you had something to ask me. What is it?"

I waited expectantly for the please-don't-use-this-information-in-your-story request. It happens quite often. People think it's just big-time journalists who have politicos and wealthy people requesting special favors. But though the sphere of influence may be smaller, there are proportionately just as many VIPs—or people who think they are—in small communities. And the stakes for them are just as high—maybe higher, because small-town people can neither run nor hide from the facts, or the gossip.

But Kent's request surprised me when it came.

"I know you'll be using the information about Jancee Reynolds being at our poker group. There's no point asking you not to. I can't even ask you not to use our names—the reasonable expectation of privacy argument won't work. Half the town knows that we all get together for a game every week. We've been doing it for years. I just wondered if you could tell me when the story is coming out? I'd like to talk to my wife before she sees it online. She's been out of town all day."

His ask was reasonable, and I found myself feeling a little sorry for him, thinking about the conversation he'd need to have with his wife.

"I'd say you have about an hour, maybe a little more. I just drove into the parking lot. Troy and I will be putting our notes together. The story will go up as soon as it's written and edited."

"All right, thank you. I appreciate it."

"Are you sure we shouldn't have a double byline?" Troy asked, looking over Miguel's shoulder. We were in the newsroom waiting for Miguel to finish editing our story. My mother and Gabe were there, too. We were all going to McClain's to celebrate the scoop.

"I'm sure. The 'additional reporting by Leah Nash' credit is how it should be. You did more than half the work, and you supplied the key piece, Lewis. Publish it as is, Miguel."

A shout of "Yes!" went up from all of us as he did.

Then my mother said, "I feel sorry for Kent Morgan. He should have gone to the police, of course, but I can understand why he didn't."

"I can too, but it was still pretty self-serving. If I were his wife, I wouldn't be so mad that it happened. I mean that was on Wes, it sounds like. What would really upset me is that he lied by omission and didn't tell me the truth until he was forced to by a newspaper story."

"Well, maybe he was waiting for the right time, but you and Troy figured things out before that ever came," Gabe said. "You two got a lot of mileage out of a red sequin and a pair of high heels."

"And now we're ahead of *GO News*. For once."

"Andrea will not be happy, but Sheriff Lamey might be," Miguel said.

"What's in our story that would make Lamey happy? Tell me, because whatever it is, I'm taking it out," I said, only half-kidding.

"You named the names, so now he isn't the bad guy to Kent Morgan and his friends. Sheriff Lamey didn't out them, you did."

"That's true, I guess. But I don't mind being a minor player in Lamey's power game—if it means we beat Spencer Karr."

I did a high five all around, but Troy's return was surprisingly lackluster.

"What's up with that, Troy? You should be dancing in the streets."

I realized too late that I had given my mother a cue to burst into the iconic Motown song, "Dancing in the Streets." I tried to move on but she'd already swung into her sixties dance steps as she belted out the lyrics and pulled Troy to his feet to join her.

Troy likes my mother, and this wasn't the first time she'd broken into song in the office, so he gave it a half-hearted try, but he looked miserable. Miguel rescued him by cutting in to finish out the song and dance fest with my mother, who had also induced Gabe to join in. Gabe is a very good dancer.

As Troy stood with me on the sidelines I asked again, "What's going on? You look like you just got asked to hand in your torch on *Survivor*. Troy, we got a solid story today. We found out Jancee's identity, and where she probably was the night she died. And we did it before the cops or *GO News!* Why aren't you deliriously happy?"

"I'm happy. I am. It's just, once we published the story, it hit me how bad this is going to be for Lewis. I sort of tricked him. And now he's probably in trouble with his boss, and his fiancée, plus all the guys he plays cards with. I feel like I used a friend."

"Okay, no. First, if he's in trouble you didn't put him there. His own decisions did. If he was so disturbed when Jancee showed up, he could have left. If he felt so guilty, he could have got in front of things by telling his fiancée when it happened. And most importantly, he didn't have to go along with the group and lie by omission to the cops."

"But—"

"I understand you feel bad. And I suppose Lewis could be mad at you now. But he seems like a basically okay person. When he thinks about it, he'll know it's on him, not on you. If you stay in reporting, you're going to run into a lot more times when you have to weigh friendship against getting the story out. If you want to do the job right, truth has to win. Now, forget about Lewis and whether or not he's mad at you. Enjoy this, Troy. You scored your first major scoop today."

I turned to the others, who were still laughing and comparing dance steps.

"Hey, you guys! We've got a date at McClain's, and I'm buying the first round. Let's go!"

17

It's possible that my fondness for McClain's dark and shabby interior stems from my fondness for the noir films of the forties. McClain's looks like a place where a sleepy-eyed private eye would go to meet the gangster's girl he can't get out of his mind. The bar is long, dark, and well-polished, and the most "fancy" cocktail you can order is a Brandy Old Fashioned—which is basically the state drink of Wisconsin.

We arrived during that lull between after-work drinkers leaving and evening regulars arriving. We pulled a couple of tables together, because Miguel, friendly soul that he is, had invited Courtnee to join us and Miller Caldwell as well. Sherry Young, a cute waitress who loves Miguel and hates me, was at the bar with her back to us, talking to Davey the bartender.

"Hey, Sherry, we're celebrating here. How about taking our orders? First round is on me," I added.

She barely nodded in acknowledgment, then headed straight toward Gabe, also a favorite. While she flirted with him, I turned to Miller, who had taken a seat on the other side of me. He smiled, showing both his perfect white teeth and a warm light in his bright blue eyes. He's started wearing his graying hair, still parted on the side, a little longer and looser and it suits him. He still looks like what he is, a wealthy businessman, but he has a sort of mid-life Robert Redford vibe going now.

"So, I'm curious. Did Kent Morgan ask you to kill the reference in the story to him and his poker game before he called me?" I asked.

"He called me, but not to ask if we'd kill the story. If he had, I would've told him that the editorial side of our partnership is your bailiwick. He was worried about his brother, Wes."

"You mean because Wes is the one that set Jancee up to come to the party?"

"Exactly. I gather Kent has been pulling him out of trouble for most of their lives."

"Did he ask you to keep his brother out of the story?"

"No, I think he just wanted to talk. He feels embarrassed and a little ashamed by the whole thing. We're not close friends. So, I suspect he may have called me because he knows I'm no stranger to public humiliation," he said with a wry smile.

I knew Miller was referring to the painful period when he had come out as a gay man after a lifetime hiding it. He'd given up a run for the state senate, ended his marriage, and almost lost his relationship with his children—all in the public eye.

"Well, if he was looking for a lesson in how to move through a tough time with courage, he couldn't find a better man to ask," I said.

He lifted his hand slightly and shook his head in denial.

"I made a lot of mistakes. I hurt my children and my wife deeply. I've been fortunate that they had the generosity to move past their pain."

"Well, your kids did anyway."

"I can't fault Georgia for her anger. I put her in a terrible position."

"Maybe you can't, but I sure can. She did her best to turn your kids against you. She trash-talked you all over town. She—"

"Leah, I appreciate your partisanship, but I don't blame Georgia for lashing out. I just hope that she's happy in her new life."

"All right. Sorry. It's your ex-wife, your life," I said, though what I thought was that with the amount of money Miller had settled on her, even Georgia would have to work hard at not being happy.

"So, how long do you think it will be before *GO News* follows up with something sensational on the investigation? Spencer Karr won't enjoy taking a backseat to the *Times*. He has a very strong competitive streak."

"Oh, they'll probably come out with something later this evening. Most likely a rehash of what we already printed. I'm pretty sure Andrea won't get any more from Kent and the other guys than we did. Probably less. I know Dan won't give her much. I think we can bask in our glory for at least a couple of days."

But our basking ended just then as Miguel jumped up and nearly knocked Sherry down in his rush to get to me. He held out his phone, a look of shock on his face that I matched with my own as soon as I scrolled down the screen.

It was a great photo—good composition, good lighting. It captured the action perfectly.

Unfortunately, the action was Dan Cooper delivering an upper cut to a smaller man, while a scantily clad, very young, very pretty woman looked on. I had no doubt it was Jancee Reynolds. Details were sharp and clear: the Tanner's logo behind the bar, the bottle of Sprecher's Root Beer next to an empty plate—the blood running down the face of a man Dan had obviously just punched.

"Oh, no," I said with a groan. "Where did they get this picture? Oh, geez, the cutline!"

Dan Cooper, father and campaign manager of sheriff candidate David Cooper, delivers a punch to Dewey Redding of Bear Creek at Tanner's Gentlemen's Club in a fight over murder victim Jancee Reynolds, who looks on.

Dan hadn't said anything about the bar fight when he told me about meeting Jancee. I cringed inwardly, remembering my lecture to Troy about checking out what a source tells you—even when the source is a friend.

There was a second photo. Dan stood next to Jancee. Her hand was on his arm. The two watched as a young guy built like a bull, identified as

Ricky Travers, held Dewey Redding by his belt and the back of his shirt. He appeared to be literally throwing him out of the bar.

I handed Miguel's phone back to him.

"I can't read the story. Spare me Andrea's breathless prose, Miguel, just give me the gist."

"Okay. Mmm. Uh-uh. Oh-oh."

He looked up, shaking his head. "It's not good. The story says Dan is helping police with their investigation, that he was a close friend of the 'sexy young stripper.' "

"Oh, boy," I said.

He nodded. "But listen to this that Andrea wrote. 'At this time police are not considering David Cooper, son of the victim's close friend Dan Cooper, a suspect in the murder of Jancee Reynolds.' "

"I have to hand it to her. The way Andrea's written that non-denial denial makes it sound like Coop *is* a suspect."

"I told you at the Eldorado, *chica*. Andrea, she never lets go, and she really does not like you. Even a little bit. She knows this story will make you crazy."

"It's both of them, her and Spencer. They're both unprincipled pseudo-journalists. But they're clever about it. They can't be accused of libel, because it very clearly says Coop's not a suspect. But the takeaway for lots of people will just be Coop's name in connection with a murder. And that fight! Those photos!"

"Dan didn't say one word about getting into a fight at a strip club. I just gave Troy a big lecture on trust but verify. Turns out I'm the one that needed the reminder. Geez, why didn't Dan tell me that? And where did those photos come from?"

Choosing to answer the easier question, Miguel replied, "It says 'photo courtesy of Monroe Mepham.' "

"I don't recognize the name. It wouldn't surprise me if Spencer hired someone to follow Coop and Dan around on the off chance they could get an embarrassing photo for the paper. I'm not serious," I added as he gave me a look. "Not totally, anyway. But how did they get the photos so fast?"

By then everyone at the table had their phones out and was checking out the story. A low-key buzz was circulating as each of them skimmed the article and shared their thoughts with the person next to them.

"Hey," I said, standing up, "I don't know what's really going on here, but you can believe it's not what *GO News* published. I'm leaving now to check a few things out with Dan Cooper and find out what the real story is. Meanwhile, you guys help Troy celebrate himself. It's because of him we beat *GO News* for the first time in a while."

All eyes turned to Troy. Even in the dim light, I could see his wide smile as Miguel lifted his drink and said, "To Troy's big story!" Everyone clinked glasses. I swallowed what was left of my drink and said, "Okay, have another round on me. Or better yet, have one on Miller. See you guys later."

I grabbed my jacket from the back of my chair and slid my arms in it as I headed to the door. Courtnee stopped me as I hurried by her.

"But, Leah—"

"What, Courtnee? I have to get going."

"What if it is?"

"If what is?" I snapped impatiently.

"The story in *GO News*. What if, you know, that *is* the real story? Like if Coop's dad really is hot for a stripper? And that's why he beat up somebody at Tanner's?"

I didn't bother to answer. But for once it wasn't because Courtnee was being mind-numbingly stupid. It was because I was afraid she might not be.

18

When I got to Coop's he had a glass filled with ice in front of him, into which he was pouring a double shot of Bulleit. His father was working on a tall glass of Sprecher's Root Beer. Coop looked grim. Dan looked embarrassed.

"Dan. What is going on? When I asked you about Jancee Reynolds, how could you not tell me about the bar fight? And holy hell, how are there photos of you punching some guy out? How?"

"It was the DJ. He was setting up for his shift. I didn't notice him taking pictures, but that's his name on the photo credit. Monroe Mepham."

Although I hadn't recognized the name when Miguel had given it to me, my brain now made the connection.

"I know that guy. Well, I know who he is, anyway. He's married to Cole Granger's sister."

The Grangers are Grantland County's low-rent version of the Sopranos. A mix of native Wisconsinites and Kentucky transplants, they're a sprawling brood of blood relations, in-laws, and possibly a few cousins who married. Their activities run the gamut from sketchy to criminal. Most of them aren't disciplined or smart enough for big-time crime, but a few operate on the edges. They're the local go-to for anyone interested in making serious bad guy connections in Madison or Milwaukee. Cole

Granger is smarter than most of his clan and runs both sides of the street—
sometimes an informant for the cops, sometimes shepherding a small-time
criminal enterprise of his own. He's helped me out a time or two—though
I'd never make the mistake of thinking he's a friend.

"Thanks to Monroe, I guess I just got my fifteen minutes of fame. Not
exactly what I'd like to be known for—bar brawling," Dan said, with a weak
attempt at a smile.

But I wasn't in the mood for even a slight attempt at levity.

"Dan, there's nothing remotely funny about this situation. Don't you
see? Those photos make your it's-no-big-deal explanation for knowing
Jancee seem like a lie. It's pretty bad for the paper, too. It makes Troy and
me look like half-assed reporters who didn't bother to get all the facts. And
I guess I'm the guilty one there. *GO News* has a bigger budget, fewer
expenses, and way less scruples than the *Times* does. What we have going
for us is credibility. A story like the one we just ran kind of throws that
advantage out the window."

When I stopped to take a breath, Dan had a chance to respond.

"I don't know what to say. I had no idea those pictures existed. Believe
me, I am so sorry I didn't tell you everything. I didn't think the fight would
ever come out. There were only a few people there: me, Jerry the bartender,
the guy who was bothering Jancee, and Ricky. The fight didn't relate to
Jancee's death. It was months ago, and I guess I thought, 'What happens in
Tanner's stays in Tanner's.' " He gave a half-hearted laugh.

"It might have, if Monroe Mepham wasn't there taking photos for
posterity."

"I'm sorry," Dan repeated. "I didn't think it would turn into a big thing."

"Unfortunately, it definitely did. Detective Fike must have checked
things out at Tanner's after you left. Somebody, probably your friend
Monroe, gave him the bar fight details and showed him the pictures. Once
Fike talked to Lamey, he tipped Andrea off and the DJ made a few bucks on
his photos."

Dan looked like he was about to cry. I knew the feeling. I put my lips
together and blew out a long sigh that made my lips vibrate before
speaking again.

"Dan, I'm sorry for harshing on you. I'm projecting, I guess, taking out my anger at myself on you. It's not your fault that I was so eager to get the story up that I didn't check it out more. Tell me again, please, about how you met Jancee Reynolds. Only this time include the *Fight Club* parts."

"All right. It happened almost exactly like I told you," Dan said. "Ricky and I were eating lunch. The bartender, his uncle Jerry, was there. Ricky left to get a tool he forgot. I was still eating. Jancee came in and Jerry introduced us. He went to the back room for something. I chatted with Jancee. When Jerry came back he and Jancee started talking. I wandered over to see the DJ, Monroe Mepham.

"He was showing me his sound equipment. There was a commotion by the bar. I looked up and saw a guy grabbing Jancee by the arm. She pushed him away, but he grabbed her again. I didn't start the fight. I just walked up to them and said, 'Hey, now, the lady asked you to go. I think you should.' Then he said something like, 'Oh, yeah, old man? You know what I think?'

"Then he sucker-punched me on the side of the head. His aim was off enough that I came back with a good right cross. I would've let it go there, but he kept coming at me. Lucky for me he talked tougher than he fought. We were both about tapped out. I was ready to let it go and have both of us walk away. Then Ricky showed up. That kid is built like Reggie White in his heyday. He picked the guy up by the back of his shirt and his belt, carried him to the door, and then heaved him out. The guy didn't come back."

"What happened then?"

"Jancee came over and said thanks. Then she went outside to see how Ricky was. Jerry gave me a towel. I took it to the restroom, cleaned up a little, came back out. Ricky and Jancee were sitting at the bar. I asked Jancee who the guy was. She said he was just a jerk who thought a tip bought him more than he was entitled to. Ricky said he was sorry it happened. I thanked him for the exciting lunch, and I left. I never spoke to Jancee again, and I haven't talked to Ricky since then, either."

"You're sure Monroe Mepham doesn't have a follow-up photo of Jancee giving you a thank-you kiss?"

"She didn't. But I don't know if he has any more photos."

I thought for a minute. "Well, I doubt he does. *GO News* would have bought anything he had on offer, and they would definitely have printed one of you and Jancee in a more compromising position if they had it."

"Dad, when you told me a couple months ago that you fell off a ladder cleaning your neighbor's eavestrough, was Tanner's bar where you really got banged up?"

Dan gave Coop a shame-faced look.

"I didn't want you to know your old man was getting into bar fights. I thought it would go down better if I said I was helping out a friend. I didn't know it would come back to haunt me—and you."

"Okay, Dan, now this is absolutely it, right? No follow-up fights, no chance meetings where Jancee threw herself into your arms in repeat gratitude in front of witnesses—with cameras?"

"No, nothing else. I swear. What are you going to do with this now, Leah?"

"We'll do a follow-up story. Before we can we have to check with Ricky for his version of the events. His uncle Jerry, too. It's not that I don't trust you, Dan, but—"

"I know. Trust but verify. I deserve that, I guess."

"It's not a matter of you deserving, it's more a matter of me remembering to follow protocol. I'll try to talk to Monroe the DJ, too."

"I'm sorry you have to do extra work. I'm sorry I didn't tell you about the fight," Dan said again.

"Forget it, Dan. Like I said, I should have fact-checked even a friend, and I didn't. That's on me. But I'm not going to let *GO News* make it look like you're some sad old guy who fell in love with a stripper way less than half his age. Which they'll try to do. And I for sure am not having the sheriff's office tag you as its number one murder suspect."

The shocked look on Dan's face made me realize I had said the quiet part out loud.

"You can't be serious! I didn't kill that poor girl. Why would I?"

Emotion raised Dan's normally low voice to yelling-at-a-deaf-person levels.

"Of course you didn't. But think about it from Lamey's point of view. One, you started a bar fight to protect your girl; two, you hid that fact from the cops; three, those photos! You look, pardon the phrase, like you want to kill Jancee's tormenter. To a lot of people that might seem like you're a jealous man defending his woman."

"That's ridiculous. She was only nineteen years old, still a teenager. And Dewey had just sucker-punched me. You bet I was mad at him. And if I loved Jancee, why would I kill her?"

"Because later she dumped you, maybe?"

"That still wouldn't make me kill someone I loved."

"Not you, maybe, but spurned love is a pretty common murder motive. Lamey can run pretty far with it before it's proven untrue. It will make a great diversion from actual campaign issues. He'll get plenty of help from his personal propaganda machine, *GO News*. And Coop's name will be tangled up with yours all the way through this."

"So what can I do? How can I fix this mess?"

"You can start by talking to Detective Fike and coming clean with what you just told us."

"Right. I'll do it tomorrow."

"I'll go with you, Dad."

"Not a good idea," I said.

"It's a worse idea to let him hang out there alone when he was just doing what he thought was right," Coop said.

"He doesn't have to be alone. He can take Gabe with him. He'll make sure Detective Fike and Lamey don't back Dan into a corner, and don't put words in his mouth."

"I can do that, too," he said. "He's my father."

"That's the point. You need a little distance from this."

He had crossed his arms on his chest and was wearing his stubborn look.

"Coop, I'm not offering you thirty pieces of silver to betray your dad here. I'm just saying let Gabe handle Dan's interactions with the sheriff's office. It's what he does, right?"

"Excuse me," Dan said. "I can still make up my own mind about what I'm going to do. I don't need you two fighting over what's best for me. Leah, I'll take your advice. I'll call Gabe."

"Excellent," I said. "And Coop, if it will make you feel any better, you can make your comment to the *Himmel Times* right now. My question is: 'Mr. Cooper, do you have anything to say about your campaign manager, who is also your father, being interviewed as a person of interest in the murder of Jancee Reynolds?' "

Coop didn't hesitate.

"Yes, I do. My father is a great man, and a great campaign manager. The sheriff's office is obligated to check into every possible lead. I know that a well-run investigation will show that things happened exactly as my father said."

"Good answer," I said.

Coop reached across the table and patted his dad's hand.

"Don't worry. Everything will be fine. *GO News* may go a little crazy for a few days, but we'll be okay. I wouldn't want anyone else to be my campaign manager—or my father."

19

I started for the newspaper office to meet Troy, then decided to take a quick detour to see if Gabe was back home from McClain's. I wanted to forewarn him that Dan was going to need some lawyer-type help.

"From your expression, I'd say Dan wasn't able to make the GO News story go away with a few quick words of explanation," he said as he opened the door.

"Nope, he sure wasn't."

"Come on in and tell me all about it."

"That's what I'm here for, but first I could use a hug."

"Happy to oblige."

After he did, I followed him into the living room. He nudged Barnacle so I could have a seat on the couch. Gabe's place is usually pretty tidy and Barnacle is generally the only thing he has to pick up when he has guests. It's furnished in what I'd describe as comfortable minimalist—a cushiony light tan sofa long enough to lie down on, an end table, a high-backed wing chair that's good to read in, a coffee table, a bookshelf, and a small fireplace.

"You'll probably get a call from Dan in the morning. Or maybe even tonight yet," I said.

"Why's that?" he asked as he sat down and half-turned so he could face me.

I gave him the whole story, ending with my advice to Dan that he contact Detective Fike and come clean about things before Fike called him.

"Also, I told him to get in touch with you first."

"Yeah, he definitely needs someone in there with him. What's Dan's alibi?"

"His alibi?"

"Yeah. Where was he last Monday night? Jancee Reynolds' body was found Saturday. The medical examiner said she died four to seven days before that. The poker party was Monday night. I think it's safe to assume the police will be looking for alibis for Monday night or early Tuesday morning. Where was Dan?"

"I didn't ask him. I was more focused on telling him how bad he messed up."

"It'll make things much easier for him if he has a good one."

"He's staying with Coop. They probably watched a movie or some sports thing and went to bed."

"Given that they're father and son, that won't make the greatest alibi."

"Yeah, I see that. But according to Dan, the bartender and Dan's friend Ricky can confirm that he met Jancee for the first time the day of the fight. That should help. Why would he kill Jancee when he only met her once, weeks ago?"

Gabe just looked at me, waiting for my brain to kick into gear.

"Wait a minute. Ricky and his uncle can confirm that Jancee and Dan *met* for the first time on fight day. They can't know for sure what happened after that day, right? Dan and Jancee could have been seeing each other but keeping it quiet."

"Detective Fike will be thinking along those lines, I'm sure."

I flopped back against the couch with a loud sigh. "Geez Louise. This isn't how I saw this day turning out when Troy and I were flipping Lewis Webber."

"Why don't you stay over? I'll try to make you feel better."

"It's tempting, but Troy's waiting for me at the office. Plus, I have a crazy day shaping up for tomorrow. I need to do some work on my book before Clinton starts getting really nervous. Then I have to make a trip to Tanner's to nose around. If I'm lucky I might be able to talk to the owner, the bartender, and maybe the DJ. I want to talk to Detective Fike, too."

"Doesn't sound much like you're pulling back from day-to-day involvement with the paper. Can't Troy or Miguel do that?"

"Miguel's doing Maggie's job plus his. Troy doesn't have enough experience. Every day that Lamey and *GO News* can keep Coop's dad in the news is a bad day for Coop's campaign. How about getting together Friday instead?"

"That would be great, except I have to go out of town on Friday. I won't be back for a few days."

"You just got back on Saturday."

"I know, but something came up."

"Business something, or personal something? Is there anything wrong, Gabe?"

"No, nothing. It has to do with my friend, the one I went to see in New York."

"Okay, well, I hope you can get him sorted out this time. When will you be back?"

"It should be just a few days. I'll know better after I get out there."

"You *are* going to tell me what the big mystery is at some point, right?"

"Yes, and I promise that will be soon."

"All right. Will I see you before you leave?"

"Sure. Dinner Thursday? I'll cook."

"Your world-famous stuffed shells?"

"Count on it."

Troy was waiting patiently when I got back to the office. He started to tell me what he'd done so far, but I held up my hand to stop him.

"Wait a sec. I have to say this. It's pretty embarrassing, so let me just get it all out there. I did with Dan Cooper exactly what I told you not to do with Lewis Webber. I know Dan, and I trust him. I really wanted to get the jump on *GO News*. So, I didn't confirm his story by checking it with the bartender at Tanner's or with Dan's friend Ricky Travers. Which is why *GO News* had the fight story today, and why we'll be playing catch-up tomorrow. So, both of us should have been listening to the lecture I gave you about sourcing and checking, I guess."

Troy looked like he wasn't sure how to respond. Should he agree that I had made a significant mistake and displayed all the expertise of a first-year journalist? Or, should he tell me it wasn't that bad, when it clearly was? Or, should he just nod and move on? He chose door number three.

"Okay. I tried again and this time I talked to both the poker players who didn't return my voicemail, Richard Pullman and Greg Vogel. They both yelled at me for the story we ran. But they confirmed what Lewis said about Jancee at the party, and also that all four of them—Lewis, Richard, Greg, Eric Tripp—rode to Kent's cabin and back together. And they were all at the bar in Omico until closing."

"Okay, good."

I gave him what I had from Dan.

"We're not ready to write this yet. We need to talk to the bartender and to Ricky Travers. Not just to confirm Dan's story. I want to know why Ricky jumped into things, when Dan said the fight was pretty much over. Maybe it was personal. Maybe Jancee Reynolds was his girl."

"You mean now?"

"No, it can wait until tomorrow. We'll take a road trip to Tanner's."

"I'm supposed to interview the Hailwell school principal tomorrow morning."

"That's all right. I think Tanner's is more an afternoon kind of place. Let's call it a day for now. We'll see what tomorrow brings."

20

Wednesday morning arrived dark and chilly, with a slight patter of rain hitting the windows. I burrowed deeper into the covers when my alarm went off. Then I remembered I hadn't set my alarm. I thrust my arm out from under the covers and grabbed my still ringing phone. Troy. I bolted upright. Something big must have happened for him to call at six-thirty in the morning.

"Troy! What's going on?"

"Nothing. I just wanted to tell you I'm in the office. So we can go over things now if you want. Are you still in bed?" The question came out on a somewhat incredulous note.

I stared at the screen for a second as my sleep-dulled mind came slowly to full consciousness. I was on a FaceTime, not a regular, call with Troy. There was a look of surprise and (I felt) judgment in his earnest brown eyes as they took in my bedhead hair and the slightly stupefied expression on my face. I quickly turned off the camera.

"I salute your dedication. But never call me on FaceTime before breakfast. In fact, never call me on FaceTime."

"I'm sorry. I thought it was later. I rode my bike in this morning and I must have pushed it faster than I realized."

"Wait, what? You live halfway to Omico. You rode ten miles before work? Why?"

Too late I realized I shouldn't have given him the opening. I don't know Troy all that well, but I do know he loves to talk about his passion for biking. A lot, and at length.

"I hit a deer last week. My car's at Bang Bang Bump Shop until Thursday, at least. So, I thought what a great time to get in some extra biking. I used to be able to do ten miles in twenty-nine minutes, but my time is slower now. But what's so great about biking is anybody can do it. It doesn't have to be like a race. For my Eagle Scout project I organized a biking program for senior citizens. Some of them were in their eighties. They loved it, and they really got in shape. You should try it."

I didn't answer for a second, beguiled as I was by the image of young Troy leading a group of senior citizens toward super fitness on their bikes. He took my silence for affront and began stammering an apology.

"I don't mean you're out of shape. Or old. I just meant it's good for anybody, not you, specifically. I could put a training program together for you, if you want. We could train together, or—"

He was in full nervous ramble. I put him out of his misery.

"I appreciate the offer, but I'm pretty busy these days. Though thanks to your courtesy early wake-up call, I can get a head start on things this morning. I'm going to take my shower and have some breakfast right now."

"Okay. Yes. Sure. Sorry. About calling so early, I mean. I could go to the Elite and get a chai latte for you. Mrs. Schimelman told me that she'd have *heidesand* cookies today. I could get some of those, too."

"*Heidesands*? Yes, please. All is forgiven, Troy. I'll meet you downstairs shortly."

Heidesand is a round shortbread-like cookie that Mrs. Schimelman, owner of the Elite Café, only makes from late fall through the holiday season. They're worth leaping out of bed and rushing through a shower for.

It was quarter after seven when I got to the newsroom. Troy had placed two *heidesands* on a paper plate on his tidy desk, with a napkin and my chai latte beside it. As I sat down, he handed me a spreadsheet.

"What's this?"

"I set it up last night when I got home. It's so we could both keep track of things. Because we're working on this story together. I put a shared folder on Dropbox we both can use. I like to print the spreadsheets out, too, and file them until after the story is done.

"See, here's the column where we list the people we interview. Then all the way across are columns where we note if you or I did the interview, when we did it, what page the notes are on in our notebooks, if we recorded it, what we named the recording, if the person was hostile, helpful, or neutral, if we need follow-up, if the interview is off-the-record or on-the-record, and so on. We can look at a source's name and by following his or her row all the way across, we'll know exactly where we are!"

"Troy, this is quite something. The thing is, though, I don't usually use a spreadsheet to track a story. I just keep my notes, and then I organize them on a legal pad when I'm ready."

He looked as though I'd just said, "I don't really believe in gravity. Watch me step off this cliff."

Still, he did his best to rally.

"Oh. Cool, sure. Yeah. I mean it's just something I like to do because—"

"Hey, you do you, Troy. I just don't see this working for me. I'm not as ... structured in my approach as you."

He folded the spreadsheet, which was printed on legal size paper to accommodate its extreme detail, as carefully as a Boy Scout might fold the flag at the end of the day. He laid it to rest in a folder in the filing drawer in his desk.

"Yeah, sure. I understand. But if you change your mind, it'll be in the Dropbox shared file. I always print out an updated copy when I get to the office, too. It's in my file drawer. In case you want to look at it," he said, hopefully.

"All right, thanks, I'll remember that."

"So, I thought I'd check with Lewis and see if he talked to the sheriff or Detective Fike and ask how it went. And then I'll go do my interview in Hailwell."

"Sounds good. What are you doing for a car?"

"The bump shop is lending me one until mine is done."

"All right then, sounds like we're set. I'll see you back here around eleven-thirty or so and we'll hit the road for Tanner's."

<hr />

I worked my flying fingers to the bone all morning and didn't even stop for lunch. I was beyond hungry when Troy and I started for Tanner's. The day had taken a turn for the better, with bright sun and a light breeze drying up the puddles left by the early morning rain.

"I'm just going to pick up a Diet Coke and a burger. Do you want anything, Troy?" I asked as I pulled into the drive-through lane of McDonald's.

"No. I already ate, and I have a water with me," he said, pulling a bottle out of the backpack that he always carries. Luckily no one was ahead of us, so my need for sustenance didn't delay us much at all.

"Could you hold this for me?" I tossed the burger bag to Troy before we pulled onto the street. "So, how did it go in Hailwell today? Oh, and would you unwrap that burger please, and hand it to me? Thanks."

"It was fine. The new principal seems nice. I think I can do a decent feature on her, and I got a good photo to go with it."

When he handed me my burger, the wrapping was still on it, neatly folded back to catch any ketchup or mustard that oozed out.

"Thanks. Did Lewis talk to Detective Fike and/or Lamey?"

"Yes. Detective Fike. It went all right, I guess."

"Is Lewis mad at you?"

"I'm not sure. I told him I was sorry it had to go the way it did. He *said* it was okay, but I don't know ... I guess I'll just have to wait and see. He said his fiancée is mad at him. And he hasn't talked to her father—his boss—yet. I still feel bad I got him into this."

"Troy, I thought we hashed that out last night. Lewis got Lewis into this, not you. And if his fiancée really loves him, she'll get over it and come around, and so will her father. And if she doesn't, maybe she's not the one. Would you hand me my soda?"

When he did, I sipped so deeply on my straw that the sudden rush of carbonated beverage made my nose tingle and my eyes water. I like a drink that shakes you up a little.

"Just what I needed," I said when I finished.

"You know, there are a lot of studies that say diet soda is worse for you than regular soda, especially for your bladder and kidneys. It acts like a diuretic. Water is the best thirst quencher."

"Soda is made with water. It's like enhanced water, the way I see it. Besides, I drink water-water, too. Sometimes, I just like to punch it up a little."

We drove in silence as I ate my burger and alternated it with sips of Diet Coke. When we reached the turnoff for Tanner's I said, "Troy, you might want to avert your eyes and cover your ears against the sucking sound of my straw. I'm about to slurp up the last bubbly bit of my enhanced water. Tanner's is just down this road."

21

Tanner's Gentlemen's Club is in the northeast corner of the county, about twenty miles from Himmel. Though I'm a Grantland County native, I'd never felt the need to visit it before. Troy assured me, unnecessarily, that he wasn't a regular patron either. A large billboard featuring the strip club's name and its logo—the silhouette of an impossibly slender yet extremely voluptuous woman—pointed the way. We followed the bumpy gravel road for a few minutes before arriving at Tanner's.

At the edge of the parking lot, a portable marquee sign proclaimed: Tanner's Home of Wisco's Most Beautiful Ladies!!! Today's Special: Fried Cheese Curds!!

Tanner's itself was a dull gray L-shaped building.

"It's kind of depressing looking, isn't it?" Troy asked.

"Agreed."

It was so dark inside that it took a few seconds before our eyes adjusted to the gloom. A faint light and the sound of furniture scraping across the floor led us to the main part of the club. A man behind the bar was shouting in the direction of what I took to be—from the sound of dishes clattering—the kitchen.

"Nadine, you let me know when that damn distributor's truck shows up. They shorted us a case of Miller last week!"

"I'm not your stock boy. I can't take care of my job and yours, too!" The voice that shouted back was high-pitched and irritated.

Shaking his head in disgust, the man turned around, muttering some not very nice things about Nadine.

I strode up to the bar, Troy right behind me.

"Hi. I'm looking for Jerry Travers."

"You found him. Who're you?"

His voice was gruff, but not unfriendly. He was a big man, wearing a red polo shirt with the Tanner's logo on the pocket. His bald head was offset by a well-trimmed salt-and-pepper beard.

"Mr. Travers, my name is Leah Nash. I'm with the *Himmel Times*. This is my colleague Troy Patterson. We're working on a story about the Jancee Reynolds murder. Do you have a few minutes?"

"Yeah, that's a real bad deal," he said, pulling a towel out from under the bar and wiping down the wooden surface. "But like I told the cops, I don't know anything about it."

"We're hoping to talk to people who knew Jancee. We're doing a story on her as a person, not just as a murder victim. Can you tell us a little bit about her?"

"Yeah, okay. I guess I can do that. Jancee was all right. The customers liked her. Some of the girls didn't. I didn't have any problems with her. She was always there with the tip-out, no complaints."

"Tip-out? What's that?" I asked.

"The dancers, they pay for their spot on stage and then they keep all their tips. They 'tip out' from their tips to the rest of us—you know, the bartender, the bouncer, the DJ. We do our jobs right, it keeps the customers in a good mood. The girls have a better shift when the customers are happy. Some of the girls bitch about tipping out, but Jancee never did."

"Wait a minute. Are you saying that the dancers have to pay to dance? Doesn't the club pay them as employees?"

"Nah. Well, maybe some clubs do, but a lotta clubs like this, the dancers get somethin' on a W-9 for taxes. You know, like as though they're independent contractors. But the real money comes from the tips."

"How much money are we talking?"

"At Tanner's, we get a mostly local clientele, a lot of just regular guys.

Most of them, they're not real big tippers. Some of them don't want the wives to know they come out here. They can't afford to be dropping too much money or the questions start coming.

"Still, the real pretty girls, the young ones like Jancee, they make out all right. Maybe average a hundred, a hundred and fifty dollars a night after tip-outs. Course some nights, I see girls go out of here crying, 'cause they didn't even make their stage fee. Then they start their next shift in the hole. But like I said, girls can have real good nights, too. 'Specially during deer season. You get a lot of hard-drinking, happy guys. They're more likely to pay for private dances, too."

"You said the customers liked Jancee, but some of the girls didn't. Why's that?"

He shrugged.

"Competition. One girl gets a lap dance that means another one don't. Jancee was a looker and young. Some of the girls, they been around the block. They know they're not going anywhere but downhill from here. Maybe wind up in the kitchen like Nadine. You got to be able to bring the customers in, it's as simple as that."

"Jerry—can I call you Jerry?"

"That's my name."

"Can I get a Diet Coke? Lots of ice? I'm really parched."

Troy gave me a sideways glance. I pretended I didn't see it. Ordering a drink gave me a way to make Jerry even more chatty without offering an outright bribe.

"Thanks, how much do I owe you?" I asked as he handed me the soda.

"Five bucks."

I slid a ten-dollar bill over to him. "Keep the change."

He smiled his thanks. We were friends.

"So, Jerry, what did you think of the story that ran in GO News yesterday? The one about the fight here a few months ago over Jancee?"

"Didn't see it. I don't pay much attention to the news."

"But you remember what I'm talking about, right?"

"Yeah, there was a little dust-up. No big whoop, just old Dewey acting like an a-hole. The bouncer threw him out, told him to stay away. Hasn't been in since."

"The bouncer, that's Ricky Travers?"

"Yeah, he's my nephew. He's just part-time. Got himself in a carpenter program over in Omico. He'll have a real good trade when he's done."

"The other guy in the fight, Dan Cooper, he's a friend of mine. A friend of Ricky's, too. You probably know him," I said, squirming a little on my seat. Even though I'd carefully taken only small sips of Diet Coke, combined with what I'd had on the way over, I was feeling some pressure. But I didn't want to risk losing Jerry's nice flow of information with a bathroom break. Or prove Troy was right.

"Yeah, I know Dan. Not that well, but he's good people. He's the one that got Ricky into that carpenter program."

"Did you know that he's in kind of a bad spot right now? Because of the story and the photos *GO News* ran yesterday?"

"Yeah? How's that?"

"*GO News* made it seem like he fought with Dewey because he was involved with Jancee. The cops investigating the case are interested in him as a possible suspect in her murder."

Jerry seemed taken aback at the idea.

"That's crazy. Dan and Jancee? No way. He just met her that day. I oughta know, I introduced them. He was only trying to help Jancee because Dewey was bothering her."

"Is Dan a regular customer at Tanner's?"

"Never saw him in here before that day. Fact is, I offered him a ticket for no cover charge and a free drink at the bar, after he got Ricky into that program. He turned it down, but nice. Said he didn't get out this way enough to use it. I knew he meant he wasn't a strip club fan."

"I see. Well, just how did the fight start?"

"Dewey was talking to Jancee. Things started to get a little loud. Dewey had her by the arm and she pushed him away. He didn't like that. Dan came up and tried talking to Dewey. I was just about to offer Dewey a free drink to get him to sit down and then *whomp!* Dewey sucker-punched Dan. Dewey's not big, but he's quick. He got in a few good licks, but Dan's in good shape for a guy his age. He about had Dewey in line, then Ricky showed up and finished things off, sent Dewey on his way."

"What happened after that?"

"Nothing. I gave Dan a towel—he was bleeding a little but nothin' too serious. He went in the bathroom and cleaned off. When he came out, Ricky apologized for the ruckus. Dan told him to forget it, and he left. I haven't seen him since."

That jibed pretty well with Dan's story.

"Do you think it's possible that Jancee was so grateful to Dan that maybe *you* didn't see him again, but *she* did?"

"You mean like dating him? Nah. For one thing, she was way too young for him. He could've been her grandpa. And Dan wasn't the kind of guy she'd go for anyway."

"What kind would she go for?"

"I don't think anybody from around here, to be honest. Jancee had plans."

"What sort of plans?" I shifted on my bar stool, trying to find a spot that eased the urge to pee.

"She wanted to get out of here. Had the idea she was going to Chicago, get a job at a big club, make big money. I dunno. Maybe she would have. She had the looks, and she was tough enough to do what it takes. Dan wasn't anybody she would've wasted time on. He wasn't rich enough for one thing, and he wasn't young enough to make things fun."

"Was there someone who was rich enough or young enough to catch her interest?"

"I don't know if he caught Jancee's interest, but she sure caught his. Wes Morgan is a regular here, and I'll put it this way, Jancee always had plenty for tip-outs the nights Wes was here."

"Jerry!" a voice screeched from the kitchen. "Your damn beer is here. The truck just pulled up out back. Come back here and take care of things, I don't have time for it."

I was actually grateful that an outside force was bringing the conversation to a quick end.

"Wait a sec, Jerry," Troy said. "Is Ricky coming in today? We'd like to talk to him, too."

Although it was an absolutely appropriate and necessary question, I wanted to kill Troy for extending the conversation wrap-up. I stood and tried not to shift back and forth on my feet like a five-year-old struggling to hold it.

"No, he's working at his real job, at the construction company."

"Where can we find the owner, Krystal Gerrard?" Troy asked.

"Her office is through that door over there, and down the hall. It's the first door on the left."

"Jerry!" Nadine bellowed again.

"I better go," he said, stepping out from behind the bar and hurrying away.

I had spotted a restroom sign on the far wall and I took off as fast as Jerry had. A surprised Troy called to my retreating back, "Jerry said Krystal Gerrard's office is down that hall."

"I know, Troy, but you're right. Diet soda is a diuretic."

22

As soon as I rejoined Troy he said, "Wes Morgan lied when he told Lewis and the other guys that he barely knew Jancee. That's pretty interesting, don't you think?"

"Yes, I surely do. Now let's see what Krystal Gerrard knows about it."

But when we found the door marked "Office," no one answered our knock.

"Okay, let's do this. We'll walk down to the rental cabins where some of the dancers live and see if we can find anyone to talk to about Jancee. Then we'll come back and try again here."

The small cluster of cabins that Tanner's rents to its dancers is about a hundred yards north of the main building. They're leftovers from a time when Tanner's was a motel. Back then it catered to families willing to pack two adults and assorted kids into a two-hundred-square-foot knotty pine cabin in exchange for $20 a night. For that amount, vacationers also got access to a small, weed-choked inland lake.

Outside of one cabin, a young woman knelt near the front door, trying out different placements for several pots of bright yellow and white chrysanthemums.

"Those are really pretty mums," I said as Troy and I approached.

She turned her head to look up at us, causing her shoulder-length, copper-colored curls to bounce a little around her heart-shaped face.

"They are, aren't they? I'm trying to make the place look a little homier."

She stood and brushed her hands off on her jeans, then stepped back to survey her handiwork.

"Doesn't really help much, does it?"

Her voice was high and light and she giggled a little at the end of her question. She looked about twenty years old, max.

"I think flowers always look nice. I'm Leah Nash and this is Troy Patterson. We're with the *Himmel Times*. We're working on a story about Jancee Reynolds. Did you know her?"

Her mouth formed a little "O" and her dark brown eyes misted over. It made me feel a little happy for Jancee. At least someone had cared about her.

"I did. I still can't believe she's dead. Jancee was the alive-est person I knew. I'm Sus—I mean Summer—Bradley. My real name is Susannah—after my grandma—but I changed it to Summer. It's a better dancer name, don't you think?"

"They're both pretty names," Troy said, earning himself a smile.

"Aw, thank you. You're sweet."

"Do you have a few minutes to talk about Jancee?"

"Yeah, sure. I'd like to talk about her. I'd invite you in, but the cabin's just about big enough for one person."

"No problem. It's nice enough to sit outside."

"Great. Can you get those chairs and set them up?" Summer asked, pointing to a set of plastic lawn chairs stacked against the cabin. "I'll get some water for us. Sorry, I don't have soda. I used to drink it, but Jancee told me that it's really bad for you."

Troy couldn't resist raising an eyebrow at me.

"How well did you know Jancee?" I asked, once we were seated with our healthy water in reach.

"We weren't besties or anything, but I liked her."

"Did she talk to you at all about her life before she started working at Tanner's?"

"A little. She didn't have any family. She was in foster care for a while. I guess it was pretty bad. She ran away a bunch of times. She got out for good when she was fifteen. I asked her who took care of her. She said nobody. She took care of herself."

"That sounds a little bitter—and sad. Is that how Jancee was?"

"No, she could be really funny. When she used to imitate Krystal she made me laugh my butt off. And she helped me a lot when I first got here. This is my first job dancing at a club."

"Why did you become a dancer?" Troy asked.

"Oh, you know. I'm not a brain or anything. My mom always says I'm sitting on my biggest asset," she said, giggling. "She was a dancer before she got pregnant with me. She told me I should use what I have before I didn't have it anymore. I tried waitressing right after I graduated. I kept messing up the orders and dropping things, and I got fired. So, I got hired at Tanner's and here I am."

"Do you like it?" Troy asked.

She shrugged. "It's all right. I'm not really, like, a planning kind of person, like Jancee. I'll just see whatever happens. For now it's okay."

"Jancee was a planner? How do you mean?" I asked.

"Well, like she wanted to go to Chicago, real bad. Her friend Fauna used to work here and she moved to a Chicago club. She told Jancee she made twelve hundred dollars some nights. So Jancee, she was saving her money —I mean like almost all of it—she hardly spent any. But she said if you want to get ahead, you have to make a plan."

"Why did she need money to leave? If she thought she'd make so much in Chicago, why wouldn't she just go?" Troy asked.

"Jancee said she already did life on the streets once. She wasn't gonna do that again. She wasn't going anywhere until she had enough to take care of herself, in case things didn't work out like she wanted them to. She already had like five thousand saved up. She took it out of her purse and showed me once. I never saw that much money at one time in my life!"

"She kept it in her purse, not the bank?" I asked.

"She said it came too hard to trust it anywhere but with herself. She had this little cross-body bag and she wore it all the time except when she was working. I don't know, she probably even slept with it!" Summer giggled a little and then her eyes widened.

"Is that what happened? Did somebody kill her to steal her money?"

"We don't know why she was murdered. But from what I understand, no money was found with the body."

Tears had welled up in Summer's eyes and they began spilling down her cheeks.

"Summer? What's wrong?"

She wiped her eyes against the sleeve of her jacket and gave me a watery smile.

"It's just that she worked so hard, and she was so proud that she saved all that money. And now it doesn't matter. She's dead, and it's all gone, and it was all for nothing. She might as well have given it to Monroe."

"Monroe? Do you mean Monroe Mepham?"

She nodded vigorously, setting her curls flying.

"He asked Jancee for money? Why?"

"Oh," she said, sniffling a little. Troy reached in his pocket, then handed her a handkerchief. Of course Troy would be the only millennial male in Wisconsin who still carried a handkerchief. Summer smiled at him through her tears as she accepted, and then blew her nose.

"Jancee and Monroe had a thing for a while."

"A thing? You mean they were in a relationship?"

She looked at me kindly, as though I were an elderly aunt.

"No. They just had sex with each other. Monroe's an asshat. Jancee knew it, but he's pretty cute. Tall, good body, curly brown hair, nice mustache."

"But Monroe and Jancee weren't still having a thing when she died, is that right?" I asked.

"She stopped it when she found out he had a kid."

"It didn't bother her that Monroe was married?"

"No, she figured it was his wife's problem if she couldn't keep him home. But she didn't like Monroe cheating on his kid."

"Monroe asking her for money, was that recent?"

"Yeah, maybe two or three weeks ago? He got in some kind of 'misunderstanding' with his supplier, he told her. Wait, you won't put this in your paper, will you?"

"I don't know yet, but if I do, I'll get it from other sources and won't link it to you."

"Okay. He's not like some big dealer, but Monroe sells a little weed, sometimes pills. I get weed from him sometimes, but not pills," she added hastily. "I don't go in for that."

"Did Jancee?"

"No, she said drugs make you stupid. I guess they do. Monroe told Jancee he could get beat up real bad if he didn't come up with five thousand dollars."

"She wouldn't give it to him?"

"No, she said she worked too hard for her money."

"How did Monroe take that?"

"He was pretty mad, I guess. I heard he asked a couple of other people at Tanner's for the money. It doesn't seem like anyone would be dumb enough to give it to him. But he must've found it somewhere, because he didn't get beat up as far as I know, anyway."

"Summer, have you talked to the police about this?"

"I haven't talked to them about anything. They were here this morning, but I was off last night, so I stayed at my boyfriend's in town. Someone talked to Lorna, though. She's one of the other dancers. She hates—hated Jancee. She probably said a lot of bitchy things about her."

"Why didn't she like Jancee?"

"Jealous. Jancee was kind of the star performer. Which Lorna used to be, I guess. Plus Lorna and Monroe were together before Jancee came."

"After Jancee dropped Monroe, did she have a thing with anyone else?"

"Not that I know of. Wes Morgan was always after her, but she wouldn't go out with him."

"Why wouldn't Jancee go out with Wes?"

"She didn't like him well enough, I guess. He's kind of old, too."

"Jerry the bartender said Wes was always here the nights Jancee danced, and that he always tipped her really well."

"Sure. She was always really nice to Wes, when she was working. You have to be, that's our job. But just to go out with him? No, she wasn't interested."

"So, there wasn't anyone else—no other customers, no one that worked here that Jancee ever talked about?"

"Well, there was Ricky, but not like you mean. Not like a boyfriend."

"Ricky Travers, the bouncer?" I asked.

"Yeah, he had a bad crush on Jancee."

"Tell me about that."

"Ricky, well, he's kinda young for his age, and Jancee was kinda old for hers. She let him hang around, but he wasn't ever somebody Jancee would take seriously. He's cute, like this big, clumsy puppy. He was always trying to do stuff for her."

"Like what?"

"Oh, like her car. It's a junker. Something's always wrong with it. Ricky worked on it a lot, for free. That's it over there," she said. She pointed to a blue Ford Fiesta with a big dent on the driver side door, a cracked windshield, and red cellophane taped over one rear taillight.

"And he brought her little presents like perfume or a bracelet or flowers. Stuff like that."

"It sounds a little like he was stalking her."

"No, it wasn't that way. He just really liked her. I said one time that maybe she shouldn't let Ricky hang around because he might get the wrong idea."

"What did Jancee say?"

"That Ricky liked to give her things and she liked to get them, so it was a win-win. I guess that makes her sound kind of mean, doesn't it? But she wouldn't go out of her way to hurt somebody. It was more like she just looked out for herself. Ricky, I don't think he has much experience with girls. So, maybe he just didn't know that Jancee was kind of using him."

"Summer, do you have any pictures of Jancee? We don't have anything to run with the story, and it would be nice to have one that showed her in a happy moment—to help people think of her as a person, not just as a murder victim."

"Sure, I have a couple of good ones."

She pulled out her phone and scrolled through until she found what she was looking for, then handed it to me.

It was a selfie of Summer and Jancee together. They leaned in close, with their arms around each other. Both of them were making those smooshy-lips teen girls do when they try to look sexy. And that's what Jancee had been—a teenager still, despite the heavy makeup, and the red-sequined halter-top dress, and the knowing eyes.

"Summer, was this photo taken last Monday?"

"Yeah. It's the last time I saw her. She wanted to borrow my car, because, of course, hers wouldn't start. And she had to be at a party—the party Wes set up with her. But I needed it to go home to Trefry for my mom's birthday. I felt bad. So I let her wear my necklace. She really liked it. She was into fairy things. Make the picture bigger, and you can see the fairy charm," she said.

I expanded the photo. A delicate gold fairy accented with tiny diamonds rested between Jancee's pushed-up breasts. "Very pretty."

"This probably makes me sound sort of self-centered, with Jancee being killed and all. And I don't mean disrespect or anything, but do you think I could get my necklace back? My grandma gave it to me, is all."

"I don't know. The police didn't release any information on a necklace."

I was about to tell her I'd look into it. Troy, however, spoke before I could.

"I'll see what I can find out," he said.

"Would you? Oh, that would be so great, thank you!"

She rewarded him with a brilliant smile.

"This is a cute photo of the two of you, but it would be hard to crop. Do you have any of Jancee alone?"

"Yeah, just swipe to the next one over. It's a nice one."

It was. Jancee wore a pastel blue tank top, denim shorts, and white tennis shoes. Her long blonde hair was pulled into a loose ponytail. She was sitting on a dock with her arms loosely wrapped around her knees, which were drawn up to her chest. Next to her was a small leather purse—I assumed it was the one Summer said she was never without. Jancee's head was tilted to the side and she was smiling. She looked young. She looked happy. She didn't look like someone who was going to wind up dead in a dark wood on a cold October night.

"Yes, this is a great picture. Can I Airdrop them both to my phone?"

"Sure, no prob."

"Did Jancee do a lot of private parties like the one the night she was killed?" Troy asked.

"Some, not a lot. Most of us do. Krystal books them. We have to split the fee with her. Jancee didn't like that. I told her that if Krystal found out she was—"

Just then a door slammed on the cabin next to Summer's, and as we all looked up, a tall brunette wearing skin-tight jeans and a low V-neck sweater walked toward us.

"Hi, Summer. Who are your friends?"

The words were innocuous, but the tone carried a note of suspicion.

"Oh, hi, Lorna. They're just some people that wanted to talk about Jancee."

Lorna's shrewd eyes narrowed. "Just people—or newspaper people?"

"We're with the *Himmel Times*," I said. "We're talking to some of Jancee's friends for a follow-up story. Do you have a few minutes?"

"No, I don't. And Jancee wasn't a friend. I don't know anything about her."

She turned her attention back to Summer.

"Does Krystal know you're talking to reporters? She won't like it. You might just find somebody else gets your Saturday night shift this week."

She turned and walked away without saying goodbye.

"What's up with her?" I asked.

"Oh, Lorna's like that. She's always kind of salty. She doesn't like me because she thinks I 'stole' one of her regulars. Can I help it if he wanted a lap dance from me? She's probably going straight to Krystal to tell on me, though."

"Are you going to get into trouble for talking to us?" Troy asked.

Summer shrugged.

"Maybe, but so what? I can always go back to my mom's if Krystal kicks me out. I might anyway. With Jancee gone, it's not gonna be as fun anymore."

I glanced at my watch just then. It was almost three, and we still hadn't talked to Krystal. And now I wanted to talk to Monroe, too. But there was more to come from Summer, I was sure. I picked up my water and swigged it down in one long gulp, while Summer showed the Jancee photos to Troy.

"For some reason I just can't get enough water today," I said as I finished. "I don't want to be a bother, Summer, but could I have another bottle, please?"

"Oh, sure. I buy it by the case. I'll get you one."

As she went in I seized the moment to instruct Troy.

"We're running out of time. I'll go see Krystal. You lead Summer back to talking about Krystal's private party scheduling. I think she was about to say something about Jancee doing her own thing when Lorna interrupted. Try to find out if Jancee set up her own party directly with Wes Morgan. And see if Summer knows who Jancee got to drive her to Kent's cabin."

"Okay, I've got it. Don't worry, I can do this."

"I'm counting on you. I'll meet you in the parking lot. Good luck."

23

When I entered the building Lorna was walking away from Krystal's office. She must have zipped over to narc on Summer as fast as her stiletto heels could carry her.

The office door was half-open. I tapped it and walked in.

Krystal Gerrard raised her eyes from the spreadsheet on her desk. She wore reading glasses on a chain, and a dark green cardigan over a white blouse. Her highlighted dark blonde hair was cut short in an asymmetrical style. Her lips were carefully outlined and filled in with a dark coral shade of lipstick. Her middle-aged face was meticulously made-up.

She was very attractive, but she looked more like a fiftyish Talbot's customer than a strip club owner. I had been expecting someone with a platinum dye job with roots, a haggard face lined by too much time in a tanning booth, and a cigarette, if not hanging from her blood-red lips at least burning in a nearby ashtray. Did I mention I watch a lot of old movies?

"Krystal Gerrard?" I asked, just to make sure.

"Yes, who are you?"

"I'm Leah Nash, with the *Himmel Times*. I'm working on a follow-up story about the Jancee Reynolds murder. I'd like to ask you a couple of questions if you have a minute."

"I already told a reporter from your paper that I don't know anything about it."

Her voice was brisk and she returned her gaze to her spreadsheet. There was no visitor's chair in the office, so I stood my ground just inside the door.

"But you knew Jancee. Weren't you worried when she just walked away from here and never came back? Left everything behind?"

"I wasn't worried about her because the girls here show up for their shifts, or they don't. If they don't show, they don't work here again. I run a business, not a sorority house. Most of the girls who work here aren't reliable. It's either boyfriends, or pregnancies, or drinking, or drugs, or just laziness. But there's always another girl to take their place. Now, as you can see, I'm busy."

"The night she died she worked at a private party for Wes Morgan. I know you schedule them for some of the dancers."

"So? It's not illegal. It's just private entertainment."

"Did you book Jancee for the party that night?"

"No. She must have done that on her own."

"Did Wes Morgan ever book any parties with you?"

"I don't talk about my customers. And I'm done talking to you."

She picked up the receiver from her desk phone.

"I'm about to call my security manager. For the record, I have no comment to make on Jancee Reynolds or her death. Don't make the mistake of coming again." She began to punch in a number on the phone, and I took that as my cue to leave.

———————

When I left Krystal's office I decided to go out through the main entrance on the chance I might see Jerry behind the bar again. I wanted to find out if he had heard anything about Jancee setting up her own client base for parties.

He wasn't there, but a man who answered to Monroe Mepham's description—tall, fit, light-brown curly hair, a kind of retro 70s mustache— stood in the corner doing something with sound equipment.

"Monroe?"

He looked up and smiled. I could see why Jancee had found him attractive.

"That's right. Who are you?"

"Hi, I'm Leah Nash. I'm with the *Himmel Times*."

"Sorry, can't help you. I've got a deal with *GO News* for my pictures. They get first right of refusal."

He made it sound as though he were genuinely sorry he couldn't help.

"Do you shoot a lot of photos for them?"

He shrugged.

"I'm pretty good with a camera. If I see a car accident, or fire, something interesting, I shoot it. It's not my main gig."

Again he flashed a smile with practiced charm. He ran a hand through his curls, just enough to fluff them up a little, like a male bird fanning its tail feathers. He leaned just a little more into my personal space.

"Mostly, I DJ."

He reached inside his wallet and then handed me his card. I didn't foresee any DJ-ing needs in my future, but I never turn down a phone number. In my line of work, you never know when you might want it.

"Thanks. Do you work just locally?"

"Mostly, now. I used to do some gigs in Green Bay, Madison—even Milwaukee. I had plans to move on to the Chicago scene. Still might."

"Why haven't you?"

He shrugged.

"My girlfriend got herself pregnant. We got married. Had the boy, and then you know how it goes. Hard to hang onto your dreams when you've got a wife and kid."

I forced myself not to make any virgin birth comments when he said that his "girlfriend got herself pregnant," as though it were something in which he had no part. But I couldn't not say *anything*.

"For some people, marriage and a family are the dream."

"Oh, for sure. Don't get me wrong. Austin's a good kid. But marriage isn't always a picnic. You have to give up a lot."

"Is that why you had an affair with Jancee? Because you felt like having a picnic?"

"Uh-oh, now she's mad," he said, looking around for affirmation as though we had an audience.

"I don't know who you've been talking to, but yeah, I won't deny that Jancee and I were friends. I'm a friendly guy. Ask anyone, that's what they'll tell you." He tried a rueful version of his smile out on me.

"How do you feel about your 'friend' being choked to death and having her body dumped in the woods like a sack of trash?"

"I'm pretty torn up about that, of course. It's a terrible thing."

"Jancee broke off your affair when she found out you had a kid. How did that make you feel?"

"Look, I've been nice to you, but you're not being very nice to me. Jancee and I had some fun, but it's a long stretch to call it an affair. She knew I was married and it didn't bother her. Then she got all hung up when somebody told her I had a kid. All right, I can respect that. No worries."

"Did you see Jancee a week ago Monday? The day she was killed?"

Anger flared in his eyes, and he wasn't very friendly anymore.

"I haven't seen Jancee except at work for months. Anyone who tells you different is lying. You can tell your boss I don't have any photos to sell your paper or any story to tell about Jancee."

He turned away then and began pulling at wires and turning dials but I was sure it had nothing to do with adjusting sound quality.

"Just one more thing, Monroe. There's a kind of coincidence that's bothering me. I heard you owed some pretty nasty people a fair amount of money, five thousand dollars, I think it was. You were scared enough to ask Jancee to help you out, but she refused, even though she had just about that much ready cash. But it looks to me like you're just fine, no sign of any broken bones. No bruises that I can see either. And the money Jancee had in the purse she always carried with her is gone. I'm trying to figure out if those two things are connected. Can you help me out? Did Jancee change her mind and give you that money?"

"I don't know what you heard, or from who, but I never asked Jancee for any money, and I don't know anything about what happened to hers. And I'm done talking to you. And I'm out of here."

"I guess we'll just have to connect another time," I said to his retreating back.

"I don't have much to report," I said to Troy as he buckled his seatbelt. "Monroe corroborated that he and Jancee had a thing, but he insisted it was casual. He denied asking her for money, and he wasn't nearly as charming at the end of the conversation as he was at the beginning. I think it's worth doing some more digging on him. I did confirm he's a sleaze ball, though."

"What about Krystal Gerrard?"

"She's pretty hard-ass. But I would have tagged her as a middle manager at an insurance company, not a strip club owner. I need to reexamine my biases. She wasn't worried when Jancee didn't show back up, because 'girls' come and go. That's about all I got before she threw me out. Did your boyish charm help you get anything more from Summer?"

"Lots more. Also, she said to give you the bottle of water you wanted, and that you should get your blood sugar tested in case you have diabetes like her mother," he said, reaching down and pulling it out of his backpack.

"She's kind of a sweet kid, isn't she?"

"Yeah, I liked her," he said.

"I noticed."

He pushed his glasses up on his nose and flipped his notebook open.

"Summer doesn't know how Jancee got to the party at Kent Morgan's. She thought probably Wes picked her up, because Ricky wasn't working that night. But then she said Jancee could've called Ricky. Wes Morgan comes to Tanner's at least once a week, sometimes more. He tips all the dancers pretty well, but when Jancee worked, he always paid her for a lap dance, too. But as far as Summer knows, he was just a good customer."

"Well, that's the key phrase, isn't it? 'As far as Summer knows.' Did you get any details from Summer about how Krystal's side business works?"

He nodded.

"Krystal schedules them, collects the fee, provides transportation—that way the driver can be sort of security for the dancer. She takes half of the flat fee she charges the customer, but the dancer gets the other half and keeps all the tips. Jancee didn't like Krystal getting half the money. She started booking on her own. That's what she did with Wes. There's something else. Krystal doesn't just book dancers for bachelor parties and birthdays. She has an escort service, too. But it's small, and not very many people know. She picks the girls she wants to use. Jancee was one of them."

"When you say escort, do you mean call girl?"

"Yes. But Jancee started going on her own there, too. But just with one guy. He was kind of kinky, Jancee told Summer. But she didn't care because she charged him double the fee Krystal did for her 'clients,' and he tipped on top of that."

"That sounds like it might be some serious kink. Did Summer say?"

He hesitated, whether out of concern for his own tender sensibilities or mine, I couldn't tell.

"Don't worry, I can take it."

"BDSM. That's bondage, discipline, sadism, masochism. Or bondage, dominance, submission, masochism, some people prefer to say."

"I know what it means, Troy. Go on."

"Okay, yeah, well."

When I glanced over at him, he was staring intently at his notebook and studiously avoiding eye contact with me.

"Don't worry, my shell-pink ears can take whatever you have to say."

"Well, Jancee was strangled, right? And Summer said that Jancee's client was 'a choker.' There's this BDSM thing called erotic asphyxiation, or breath play. It's the restriction of breathing during sex by cutting off your partner's air supply temporarily to increase orgasms. I looked it up online while I was waiting for you."

"Are you thinking that maybe Jancee had a date after the poker party with her private client who was into choking? And something went wrong?"

"It could be, right?"

"Yes, Troy. It could."

24

"I thought we were going to see Wes Morgan and Ricky Travers at Morgan Construction. Why are you driving back to the office?" Troy asked as he realized where we were going.

"Because it's almost four, and you have to shoot the girls volleyball game today. I'll drop you off at the office so you can get your car. You might be a little late, but not too bad."

"But one of the stringers can do it, can't they? I mean, this is a more important story, right?"

"It's a more interesting story. But to all the kids on the team, and their coaches, and their moms and dads, and grandmas and grandpas, this game is important, too."

I was reciting almost verbatim a speech a boss had given me once when I had complained about the dullness of my assignments. It didn't make Troy feel any better now than I had then.

"But I've been here for almost nine months. This is the first big story I've even come close to. I can phone the coach for the score and some details about the game later, and some of the parents will have photos. I can track those down."

"Troy, I think—"

"Don't take me off the story, please. I got Summer to tell me about the escort service and Jancee's client who likes to choke women. I want to ask Wes about the BDSM stuff and see how he reacts, and—"

"Troy, hold on. You're not 'off the story.' And it's too soon to ask Wes about the BDSM stuff. We need to do some digging there first. I don't want to tip our hand just yet. You won't miss much there. As for Ricky, I'm afraid two of us together might unnerve him, and then we wouldn't get anything. There's still a lot of other news in the county to cover. We don't have the luxury of putting you exclusively on one story."

He nodded stiffly. I knew he was both angry and disappointed. I understood. I'd feel the same way.

"Listen, when Maggie's back, things will be a little different."

"The story could be over by then."

"Maybe. But there's always another one. That's how news works. Right now, I need you to do the things I know you can handle well, because—"

"Because you don't think I can handle this," he finished for me. "It's all right. I get it. But I can do more than you think."

I was glad he'd interrupted me, because I wasn't exactly sure how I was going to end that sentence tactfully. He'd done fine with Summer, but she wasn't exactly a tough interview. And she was peripheral to the story. But Wes Morgan could be the epicenter. Wes had already stonewalled him once. I didn't reply. Nothing I said would make him feel any better.

I really don't like the people managing part of owning a newspaper. Mostly because I'm not very good at it.

Wes Morgan's construction office in Omico wasn't impressive at first glance. Or at second or third, either.

Gold lettering across the front of the dark green building proclaimed it to be "Wes organ Construction."

The "M" in Morgan wasn't completely gone. An abandoned bird's nest rested on the part that remained in place. A dark green pickup with the company logo on the door was parked in front of the building. I could see an equipment garage behind the office. When I opened the entrance to the office, I walked into a small reception area. The woman seated at the desk to my left looked at a computer screen as she hunched her shoulder to her neck to hold the handset of her phone. She glanced at me and held up a hand to indicate she'd be with me in a minute. Behind her was a closed door I assumed to be Wes's office. A metal-framed love seat with cushions in the same dark green and gold the building sported was available for visitors. Two chairs of the same design completed the seating arrangement.

I didn't sit, however. Instead I walked over to look at the photographs mounted on the far wall. They seemed to be examples of work done by Wes Morgan's firm. There were a few houses, an office building, a drive-in bank, and a very nice photo of Kent Morgan's cabin. But the photo that held the center spot looked out of place.

It was a close-up of two happy fans in the stadium at Lambeau Field. I deduced the location by the Packers gear the men wore, the big grins on their faces, and the sea of green and gold behind them.

"That's Wes and his brother," said a voice at my elbow.

The woman who had been on the phone stood next to me. She wore jeans and a dark green polo shirt with the company logo on the left. Her shiny, brown, shoulder-length hair was held back by a headband. She was several inches shorter than me.

"Oh, yeah, I can see it now. When was it taken?"

"Sixteen years ago. Don't ask Wes about it, or you'll get the whole play-by-play of the Packers/Seahawks game, January 2004. Al Harris won it for the Packers against the Seattle Seahawks in overtime. Wes scored tickets for himself and his brother, and I've heard the story so often I could recite it in my sleep. You probably noticed, it's all about Packers green and gold around here. Don't tell anyone, but I'm not a Packers fan. I'm from Pennsylvania. I'm a Steelers gal through and through."

"Your secret's safe with me. I'm from Wisconsin, and I've never watched a Packers game all the way through. I'm Leah Nash, by the way. I'm hoping to see Wes, if he's in."

"I'm Sandy Eldridge, Wes's office manager. I recognized you when you came in. I was at the talk you gave at the library last summer. You signed a book for me."

I've done events at all the libraries in the county, and I appreciate everyone who turns out. I just don't remember most of them. It seems rude to say that, especially when they make a point of letting me know we've met. So I've come up with an all-purpose response that seems to work.

"I'm glad you came out for it, Sandy. I hope you enjoyed the book."

"Oh, I did. I love true crime. And the part about your sister and your dad—that really got to me. I'm trying to talk my book club into reading it, but we're kind of in a Nazi phase right now. I mean reading books about Nazis in World War II, not that the book club is full of fascists. Though I'm not quite sure about Barbara."

She grinned, and it made her look younger than the mid-forties I had pegged her for.

"So, how come you want to see Wes? It's about that murdered girl, right? Leave it to Wes to get mixed up in something else his brother will have to clean up."

Sandy was not striking the protective note I had expected from a loyal staff member.

"What do you mean, 'leave it to Wes?'"

"I mean, if there's a way to screw things up, Wes will find it. You'd think a guy could set up a boys' night out for his brother and some friends without having it end with a dead stripper and everybody's name in the paper, right? Not Wes. He really did it up royal this time. I don't know how Kent puts up with it."

"Puts up with what?"

"Everything. Before this, he had a bar that went belly-up. Now, seriously, how can a bar not make it in Wisconsin? Then Kent helped him get this place going. He's always bailing him out."

"But the construction business, Wes is doing all right?"

She shrugged. "Not really."

"How's that?"

"I'll give you that Wes knows construction. So you'd think with his brother helping with the financing and steering business his way, he'd be a big success, right? Nope. We're always teetering on the edge. Without Kent propping him up, we'd probably fall right over."

"What's the problem?"

She raised an eyebrow.

"Being Wes, I guess. Why is Alec Baldwin big time and Daniel Baldwin never made it past wannabe? It seems like the harder Wes tries, the more he screws up. But to be honest, Wes isn't that much of a trier. He thinks he's smarter than he is, that's part of his problem."

"Wow, Sandy. It doesn't sound as though you like Wes very much. Why do you work here?"

Again she shrugged.

"The job's not hard, we never stay past five. Wes doesn't mind if I need to take time off for my daughter. I'm a single parent. I don't have to work weekends either. That works for me. Wes is all right, I guess. I don't have anything against him personally. I just say it like I see it."

That clearly being the case, I tossed in another question for Sandy to weigh in on.

"I hear Ricky Travers is working here, is that right?"

"Yeah, he's doing his apprenticeship. Why?"

"He's a friend of a friend of mine. How's he doing?"

"He's a nice kid. Does good work, from what the guys say. Pretty quiet, but that's a nice change from some of the loud mouths around here."

She looked at the clock on the wall behind me.

"Oh! I've got to get going. Have to pick up my kid at four-thirty. Wes will be scooting out of here pretty quick, too. It's Fish Fry and Packers Trivia Night at Stan's Bar. Wes likes to get there early to get his 'lucky table.' You better go on in if you want to catch him."

"You don't need to buzz him, tell him I'm here to see him?"

"Nah, just tap on the door and go on in. Sometimes he likes to show off for visitors and tells me to make coffee or bring water in. I don't have time today, or I'll be late for my daughter. Hey, it was nice to talk to you. I can't wait for your next book. I'm a big fan."

"Thanks, Sandy, nice talking to you, too," I said to her retreating back.

I rapped lightly on Wes's door.

"Yeah?"

25

He had been leaning back in his chair, but Wes crashed forward with a thud as I shut the door behind me and moved toward his desk. Behind him was a bookshelf filled not with books, but with Packers memorabilia—mugs, coasters, bobble-heads and a mini-Packers autographed helmet in a plastic display case.

"We haven't met, Wes, but I'm Leah Nash, with the *Himmel Times*. We're doing a follow-up story on Jancee Reynolds. I just have a few questions for you, if you've got a minute," I said with a smile. I had decided to go with the friendly approach—to start, anyway.

It was easy to tell he and Kent were brothers. They shared the same coloring and features. But Wes was like the generic brand of Kent—kind of the same, but not really. His hair was blondish, rather than bright blond like his brother's. His blue eyes were the color of washed-out denim, not the azure blue of Kent's. Where Kent's jawline was strong, Wes's chin was just this side of receding. He wore a V-neck sweater in the ubiquitous dark green with the gold company logo over a white T-shirt.

"You should have made an appointment. I'm on my way out. I don't have time to talk," Wes said.

"I get it. Nobody likes talking to the press. It's starting to make me feel bad about myself. But just a couple of questions and I'll be on my way. Does it help if I tell you I'm a fellow Packers fan? Awesome picture of you and your brother in the reception area. Looks like you had prime seats. What game was that?"

I tried another smile out on him. But it was the Packers reference that worked.

"You saw that, eh? I scored the tickets for that game. Won a bet, broke the guy's heart but got me and Kent seats on the fifty-yard line at only the best game in history. It was legendary."

He proceeded to recount the key moments of the game for me, as Sandy had warned me he would. But he was getting decidedly more relaxed so maybe it was worth it. I nodded and injected "Oh, wow!" and "You're kidding!" and "You were so lucky!" here and there to make it seem as though I was actually listening. I tuned back in as he seemed to be winding down.

"… on the way home we stopped at a bar in this little podunk town. Wall to wall green and gold, guys buying us drinks just because we'd been at the game in person. It was lit."

There is something ridiculous, even pitiful, about middle-aged guys trying to be "cool" by appropriating the words a younger generation uses. Now that we had established Packers rapport, I worked hard not to dispel it by a scornful look on my face.

"Well, that's a once-in-a-lifetime experience, for sure. You and your brother are pretty close, aren't you?"

"Yes, we are."

"So, that's why you wanted to surprise him with a dancer at his birthday?"

"Kent's a great guy. But he's too serious. I just wanted him to loosen up, have a few laughs with the guys. I just hired Jancee for fun."

"But he didn't think it was very much fun, I take it."

"It was fine, but he just can't relax. And then all this other stuff happened. I didn't mean to get him and all the rest of us in the paper. It was just supposed to be a guys' night out. That story your paper ran cost me three jobs today. People are funny, they don't like to do business with a guy linked to a murder."

I could tell that our Packers bond had slipped away. Friendly wasn't going to cut it. Time for real me to come out.

"I can understand why you didn't want the story in the paper. I wouldn't either. But a young woman was choked to death. You were the person who invited her to the last place where she was seen alive. That makes you part of the story."

"I didn't 'invite' her. I paid her to come and dance. That's all. I barely knew who she was. And I don't know anything about what happened after she left. Listen, a girl like Jancee, well, it's not that surprising, is it, what happened to her?"

"What do you mean 'a girl like Jancee?' What kind of 'girl' is that?"

"You know what I'm talking about. A girl who teases men for a living? Who can be surprised at what happened to her? It's sad, sure. But it's got nothing to do with me. Or any of the rest of the guys. It was just our bad luck that she got herself killed that night."

"Well, it has at least a little to do with you, doesn't it? Or isn't it true that you're a regular at Tanner's?"

I had already pulled out my notebook, and now I flipped back and forth through the pages, as though looking for some damaging piece of information to spring at him. He eyed me nervously, then apparently decided a flat-out denial wasn't a good idea.

"I don't know what you mean by 'regular.' Sure I go to Tanner's sometimes, like a lot of guys do. Nothing wrong with that. It's not illegal."

"No, it isn't," I agreed. "But I heard Jancee was a particular favorite of yours. Is that true?"

"No. She was a good dancer. I liked the way she moved. So I hired her for the party. But it wasn't anything personal."

"Really? Because a couple of people told me that you seemed to be pretty taken with Jancee—that you kept asking her to see you outside of work."

"I don't know who you've been talking to, or what you think you know, but—"

"That's right, you don't. So it's probably a good idea to tell me the truth. You're already part of the story, Wes. Answering a few questions is a good way to have your say. It's your chance to set the record straight. So, did you pressure Jancee to go out with you?"

"No. I didn't 'pressure' her. I asked her a couple of times if she wanted to go have a drink with me after work, but she said no. She didn't date customers. That was fine, I understood. And it's not like I can't find a girl when I want one."

"Okay, but did you ask Krystal Gerrard for Jancee, specifically, when you set up the party for Kent?" Sometimes it's good for reporters, like lawyers, to ask questions they already know the answers to.

"I didn't have Krystal schedule it. I did it direct with Jancee."

"Why would you do that? I understand Krystal makes it easy for customers. Does the scheduling, collects the fees, takes care of transportation for the dancers, takes care of everything. Why didn't you go through her?"

"Because Jancee said she could do it direct and then she wouldn't have to give Krystal a cut of the money. It didn't matter to me one way or the other."

"But then did you have to give Jancee a ride that night? Her car wasn't working."

"No, I don't know anything about that. I told her where to park behind the cabin so the guys wouldn't know she was there. I don't know what she drove. I didn't check."

"Did anyone besides you know Jancee was going to be at Kent's that night?"

"No. It was a surprise. A joke really. I thought the guys would like it."

"So you said. Did they enjoy it? Were they surprised?"

"Some did, some didn't," he said. His voice had become truculent.

"Lewis Webber didn't. He doesn't think Kent did, either."

"Lulu is a scared little rabbit."

"It wasn't just Lewis who didn't like it. I talked to Kent. He told me he wasn't happy about it. And Lewis said that he and the rest of the guys left because you and Kent got into an argument."

"That's not what happened."

I flipped through my notebook officiously again, then looked up as

though I'd confirmed a point I wanted to check. "Are you saying you and
your brother didn't argue?"

"No, I'm not saying that. Kent was mad, yeah. We had words, but it was
no big deal. We worked it out. I ended up staying the night with him at the
cabin, in fact. He thought I'd had too much to drink to be driving. It wasn't
true, but I stayed to make him happy. There wasn't any big fight."

"That turned out to be lucky for you, didn't it? Staying at the cabin, I
mean."

"How's that?"

"Because Kent's your alibi, right? I mean, you were sleeping it off at your
brother's place while Jancee was getting dumped in the woods fifteen miles
away."

"I don't need an alibi, because I didn't do anything to Jancee. I told the
other reporter, I told the cops, and I'm telling you, I don't know how Jancee
got to the cabin. I don't know what happened with Jancee after she left.
This is why I didn't want to go to the police in the first place. Now, thanks to
your paper, I'm getting dragged into something that has nothing to do with
me." His voice had gotten quite loud, and his cheeks were very red.

"All right, all right, I've got it. You convinced me."

He hadn't, of course, but I thought it was time to bring out good Leah
instead of bad Leah for a bit.

"But, Wes," I continued in a conversational voice, "Jancee asked to
borrow a friend's car, but she wasn't able to. So don't you wonder how she
got there? And how she left? You must have thought about it."

"Well, if you really want to know ..."

"I do."

"I'd ask Ricky Travers. He had it bad for her. She had him wrapped
around her little finger."

"He works for you, doesn't he?"

"Yeah, but he's a part-time bouncer at Tanner's. He was always following
her around, trying to get her to pay attention to him. If I were you, that's
who I'd be talking to. Now, I talked to you more than I should have. I've got
things to do."

He stood up, and I could tell I wasn't going to get anything else, at least
for the moment.

"Thanks for your time."

"Just so we're clear, I've said all I'm going to about Jancee Reynolds. How many ways can I say that I don't know anything?"

"I think you about covered them."

As I left the building, a sheriff's office car pulled up. Maybe Wes wasn't going to make it to Stan's in time to get his lucky table after all. I waited by my car for a minute to see who got out.

The man who walked toward me was tall and thin. His reddish-gold hair was very short, almost a buzz cut. He wore a shirt and tie under a windbreaker with a sheriff's office logo on the front. As he got closer I could see that his eyes were a light blue. He looked like he was somewhere in his thirties.

"Ms. Nash, isn't it? Sheriff Lamey said I'd probably run into you at some point today. I'm Detective Owen Fike."

"You can call me Leah. And is it Detective Fike, or Owen, for you?" I asked as he shook my hand.

"Leah it is, then. You can make it Owen for me."

So far, he seemed okay.

"I understand you're in charge of the Jancee Reynolds case. How's that going?"

"It's going. I'm kind of surprised the owner of the paper is covering the story. Isn't the police beat below your pay grade?"

"We're short-staffed at the moment. Besides, I always enjoy seeing the wheels of justice at work. Right now, I'm a little surprised to see that Acting Sheriff Lamey has them turning in the direction of Dan Cooper, just because he knew Jancee Reynolds."

"Is this an on-the-record conversation?"

"No, more a getting-to-know-you chat."

"Okay, first off, it's a little more than just knowing Jancee Reynolds. Mr. Cooper hid the extent of his involvement with the victim. And he lawyered up pretty fast for someone who has nothing to hide. That's why he's a person of interest—not a suspect—at this point."

"Have you led a lot of murder investigations, Owen?"

"Enough to know what I'm talking about."

"So then you know it's just commonsense for a 'person of interest' to have a lawyer with him when he talks to the police. Especially in this case, when the acting sheriff has a very personal reason for focusing on Dan Cooper. Has he recused himself yet?"

I could hear my voice getting just a bit less friendly.

"No, he hasn't. That's his prerogative. But I'm running the case. And I don't have a stake in which way this turns out. I'll call it like I see it."

"Even if it would help the guy who hired you keep his job?"

"Even then. I don't play politics."

"I hope that's true. Because if you're a smart guy, and I have no reason to think you aren't, it won't take you long to see that there are several more likely suspects for you to investigate than Dan Cooper."

"Do you want to share your thoughts about them?"

"You go first."

He smiled for the first time.

"I guess what I've heard about you is true."

"What's that?"

"I think that's something I won't share either."

"Okay, let me take a guess about one of your leads. You can blink three times if I'm right. You're here to talk to Wes Morgan. That seems like a good idea to me."

"I wouldn't jump to conclusions if I were you. And much as I've enjoyed our conversation, I'm not one of those cops who likes to get too cozy with the press, so don't expect any inside information from me."

"And as much as *I've* enjoyed our conversation, I'm not one of those reporters who tries to curry favor with cops by backing off when they should be pushing hard."

"Understood. Nice meeting you, Leah. I'm sure we'll see each other again."

"I'm sure we will, Owen."

26

Well, I didn't hate Owen Fike. And it was possible that he wasn't under Lamey's thumb. I'd have to wait and see. I was curious about where he'd come from, and why. It's not like the Grantland County Sheriff's Office is a big step up on a cop's career path. Most lateral transfers are because there's more money to be made in a bigger county—which we weren't. If someone transfers into Grantland County, it's usually because a spouse got a job here, or because there was some kind of problem at the old place. When I had time, it might be worth checking into that.

As I was leaving, a black pickup detailed with vivid orange and yellow flames on the sides and around the tailgate pulled in. I recognized the driver easily from his photo. Ricky Travers.

Maybe he was the person Owen Fike had come to see, not Wes. But now, I could get to him first. I honked my horn and motioned with my hand for him to pull over. As he parked his truck and got out, I walked up to meet him.

"Ricky, hi. I'm Leah Nash from the *Himmel Times*. I'm also a friend of Dan Cooper's."

He was about six feet four, maybe even an inch or two more. His build was big—not jacked like he spent hours at the gym, but big like he used his muscles hard every day. He wore jeans, steel-toe boots, and a dark green windbreaker with the gold Wes Morgan Construction logo. Summer had described him as a puppy dog, but I couldn't see it, except in his eyes. They were big and a soft warm brown, with thick lashes. The look in them was wary.

When he shook my hand, the shy smile he gave me revealed metal braces. I found it rather endearing. He didn't look much like a menacing strip club bouncer.

"I feel bad that picture got online," he said. "The one with me and Dan and Dewey Redding, I mean. I don't know why Monroe is such a dick. I hope he gets caught someday."

Ricky's voice was surprisingly soft for someone with a physical presence as big as his.

"Caught for what?"

"He, well, never mind. I probably shouldn't say."

I was pretty sure I knew what Ricky was referring to, but I didn't want to put words in his mouth.

"Ricky, don't leave me hanging. What's Monroe doing?"

"You don't have to tell anybody, like the cops or anything? If I tell you, I mean."

"Are you asking to go off the record?"

"What's that?"

"It means that I can't use what you tell me except to help my own understanding of things. It won't go into print. On the record means I can report on what you tell me. Though it doesn't mean that I'll use everything you say. Just if it's relevant to the story."

"Off the record, then."

"All right, tell me."

"Monroe sells on the side."

"You mean drugs?"

"Just weed mostly."

"Who does he sell to?"

"The dancers, some of the workers. Some customers, too, I think."

"Not you?"

"No. I don't drink and I don't use drugs, not even weed. My mother was a user. That's how she died. I never knew my dad. That's why I wound up in foster care, until Uncle Jerry got me out."

He said it matter-of-factly, with no trace of anger or resentment.

"I'm sorry that happened to you."

He shrugged his beefy shoulders.

"It's okay, some of the homes were all right. But the last one wasn't. That's when Uncle Jerry got me out. He says it's none of our business what Monroe does. Just keep our heads down and do our jobs. So, that's what I do. But I felt real bad when I saw that Monroe put those pictures in *GO News*. Dan wouldn't even have been there if he wasn't helping me."

"You don't like Monroe much, do you?"

"No."

"Ricky, did you know that Monroe and Jancee Reynolds used to have a thing?"

His face clouded over.

"Yeah, I knew."

"You were a good friend of Jancee's, weren't you?"

"I tried to be."

"Did Jancee ever say anything to you about Monroe?"

"One time she told me he was an asshat, but that at least he didn't pretend to be anything else."

"Did Monroe treat Jancee badly?"

"I think he treated Jancee *and* his family bad. He's married. He has a little boy. He should be faithful to them."

I wasn't surprised that Ricky chose the old-fashioned word "faithful" to describe what Monroe's behavior should be. It was an apt description of his own behavior toward someone he loved—Jancee.

"I agree, Ricky. Did you hear anything around Tanner's about Monroe being in a financial bind recently? Or did Jancee say anything to you?"

"She didn't, but I heard it around. He was asking for a big loan."

"How big?"

"I don't know for sure, but somebody said five thousand."

"Do you know if he got it?"

"I guess he must have. He was saying that he'd get beat up if he didn't get the money. He didn't look like that happened."

"Ricky, let's go back on the record now, okay?"

He nodded.

"Dan told me that he met Jancee for the first time the day of the fight, and it was the only time he ever saw her. What do you remember about that day?"

"Dan came to help me put in a window in one of the cabins, and then I bought him lunch. My Uncle Jerry, he's the bartender at Tanner's, he introduced Jancee to Dan."

"I talked to your uncle already, and that's what he said, too. But do you think Dan and Jancee might have gone on seeing each other after that—only they kept it quiet?"

He had started shaking his head before I finished.

"Dan's great. But, well, he's old. And anyway, Jancee, she had plans."

Again, that was the same thing Jerry had said, and Summer, too.

"You mean plans to move to Chicago?"

He nodded.

"Yeah. I didn't want her to, but now I wish she had. She'd still be alive then." His eyes were bright with unshed tears and he blinked them away.

"Were you Jancee's boyfriend?"

"No. I wanted to be. But she said I was too young. I'm twenty-one. She was younger than me! I tried everything I could think of for her to like me. I even got braces, so my teeth would look better."

He bared his teeth to give me a better view of the metal bands.

"I wanted the invisible kind but my dentist said these were better on account of my teeth were extra twisted. I know they look stupid. But I thought when I got them off and they were all straight, Jancee—well, it doesn't matter now. She liked me. Just not the way I liked her."

"Summer said that you bought Jancee presents, and you ran errands, drove her places, did all kinds of nice things for her. And you even spent all that money to get braces because of her. Didn't it make you even a little angry that she kept turning you down?"

"It made me sad. Not mad. I loved her, but she didn't love me back. You can't help who you love, can you? I just liked to be around her. Now I never will be again."

He was as open with his hurting heart as a child. Dan had said that Ricky had been an easy target for his classmates. That he had gotten into some trouble when he finally had enough and fought back. Could one last turn-down from Jancee have turned his hurt into rage? Could he have become as consumed with anger as he was with love and turned it on Jancee? I didn't want to think so. But I had to acknowledge the possibility.

"Ricky, Jancee's car wasn't working the night she died. Did she call you for a ride?"

"No." He shook his head for emphasis.

"Do you think your boss, Wes Morgan, drove her to his brother's cabin for the party?"

"I don't know. I don't know anything about it. That is, I know she did some parties and other stuff. But I didn't know that Wes hired her. He never said. Jancee never told me either. I didn't know anything about it." His repeated denial flashed a warning sign in my mind.

"I understand that some of the dancers do escort work, off the books. Is that what you meant when you said 'parties and stuff?' Did Jancee do escort work?"

"Can we be that off-the-record thing again?"

I nodded.

"Did Jancee do escort work?"

"I guess."

"How did you feel about it?"

"I didn't like it."

"Did you tell her that?"

"Once. But she said it was her life. She didn't need anybody telling her what to do. If I didn't stop, she didn't want me around anymore. So, I stopped."

"Ricky, Jancee was someone you really cared about, loved, even. And it didn't bother you that she was having sex with other men for money? It didn't make you angry?"

"It's not like she loved them. She didn't even like them, she told me. It was just her work. They had to pay to spend time with her. I got to spend time with her for free."

It was sad to me how little a nice kid like Ricky had settled for.

"Let's get back on the record, Ricky. You said you didn't drive Jancee to Kent Morgan's cabin. What were you doing that night?"

"I was just home. I was real tired when I got back from work. I ate some supper and watched Netflix and then I fell asleep on the couch. Uncle Jerry had to wake me up when he got home." He spoke the words quickly and in a slightly raised voice, like a child reciting memorized lines for a school play.

"That sounds like my kind of night. Except I don't have an Uncle Jerry to get me up off the couch when I fall asleep watching Netflix. What time does Jerry get home?"

"He works different shifts. Mondays he gets home late, around two-thirty, usually. But I don't understand why you're asking me so many questions. I don't know anything."

"I just have one more question. Weren't you worried about Jancee, when she didn't come back to Tanner's?"

"No, because she—" He stopped himself.

"Because she what, Ricky?"

"Because she told me before that she was going to Chicago someday. I thought she just went."

"Weren't you hurt that Jancee didn't tell you goodbye?"

"No. That's just how she was. But I have to go now."

"All right. I didn't mean to keep you. I'm just trying to get a picture of what was happening the night Jancee died, that's all. Look, here's my card. In case you think of anything else you'd like to tell me. Can I get your number, too?"

He took my business card, and then repeated his phone number for me. He looked and sounded so forlorn that I touched him on his arm and said, "Ricky, I'm sorry for your loss. Thanks for talking to me."

His eyes filled with tears again, and this time he couldn't blink fast enough to keep them from running down his cheeks.

"Are you okay?"

"Yeah," he said, quickly wiping his sleeve across his eyes. "You're just the only one that ever said that to me."

"Said what?"

"That you're sorry for my loss. I loved Jancee, even if she didn't love me back. It *is* my loss. Thank you for knowing it."

"You're welcome, Ricky."

27

On my way back to the office, my phone rang. Gabe.

"Hi, I was just going to call you. Did Owen Fike and Lamey back off after you went in with Dan today?"

"They might have, except we ran into a problem."

"What?"

"His alibi. He says that the night Jancee was killed, he was with a friend from around ten o'clock until two a.m."

"What's wrong with that? I suppose it's possible that he could have arranged to meet Jancee at two a.m., but it's not very likely. What did Lamey say?"

"Fike did the interview, Lamey just hovered. The problem is that Dan won't name the friend."

"Why not?"

"I don't know. He said it was up to his friend whether he could reveal that or not. He wouldn't even tell me. Do you think he was with a woman?"

"Coop never said Dan was seeing anybody, but I guess he could be. But why wouldn't he say that? He's not married."

"Maybe she is."

"Ohhh."

"Yeah."

"Did you tell him he has to talk to his friend? That the longer he doesn't offer a solid alibi for the night Jancee was killed, the more time *GO News* and Lamey have to mess with Coop's campaign?"

"I did. He said his hands were tied. Maybe you and Coop can take another run at him, see if you can get him to change his mind."

"Oh, we will. Well, I will. I can't really speak for Coop. He and Dan are both equally stubborn. But possibly, it won't matter. Troy and I turned up some really interesting information about Tanner's today. I think that's the centering point for this whole thing. Oh, and I met Owen Fike today. He—"

"Leah," he interrupted. "I want to hear about your day, but I can't at the moment. I'm actually driving to the airport right now, and I'm nearly at the exit."

"What? I thought you weren't going until Saturday."

"I wasn't, but things changed for my friend and I've got to get there tonight. I'm really sorry about dinner tomorrow night. I'll make it up to you."

"You know how you can make it up to me? Just tell me what's going on with you."

"I told you, it's my friend—"

"We just agreed that was a lame answer from Dan. It's just as lame from you. Your friend has a problem. All right. What's the problem? Why do you have to go to New York twice in two weeks? And why do you suddenly have to upend your plans and zip out there today, instead of Saturday? What's going on?"

"I promise I will absolutely tell you everything when I get back. I just can't get into it right now. Trust me, please?"

I sighed heavily to make sure he got that I wasn't happy. But then I said, "All right. I'll trust you. But I really don't like being kept in the dark."

"You won't be soon. I'm at the airport. I have to go. I've already talked to Miller. If anything comes up with Dan, he'll handle it. Try to get Dan to name his friend. I'll talk to you soon."

"But—"

And he was gone, which seemed to be becoming a habit with Gabe.

"I'm telling you, Miguel. I saw them. Well, maybe not them, but I legit saw Dan's car. I can put two and two together. We should tell Leah."

"Courtnee, I want nothing to do with that narrative," Miguel said.

"What narrative is that?" I asked as I walked into the newsroom. Courtnee was lounging against Miguel's desk as he tried to work.

"Leah, you'll never guess who Coop's dad is having an affair with. Wait, is it an affair if you're not married?"

Given my conversation with Gabe about Dan's alibi, for once I actually wanted to hear what Courtnee had to say.

"Who?"

"Marilyn Karr!"

"Dan and Marilyn? No. Where did you get a ridiculous idea like that?"

"I got it from myself. I saw them. Twice already."

"Saw them what? Sitting in the same pew at Mass? Standing in the same grocery line? Courtnee, I'm embarrassed for you, that is some seriously weak tea."

"You don't have to be so salty, Leah. What if Dan marries Marilyn? Then maybe she won't hate your mom so much for breaking up her marriage to Paul."

"My mother didn't break up Paul and Marilyn's marriage. They were already divorced. And—wait, why am I even talking to you as though you have actual facts that you're sharing?"

"But I do," she said, whining out the word "do" like a toddler about to have a temper tantrum.

"I do have facts. My boyfriend Oliver saw them, too. When we were coming from Whisky Jack's in Madison, we drove right by Marilyn's house. There was Dan, walking out of her front door. At like two in the morning! We *both* saw him. You can ask Oliver. And I saw them again myself last night, in the parking lot behind the Starlight Lounge in Hailwell. They were in Dan's truck."

"Okay, now I know you were hallucinating. Dan wouldn't have been at the Starlight. He doesn't drink. Even people who do don't go there. It's the skeeviest bar in the area. What were you doing there?"

"I went with my Aunt Stella to look for my Uncle Chuck. She thinks he's cheating on her with a waitress. But he wasn't there. But when we got back to the parking lot, Dan Cooper and Marilyn Karr were in his truck. For real!"

"Courtnee, it had to be someone else. Dan's been in AA for about a hundred years. You made a mistake."

"I didn't."

She began repeating her tale of Dan and Marilyn's assignations as though repetition would make them true.

I wasn't listening, though, because something had suddenly clicked in my brain.

"Courtnee," I said, grabbing her by the shoulders to get her attention. "Stop talking and just answer me."

"How can I answer you if I stop talking? Anyway, I thought you didn't want to hear what I had to say. You said—"

"Forget what I said. When did you see Dan coming out of Marilyn's house? What day?"

"I don't know if I can remember now. You were so mean to me," she said in a pouty voice. I wavered between begging her and shaking her.

Miguel, who had been observing, could see that I was leaning toward shaking her. He stepped in.

"Courtnee, what day did I go with you to buy your fabulous sling-back kitten heels? You said you were going to wear them to Whisky Jack's that night."

Leave it to Miguel to pin Courtnee's memory recall to her favorite subjects—herself and her shoes.

"My new gold ones with the pointy toes and the cute little bow! I love them so much. That was last week. Last Monday at lunch hour. Oh, so it was last Monday when I saw Dan with Marilyn."

"You're sure?"

"Totally, but—"

"Okay, I gotta go. Thanks, Courtnee. I owe you one."

"Really? Because I'd like you to—"

"Catch me later. I have to go."

28

It had hit me with a jolt after I heard myself say to Courtnee that it couldn't have been Dan in the Starlight Lounge parking lot. It's true that Dan never drinks, and he wouldn't go to the grossest bar in town even if he did. But Marilyn Karr drinks. A lot. And she might choose to go to a bar where she could be pretty sure she wouldn't run into any of her high-class friends. I ran the theory through my mind as I drove.

If Marilyn was trying to quit, she might have called Dan the night Jancee died. Dan would have dropped whatever he was doing and gone to help if he could. I'd heard him say many times that the AA member who was there for him when he reached out for help had saved his life. And Dan is seriously committed to paying it back. And also to the anonymous part of Alcoholics Anonymous. If Marilyn was his alibi for last Monday night, there's no way he'd reveal her name without her permission.

I realized as I parked in the driveway and ran up the flagstone walk to Marilyn Karr's front door that I had no idea how I was going to approach this. But sometimes it's better not to have a plan. I rang the bell and waited.

"Leah? What are you doing here?"

Marilyn looked bad. Her auburn hair showed half an inch of gray roots, which was something I'd never seen on her before. Her skin without makeup was pasty and dull. Her eyes were puffy with dark circles. She, who always dressed fashionably, was wearing yoga pants and a faded blue shirt with what looked an awful lot like a red wine stain on the front. Her feet, long and veined, were bare. I didn't realize I'd been staring until she said, "Well? What is it?"

"Oh, sorry, Marilyn. Could I come in and talk to you for just a minute?"

"Talk to me?"

I waited for her to follow up with some nasty zinger about my mother, or the paper, or me. Instead she looked back at me through slightly out-of-focus eyes.

"Yes, it won't take long at all. I just want to check something with you, something Dan Cooper said."

The mention of Dan's name seemed to prod her to pull herself together.

"What's he said? He's lying. I don't know anything about it. Is it that girl? That stripper? I'm not saying anything for you to put in that, that, that ..."

She sputtered to a stop temporarily, searching for the word. As she swayed a little, I realized that she was drunk. Not sloppy, fall-on-your-face drunk, but heavy-drinker-faking-sober drunk.

"That what? That weekly newspaper that I own, the *Himmel Times*? Actually, Marilyn, I'm working on a story about Dan, and the way he's helped so many people achieve sobriety. I want you to be part of it. That's why you've been meeting with him, isn't it? To see if he can help you with your drinking problem."

"What are you saying? I do not have a problem. You get out of my house now."

"Marilyn, Dan is in trouble and he's not going to get out of it unless he produces an alibi. And I know you're it. He was with you."

"That's a lie. He's lying if he said that. And I have no idea what a handyman does with his evenings."

She spoke slowly, careful to pronounce each word distinctly, with no slurring.

"He didn't say that. He wouldn't. But I know you called him last Monday night. I know he came to your house. Were you as drunk then as you are now? Or worse? Probably worse, because he stayed so long."

I knew I was right because she was struggling to keep her expression neutral.

"I don't care if you do anything about your addiction to alcohol. But Dan does. That's why he spent four hours or more with you the night that Jancee Reynolds was killed. Now *GO News* is doing its best to imply that Dan was mixed up with Jancee Reynolds, and that he's hiding something. But does Spencer know what he's hiding is that Dan was with you?"

Again no answer, but she was blinking and squeezing her eyes, probably trying to keep her concentration. Though she could also have been trying to keep the tiny bit of her conscience that still existed from bursting out and telling the truth.

"Dan won't say that he was with you, because he cares that much about your anonymity. It's for you to tell. He never will. And as long as he doesn't, your son will make it look as though Dan has something to hide, when it's really you. Art Lamey and Spencer will keep rumors about Dan out there to cause problems for Coop's campaign as long as they can. How do you think Dan feels, knowing that to honor his commitment to you, he has to hurt his own son? How would you feel if it were you?"

Her eyebrows were drawn together in a frown, which I hoped meant she was thinking about it.

"You could either tell Dan it's all right to reveal that you're the friend he was with that night or call the sheriff's office yourself and talk to Detective Fike. How hard is that?"

That seemed to rouse her.

"Oh, of course *you* don't think it's hard. You and your mother would love to have me humiliate myself. Well, I won't. I won't have people whispering behind my back, looking down on me, pitying me. The way they did when Paul left me. I am not a common drunk. I am Marilyn Montague Karr."

"Marilyn, please. Most people these days understand addiction. You might be surprised how many would support you. Besides that, no one would even have to know. You're an important person in the community. With your influence, you could keep your personal issues quiet. You wouldn't even have to spell it out for Detective Fike. You could just say that you and Dan are seeing each other. Who's to prove you're not?"

"Don't be stupid. Why would I be seeing Dan Cooper? No one would believe that I was involved with him. You're just trying to get some kind of gossip for your paper. If you print anything like that, I'll sue you for slander."

"Marilyn. For one thing, it's libel if it's in print. So, you'd be suing me for libel. It's slander if I talk trash about you. It's neither one if it's true. But all I want to do is shut down the *GO News* insinuations about Dan."

"That's what you say. But how can I trust you? You're just like your mother. She's always hated me. Because I married a man of substance, someone with standing in the community, while she married your weak, feckless father. She turned my husband against me. And now you can't wait to run to her and tell her all about this. Give your mother and Paul something to talk about. *Poor Marilyn, did you hear? She's out of control. She's a drunk.* They'll laugh at me. I will not be a laughingstock."

Her lips trembled on the last word. I thought she was going to cry, but she swallowed hard and clenched her fists at her sides instead. Marilyn is the kind of person who thinks things like drug addiction or alcoholism are character failures, not illnesses. She's also the kind of person who doesn't forgive anyone—maybe especially not herself—for failure.

"No one is going to be laughing at you, Marilyn. Please, do the right thing by Dan. You know he always will by you."

"*Chica,* where are you? You zoomed out of here so fast. What's happening?"

"I'm on my way to Coop's, but I just left Marilyn Karr's house. I had a flash of insight while Courtnee was babbling. Really, I shouldn't be so snarky about her, I suppose. She may have provided Dan with an alibi for Jancee's death."

"You mean it's true, Dan Cooper and Marilyn? Wait. If Dan and Marilyn get married, and Carol and Paul get married, who will get custody of Spencer, you or Coop?"

"Don't even go there. I know why Dan won't say where he was the night Jancee was killed. It's got nothing to do with romance. But it's a solid alibi for him."

"Is it AA?"

"What a smart boy you are! But it's complicated. Hey, we've got a lot of catching up to do. After I'm done at Coop's how about if I swing by Bonuc-ci's, pick up a pizza, and we can have an eat and talk at my place in about an hour?"

"I can't. I have to cover the special meeting at the Hailwell school board tonight."

"But we don't usually cover those in person. Can't you just do a phone follow-up?"

"Not tonight. Lots of parents are mad at the football coach. I want to get the story up online right after the meeting. It won't be good. I mean, it will be a good story, lots of conflict, but not good for the coach."

"What about a stringer?"

"No one available."

"What about Troy, he must be done with girls volleyball by now?"

"No. I think we should talk about Troy, but when we have time."

"All right, how about this? You go to Hailwell and get the story; on the way back, *you* pick up the pizza at Bonucci's. We'll have a late dinner and rehash our days and settle all problems."

"*Perfecto*. See you soon."

29

Dan's car wasn't in the driveway when I reached Coop's house, which was good because I wanted to talk to Coop alone.

"Your dad's not here, is he?"

Coop was standing at the sink rinsing off his dinner dishes. He put them in the drainer before turning to answer.

"No, he's taking some yard signs around. He had a bunch printed off with the campaign donation from Kent Morgan."

"I kind of like that guy. Not his brother, Wes, so much."

"Did something happen?"

"I'll tell you later. First, did Dan tell you what happened when he and Gabe met with Owen Fike and Lamey?"

"You mean about his alibi? Yeah, he told me."

"Coop, I think it has to be—"

"AA," he finished for me. "Yeah, I agree. Dad will tell anyone his personal story about drinking if they want to hear it, but that's it. Nothing about who's in AA, who he sponsors, who the call in the middle of the night is coming from. He never even told Mom. He's always been like that."

"Yeah, well, thanks to Courtnee—and I bet you never thought you'd hear that phrase come out of my mouth—I know who Dan was with. Marilyn Karr. Courtnee saw him coming out of Marilyn's house very late the night Jancee Reynolds died. And she saw them another time in the parking lot at the Starlight Lounge. I just came from Marilyn's. Man, she looks rough. But she wouldn't agree to give Dan permission to give the cops her name. She won't go to the sheriff's office herself, either."

"Because she doesn't want people to know she's got a problem, right?"

"Yeah. I don't think she realizes that for the last couple of years people have been speculating about when she's going to get arrested for drunk driving or smash her car up. Why do you suppose she reached out to Dan? She was her usual snotty self when I said she could just say she was with him, and let people think they were a couple. Like your dad isn't good enough for her."

"Dad's done a few jobs at her house over the years. He likes to talk while he works. He probably told her his AA story. She might feel like she didn't have to keep up a front with him, because he's not in her social class. Dad couldn't care less about stuff like that."

"Do you think it's worth telling your dad that we know he's covering for Marilyn? Remind him that *GO News* will keep pumping out variations of the Cooper's-campaign-manager-questioned-in-stripper-murder stories until Lamey or Owen Fike says he's not under investigation anymore?"

"No, it won't change his mind. Anonymity is a really important AA principle for him, you know that. And you saw how bad he felt when *GO News* ran with the Tanner's photo. If I pressure him to name his alibi because it's hurting the campaign, he'll just resign. I don't want that. I'll just keep putting the message out there—I'm qualified, I can do the job, and I care about the people in Grantland County. If that's not enough, well, so be it."

"You know, Captain America, if you were running for an open spot on the Avengers team, your noble sentiments might work. But you're running for sheriff against a nasty little man. I'm not sure lofty principles are going to be enough. I want you to win, Coop!"

"Leah," he said, with a touch of exasperation in his voice. "I want to win, too. But I have to do it my way. Trust me, okay?"

"Yeah, yeah, all right. You're the second person to ask me to trust them today."

"Who was the first?"

"Gabe. He's making his second mystery trip to New York in less than two weeks and he won't tell me why, except he's helping a friend."

"What's the matter, *don't* you trust him?"

"Yes, sure I do. I just don't like being kept out of things."

"Oh, I know that all right. When's he coming back?"

"He wasn't sure, probably Sunday."

"Well, you have plenty to keep you busy right? What's going on with the Jancee Reynolds' story? I know you didn't confine it to checking out my dad's alibi."

"Right you are, my friend. It's going great guns as a matter of fact."

I gave him a quick rundown on what Troy and I had found out during our round of interviews.

"I know Tanner's runs a side business scheduling dancers for private parties, but I haven't heard anything about the escort end of things. Must be Krystal Gerrard is pretty careful. You're going to share what you have with the sheriff's office, right?"

"Eventually."

He lowered his head slightly and gave me a look from under eyebrows drawn together in a frown.

"Coop, as a master of 'the look' myself, I can tell you, it's not going to work on me. At least not coming from you. It's not my job to hand everything I find out over to the sheriff, especially before I've figured out how it fits together."

He sighed, but he knew I was right—from a reporter's point of view, if not from a cop's.

"How much do you know about Monroe Mepham?"

"You mean besides he's the jerk who gave Dad's picture to *GO News*? He's married to Cole Granger's sister. Their son Austin is the one James Shaw mentors."

"Yeah, I remember all that, but I was hoping you might have some criminal-type information to share."

"I haven't had any run-ins with him personally, but I know he did some county jail time for selling weed a few years ago."

"I'm hearing he's still in the business, not big time though. Just dealing to some of the dancers and customers at Tanner's. Also, he and Jancee

Reynolds were together for a while, but she dumped him when she found out he had a kid. He moved on but came back around to hit her up for money the week before she died. He tried other people at Tanner's, too, according to Ricky Travers. Told everyone a hard luck story that he was going to get a beat down or worse if he didn't come up with it. He's still here, and he didn't get beat up, so he must have found the money. The interesting question is where."

"What are you getting at?"

"Jancee had at least five thousand in cash in a purse she kept with her all the time. But no purse was found with the body, according to Ross. The cops are keeping that quiet, though. So, where is the cash? My thoughts turn to Monroe. He needed the money, she turned him down. Did he find a way to get it from her anyway?"

"That's thought-provoking."

"Isn't it? And it's not my only provoking thought. What about Wes Morgan? You know him, too, right?"

"Barely. Not enough to judge."

"Oh, it's all right, be a little judgy. He came down hard when Troy talked to him on the phone about Jancee Reynolds. He alternated between threatening and friendly when I visited him today. I don't like him much as a person, but he'd make a nice murder suspect. Do you see him as someone into BDSM?"

"What? Where'd that come from?"

"It ties in with the escort service. Jancee went out on her own. She started seeing a client who booked and paid her direct, because she was happy to accommodate his special needs. He was into BDSM, specifically into choking women, otherwise known as breath play."

"And you think that's Wes Morgan?"

I shrugged. "Maybe. What do you think?"

"I have no idea. I asked a few people about him after Dad mentioned Wes. All I got is that he cuts corners on jobs sometimes, he spends more than he makes, and his brother bails him out a lot."

"That's not much help. Can I give you some constructive feedback?"

"Can I stop you?"

"You do fine on the 'protect' part of Protect and Serve, but I'd really like you to take the 'serve' part more seriously when it comes to me."

"That could be a full-time job."

"But you'd love it. Ask any of my employees. Well, maybe not Troy. At least not today. Hey, want to come to my place for dinner tomorrow night? Gabe was supposed to cook for me, but with him skipping out, I'll have to fend for myself. Want to fend with me?"

"Sure. Can I bring something? A backup box of Honey Nut Cheerios?"

"That joke never gets old for you, does it?"

"I'm a fan of the classics."

30

I headed straight for the refrigerator as soon as I walked through the door of my apartment. Miguel wouldn't be arriving with the pizza for another hour or two, and I was getting hungry. I put together a cheese plate with some crackers and poured some Jameson over ice for a solo cocktail hour while waiting. Then I settled myself on my window seat for some thinking.

On the whole, I was pretty pleased with the day. Our visit to Tanner's had paid off. Not only was Dan's story corroborated, we picked up new information on Wes Morgan and Jancee. Plus, we now had the very interesting news that Tanner's owner Krystal Gerrard was running an escort service, and that Jancee had set up shop on her own. At least for one very special client. And that could be Wes Morgan. He might have killed her out of anger at her constant rejection. Or there might have been an accident during a paid session of breath play.

And then there was Monroe. He had a couple of possible motives, too. He said that it was casual with Jancee, but maybe it wasn't. Maybe he wanted her back, she refused, and he killed her. Or maybe it was money. She had it. He needed it. He killed her for it.

I didn't want to think too hard about the third suspect we'd turned up. Ricky. But I had to admit the possibility that he had killed Jancee either out of thwarted love or jealousy.

I tapped my legal pad with my pencil while I thought some more. One thing seemed clear. Jancee's killing wasn't planned. Strangling her with her own purse strap spoke of impulse, not planning. And I could see any one of the three being in a situation where their emotions, not their thinking, had taken hold.

A knock on my door meant Miguel had arrived. I hurried to greet him—and unburden him of the Bonucci's pizza.

"Hey, you! I'm always glad to see you, but never more than when you're bringing me Bonucci's. Get some plates out, will you? I'm just going to stick my face in the box and start eating."

I was only half-kidding, the pizza smelled that good.

"So, what happened at the school board?" I asked when we were seated across from each other in the kitchen.

"Very crazy. Parents yelling, coach yelling, students crying. In the end, the coach resigned. I already posted it online. You can read it all later. Now, tell me everything about the Jancee Reynolds story."

Between bites of pizza I told him.

"Do you think *GO News* knows about the escort service? Monroe Mepham gave them the photos of Dan. Would he tell them that, too?"

"According to Summer, it's a small operation, low-key. I can't imagine Krystal confiding in Monroe. But even if he knows about it, I don't think he'd risk losing his legit job as a DJ, and possibly exposing his illegit job selling weed, for a one-time fee from Spencer for passing along a news tip."

"Do you think it's Wes, or Monroe, or Ricky who killed Jancee?"

"I was thinking about that before you got here." I gave him the motives I'd come up with.

"Do they all have alibis?"

"Wes does, but it's his brother, so that's not totally solid. Ricky does, but it's not good. He was asleep on the couch until his uncle woke him up. But he could've covered a lot of ground that night before Jerry got home. Monroe, I haven't gotten into yet. I feel like Tanner's is the epicenter of this murder story and I want to find out more."

"You and Troy already found so much today. An escort service? BDSM? Strip club dancers? This could be a very big story. But not a very family-friendly story," he added.

"It's not even a very Troy-friendly story. You should have seen him trying to explain bondage and breath play to me. I didn't laugh, because that would have been cruel, but it was pretty funny."

"*Chica,* I want to tell you something about Troy. I don't think he will like me saying it, but you should know."

"What is it?"

"Troy came back from girls volleyball while you were with Marilyn Karr. He feels very, very unhappy."

"Because I made him cover volleyball instead of letting him go with me to see Wes and Ricky?"

"He thinks that even when he does good, like with Lewis Webber, you don't think he's good enough."

"But I told Troy he did a good job with Lewis. I trusted him today to interview Summer alone. What does he want from me? I'm a writer, not a life coach. He's going to meet a lot tougher bosses in newsrooms than I am."

"Maybe tougher, yes. But maybe not so ... so ..." He floundered for a second, then settled on "in charge."

"If you mean controlling, you can just say that."

"Okay, controlling," he agreed, a bit too quickly for my taste.

"You know you only let him interview Summer alone because you wanted to talk to Krystal Gerrard. But Troy got more from Summer than you did, right? But when you go to Omico to talk to Wes and Ricky, you make Troy cover volleyball. He was right, he could have gotten photos from some of the parents there and quotes from the coach. He really didn't have to be there. You're very tough on him. I think you need to give him more respect."

He cocked his head and looked at me, one eyebrow raised. When Miguel takes me to task, I feel compelled to listen.

"Is that Troy talking, or you?"

"Maybe both of us?"

"I thought I was doing a good job mentoring him. Stop looking at me like that. All right, I probably should have let him go with me. And I should let him off the leash more often. It's just that I don't want the story to get away."

"But you have the big thing *you* wanted, right? You know Dan is telling the truth, and you know his alibi is solid. Maggie is coming back Monday. I can work the Jancee story with Troy. You trust me, don't you? And I don't make Troy nervous."

"Yes, I trust you. And I should spend some time figuring out how to pressure Marilyn into confirming Dan's alibi. *GO News* won't let up until she tells Owen Fike or Lamey that she was with Dan. Or until Owen makes an arrest that isn't Dan."

"That's right. You can just let go and let Miguel. I will help Troy, and that will help you. We can't afford to lose him. Who else would work for the *Times* salary?"

He was joking but it stung a little, because it was true. Getting Miguel's —and everyone else's, but especially Miguel's—salary up where it belonged was always on my mind—and my conscience.

"Troy has an idea he's working on right now," he said.

"What is it?"

"He wouldn't tell me. But he is very excited. I told him to go for it. That he can't wait for your permission, that he needs to take action. I told him I never ask."

"Oh, so now you're conspiring with staff to manipulate me. What's next, armed rebellion?"

"Never. It's not manipulating. It's giving you what you need and helping Troy get what he wants."

"We'll try it your way. I'll write up my notes for both of you. Then, I'll just sit back and be a resource. No, not even that. I'll be a silent beacon of encouragement and hope. A shining light for all young journalists to turn to in these uncertain times. Does that make you happy?"

"You make me happy, *chica,* even when you are salty. Because I know the real you."

It both pleased and disturbed me that what he said was true.

31

When I make a promise, I keep it. Or at least I give it a good hard try.

I got up early and typed up all my notes from the past few days—I didn't put them into Troy's spreadsheet format, though. He could do that part himself. Instead I set up a Dropbox folder to share with both Troy and Miguel, and dropped in the files as I repeated, "Let go and let Miguel."

Then I started plotting out a way to make sure Marilyn did the right thing so Dan—and Coop's campaign—would no longer be part of a strip club dancer's murder story. I had just had an inspiration that I wasn't sure I should act on when my phone rang.

"Hi, Miguel. Everything's in a fold—"

"Leah."

I stopped talking immediately. It's always serious when Miguel calls me Leah instead of *chica*.

"It's Troy. A car hit him on his bike. I think it's really bad."

"What? Where are you? What happened?"

"I'm at the hospital. I—"

"Never mind. I'll be there in ten minutes."

"Miguel, what's going on? How bad is it?"

I had found him in a small waiting room off the ER receiving area at Caldwell Memorial Hospital in Himmel. His hands moved back and forth on his thighs. The zhut zhut sound of corduroy being rubbed was a backdrop to our anxiety.

"I think it's bad. I think it's really bad."

"Okay, you think, or you know? Have you talked to a doctor?"

"No. A nurse told me they are doing tests and we just have to wait. I'm so worried. I want to know what is happening."

"Yes, sure. So do I. How did you find out about it?"

"I heard it on the scanner. A bicyclist down on Hondell Road. A hit and run. My heart, it just started going so fast. When I got there, the ambulance was already leaving. Charlie Ross was there. He told me, he said ..."

A sob escaped him, and he didn't finish. I slipped my arm around his shoulder.

"Hey, it's okay. Take your time."

"He told me it was Troy. He was riding his bicycle and somebody hit him, and they left. They just left him there lying by the side of the road. *Dios mío.* I told Charlie I know Troy's *mamá* and I should call to tell her, but I was crying, and he said no, he would do it. She should be here soon. His bike. It was all broken. And Troy, he must have been so broken, too. What if he, what if Troy—"

Although my own mind was running down the same dark corridors, I didn't want him to know that.

"Miguel. Don't do that. Troy will be fine. I'm sure he will. He's young and he's strong. Now, tell me again. You said Troy was on Hondell Road when it happened?"

"Yes. A man was driving to coffee at the Polka Dot Diner. His headlights picked out the bicycle reflector. He pulled over and saw Troy. It wasn't daylight yet, about quarter to seven. He called 911."

"What was Troy doing way out there?"

"Sometimes he does morning bike rides before work, for his fitness plan."

"Yeah, I suppose that could be it. He offered to set me up a training plan the other day."

I flashed back on the memory of Troy telling me about it and wished I hadn't teased him.

"I guess it doesn't matter right now why he was there. He can tell us when he feels better, right?"

Miguel gave a half-hearted smile and then very uncharacteristically for him subsided into silence. I couldn't think of anything uplifting to say, so I did, too.

"What are the chances you'll be able to find who did this to Troy?" I asked Ross. He had shown up to see how Troy was doing while Miguel was getting some coffee from the cafeteria.

"I don't know, Nash. I hate these hit-and-run sons of bitches. We don't have much to go on. No one saw it. We called in the State Patrol reconstruction unit to investigate the scene. It didn't look to me like there was much to see. But they're the experts, not me. It's a bad deal," he said, rubbing the side of his face with his hand.

As we spoke, a commotion started in the outer reception area of the ER. We walked out to see what was happening.

"Where's my son? I need to see my son! Troy Patterson, where is he?"

A tall, slender woman strode to the front desk as she shouted. Her light brown hair was caught up in a loose knot on top of her head, which bobbed and threatened to fall down as she hurried across the room. She was followed by an older man with close-cropped silver hair and a worried expression on his face. As she reached the desk, the woman began rapping with her fingers on the glass sliding panel that separated the admissions clerk from the rest of the room.

Ross jumped up and hurried to the reception area to get her. I watched as he put his hand on her arm and said something to her and the older man. They both nodded. I went back into the waiting room as Ross guided them there. Miguel came in right behind them.

"Mary! Gordon! I am so sorry," he said.

He hugged Troy's mother and then embraced the older man while Ross and I looked on. Then Troy's mother turned to Ross again.

"We called on the way down but they said they didn't have any information they could give us yet," she said.

"I told Mary not to worry. That's how hospitals are. They just want to be able to give us complete information. It doesn't mean anything is wrong. I'm Troy's grandfather. Gordon Fuller. Mary is my daughter," he added, nodding in the direction of Ross and me.

"A nurse said they're still doing tests," I offered.

"Who are you?" Mary Patterson asked.

"I'm Leah Nash. I'm—"

"Never mind. Now I know who you are."

I almost got frostbite from the icy glare she gave me. She directed her attention to Ross.

"Detective, what can you tell us about the accident?"

Ross gave her what he knew, which wasn't all that much.

"I don't understand how it happened. Troy's an avid cyclist. He's ridden all over the state. He's used to riding with traffic. He's very careful," she said.

"Well, it was still dark. Could be the driver wasn't expecting to see a bicycle out there at that time and wasn't focused like he—or she—shoulda been. I'm hopin' your son can give me more details when—"

"Mrs. Patterson?"

We all turned to the doctor who had appeared in the doorway, each of us trying to read the news by the expression on her face. Troy's mother stepped forward.

"Yes. I'm Mrs. Patterson. My son, Troy, is he—"

"Given the circumstances and his injuries he's doing pretty well."

We all breathed a sigh of relief.

"Oh, thank God," said Troy's grandfather.

"They're just finishing setting his arm. He has a fractured ulna, multiple lacerations and bruises on his legs and body. But his vitals are good. His bloodwork came back fine. So did his CAT scan. He was wearing his helmet and that probably saved his life," she said with a smile.

"Can we see him?"

"If you keep it short. No more than five minutes. He's on pain medications. Don't expect a lot from him," the doctor said as she left.

"Mrs. Patterson, Mr. Fuller, I know you're itching to see Troy. But if I could just get in ahead of you for one minute, just to ask a couple of questions to get me goin' on this investigation. It could help a lot. I won't take long, I promise."

"I suppose," Troy's mother said. "If it helps you find out who did this to my son. But just for a minute. If you take too long, I'll come down and throw you out myself."

"You got a deal, thanks."

When Ross left, I sat down in a corner chair and tried to be invisible. I wanted to wait for the chance to see Troy, though I wasn't sure his mother would allow it. I couldn't figure out why she seemed so angry at me. Sure, a lot of people don't like me, but that's usually the result of knowing me. It's pretty rare when someone hates me at first sight.

"Ms. Nash."

Oh-oh. My cloak of invisibility had failed me again.

"You can call me Leah," I said, offering up a friendly smile.

"Ms. Nash," Troy's mother repeated. "Troy would be mortified if he knew I was saying this, but I think it's long overdue. My son admires you, tries his best to do a good job for you, but you can't be troubled to give him an ounce of encouragement. Troy is very bright. He's always done well academically. He loves being a journalist, but you don't have faith in his abilities. Why is that?"

I was taken aback. It was the first time a staff member's mother had requested a performance review.

"Mrs. Patterson, I agree, Troy's very bright. I think I've told him when he's done a good job—and when he hasn't. But I don't feel comfortable talking about his job performance with you. That's between me and Troy."

"Well, I don't believe you're being fair to him. My son deserves to be happy in his work, don't you think? And how can he be, if you undermine his confidence?"

I tried breathing in and out very slowly to avoid an answer that I'd regret. Mary Patterson had just been through a very emotional experience. She had come close to losing her son. Maybe I was the place where she needed to project the anxiety and anger that had no other outlet at the moment.

"Mary, do you think this is really the time for this discussion?" Troy's grandfather put his hand on her arm to settle her down.

Miguel, meanwhile, who is a fan of family drama, was watching with great interest.

"Yes, Dad, I do. Troy has worked his heart out and I'm tired of hearing him beat himself up because he can't please his boss." She stopped suddenly, her attention drawn to a flurry of activity outside of the waiting room. There was the sound of feet running down the hall and quick, sharp voices.

Ross came rushing in.

"It's Troy. He was okay. I was talkin' to him, and he was good. But then it was like he had trouble makin' the words come. He looked real funny. I called the nurse and got outta the way."

Mary Patterson let out a gasp and grabbed for her father's arm.

Ross physically restrained Troy's mother from running into the hall to find her son.

"Take it easy, Mrs. Patterson. You'd only be in the way, slow things down. Someone will be here as soon as they can."

"But you were there, what happened? They said he was fine. They said we could go see him. What's wrong with my son?"

Her voice ended on a wail, but she stopped fighting Ross's hold. He led her over to a seat. Troy's grandfather sat on the other side of her, trying to calm her down. Miguel and I exchanged worried glances but stayed where we were on the far side of the room.

After about half an hour that seemed much, much longer, a doctor appeared in the doorway. Troy's mother looked up and the terror on her face was awful to see. She and Troy's grandfather both stood, holding tightly to each other's hands as the doctor approached.

"Troy began to deteriorate clinically. We had to intubate him to protect his airway. We did a repeat CAT scan. It showed a subdural hematoma. That means a bleed in the brain. We're not equipped to deal with that here.

Troy will need a craniotomy. We're going to airlift him to a trauma center in Madison."

"Can we see him?"

"Yes, for a minute, but he isn't conscious."

"I want to go with him," Troy's mother said.

"I'm very sorry, but you can't. Space is too limited, and the medical team has to be able to focus on your son."

Overhead we heard the sound of a helicopter approaching. Mary Patterson let out a small moan.

"Troy's a very strong boy. He's going to be all right, isn't he?" his grandfather asked.

"We'll do everything we can to help him."

"Dad, we have to go. I have to see Troy. I have to tell him it'll be all right."

32

"Oh, Leah, that's terrible! And what his poor mother must be going through," my own mother said.

Miguel and I had returned to the office and updated everyone on Troy's situation. Although I'd been surprised to see that "everyone" included not just Courtnee and my mother, but also Maggie, and Allie Ross. Why Allie was there on a school day, and why Maggie was there when she was supposed to be convalescing on her couch, I hadn't had time to ask.

"How could anyone just drive away? Just leave Troy there?" Allie asked, her blue eyes filled with tears.

"Some people don't care about anyone but themselves, Allie," I said.

"Agreed," Maggie said. "But it might have been someone who just panicked and drove away without thinking. Then they got too scared to go back."

"But they could at least have called an ambulance," Allie said. She sniffled as she tried to process the concept of a sense of self-preservation so strong it could leave another human being broken by the side of the road.

"I have all the feels for him," Courtnee chimed in. "But riding his bike in the dark? In the winter? That's cray. But, like, I hope Troy's gonna be okay, anyway."

"He had a light on his bike, and he was wearing a helmet. And it's fall, not winter. There's no snow yet. And bicycles have as much right on the road as cars," Allie said, leaping to his defense. "It's not Troy's fault that some dumbass driver decided to run over him."

"Sorry. I forgot Troy's your secret geek crush," Courtnee said.

Allie blushed, because she does have a not-so-secret crush on Troy. But before I could put Courtnee in her place, Allie spoke up.

"I like Troy, yes. Because he's smart, and he's nice, and at least he's not a narcissist like you," Allie shot back.

Courtnee stood speechless, blinking her large blue eyes as though a pet rabbit had just taken a bite out of her hand. I was enjoying the moment, but my mother stepped in not so much to smooth things over as to get everyone moving.

"Courtnee, I've got some spreadsheets that need updating. I'll show you what I want," she said, taking Courtnee lightly by the elbow and leading her to the reception desk out front.

Maggie took over as they left.

"Allie, I didn't call you in on your day off from school to argue with Courtnee. After eight months here I'd think you'd know that's a lost cause. You were my first call when I heard you were off school for two days. But if you're too upset to work, tell me now. Do you need to go home?"

"No, Maggie. I'm good," she answered firmly, discreetly wiping her eyes on her shirt sleeve and moving over to the desk and computer set aside for stringers to use.

Next Maggie turned to Miguel, pulling her glasses off her nose as she did and pointing one of the bows at him.

"I assume you're going to file something more online about Troy's accident. And you'll pick up what Troy was working on with Leah—the murdered dancer story, right? And I need a complete briefing on that."

"Yes, Maggie," Miguel said promptly, glancing over and giving me a small grin.

"What's funny about that?" she demanded.

"Nothing, Maggie. Glad to have you back. The story budget for this week is on your desk," he said.

"Maggie, you have no idea how happy I am that you're here, but should you be? I thought your doctor said Monday, not Thursday."

"I feel fine, Leah. I can't watch one more daytime TV show, do one more crossword puzzle, or take one more visit from the Homebound Visitation Committee from church, bless their hearts. We've got a paper to get out and it's not getting done standing here. Let me know by four how much space to hold for a follow-up on Troy, and if you've got more to add to the Jancee Reynolds story. And Miguel, I want that briefing ASAP."

"You'll get it, Maggie," I answered for him. "But first Miguel and I have to grab some breakfast. We've both been going since early this morning. We'll pool our resources and he can update you within the hour. Okay?"

"Okay," she said. Then she perched her glasses on top of her thick gray bob, where they reside most of the time, and marched into her office.

"The first thing on my list is to see Spencer Karr. I'm going to try some friendly persuasion to get him to back off Dan."

I had taken Miguel up to my place to grab some of the breakfast neither one of us had had. We were plotting our strategy for the day over bowls of Honey Nut Cheerios.

"You, Spencer, and friendly don't go together. What are you planning to do?"

"Well, my friendly persuasion is going to be followed by a brisk round of hardball that I think Spencer will respond to. Though it revolves on the premise that he loves his mother, and that's not a sure bet with him."

"Oh, I would like to watch that!"

"Sorry, it's a two-person game, no spectators allowed. But I'll have the results by four o'clock today. I'll fill you in then."

"I can't wait. My money's on you. Now, what is second on your list? That I should find out more about Tanner's?"

"You *were* listening to me last night. Sometimes I can't tell if you're paying attention to me, or mentally planning a fashion makeover."

"Both, *chica*, always both."

"I'd like you to talk to Summer. Try to get more specifics from her on the escort aspect of things, and about Jancee going rogue with her own parties and her special escort client. Try Krystal, too. She threw me out, but you may have better luck."

My phone rang.

"Gabe, I'm glad you called. Something awful happened here." I filled him in on Troy.

"Oh my God! Will he be all right?"

"I don't know. We probably won't hear anything until later today. I hope so."

"I'm so sorry. I'll be thinking about him, hoping everything goes well."

"Thanks, he can use all the good thoughts he can get."

"Listen, I just wanted to let you know that I'll be back on Saturday instead of Sunday. And I have a surprise that I hope you'll be happy about. I'll explain everything when I see you. I promise. Can you do dinner on Saturday?"

"Yes. But you're going to keep me in suspense until then?"

"Have to. It's too much to tell over the phone. I'm sorry, I've got to go, but I'll call you tomorrow. We can talk longer then. But keep me posted about Troy. I'll keep my fingers crossed for him."

"Yeah, thanks. Toes wouldn't hurt, too. Bye."

"Well, that was interesting," I said to Miguel.

"What?"

"Gabe had to go back to New York last night, but he wouldn't or couldn't tell me why. Something to do with his mystery friend. He wasn't sure when he'd be back, but now he's coming home on Saturday and says he has a surprise."

"Oh, I love surprises! Maybe he is taking you on a cruise."

"Miguel. Why would he be taking me on a cruise?"

"Because a cruise is very romantic, *chica*. The ocean, the night sky with stars, the—"

"The norovirus running through the passengers, the people I don't want to sit with, the dressing up I don't want to do. No, Gabe knows me better than that. I hope it's not something bad."

"Why would it be bad?"

"Surprises aren't always good, you know. I guess I'll find out Saturday."

"I wish we knew about Troy now."

"Yeah, me, too, but I'm sure it will be hours before we hear. Don't look so worried. It's serious, sure, but Troy is healthy, he's very fit, he's got the strength to come back from this. And trauma centers know how to treat stuff like this. He's right where he should be. I just have a good feeling about it."

"Really?" Miguel said, his face brightening a little.

"Absolutely," I said.

It's not always bad to lie to someone, is it?

"Now, what I'm going to do while you work the Tanner's angle is pay a visit to Kent Morgan."

"Kent? Why?"

"Everyone I've talked to about Wes—Lewis, Sandy his office manager, Dan Cooper, Miller—has said the same thing. Kent is constantly bailing out his younger brother. So the more I think about it, the more possible it seems that he's stepping in again to help his brother with an alibi."

"You think Kent Morgan lied?"

"Maybe. Or possibly Wes stayed at the cabin, but he slipped out and back in during the night without his brother knowing."

My phone rang again. This time I didn't recognize the number.

"Maybe it's about Troy," I said.

Miguel leaned forward on his seat, his body tensed.

"This is Leah Nash."

"Leah? This is Lewis Webber."

I shook my head and moved my hand to indicate to Miguel that it wasn't the call we were waiting for.

"Lewis, how are you?"

"Is it true? I heard that Troy Patterson was killed in a car accident this morning."

His voice was tight and anxious.

"No. Troy is badly injured, but he's not dead." I explained what had happened. "His mother and grandfather are at the trauma center with him."

"Are Drew and Erica, too?"

I didn't know who he meant at first, then remembered that Erica was

Troy's older sister, the one who had once dated Lewis, and Drew was Troy's brother, who'd been a medic in Afghanistan.

"They weren't at the Himmel hospital, where Troy was taken first. They might be in Madison, I don't know."

"Do you think Troy's going to be all right?"

"I hope so, Lewis. I haven't heard anything yet. Do you have his mom's phone number?"

"No, but I have his grandfather's."

"He might be the better one to talk to. Troy's mom was pretty shaken."

"I can't believe it. I was just talking to him last night. He still thought I might be mad at him because of the story and everything. I told him I wasn't. We—"

"Wait. You talked to him last night? When?"

"Well, not night really. He called me around five or five-thirty. He just asked how I was doing—you know because of everyone knowing about me being at Kent's. And then he asked me if I knew where Wes hung out in the evenings—if he had a favorite bar or anything, because he had a couple of follow-up questions to ask him."

"What did you tell him?"

"That there's this place here in Omico, a sports bar called Stan's. Wednesday is Packers Trivia Night. Wes calls himself the King of All Things Packers. He does know a lot. But he always drinks so much, and brags so much, hardly anyone wants to play on his team. I told Troy he should go and show Wes who's the real king. Troy really knows his Packers trivia. He's like the guy in that movie—the one who can remember things—only about the Packers. *Rain Man,* that's the one."

"Did Troy say if he was going to go or not?"

"He said he might go over. That if he bought Wes a drink or two, he might be more willing to talk to him."

"But you don't know if Troy actually went or not?"

"No. Why? Is it important?"

"No, no. I'm picking up where Troy left off, and I just want to be sure I don't miss any leads he was working on. That's all. I'm sorry, Lewis, I have to go, but if I hear anything about Troy, I'll let you know."

"Oh, sure. All right, thanks."

33

"Troy's friend Lewis, what did he tell you?"

"That Troy planned to see Wes Morgan last night. That he wanted to ask Wes some follow-up questions."

"Do you think he did?"

"I do. But I know how to find out for sure. Hold on a second."

I grabbed my laptop and opened the shared Dropbox folder Troy had set up for the two of us. There it was, the spreadsheet he had so proudly showed me, neatly labeled "Interviews, Jancee Reynolds Story."

Troy had been so excited to show me his spreadsheet, to show me how organized he was, how ready to do the job. I thought about how quickly I'd dismissed his idea.

"*Chica,* what's wrong?"

I blinked away the tears that had surprised me by springing to my eyes. Leave it to Miguel to notice.

"Oh, it's just this damn spreadsheet. It's so Troy, isn't it? I wish I'd been more patient with him."

"Does his spreadsheet have Wes on it?"

"Yes," I said, as I found his name. "But it doesn't help much. Troy ticked the column for notes, and on the record, but no details on what they talked about. We need to get hold of his notebook, and his phone if it survived the accident. Troy usually records, too. I'll bet his mom has it."

"Not the police?"

"I don't think so. I'll check with Ross, but it's an accident investigation and Troy is the victim not the suspect. It seems like they'd give his personal stuff like his phone, notebook, wallet, and things to his family. If that's the case, you'd better be the one to ask his mother for them. If I do, she's sure to say no."

I fell silent for a minute. Then it hit me. I opened the calendar app on my phone and pulled up Troy's. We're all supposed to keep *Times* work appointments updated on the app so Maggie knows where everyone is. Troy is the only one who always remembers to do it.

"Miguel! Troy had a meeting scheduled this morning at seven, at the Polka Dot Diner. That's why he was on the road, that's where he was going."

"Does it say who he was meeting?" Miguel asked.

"No. It just says Polka Dot, seven a.m. But what if it was Wes?"

"Why would he meet Wes if he already saw him at the bar in Omico?"

"Let me think a minute." I paused while I tried to put myself in Troy's place.

"How about this? Yesterday, Troy thought I was making the wrong call when I told him it was too soon to ask Wes about escorts and the BDSM angle—that I wanted to lay some groundwork first. Then later he tells you he's got an idea that he's going to run with. His plan was to ask Wes about the escorts and if he was Jancee's private client. He wanted to show me that he could be an aggressive reporter, that he could take the lead, that he could be right and I could be wrong. Only his questions hit too close to the bone and it freaked Wes out. Wes has a bully's temperament, so he blustered and shouted and blew Troy off."

"But then why would Wes meet Troy the next morning?"

"Because after he thought about it, he realized he had to divert Troy's attention. He needed to get Troy focused on someone else and away from the whole BDSM thing. So maybe he texted Troy with a pretend apology, and said he wanted to meet him this morning, because he had some information."

"Like what?"

"I don't know, like throwing Ricky under the bus, maybe. When I talked to Wes, he pitched Ricky to me as a suspect. He could've planned to expand on that idea with Troy. And Troy would definitely have agreed to a meeting ..."

I paused as a vague idea took shape in my mind.

"Miguel," I said slowly, "what if Troy's accident wasn't an accident? What if Wes Morgan knew where Troy would be? He could have waited off a side road for Troy to pass, then zoomed up on him, knocked him off his bike, and driven on his way."

"But he couldn't know that it would work—that Troy would be killed, I mean. And he wasn't, *gracias a Dios*."

"But he almost was. Wes might have thought it was worth a try. It wasn't very risky—a dark road, not much traffic, early in the morning. That part worked. Nobody saw who hit Troy. It didn't kill him, but even so, it bought Wes some time to figure out his next move."

"But how would Wes know what road Troy would take? Or that he would be biking instead of driving?"

"Troy was trying to cozy up to Wes in a bar, right? He would've bought a round or two of drinks. What happens when Troy drinks even a little?"

"He talks a lot."

"And what does he talk about most?"

"Biking," Miguel answered. "Where he rides, how long he rides, how fast he rides."

"Exactly. So later, when Wes texts to set up the meeting, maybe he asks him if he'll be riding his bike there, and what road he'll take. Or Troy just volunteers it. Or, Wes takes an educated guess based on where Troy lives and where the diner is. I don't know. I don't even know if it happened, but I think it's possible. Don't you?"

"Possible, yes, okay."

"I'm not saying it's for sure. But now I think I'm going to see Wes first, instead of Kent. If he tried to kill Troy earlier today, he might be a little off his game when I pop in unexpectedly. And I'll call Ross, too, and ask who has Troy's notebook and phone. Oh, and I want to talk to Cole Granger, too."

"Cole? What does he have to do with this?"

"Nothing that I know of yet. But there is the Monroe connection. I'm not going to put all our eggs in the Wes basket."

"We're going in a lot of directions. Wes, and Monroe, and Cole, and Tanner's, and—"

"I know, but it's just where we are right now. I'm open to suggestions, Miguel."

"I don't have any, *chica.*"

"Then we just keep plugging along until one of us has a good one. But before I do anything else, I'm going to pay a quick visit to Spencer Karr. You'd better go down and give Maggie the briefing she's waiting for."

34

I mentally rehearsed what I was going to say on my way to the *GO News* office, which is only a few blocks from the *Times*. There was no point in trying to reason with Spencer. The only thing that might get him to back off was to hit him as hard as he liked to hit other people. I just had to hope beneath the moral wasteland that was his soul, there beat a heart that cared for at least one other person in the world, his mother.

A young woman with purple hair, heavy eye makeup, and a tight black leather dress sat at the desk in the minimalist black and white reception area of *GO News*. She put her hand over the phone she was talking into, but managed to get out only an irritated "Can I help you? Wait—" before I had breezed past her. I knew exactly where I was going.

The door to Spencer Karr's office was open. I marched in and stood in front of his desk. He made an elaborate production of not noticing me, then looking up from his computer and over the top of his glasses when I rapped on his desk.

"Leah, it's too bad about Troy Patterson. My condolences."

His words were rote and his expression blank.

"Thanks, but if I needed condoling I sure wouldn't come here."

"Oh. All right then. I'm sorry, we're fully staffed at *GO News* right now.

But we might have an opening for a stringer if you want to leave your resume at the front desk."

"No thanks, I already own a real newspaper. Not a pretend one."

"I'd love to stop and spar with you, but I'm busy—"

"I thought you might like a heads-up on our lead story tomorrow."

"You mean a catch-up piece on something we've already run? That's the *Times'* specialty, isn't it?"

"No, this is an exclusive. It's a profile on Dan Cooper. His journey to sobriety, the way he pays back the help he received by giving it to others. It's very inspirational."

"I think the word you mean is boring. And transparent. You're doing a feel-good story to distract from the fact that your boyfriend Coop's campaign manager got a little too close to a murdered stripper."

"I disagree. Readers like stories about people who triumph over adversity. But I'll admit that the *GO News* formula—stories full of innuendo and half-truths—appeals to the streak of *schadenfreude* most of us have. We enjoy seeing the mighty brought low. That's why the sidebar is going to deliver a punch. It's an interview with your mother."

He worked hard to cover his surprise but didn't succeed.

"My mother wouldn't do an interview with you."

"Oh, but she did. I've got the notes to prove it. See, the reason I'm running the two stories together—the main story about Dan Cooper and the sidebar about your mother—is that they're connected. Because one of the people who asked Dan Cooper for help was Marilyn. And he didn't hesitate to give it when she called him—the night Jancee Reynolds was killed. No, Dan went right to her house. She's the friend he won't name to prove his alibi."

"She'd never admit that to you."

"Maybe completely sober she wouldn't. But think about it, when's the last time your mother was completely sober? And she's getting worse. Under normal circumstances, I'd feel sorry for her, and then move on. But these aren't normal circumstances. Your mother can give Dan an alibi to put an end to all the garbage *GO News* has been hyping about him. But she won't, because she doesn't want to be 'humiliated' and be a 'laughingstock' in the community. That's one of the quotes in the story."

"So, I guess Dan's commitment to anonymity doesn't mean much when he's really up against the wall, then," Spencer said.

"Oh, it means everything to him. And he's suffering because of it. Your mother could end that but she refuses to come forward. That makes me mad. But you blowing up a non-story about Dan and Jancee Reynolds to hurt Coop's campaign makes me furious. I want it to stop. Now, either you persuade your mother to go to Detective Fike and tell him that Dan was with her that night, or I run my story."

"You won't do that. Besides, Dan Cooper would never agree, and Coop won't want any part of that. He's too 'ethical.' "

He said the word like it was an insult, not a mark of character.

"I'm running the story, Spence, unless your mother goes to the sheriff and confirms that she's the friend Dan Cooper was with the night of the murder. You have until four o'clock today to let me know if I should spike it. Your mother needs help. Who knows, maybe running the story will force her to get it. But that could happen a lot less publicly if you persuade her to tell the truth."

"I don't need your fake concern about my mother."

I shrugged.

"Sorry you see it that way. Marilyn has tromped over enough people in the county to ensure a story featuring her will be very widely read. That *schadenfreude* thing, you know. Four o'clock today, or tomorrow you and everyone else can 'read all about it,' as they say."

I felt pretty good about how the encounter had gone. I'd caught Spencer off guard, and I thought I had carried off the bluff pretty well. Because bluff it was. There was no way that I would expose Marilyn to the public humiliation she feared—not so much because I'm a good person, more because Dan and Coop are. I knew both of them would be pretty unhappy with me if I did. I seemed to have fooled Spencer, however. Maybe because it was exactly the kind of thing he would do.

If I *had* managed to fake him out, it would be a glorious victory.

I stopped in the Elite long enough to pick up a chai to drink on my way to Omico. While I waited for it, I Googled Stan's Bar, and saw that it opened at eleven for lunch. That meant I could check in there before I stopped to see Wes. I tried Ross on my way over, but I had to leave a message. I got a call as I pulled into Omico, but it was Coop.

"Leah, how's Troy?"

I went through what I knew, which was basically what he'd already heard from Ross.

"But Coop, I'm thinking maybe it wasn't an accident."

"Based on what?"

I explained about Troy connecting with Wes and my growing suspicion that Wes was the person most likely for Jancee's murder.

"That's not a bad working theory. It would sure make my dad happy if it was him."

"Why's that? I didn't get the impression Dan disliked Wes when he talked about him the other night."

"It's not about not liking Wes. It's about being concerned about Ricky Travers."

"Why, what happened?"

"Ricky called Dad last night, pretty worried. He should be. He lied to Owen Fike. And got caught."

"About driving Jancee to Kent's cabin?"

"Yeah, how did you know?"

"I talked to Ricky yesterday afternoon. He insisted that he didn't give Jancee a ride, but I had a feeling he wasn't telling the truth. Why did he lie?"

"He told Dad that he was scared and that his uncle told him he should just be quiet about it. That as long as he didn't say anything, and he didn't know anything, it would be okay. It was better to stay off the cops' radar."

"But of course lying has now put him up front in the most likely suspect race. Except for your dad, of course. Though I *may* have gotten Dan off Lamey's list and also off the daily scandal beat on GO News."

"How?"

"I'd rather not say."

"You didn't kill Spencer, did you?"

"Well, dead men tell no tales, I hear. But no. I didn't break any laws, but I'm not sure your dad would approve. If I tell you, you'd have to lie to him."

"I never lie to my dad."

"Exactly. And anyway, it might not work. I'll know by four o'clock. So, back to Ricky. How did Owen get him to admit that he lied about driving Jancee to Kent Morgan's? Did a witness come forward? Or did Owen bluff him?"

"No bluff. It was true. I checked with Charlie. Monroe Mepham came in yesterday. He said that he saw Ricky and Jancee drive off together. He didn't come forward before, because he didn't want to get involved, he said. Then he realized that he couldn't lie to the police."

"That would be a first for a Granger. Remember I told you that Monroe is still dealing weed?"

"Yeah, you said it's small time to some dancers and customers at Tanner's. You think that's connected to Jancee's murder?"

"I don't know if it is or not. But it feels like Monroe might be a bigger part of things there. That he's not just a part-time DJ, I mean. He had a fling with Jancee. He was in a financial bind—maybe he cheated a supplier or something like that. The Grangers aren't hardcore bad guys, but they play with some who are. And Monroe didn't strike me as particularly bright. I've got to go. I'm making a surprise visit to Wes at his office. No, don't even say it. It's daytime, his office manager is there, he's not going to try anything. I'll be perfectly safe. I have a plan. I'm going to make sure he realizes that Troy isn't the only one who knows about the escorts and Jancee's special client. I know, Miguel knows, Maggie knows. That way, if he really did try to take Troy out, he won't try it again, because he can't kill everybody."

"I wasn't going to say anything but watch yourself. Call me if you hear anything more about Troy."

"I will."

35

Stan's Bar was pretty nondescript on the outside. A plate glass window had the name "Stan's" in gold lettering arced across it, but that was all there was to let you know where you were. A solid wooden door led into a square room and a sign invited me to seat myself. I took a stool at the long bar, which ran nearly the length of the far wall.

"What can I get you?"

The bartender had dark hair that was streaked with gray and pulled back in a French braid. She wore a white shirt with rolled-up sleeves and a black and white striped apron over black chinos. It was one of the better bartender looks I've seen.

"Just a Coke, thanks. I'll scoot out before things get busy."

"You've got plenty of time. It's always pretty slow until around four."

"Wes Morgan says it's really jammed on Wednesday nights. Is that true?" I asked as she handed me my drink.

"Oh, yeah. Packers trivia really pulls them in. I worked last night and the place was hopping. Wes is a friend of yours?"

The way she asked I had the feeling that wasn't a plus in her eyes.

"No, just a work acquaintance. If you know Wes, you know he's always saying he's the king of Packers trivia. I told this friend of mine, Troy, that he should stop in sometime and wipe the floor with him. Troy's the real thing when it comes to the Packers."

"Real young-looking guy? Freckles, brown hair, glasses?"

"That's him."

"He was in last night. And he was with Wes. I waited on their table. He didn't stay past the first round of trivia, though. Wes neither. Looked like they got in some kind of argument."

"Really? Troy's not usually a fighting man."

"They were joshin' it up when I served them the first couple rounds, but Wes probably started acting like a jackass. He can't help himself. He could get Gandhi to throw a punch at him."

A couple came up to the bar then and she left to wait on them. I put some money on the bar for my drink and a tip and left without finishing my Coke. I had what I came for, verification that Troy had been with Wes the night before.

The same green pickup that had been in the parking lot the day before was in front of Wes Morgan Construction when I arrived. That was a good sign that Wes was in the office. Before I went in, I quickly scanned the front and sides of the truck, looking for chipped paint, scratches, dents, anything that might indicate it had recently had a close encounter with a bike. I saw nothing beyond normal wear and tear. But would Wes have been stupid enough to run over Troy and then keep driving the same vehicle around?

"Well, hello again. Looks like you're getting to be a regular around here." Sandy Eldridge smiled as I came through the door. "Didn't you get a chance to talk to Wes yesterday?"

"I did, Sandy, thanks, but I have a couple more questions for him."

"He's on the phone now," she said, glancing down at a light on her desk phone, "but he shouldn't be long. Hey, I heard one of your reporters got hurt real bad in a hit and run this morning. I'm sorry."

"Thank you. Yes. Troy Patterson. He was riding his bike on Hondell Road when he got hit. Whoever did it left him lying by the side of the road. He's in surgery at the trauma center in Madison right now."

"Hit-and-run drivers are the worst. I mean, I understand distracted driving, it can happen to anybody. You know, you reach down to turn up the heat or grab your coffee. It just takes that few seconds and then bam! I rear-ended a car once because I turned around to hand my daughter her binky. Nobody got hurt, thank God, but I didn't just drive away! Well, I hope he'll be all right."

"Yeah, me, too."

"Oh, it looks like Wes is free," she said, noticing the light on her phone had gone off.

She pushed a button to tell Wes I was there. Apparently mornings called for more formal office protocol than afternoons, but I didn't wait for his answer.

As she said, "Leah Nash is here to see you," my hand was on the door-knob and I was already turning it. I stepped into his office just as Wes was telling Sandy to say that he was too busy to see me.

"Sorry to bother you, Wes. This will just take a minute."

"I told you yesterday, I already said everything I know about Jancee Reynolds. I don't have time for this. I'm very busy."

He proceeded to pick up, put down, and push around some papers on his desk in imitation of what he understood busyness to be.

"It's not about Jancee, Wes. It's about Troy Patterson."

He stopped mid-paper shuffle.

"Troy Patterson? Doesn't ring a bell."

"He's a reporter for the *Times*. He did the story about your poker group and Jancee Reynolds. Someone saw you two together at Stan's last night."

"Ohhh. Oh, yeah. Troy. Right, that guy. Forgot his name. He said he was a big Packers fan, knew everything there was to know. We had a couple drinks together before he told me he was the reporter who put me in the paper. I would've told him to get lost, but he was buying the drinks. He told me his boss was the one who said he had to include me in the story."

I wasn't angry at Troy for throwing me under the bus. For the sake of a story, you do what you have to do.

"That made sense to me. Miller Caldwell owns the paper. Him being gay and all, he probably didn't get that we were just regular guys having some fun with Jancee. Is that why you're here, Miller's making you beat that dead horse, too?"

It was galling, but at the same time helpful, to have Wes forget that women can be bosses, too.

"Miller's a pretty good boss, but he does think this is an important story. Especially now, if Troy's accident had anything to do with his reporting."

"What accident?"

I looked at him closely for signs that he was feigning ignorance, but he was playing it cool.

"Troy was injured in a hit and run this morning on Hondell Road. We can't figure out what he was doing out there so early in the morning. It's way out of his usual biking circuit. Did he say anything to you about it last night that could give us a clue? He's still working on the Jancee Reynolds story with me. I'm wondering if his being out there had anything to do with that."

"I didn't hear about the accident. How bad is he hurt? Will he be all right?" Wes seemed genuinely surprised.

"I don't know. I hope so. It's very serious. He's in surgery right now at a trauma center in Madison. The police are investigating."

"But it was an accident, right? I mean, you said a hit and run. Were there any witnesses—any idea who did it?" Wes asked.

Okay, now that seemed a little more like someone who had a vested interest in gathering all the information he could about how the police were viewing things.

I shook my head. "No. It was around six-thirty or so this morning. A man on his way to the Polka Dot Diner found him. There wasn't anyone around when he did. And Troy was in and out of consciousness so he wasn't able to tell the police anything."

"I see. That's a tough one. Sorry, but I don't know anything that could help you. So—"

"I know you're busy, Wes, but this is really important. If we knew where Troy was headed, we might find a connection to a lead that he was checking on. It's thin, I know, but it's all we've got. Are you a cycling fan like

Kent? If so, Troy must have really bent your ear. He loves talking about riding."

"No. You wouldn't catch me spending four thousand on a bicycle. He didn't say anything at all about it."

"It was a short night, though, right? Neither of you stayed past the first round. What happened?"

He laughed uncomfortably.

"What? Did you have cameras on us? Troy thought he knew more than he did. We didn't see eye-to-eye about some answers. Things got a little heated, so we both called it quits."

I made a show of leafing through the notes I'd been taking, as though to make sure I had everything covered.

"Okay, then. So, Troy didn't talk to you about cycling at all. He ran into you by chance, you guys had a couple of drinks, some Packers talk, and then you both left early."

I nodded as if satisfied and said, "Okay, that's it, I guess."

I flipped my notebook shut and shoved it in my purse.

"Thanks for your time, Wes. Sorry to interrupt you on a busy day."

He didn't actually say, "Phew!" but his face had the relieved look of someone who had successfully traversed a field full of cow pies. Until my last question.

"Oh, just one more thing. Did Troy ask you about Jancee Reynolds having a side hustle as an escort, and if you ever used her services? You know, like you did when you set up the birthday party directly with her?"

His face flushed and he stood up.

"No, he didn't. And I don't appreciate you doing it now. I tried being nice. I tried cooperating. But this is the last time you come to my office, understand? Any more questions, you can ask my lawyer."

"Sure thing. Have you got a name and number for me?"

"Get out."

36

When I finished with Wes, I tried Monroe Mepham, but he didn't answer and his voicemail was full. Next, I called Jerry Travers to see if he knew Monroe's schedule for the week. An impromptu in-person visit would probably work better than a phone call anyway.

"He's usually here on Fridays and Saturdays. Krystal would know for sure. You want her cell number?"

"Yeah, thanks."

He rattled it off, and then he said, "You musta heard about Ricky. That he lied to that detective."

"I did. That wasn't a smart thing to do."

"That's on me. My experience with cops hasn't been the greatest. When they found Jancee, and Ricky told me about driving her that night, I told him to just keep quiet, not to tell the cops anything. Nobody had to know but him and me. He's a real smart boy, but you gotta give him time to think. I knew if he got nervous and said the wrong thing, the cops would go after him, even if he didn't do anything wrong. Looks like I gave him some real bad advice."

"I'm sure you meant well, Jerry."

"Could you just kinda look out for him? I mean, I know you're not with the cops or anything, but don't put any story in your paper like he did something wrong. Because he would never hurt anybody. I'm real worried for him right now."

I had a sick feeling that he should be. I didn't want to make him feel worse by pointing out that Ricky hadn't had a problem hurting Dewey.

"We have to report what's true, but if Ricky didn't have anything to do with Jancee's death, then we certainly won't make it look as though he did."

"Okay, okay. I probably shouldn't have even asked you, but damn I'm scared for that boy."

"I know you are. I hope things go well for him."

Next I tried Krystal's number, thinking that given her side hustle, she probably picked up unknown numbers for the same reason I usually did—you never know when a lead's coming in.

"Krystal Gerrard," she said in her brusque, make-it-quick voice.

"Krystal, Leah Nash here. I tried to reach Monroe Mepham this afternoon, but he didn't answer his phone and—"

"He probably doesn't want to talk to you. Neither do I."

"Wait, please. Can you just tell me if he's working this weekend?"

"No."

"No he's not working, or no you can't tell me?"

"You figure it out. I've got your number. I won't be picking up again."

"Leah, I told you before, you're gonna have to contain your constant desire for my attention. I'm workin.' Now, if you want to get together a little later, I'm sure we can fix somethin' up."

"Cole, this is serious. I really need to talk to you. Can you meet me for lunch or not?"

"I cannot. However, if your need is that great, you can come to the Ride EZ corporate headquarters, and I'll squeeze you in."

"Fine. I'm just leaving Omico. I'll see you in about twenty minutes."

"Now wait just a minute. If you're over that way, stop by the Starbucks and get me one of them Spiced Pumpkin Lattes. Extra hot. Like me."

"Fine. But it won't be very hot by the time I get there."

"That's all right, darlin', I still will be."

I shook my head as I hung up. Cole is absolutely a low-life, small-time conman with his eye always on the main chance. But I've discovered over time that he's fairly bright. He's not a good man, but occasionally he does good things. Still, it would be a big mistake to ever really trust him, of that I was confident.

The Ride EZ "corporate headquarters," as Cole had so grandly described it, is a pea-green cinderblock structure on the outskirts of Himmel. Immediately inside the door is a dented Formica counter cluttered with a glass jar of wrapped peppermint candies, a collection of pens in a plastic container, and a stack of flyers promoting the business. Cole himself, a thin-lipped man in his late twenties, with slicked-back brown hair beginning to curl a little on his neck, sat at the counter. His glance up at me was cocky and assured. I plunked the now lukewarm latte on the counter.

"Okay, there's your tribute, now I need some answers."

"That depends on what the questions are."

"Do we have to talk out here, with the counter between us?"

"It's Ride EZ policy to keep our clients on the opposite side of the counter. But, as you're not exactly a client, and we're old friends, I guess I could let you come back to the executive dining room."

He stood and I followed as he led me down a short hall. He gestured for me to walk ahead of him into a room on the left, furnished with a microwave on a rolling cart, a dorm-size refrigerator, and a small painted table around which sat three plastic chairs.

He pulled one out for me with a flourish, then popped his Starbucks into the microwave. When it dinged, he retrieved his latte and sat down across from me. He folded his hands together on the table, like an agent waiting to hear a story pitch.

"Why did Monroe Mepham go to the cops and tell them that Ricky Travers drove Jancee Reynolds the night she was killed?"

"What? That's it? No finesse, no polite openers, no common courtesy even? Just 'gimme what I want, son.' You need to seriously work on your people skills, Leah."

"Troy Patterson was nearly killed by a hit-and-run driver this morning. He's having brain surgery in Madison—maybe already had it. I don't want to play stupid games with you today."

"Hold up there. I didn't know that. I'm truly sorry about your friend's accident."

He sounded sincere, but he usually wasn't.

"Thank you," I said.

"In answer to your question, I'd have to say Monroe was doin' his civic duty to help the police. What other reason could there be?"

"I can think of a couple. Your brother-in-law was close to Jancee Reynolds at one time. Very close. He also hit her up for a five-thousand-dollar loan, which she refused. He told her he was in physical danger if he didn't repay some money he owed. He tried several other people at Tanner's. They refused as well. Maybe someone offered to pay him if he took a phony story to the cops."

"Coupla things, Leah. First, Monroe, he's quite a storyteller."

"So he didn't need the money? He wasn't going to get a beat-down?"

Cole chuckled and shook his head.

"Now who would Monroe be associatin' with that would put him in danger of physical reprisal?"

"Well, you. And the rest of your family, for a start. Monroe deals weed and sometimes pills. Maybe he skimmed some money he owed his dealer from sales or borrowed money against future sales but he didn't come through when it was time to pay up. You're in more of a position to know about Monroe's business problems than me."

"Now, see, there's where you're wrong. I have no idea what you're talkin' about. You need to direct your questions to Monroe."

"I would, but I can't find him. Do you know where he is? I called his cell phone, but he didn't pick up. At Tanner's they wouldn't tell me when he's working, or even if he's on the schedule. Has he gone somewhere?"

"Well, now you just refreshed my memory. I believe he's out of town."

"Why? When is he coming back?"

"Just family matters, Leah. Nothin' that's any of your business. I have no idea when he's comin' back. It's gonna be hard to reach him, too. Some of them hollers down in Kentucky there where the family lives don't get good phone reception."

"Cole, I'm curious. Don't you care at all that your sister is married to a man who might be involved in a murder?"

"Whoa! Hold up there. I'm tryin' to be understandin' here, because you got some stress about your friend's accident. But you got no business comin' here and accusin' someone in my family of a heinous crime. Where did you come up with such a crazy-ass idea?"

"Is it crazy-ass? Monroe had a thing with Jancee. Maybe he wanted to restart it and she didn't agree. Maybe he wanted to borrow money and got mad when she wouldn't give it to him. Maybe he went to the cops to point their investigation away from himself. A lot of possibilities there, Cole."

"Don't mess with me, Leah." His tone held none of its usual faux friendliness.

He stared at me hard for a few seconds. I returned his glare. It was a little bit funny, and a teensy bit scary.

Then he stood, and I did, too. He followed me as we walked in silence back to the reception area. When I reached the door, I turned back to look at him.

"I care about who killed Jancee Reynolds. And I *will* find out who it is. And if Monroe, or any other Granger, gets caught up in me finding out the truth, that's not my problem. Just so we understand each other, Cole."

"I think we understand each other fine. You take care now."

37

I wasn't very satisfied with the way my conversation with Cole had gone. I hadn't succeeded in getting him to admit anything.

I looked at the clock on my dashboard. Almost one-thirty. What was happening with Troy? How long did brain surgery take, anyway? I should have heard something. I called Ross.

"He's not outta surgery yet, Nash," Ross answered, before I even asked the question.

"But it's been hours!"

"Take it easy. The ball game ain't over yet. I talked to a doc friend of mine. He said five hours or even longer's not unusual. I'm keepin' tabs on it. I'll let you know. I got some other news for ya though. The reconstruction team finished up a little while ago. Those guys are good. Found a little piece of paint on Troy's bike. They gotta analyze it but they think they can match it to the truck that hit him. They know it's a truck from the tire pattern. They can tell that the driver didn't try to stop, just plowed right into him."

"You're saying someone deliberately ran into Troy?"

"No, I'm sayin' whoever hit him didn't try to stop. It coulda been a drunk, or it coulda been on purpose. Don't put that in, it's too early."

"Oh, before I forget, do you have Troy's phone and his notebook?"

"His mother does—not the phone, that was pretty much smashed to smithereens."

That meant we wouldn't be able to check it to see if Wes had actually texted or called Troy. But Ross might have requested the records. He's usually pretty thorough.

"Are you getting Troy's phone records?"

"Yeah, I got a request in. Could be Troy was on his phone and not paying too much attention right before he got hit. Not that it would excuse whoever hit him, but I like to get the whole picture on things."

"Could you tell me what the records say when they come back?"

"No. You want that, you're gonna have to file a formal request, and good luck with that. I told you, I walk the line until Lamey's gone. Why do you want 'em anyways?"

"Miguel and I are following up on the assignments Troy was working on. I just want to make sure we don't lose information in the transfer to us. When you get them, you could at least tell me if he was in contact with Wes Morgan last night, couldn't you?"

"Maybe. You could at least tell me why you really want to know, couldn't you?" he asked, mimicking my faux casual tone. Sometimes Ross is a little too observant for my purposes. I wasn't ready to give him my budding Wes theory yet, because with his current mindset, he'd take it straight to Owen Fike, and it was too soon for that.

"I did tell you. Miguel and I don't want to lose any leads Troy might have been after."

"Uh-huh."

I moved quickly to change the subject. "Has anything more happened with Ricky Travers?"

"You mean since Fike got him to admit that he lied about driving Jancee Reynolds?"

"Yeah, Coop's dad got a call from Ricky. I guess he's pretty scared."

"The kid should be. Lyin' like that, it's a red flag."

"Ross, don't you think it's a little odd that Monroe Mepham had a sudden attack of conscience and came in all on his own to tell Owen Fike that he saw Ricky with Jancee? Does that sound like a Granger to you?"

"Not right off hand, no. But he's just a Granger by marriage to Cole's sister. Maybe the Mephams have a touch more respect for the law."

"Yeah. Maybe. Or maybe he's trying to shift attention to Ricky, because he's got something to hide. Or maybe Wes Morgan paid Monroe to do it, because he's the one who's hiding something."

"You're never short on ideas, are you, Nash? What's all these questions about Wes Morgan, and phone records? What do you know?"

"Nothing. I have some ideas that might work out, that's all. Then again they might not. You're right, I shouldn't drag you into it. When I'm sure, I'll tell you."

"Hey, don't be trying to—"

"Oh, you're breaking up! Sorry. I'll talk to you later. Bye!"

Of course, he wasn't breaking up, but at the moment I was just riffing on ideas—Wes, Monroe, Ricky. I didn't have enough for Owen or Ross to take seriously yet.

A call from Jennifer Pilarski on her personal number popped up on my phone as I was driving into town, so I knew it wasn't official business from the sheriff's office.

"Hi Jen, what's going on?"

"Leah, how is Troy? I'm so sorry. He seems like a nice kid. Are you doing okay?"

"He's in surgery, Jen. And don't be nice to me, or I'll start crying. I was pretty tough on Troy the last time I talked to him. I didn't know it might be the last time."

"Stop that. You have to think positive. Your thoughts manifest what happens. If you think negatively, you'll bring what you don't want into your life."

"Been watching *Oprah Super Soul Sunday* again, haven't you, Jen?"

"Mock if you must but try it. I'm serious. Anyway, I also called because something incredible just happened. But I can't be your source."

"How incredible?"

"No. Swear that you're willing to go to jail for me before you reveal your source. Like those big-time reporters do."

"Are you saying I'm not a big-time reporter?"

"Do you want to hear this or not?"

"I do. Okay, I swear I will protect your identity to the death. Now what is it?"

"Marilyn Karr just came in a few minutes ago, and she's meeting with Owen Fike right now. She looks like hell, too, by the way. Something is up."

"What do you think it could be?" Of course I knew, but it was best if Jen didn't.

"All Owen's working on now is the Jancee Reynolds' case. It has to be something to do with the murder."

"Maybe she's a witness. Maybe she saw something she forgot to report. Well, I better go. I—"

"Wait a minute. Do you know something? You do, don't you? I can tell by your voice. What is it? Don't you trust me? After all the times I've trusted you, tipped you off with information?"

"Yes, I trust you, Jen. I might know why she's there. But I could be wrong. I have to get verification. And even if I'm right, before I'll tell you, you have to promise that you will speak not of this to anyone. That includes John. On pain of damaging our friendship forever."

"I don't like to keep secrets from John," she said hesitantly.

"You get an A for marital transparency. But unfortunately, you do not get the Leah Nash Top Secret Security clearance, which is required to be read in on this information. You'll have to wait for Lamey to lift the veil of secrecy, or for Marilyn to reveal it."

"Now I *have* to know what it is. Fine. I promise I will tell no one. Ever. Now tell me."

"Nope, sorry. I really can't. But watch for a statement from the sheriff later today. If it doesn't come, ask me again."

38

I tried Miguel after I hung up with Jen, but it went straight to voicemail. Hopefully that meant he was getting somewhere with his interviews. When I got back to work, I stopped in the office to see Maggie.

I found her at her desk, frowning at her computer screen.

"Hey, Maggie. How's the first day back, you doing all right?"

She turned to look at me as she pushed her glasses on top of her head.

"Leah, what about Troy? Do you have anything?"

"No update on his condition. I talked to Ross a little bit ago. He's still in surgery."

"It's gonna be bad. My mom said that if he survives he'll probably be, like, a vegetable, you know, like in a coma forever," Courtnee said.

She had come up behind me to deliver her assessment with the solemn glee some people experience when reporting terrible news.

"She's raised a blonde vegetable herself, so that makes her an expert? Your mother is a part-time receptionist, not a neurosurgeon, Courtnee. She doesn't know jack about Troy or what's going to happen. Keep your half-assed information to yourself," I said.

Her eyes widened, and because Courtnee's armor of self-esteem is rarely pierced, I knew I'd crossed the harshness line.

"I'm sorry, Courtnee. You just said what I've been fighting not to let myself think all day. It punched the wrong button for me, I guess. I shouldn't have come at you like that."

"No, you shouldn't, Leah. Don't you think I'm worried about Troy, too?"

"Yes, sure, I—"

"He said he'd babysit my little brother next Saturday so I can go to Chicago. Now what am I going to do? You're not the only one who feels bad," she said, her mouth forming a pout.

I was about to tell her what she could do, but Maggie intervened.

"We're all worried about the kid, Leah. Head injuries are bad news. But we don't have to think worst-case scenarios at this stage, right? Everybody's different, and Troy's young and he's strong."

She was repeating the same facile words of comfort that I'd offered Miguel earlier in the day. And the more time that went by, the emptier they seemed.

"Twenty to thirty percent fully recover. Sometimes it takes a few weeks, sometimes it takes months. It depends how bad it is and how fast it gets treated. I Googled it," my mother said, coming up behind me and putting an arm around my shoulders.

"I've been praying all day that Troy is one of the full-recovery-in-a-few-weeks patients," she added. "I take it there's no news yet, Leah?"

"Not about Troy, no. But Ross updated me on the accident reconstruction team findings so far." I gave them both what I had. "Also, the driver didn't even try to stop. Just full-tilt drove straight into Troy."

"Sounds like a drunk driver so far gone they didn't know what they were doing," my mother said.

"Or someone who knew exactly what they were doing, and did it on purpose," I said, and then immediately regretted it.

"Why? What could anyone have against Troy?" my mother asked.

I cast about for a way to backtrack on my answer, because I definitely didn't want to reveal my suspicions in front of Courtnee. Before I could come up with a diversion, I was saved by the Miguel.

"*Chica*, anything new about Troy yet?"

He hovered in the doorway, an apprehensive look on his face.

"No, but I'm glad you're back."

I moved swiftly over to him and slipped my arm through his and tugged him toward the hall.

"Let's go upstairs. I'll make you a sandwich and we can catch up. Maggie," I called over my shoulder as we left, "we'll get ourselves organized, then Miguel can update the story on Troy. I might have something from the sheriff's office, too. I'll know for sure shortly."

"Here you go," I said, putting a peanut butter and jelly sandwich with a side of chips down in front of Miguel, and another plate with the same at my place.

"Did you notice how I made it special? Diagonal cut, not straight across. Nice, huh?"

"Yes, I feel very special now."

"Good, because you—" I stopped mid-sentence as my phone rang. It was the call I'd been waiting for.

"Hello, Spencer. What can I do for you?"

"You can conduct your victory dance in private. It's up. A news brief saying Dan Cooper is no longer considered a person of interest in the Jancee Reynolds murder."

"Good. I didn't want to have to print the story about Marilyn."

"The thing I wonder, Leah, is if you really would have printed it, or if you were bluffing."

"Now you'll never know. Why didn't you call my bluff?"

"I couldn't afford to be wrong. You just upped the ante, Leah. Look out."

"I won't look out. I'll look forward to the next time I beat your ass like a drum. Bye."

Miguel's eyes were wide with curiosity.

"Was that about your hardball game with Spencer? What happened?"

"Just a second, I'm trusting but verifying here," I said as I looked at the *GO News* site on my phone. There it was. I looked back up at Miguel.

"This stays here, it's not for print—it's more personal than professional, okay?"

"*Chica*, you know they call me Mr. Confidential."

"No, they definitely don't. But I know you can keep a confidence if it matters. This does. Okay?"

"Okay."

"Marilyn Karr is Dan's alibi for the night Jancee was killed. He was talking her through a bad night with her drinking, trying to help her find her way to AA. She was too embarrassed, or ashamed, or whatever to go to the cops. Dan wouldn't say who he was with, because he's so hooked into the anonymity part of Alcoholics Anonymous. It was killing him to be used to hurt Coop's campaign. I explained all that to Marilyn. I asked her nicely to get Dan off the hook, but she refused. So, I took it to Spencer, with a little added incentive."

"The hardball?"

"Yep. I said I'd print a story about Marilyn's alcoholism, her reliance on Dan's help, and her refusal to help him. That is, unless he got her to go to the cops, and *GO News* ran something that said Dan was no longer a person of interest."

"And she did today?"

"She did."

"But you wouldn't have run a story about Marilyn, would you?"

"No. But I was able to convince Spencer that I'm just as much of a moral midget as he is. So, he did what needed to be done. But the drinking stuff is Marilyn's story to tell publicly, if she ever wants to."

"Of course. You did good today, *chica*."

"I did, didn't I? But it's not all good."

I filled him in.

"That looks bad for Ricky—that he lied to Detective Fike."

"Agreed, but I'm curious about why Monroe had a sudden burst of good citizenship, and why he's nowhere to be found. He might have been trying to protect himself by putting the attention on Ricky, or maybe he didn't see Ricky with Jancee at all. Maybe Wes paid him to say that, to keep the attention off himself."

"This is getting very complicated, and I haven't even told my story yet."

"That's right. Let's hear it."

39

Before he began, Miguel moved his plate out of the way to give himself plenty of room for the extravagant hand gestures that accompany his stories.

"First, your friend Summer? She got fired!"

"What? Between yesterday and today?"

"Yes! I went first to the cabins at Tanner's. I asked a woman who was coming out of one of them where to find Summer."

"Was it a tall brunette named Lorna?" I asked, thinking of the woman with the tight jeans and the shrewd eyes who had stopped by when Troy and I were with Summer.

"No, it was an older lady. She said that Summer left this morning, for good."

"I think Troy and I might have gotten her fired. Lorna is one of the dancers. She made a point of coming over to us when we were sitting outside Summer's cabin talking to her. Then a little while later, when I went to see Krystal, who should be leaving her office? Lorna. I suspected Lorna had buzzed right over to tell Krystal all about Summer's new friends. Looks like I was right. Did you find out exactly what happened?"

"*Chica,*" he said, shaking his head at me with a disappointed expression on his face.

"It was me, your Miguel, with an older lady. What do you think? Of course I know what happened. Joyce Tucker—that's her name—she spilled some tea for me. Also, her nephew lives in Milwaukee just three streets over from my cousin Raphael's restaurant. I told her ..."

"Miguel, we can get to the connections between your family tree and Joyce's later. What did she tell you about Summer, Krystal, and all things Tanner's?"

"Summer said goodbye to Joyce before she left. She told her that Krystal said she was a troublemaker, and she couldn't dance at Tanner's anymore. Summer told Joyce that she didn't mind. She would go visit her *mamá*. But Joyce feels sad, because Summer is so nice. She gave Joyce twenty-five dollars today to thank her for all her hard work."

"At least Summer shouldn't be too hard to find if we need her. Her mother lives in Trefry and that only has about three hundred people. What did you find out about Krystal?"

"She has been the manager at Tanner's for ten years. But Joyce knew her before that, from when Joyce was a house mom at Foxy's in Madison a long time ago. Krystal was a dancer there."

"Wait. Strip clubs have house mothers?"

"Some do, but not so much now, Joyce said. House moms, they bring food to the dancers, help them with costumes and makeup, keep the dressing room clean, give them a little advice, a little encouragement, you know, like that."

"Miguel, you would make a great house mom. You do some version of all those things for me."

"When you become a stripper, I'll become your house mom."

"So did Krystal and Joyce stay lifelong buds and that's why they're both at Tanner's now?"

"No. Krystal was mean to the other dancers and mean to Joyce. But she was very pretty so the customers liked her. Joyce got married to Duncan and she quit Foxy's. They started their own fair food business."

"What's a fair food business? They sold groceries at a fair price? Or they had a restaurant that sold food that tasted fair? What is this fair food you speak of?"

"Fair food—funnel cakes, cotton candy, deep-fried lasagna bites."

"Stop, you're making my stomach hurt. Joyce and her husband owned a concession truck?"

"Yes, but their fair food was 'deluxe,' Joyce said. Steak-tip dinners with potatoes *and* a vegetable. They used to go all over Wisconsin to fairs. Joyce loved it."

"So why is Joyce working at Tanner's now?"

"Because Duncan, her husband, took all their money and their concession truck and ran away to Florida with Pam, a nail technician. So, Joyce had to find a job. She applied at Tanner's—she didn't know Krystal was working there. She thought she could go back to being a house mom. But they don't have them at Tanner's. I think if I was a dancer, it would be nice to have a house mom," he added.

"And you would make a great dancer as well as a house mom. But you kind of built me up for more than Joyce's life story, Miguel. When does Krystal come in?"

"Now, almost. Krystal was the manager then, not the owner. She told Joyce she had an opening for a cleaner. So Joyce said yes. 'Not very many people like to hire old broads,' she told me. I like older ladies."

"You like all ladies. So, okay, Joyce is working at Tanner's. Did she change her mind about Krystal?"

"No, she still doesn't like her. And neither does Nadine, Joyce's friend who works in the kitchen. Now, here is the part you have not been very patient waiting for, but it's worth it. Nadine and Joyce, they think that Krystal doesn't really own Tanner's."

"Why?"

"Because Krystal only made forty thousand dollars a year when she was manager, Joyce said. How could she have enough money to buy Tanner's?"

"How much does a strip club cost, do you know?"

"I checked. For big city clubs, the listings online were from a million to four million dollars. In the smaller places like Grantland County, from a hundred to three hundred thousand dollars."

"Hmm. Even the low-end prices would be out of range for someone making forty thousand a year. And I doubt the local bank or the SBA would loan money to buy a strip club."

"No. I asked Miller. He said a business like a strip club would probably have to get a commercial hard money loan. But you have to have at least twenty percent to put down, or some collateral like commercial real estate. It would be hard for Krystal to have twenty percent of a hundred thousand dollars saved."

"I agree. But how does Joyce know how much Krystal made as manager?"

"She cleans her office. She can't help it if a pay stub fell on the floor and she had to pick it up, and just happened to see Krystal's wages, can she?"

Miguel voiced his answer in the disingenuous tone Joyce had doubtless used when excusing her snooping. Not that there's anything wrong with snooping, necessarily.

"Nadine and Joyce think that Krystal is fronting for someone else who owns the club—someone who doesn't want to be connected to it."

"Now, that could lead us somewhere interesting. Do they have any ideas?"

"Joyce said no, but I think she does. I can try again."

"Did you have time to check commercial real estate sales online to see if there's a record of the Tanner's sale?"

"Yes. Tanner's was sold to a limited liability company, Girlzelles Entertainment, three years ago."

"Did you check the LLC on the Wisconsin DFI website?"

"I did, but the Department of Financial Institutions only has the Articles of Organization. Those show the agent of record, which is Krystal Gerrard, and the organizer, which is Krystal also, but—"

"But the agent of record can be, but doesn't have to be, the owner," I said. "The organizer doesn't have to be the owner, either. Using an LLC and an agent is a good way to make the real ownership hard to find. But all LLCs have to file an annual report, and the annual report has to list the members. So, if we get the Tanner's annual report, we'll know who the member/owners are."

"I'm already there. But you can't get the annual report online. I had to request a print copy. It takes a week to ten days for it to come."

"Great work, Miguel."

"Who do you think the owner is, if not Krystal?"

"I'll put it to you this way. Who have we come across so far who would think Girlzelles Entertainment is a really clever name?" I asked.

"Wes Morgan?"

"That's where I'd put my money. If it's true, he's got himself in the middle of a hot mess: drugs sold on site, a prostitution ring, and a murder? He might have found something that his brother can't get him out of."

This time it was Miguel's phone that rang. He looked at the screen.

"It's Troy's grandfather," he said before answering. "Hi, Gordon. How is Troy?"

Miguel paced back and forth as he talked. Mostly he listened, and I couldn't glean much from what he said.

"Yes."

"How long?"

"My heart is with you. I will pray for all of you."

He hung up then. I held my breath waiting for him to tell me the news.

"Troy is in recovery. The surgery went well!"

The icy lump of fear I'd been carrying in my heart all day melted instantly.

"What did he say exactly? Is Troy awake? Can we see him?"

"He's not awake. After he's out of recovery, his family can see him, but only one at a time and just for a minute. Troy's sister Erica is there, and his brother Drew will be there by tonight."

"Can they tell if he'll recover fully?"

"Not yet. But he is alive, and the surgery was good, and we can be happy for now, yes?"

"Yes, Miguel. A big fat yes to that."

But even before the relief had made a full circuit of my body, I remembered something.

"Miguel, I forgot to tell you I talked to Ross. Troy's phone is smashed, so if he recorded anything from his meeting with Wes we won't be able to get it. Not unless he wakes up and gives us his iCloud password. And we won't be able to see any calls or texts he might have received from Wes. But his mother has his notebook."

"I'll ask her if I can have it when I go to Madison tomorrow."

40

When Miguel left I put in a call to Kent Morgan. His secretary said he wasn't in and wasn't expected back until the next day. I didn't leave a message. Instead, I tried the cell number I had for him, but that flipped immediately to voicemail.

"Kent, this is Leah Nash. I'm working on some follow-up about the Jancee Reynolds story, and I'd like to meet with you whenever it's convenient. If you could call me back, that would be great. Thanks."

I left both the office and my cell number, but I wasn't too optimistic about hearing from him. He probably wanted to stay away as far as possible from the story his brother's appalling lack of judgment had unleashed.

There wasn't much else I could do. So, I spent the unexpected gift of time on my real job, the book I was writing. I always try to be very structured when I start writing a book. I have a nice flow chart, a big calendar hanging on the wall above my desk filled with key deadlines. I keep a rough outline of the main ideas for each chapter next to me on my desk. I use a software program that tracks my word count each day to help me stay on track. Things go along swimmingly—for a while. Then something happens, usually something to do with the *Times,* and I wind up in a deadline crunch. Which is where I was.

Fortunately, I do some of my best work with a deadline looming. I sat down at my laptop and tuned everything else out. I was so immersed in my work that it took an insistent pounding on my door to break my concentration.

What the heck? If that was Courtnee, or if she'd sent somebody up here, which she was wont to do, even though I have told her a million times that I am not her lifeline for the reception desk, I would kill her.

"Just a second," I called, pausing to save the document I was working on before opening the door.

"Leah! What's going on?"

All it took was the sound of his voice for everything to come into very sharp focus. Coop. Dinner. Six o'clock. Oops.

"Coop! I forgot all about dinner. I can't believe it, I'm so sorry!"

"I guess I should have brought that backup box of Honey Nut Cheerios after all. Or we could just eat this cheesecake from the Elite that I got for dessert."

He held the box out toward me.

"Really? With raspberry sauce?"

He nodded.

"Now you're making me feel even worse. I've been looking forward to hanging out with you. I want to catch up on all your news. I want to pick your brain about some things. I can't believe I whiffed it like this. It's been a crazy day, but still ... do you think I'm losing my mind? Don't answer that. But we can still have dinner. I'm pretty sure I've got some cereal. Or cheese. I could make grilled cheese sandwiches."

"I'm a little hungrier than Cheerios, and I had grilled cheese for lunch. Why don't we just order something from Flower Drum? How does Sesame Chicken sound?"

"I remember now why we're such good friends. That sounds great. Let's get some egg rolls, too, okay? And I'm paying."

"You bet you are. I'll go pick it up."

I phoned in the order and handed Coop the money. While he was gone, I went into full hosting mode, to make up for being in full self-focused mode and forgetting to make dinner. However, I don't have a lot of hosting finesse. I almost always eat at the bar in the kitchen, and anyone who comes over joins me there. Or I sit on my window seat. I don't even have a dining table. Once in a while, if I'm feeling fancy, I might set up a tray table in the living room, for some fireside dining.

I decided to go for fancy. I set up two tray tables in front of the sofa, I turned the fireplace on, and I streamed a Lucinda Williams playlist, Coop's favorite. I got out plates, and napkins—not just sheets torn from a roll of paper towels for this party girl. Luckily, I had Leinenkugel in the fridge. By the time he got back, all was in readiness.

"I see you went fancy. Got the tray tables out. Napkins, too. I'm impressed."

"Only the best at Chez Leah for my bestie."

"I hate that word."

"Chez?"

"Bestie."

"Really, why?"

"I don't know. Aren't there words you just don't like? Besides 'no,' that is."

"Several: blouse, slacks, moist, davenport. Now, let's eat."

"So, catch me up on things," I said as we dug into our food.

"No, you first. Anything new on Troy?"

"Yes, and it's good. Well, we hope so." I gave him the latest information.

"That's great to hear. Just don't expect too much, too soon. I had a guy on a case once who was unconscious for a week before we could talk to him. It was longer than that before he could remember anything. But he was fine, in the end. Just like Troy will be."

"Fingers and toes crossed that you're right."

"What about Cole? Did you talk to him today?"

"I did, but he wasn't willing to be much help. I'm wondering if he's covering for Monroe. Not to help Monroe as much as to keep the spotlight off the Granger family enterprises in general."

"Monroe is still on your suspect list, then?"

"Yes. I still think that he could've killed her for the money, or because he wanted her back and he lost it when she told him no again."

I waited, but Coop didn't say anything.

"Well?"

"I've got an idea," he said.

Again he fell silent.

"You know, that statement is usually followed up with some detail. What's your idea?"

"You could be on to something, and I have a thought that might help you. But it's not my investigation. Is it really right for me not just to listen to you, but to actively assist you on someone else's case?"

"Yes."

He shook his head and smiled.

"You sliced right through the Gordian knot of that moral dilemma, didn't you?"

"I did, because it's not a dilemma. Just tell me what you think. You have a right to think, even if you're not running the case. Besides, it may be a terrible take on things and I'll ignore it. Even if it's spot-on, I won't give you any credit. Does that make you feel better?"

"It's not about credit. I don't want to undermine Owen Fike."

"It's not undermining him. It's helping him if you have a theory that leads to the real killer, not to the person it's most convenient to arrest."

"All right, but it's understood I'm just throwing it out there. It's not that big an idea anyway."

"Yes, yes, yes. Tell me, already."

"What if the Grangers have something to do with the escort service Krystal Gerrard is running? Ride EZ could be supplying drivers. Monroe could be one of them. Which means he also could be—"

"A driver for Jancee, if she had her own set-up, like Summer told Troy," I said. Coop's suggestion filled in some of the holes in my thinking, and I went on.

"Monroe could drive Jancee to and from her appointments with her high-paying kinky client. And he might know who that is. And if it's Wes, like I think it could be, then maybe Monroe didn't kill Jancee to get the money. Wes killed her. Monroe figured it out and tried a little blackmail. He got the money he needed from Jancee all right, but indirectly. It came from

Wes after he killed her and took her cash. But then why would Monroe go to the cops and point the finger at Ricky?"

"Maybe Wes paid him to keep the heat off himself. Or maybe Monroe took it on himself to make sure Wes had a nice long run as his blackmail victim. If Wes paid him once to keep quiet, Monroe could be pretty sure he'd be able to tap him again. But he couldn't do that if Wes was in prison," Coop said.

"True. And Cole could know about it and be seriously pissed at Monroe. Not because he's blackmailing Wes, but because Monroe's involvement could drag all the Grangers into the middle of a murder investigation."

"Well, that would fit with Cole getting Monroe out of town to keep him off Owen's radar," he said.

"What's your take? Do you think that Owen would seriously consider any of this? Because if he doesn't, it could mean that either Monroe or Wes gets away with murder, Krystal's prostitution ring keeps humming along, Ride EZ gets its cut, and everybody but Ricky lives happily ever after."

"I'm pretty sure if you talk to Owen about a prostitution ring in the county, he's going to want to check it out. And if he pulls on that thread, maybe the whole thing comes unraveled."

"Coop, see how well we can work together when you're not telling me not to get in the way? Look at all the good thinking we did. When you become sheriff, just imagine all the help I'll be able to give you."

"That's the stuff of nightmares, Leah."

I crossed my eyes at him.

"Very nice," he said. "So, what's your next move?"

"I'm not sure, except that I'm not going to Owen with any of this until I have something solid to go with my conjecture. To me, Wes is screaming prime suspect, but it could be that he's just a prime idiot who has a way of screwing everything up. Monroe makes a pretty good suspect, too. Then there's Ricky. And yes, I do realize that it could be him, even though I don't want it to be. I need to do some digging there. You know, usually when I'm chasing down a story, I'm looking for missing pieces. This time it feels like I have too many. I can't see which ones complete the picture, and which belong in another puzzle box."

"Maybe you should take a step back, give the pattern time to come clear. Also, try to stay out of Owen's lane. Journalists have one job, police have another. You can gather all the facts you want, and put together a theory that fits them, but you don't have the power to make arrests. At least not yet."

"Wait. Are you saying that under the Sheriff David Cooper administration I will have?"

"No. That is one campaign pledge I will never make. If you find something that needs action, go to the people who can take action, and by that I mean the investigator in charge."

"Maybe I should just let Owen's investigation play out. I already accomplished what I started out to do, which was to get Lamey off your dad's back, and *GO News* away from slinging mud at your campaign."

"Don't even try to pretend you're walking away. It would bother you 'til the end of time not to follow through on a story you started. Besides, you're good at sorting the pieces out. You'll get there in the end."

"Thank you!"

"You're welcome."

"And now, let's move on to the cheesecake portion of our evening. I'll get it."

41

"You know those raspberries are the design on the plate, don't you? They don't come off," Coop said as I scraped my fork across the surface, trying to get every last bit of cheesecake and raspberry sauce.

I looked up from licking my fork.

"I forgive you for your sarcasm, because forgiveness is just a part of who I am. And because this cheesecake is sooo good! Thank you for thinking to bring it. And for not reminding me a dozen times that I forgot about the whole dinner. Like I would have reminded you. Wait a minute. Does that mean you're a better person than I am? I think it actually does. And you know what? I'm not even kidding. You are."

"All right, enough. You're just trying to throw me off from asking exactly what you did to get Dad off the hook with the sheriff's office, and Spencer Karr."

"No, I'll tell you. But just be aware that the end justified my means."

I proceeded to give him the strategy I'd used on Spencer.

"I know it was borderline, and Dan might be mad when he finds out, if he finds out, but it worked. Is Dan going to find out? Are you going to tell him?"

"I won't, but I bet you will. He's going to want to go straight to the source, and he's smart enough to know that has to be you."

"Coop, I couldn't think of anything else. I tried the straight-forward way, but drunk Marilyn is as mean and self-serving as sober Marilyn. She completely rejected my plea to her better nature. That, of course, is because, like her son, she has no better nature. So, then I thought about how Spencer might handle a situation like that. I followed his playbook, and it worked. I don't want Dan to be mad at me. But I had to do it. I just couldn't stand seeing him hurting because he was hurting your campaign."

"It might not be that bad after he realizes that you may have forced Marilyn's hand, but you didn't reveal her secret to anyone except herself."

"Full disclosure, I did tell Miguel, but as much as he enjoys a juicy bit of gossip, he also understands professional confidentiality. I trust him as much as I trust you. And that's a lot."

"What about Jennifer?"

"I didn't tell her, but she's not stupid. Jen was there when Marilyn came into the sheriff's office to see Owen. Shortly after Marilyn leaves, the sheriff issues a statement that Dan is no longer a person of interest. She'll be able to connect the dots, or pick it up around the office, I'm pretty sure."

"I wouldn't have done it the way you did, Leah, but you got results. And I'm not sorry that you probably gave Spencer a bad minute or two while he decided what he cared about most, his mother or his media. So, thank you. Maybe this will take the focus off the strip club aspects of my campaign and put it back on the issues."

"So what *is* going on with your campaign? It's only a couple of weeks now until the election. Did you know Miguel isn't having a Halloween party this year? Instead, he's planning your election night victory party."

"I hope he's not disappointed."

"Don't say that. With *GO News* backing off, people can read about things that matter, like what you plan to do when you win. Besides, I've been seeing a lot of 'Cooper for Sheriff' yard signs around the county since your dad got that infusion of cash from Kent Morgan and his wife. And Mom said she's seen ads for you in her Facebook feed, too. I've had tweets from your campaign in my Twitter feed every day. Why are you sounding so down about it?"

"I'm not down. I'm just trying to be realistic. I've been finding out just how powerful incumbency is. People know Art because he's been with the sheriff's office for years. They associate him with the good things Sheriff Dillingham did, even though we know he hasn't exactly followed in Lester's footsteps."

"But people in Himmel know you and respect you and like you," I said.

"Maybe. But Himmel is less than a quarter of the county's population. I've had to reach out to Hailwell, and Omico, and half a dozen villages like Bear Creek, and Mertonville, and Gray Lake. I'm doing my best. But the plain fact is, Art's still in the lead, and the election isn't very far away. People know his name. And when they go to vote, they're just naturally going to go toward the familiar—barring any major scandal that crops up in the next fourteen days. Which isn't very likely."

"I refuse to believe that. Who in their right mind could want Lameass Lamey to be the Grantland County Sheriff? He's arrogant, ignorant, and corrupt."

"To you, yes, because you know about what he did in the Bruce Dengler situation. To me, too, because I've seen some of his shoddy work. Most people don't know about those things, and I can't cite them without the evidence to back them up. Haven't we had this conversation before? Like last week?"

"Yes, we did, I know. And I said we were working on getting to the bottom of why and how Lamey shut down the criminal investigation into his bestie Bruce Dengler. Oops, sorry, I forgot bestie is a trigger word for you. And no, we haven't got there yet. If we could prove it and run the story, that would open some eyes about Lamey."

"Let's be realistic. You were short-staffed before, and now with Troy out, it's worse. Even if you could get a story out, it might not matter. Art's good at political games. I'm not. I'm giving it my best shot, but it's a long shot, for sure."

He was trying to sound philosophical about it, but I could tell how discouraged he was. He really wanted to be the sheriff. And he really should be. But I felt helpless to help. A feeling I hate.

"Coop," I started, then stopped. I wanted to say something encouraging, but realized I had nothing.

"It's all right. Don't worry, I'll keep on fighting, and you know my dad, he never quits. Let's talk about something else."

"Okay, what?"

"So, have you talked to Gabe? Does he know about Troy?"

"Yes. He called this afternoon. He's coming home Saturday."

"That's a quick trip."

"Yes, it is. I'm having dinner with him Saturday—if he doesn't decide he has to go back to New York as soon as he gets here. He said he had a surprise for me, and that all will be revealed."

"Well, that's what you want, isn't it, to find out what all the mystery is about? Why do you sound like you're annoyed?'

"Because I am kind of annoyed. I don't like surprises, you know that."

"Yes, I do. Sounds like you haven't shared that particular phobia with Gabe yet."

"It's not a phobia. I just like things to fit, to make sense, to be part of an overall plan."

"You mean you like to control all the action, and if there are any surprises you want to be the surpriser, not the surprisee."

"I don't want to control everything, just the things that have an impact on me. And on the people that I care about. And on the people that I meet on the street. Okay. Guilty as charged, but you have to admit, there could be worse people than me in charge. In fact, I can make a pretty good case that there are."

"I won't fight you on that. In fact, I won't fight you at all. Sounds like you'll get your answers soon enough."

He stood up then and carried his plate to the kitchen and I followed with mine.

"Just put it in the sink."

"No, let's load the dishwasher, that'll save you time in the morning. You've got plenty to do."

"You're right. See how I did that? Put you in charge of my dishwashing routine? I can cede control in a nanosecond."

"About when to load the dishwasher, yes, you're very flexible."

"We understand each other. That's what makes us friends."

He smiled at me then, and said, "Thanks for dinner. This was fun."

"Yeah, it was."

42

"Kent, thanks for fitting me in this morning," I said, seated on a visitor chair in Kent Morgan's office. He handed me a cup of coffee before taking a seat on the other chair in front of his desk and swiveling it around so that he was facing me.

The executive office of Kent Morgan Financial Services appeared to have been designed with one purpose in mind: to assure clients that their finances were in safe, steady hands. Traditional furnishings—a cherrywood executive desk, a tufted leather executive chair, a thick carpet in dark green, and a glass-fronted bookcase—were a marked contrast to his brother Wes's Packers-inspired decor.

Kent himself had the same confidence-inspiring look. He wore a crisp white shirt with a navy two-button suit, a dark maroon tie, and white pocket square. His blond hair was precision-cut. I caught the faint woodsy scent of his aftershave as he leaned forward and began speaking.

"I'm sorry it had to be so early, but I've got appointments from nine o'clock on today. I'm not sure there's anything more I can tell you about that night with Jancee Reynolds. But it feels like I owe you one for not being completely honest the first time we talked. So, what is it you want to know?"

"Eight-thirty isn't too early for me, I'm an early riser usually," I said. I didn't reassure him that he didn't owe me anything, because it's always good to start with the advantage in an interview.

"I've talked to your brother Wes a couple of times—"

"Yes, he's mentioned it. I assume he wasn't very helpful?"

"You could say that."

"I'm sorry. Wes is ... well, Wes is Wes. He has a good heart, but he's had a lot of disappointments. That's made him a little angry at life."

"What kind of disappointments?"

He sighed and sat back in his chair.

"I love my brother. And it's hard to see him struggle. He had an unhappy marriage and even unhappier divorce. He's a hard worker, but he just can't seem to make a go of it in business. I've been very fortunate in my marriage and in my career. It's tough on him to have everything he touches fall apart, and seemingly everything I try come together."

He stopped talking. I waited without speaking for him to continue. I was certain he would. Kent had said that he loved his brother, and he probably did, but he was angry at him too. It was in the tightness of his voice and the careful way he chose his words.

"I've tried to help, with advice, with money, with encouragement. My wife says I'm enabling, not helping, him. That he needs to stand or fall on his own. I know he resents me, even though he needs me. Or maybe it's that Wes resents me *because* he needs me. It's very hard for me not to fix things for him. It's been that way since we were kids. I feel guilty about how lucky I've been. Now I'm starting to think maybe rescuing him isn't the way to help him at all. I might be making things worse."

"From what I've heard, you've been a great brother to Wes."

He gave a slight shake of his head and held up his hand as if to wave away what I'd said.

"Our mother died a very difficult death. Toward the end she was heavily drugged to dull the pain. But on the day before she died, she refused her medication. She was in terrible pain, but she couldn't rest until she talked to me. I was twenty, Wes was seventeen. She begged me to look out for him. She knew I'd be all right, but she was worried about Wes. He was always so impulsive, so restless. He was never a bad person. He just didn't think. I promised her I'd always be there for him. But it hasn't been easy."

This seemed like a good time to lead him back toward the night Jancee died.

"Kent, is that why you sent Jancee home early and shut down the game that night? Because he finally pushed you too far, and you had to tell him so?"

He didn't answer the question directly, but what he did say made it clear that's why he had done it.

"It wasn't just me that night. He put everyone there in a bad spot because of a stupid 'joke.' We all have families, jobs, positions in the community. No one except Wes needed that kind of juvenile 'entertainment.' That's something you do when you're in your twenties, not your forties. I admit it. I was really angry at him. I didn't want to get into it with everyone there. I took the dancer aside and paid her to leave. Wes wasn't happy, but I wasn't either. Everyone left and then we had it out."

"How did that go?"

"Not well. I did most of the talking. Wes was belligerent, and then sorry for himself, and then angry, and then sorry for himself some more. Finally, he apologized, said he didn't think it through. He told me he was under a lot of stress. He had just wanted to forget about it and have a little fun for one night. By then I was tired of hearing myself talk. I told him I'd accept his apology, if he agreed to spend the night at the cabin. He wasn't exactly drunk, but he'd had enough that I didn't want him driving. He agreed. I'd already planned to stay the night because my wife and daughter were away, and I enjoy waking up there in the morning. So, that's what we did."

"What kind of stress is Wes under?"

"His construction company is having cash flow problems. A major project he was counting on fell through and he's not sure what he's going to do. He's struggling. That's nothing new for Wes, though."

That basically tracked with what Sandy, Wes's office manager, had said.

"I know what that's like from my own business. I'm lucky that Miller Caldwell is my partner and he's steering us through some tight times."

I hoped invoking my struggles at the *Times* would keep Kent at ease and talking about his brother's problems. Instead it seemed to wake him up to the fact that he had just spilled quite a bit about his brother's business interests.

"Leah, I didn't mean to talk so much about personal family relationships. Please, don't use anything I said about Wes. I don't want him to read something in the paper that's going to hurt him, or his business. I don't want to make things any more difficult between us than they are. To be honest, it was a relief to say them out loud, but I never meant them to be for publication."

"Kent, anything not directly relevant to the story won't go in it. Also, I understand all about complicated family relationships."

"Thank you, I appreciate that."

"But there is just a question or two more that I want to ask. You and Wes both spent the night at your cabin, right?"

"Yes, I just told you that." He looked puzzled.

"I just want to make sure I have all the details. I assume the cabin has several bedrooms."

"Yes, there's a guest room and bath on the ground floor and a master suite and two additional bedrooms and a bath upstairs."

"Okay. So, you guys didn't have to share a bedroom."

"No. Even if I only had one bedroom in the cabin, we wouldn't have shared it. One of us would be on the sofa. I usually go to bed early and sleep hard. I'm also one of those obnoxious people who jumps out of bed wide awake and ready for the day. I'm not always easy to take first thing in the morning, according to my wife."

"And that's not how Wes is?"

"No. He's exactly the opposite. He likes to stay up late, he doesn't sleep well, and he's grouchy as a bear in the morning. It's always been that way."

"So, I suppose you stayed in the master suite. Did Wes sleep upstairs, too?"

"No, he always stays in the downstairs bedroom. He likes the shower in that bathroom."

"Okay, that night, you're upstairs, sleeping hard. Wes is all the way downstairs. How do you know that he was in the cabin with you all night?"

"How do I know? Well, for one thing, where else would he be? For another, he was there when I got up at seven a.m. I made coffee and some breakfast, and we ate, and then we each left. I don't think I like where you're going with this."

"Where is that?"

"You're implying that Wes left the cabin during the night without me knowing. That the reason he didn't want to stay at the cabin was that he had arranged to meet the girl, Jancee. You think that he left, went to see her, and came back before I woke up in the morning."

That was actually pretty close to what I was thinking. But I wasn't sure if Wes had stayed at the cabin and snuck out, or if he hadn't been there at all. Given his past record, it could be that Kent had once more kept his promise to look out for his brother, this time by lying and giving him an alibi for murder. Maybe that accounted for all his confessional angst.

"I asked the question, Kent. But it sounds to me like you've been thinking about the answer for a while. Are you worried that Wes met up with Jancee? Are you worried that he might be the one who killed her?"

He didn't hesitate in his answer. And he didn't get defensive or angry either.

"No. Absolutely not. Wes would never murder anyone. He doesn't have it in him. And if I thought for one minute that he had, I wouldn't hide that from the police. I am absolutely certain he was there all night. And I have no problem at all being quoted on that."

I still thought Wes was more than capable of being Jancee's killer, but I didn't think that Kent was knowingly covering for him.

"All right. Thank you for giving me so much time. I appreciate it."

He stood and walked me to the door, but as he was reaching to open it for me he stopped.

"I meant to ask, how is Troy Patterson doing? I heard about his accident. Someone said that he'd been airlifted to a trauma center for surgery. Is that true?"

"Yes, it is. He had a head injury. He was in surgery for over five hours. He came through fine, but he was still heavily sedated last time I checked."

"I'm sorry. What's the prognosis—if you don't mind my asking?"

"It's really too early to tell. Patients with injuries like Troy's can recover fairly completely—sometimes in a matter of weeks. But that's not the case most of the time. We're all trying to stay positive for him. Once he's awake, it will take some time to assess the damage, and how well he'll recover."

I had managed to get it all out without choking up, but saying those words was hard.

"I'm sorry," he said again. "It was a hit and run, I understand. Any chance of finding out who did it?"

"It doesn't seem likely, but the state accident reconstruction team is on it, so who knows? The main thing we're all focused on is Troy getting better."

"Yes, of course. When he recovers, and I'm sure he will, remind him that he's got an open invitation for bird watching out on my property, as soon as he's well enough."

"I'll do that. Thanks again."

43

Once back home I started organizing and thinking about the information I had gotten from Kent. I also worried a little about Dan's reaction to what I'd done about Marilyn. He might thank me. Or he might look out at me from under lowered eyebrows and say, "Leah, I'm disappointed in you."

That's the worst. I can withstand being yelled at, threatened, or fired. I can take a punch if need be—literal as well as figurative. But if I live to be a hundred, I will never be able to remain strong under the weight of disappointing Coop's dad.

I'd been working for about an hour when my phone rang.

"Hey, Miguel. I was going to call you later. I just finished up an interview with Kent Morgan, and it was pretty interesting. I—"

"*Chica,* something is going to happen, or maybe it did already!"

"Okay, that's a fair statement in general. But I'm guessing that you've got something specific in mind?"

"Yes! Listen, I'm telling you! I stopped at the Gas & Grub on my way to Madison. When I was inside getting coffee, I talked to my friend Judy. I think someone is getting arrested today for killing Jancee Reynolds."

"What? Who's Judy, and how does she know this? Is she connected to the sheriff's office?"

"No, no. She works part-time at the Gas & Grub."

"So what gives her inside information on an arrest?"

"Not her. She doesn't know what she knows, but I do. Gas & Grub, *chica*, Gas & Grub! It's on the corner of Bannock Road. The road where Kent Morgan's cabin is!"

He was getting a bit frustrated at my dense-headedness, but I wasn't making the connection.

"Yeah, okay, but I'm gonna need a little more."

"Judy's husband picked her up from work about eleven o'clock on Monday night two weeks ago. The Monday Jancee Reynolds was killed. When they pulled onto the road from the parking lot a truck came speeding by so fast it almost hit them. Judy took video on her phone, and she called the sheriff's office to report it."

I met his dramatic pause with a supportive, "Yes, go on."

Sometimes Miguel's wind-up to the pitch can be as long as Courtnee's. However, he usually comes through with something worth hearing.

"The person who answered told her everyone was called out to a bad accident across the county. He took Judy's contact information, but he said he didn't know when someone would be in touch. And they never were! Bob, that's Judy's husband, told Judy to forget it. But Judy decided no, because the driver of that truck could kill someone someday, driving like that. So, she called again yesterday, and early this morning, a detective came and he took her video."

"Wait. No detective would go out to interview Judy about a two-week-old minor traffic incident."

"Yes! That's what I'm telling you. When Judy called the sheriff's office, she said the truck that almost hit them had orange and yellow flames painted on it. Detective Fike, he came out to talk to her this morning. He just left before I stopped for coffee. The truck—"

"Belongs to Ricky Travers," I said, stepping on his big finish.

"Yes. I knew from what you told me. I didn't say it to Judy, but I think Ricky's in big trouble."

"He sure is. It's proof that he was on the road to Kent's cabin to pick Jancee up. Damn! His second big lie. First he said he didn't take her, then he said he didn't pick her up. I'll bet Owen's either questioning him right now or getting a warrant to search his truck."

"Do you want me to follow up before I go to Madison?"

"No, you go ahead. I'd like a first-hand report on how Troy's doing, and the sooner you can get his notebook from his mother, the better. Especially now. Things are moving. It would be nice if there's something in Troy's notes that we can use."

"But you don't think this means that Ricky is the one? That he killed Jancee Reynolds?"

"It could mean that, yes. But maybe someone else used Ricky's truck."

"Why would they? How would they?"

"Maybe killing Jancee was better planned than I thought. Someone could have used Ricky's truck to set him up."

"I don't know ..."

"It sounds weak, I get it. But I don't want to throw in the towel on Ricky yet. I'll make some calls, see if I can find out where things stand with Owen's investigation. And we'll go from there."

"Fike." His voice was crisp and no-nonsense, the sound of a busy man with lots to do.

"Owen, this is Leah Nash, do you have a minute?"

"Just about that. I was expecting to hear from you, though not quite this fast."

"Have you brought Ricky Travers in for questioning?"

"No comment."

"Do you have video of a truck belonging to Ricky Travers traveling down Bannock Road on the night Jancee Reynolds was killed?"

"No comment."

"I'll take that as a yes."

"You can take it how you like, but it's a no comment."

"How close are you to making an arrest in the Jancee Reynolds' murder?"

"No comment."

"Can you at least tell me if you have a primary suspect in the Jancee Reynolds' murder?"

"I told you when we met, I don't share information with the press. Nothing personal, that's just how I operate. Sheriff Lamey is the official spokesman for the investigation. Any information you want, you'll have to get from him. I have to go, Leah. Nice talking to you."

He hung up before I could say goodbye.

I tried Coop, on the off chance that he might have heard something, but when it went to voicemail, I decided to go directly to the source. I tried Ricky's number. Straight to voicemail. I called Sandy at Wes Morgan's office to see if she knew where Ricky was working.

"Well, that's the funny thing, Leah. He was supposed to be on a job in Hailwell today, but he didn't show up. The site manager couldn't get him on his phone, and neither can I. That's not like Ricky. I hope nothing's happened to him."

"Yeah, me, too. Thanks, Sandy."

I had a pretty good idea what had happened, and one more source to call and find out if I was right.

44

At least Ross picked up on the first ring, even if his greeting wasn't that friendly.

"Hey, what's going on over there?" I asked. "Owen Fike hung up on me. Ricky Travers isn't answering his phone. His work doesn't know where he is. Is he at the sheriff's for questioning right now?"

"Are you tryin' to get me fired, Nash?"

"What? Why—"

"Are you at your place?"

"Yes, but—"

"Hang up. I'll call you back on Allie's phone. She's there today, right?"

"I think so, I haven't—" But the line was already dead.

I ran downstairs. Allie met me in the hallway, holding out her phone.

"It's my dad, he says he needs to talk to you. But why is he calling you on my phone?"

"I have no idea," I said, taking the phone.

She shrugged and went back to the newsroom.

"Ross, why are you acting like Deep Throat in the underground garage?"

"It's not funny, Nash. Lamey just dropped the cone of silence on the whole office. Fike told him you called askin' about Ricky Travers. Lamey thinks I leaked something to you. I don't want my cell phone records showin' I called you. If he has them checked, it'll be bad enough for him to see that *you* called *me*. At least this way it looks like I'm just callin' my kid. And I can always say your call to me only lasted ten seconds because you're a pain in the ass and I hung up. Which you are."

"Your phone records? You really think Lamey is going to check those just to find his imaginary leak?"

"I don't know. Maybe I'm bein' a little paranoid. But he's really pissed that you know somethin's up."

"He's probably trying to save it for *GO News* and his girlfriend Andrea. But I don't have much, Ross. That's why I'm calling you."

"Can't help you. I'm tellin' you, Lamey is gunning for me. I'm tryin' to hang on here, hoping Coop wins the election. If he doesn't, I wanna go under my own steam, not with a firing on my record."

"He's going to win," I said, "so don't worry. How about this? Let me tell you what I know, and if it's true, don't say anything. If it isn't true, clear your throat."

He sighed.

"Okay, go."

"We got a tip—well, Miguel did—that Ricky might be arrested today. I tried Fike first and he wouldn't give me anything. Then I tried to reach Ricky on his cell, but it went to voicemail. Is he being questioned now?"

Silence.

"All right, he is. Does he have a lawyer with him?"

"Ahem."

"Okay, no lawyer. He definitely needs one. But, Ross, I'm still having a hard time seeing Ricky as a brutal killer. If you could hear him talk about Jancee—it doesn't fit."

"It wouldn't be the first time you had a hard time seein' what you didn't wanna believe," Ross said.

"I liked it better when you were holding your silence. I know, sometimes I do get the wrong end of things. But it wouldn't be so hard for me to believe Ricky killed Jancee, if Wes Morgan didn't make such a good suspect."

"Still on that track, are you? I don't think it's gonna take you far. The video isn't all Fike's got. I can't stand around all day in the parkin' lot playin' spy games with you. This is all off the record, and then I gotta go."

"What?"

"That woods where the body was found? It belongs to a couple who goes to Florida for the winter."

"Yeah, I know that. So?"

"What I guess you don't know is that the Seetons, that's their name, they had Ricky livin' with them out there for better than a year. They gave up foster care when they both retired and started spendin' six months a year down South. So your boy Ricky, he knows those woods, he knows the Seetons aren't there this time of year, and he knows there's only a coupla houses on that road. If he wound up with a dead girl on his hands, that woods in the middle of the night might seem like a great place to get rid of her."

I blew out a sigh that came all the way up from my toes.

"They've got enough to get a warrant, don't they?"

"I hear they're applyin' for one right now for both his truck and his house."

"But if Jancee's prints or DNA show up, that won't really prove anything, will it? Ricky was always giving her rides. He was like her personal Uber driver."

"Did she ride in the back end of his pickup truck?"

That landed like a punch in the stomach.

"Oh, right. You mean they're looking for evidence not that Jancee was in his truck as a live passenger, but as a body transported in the back of the pickup."

"You got it."

"And at the house?"

"They'll be hopin' to find more hard evidence to tie Ricky to Jancee."

"You mean like her missing purse."

"If he used the strap to strangle her like they think, they might be able to get his DNA off it. You think he's dumb enough to keep it?"

"He's not dumb, Ross. He's just a slow processor. If he did kill Jancee, he might have taken it back home to think through what to do with it, but I don't think he'd keep it there."

"Look, I gotta go," Ross said. "Those crime stat reports don't write themselves."

"No, just wait a minute. Please," I added. "I've got some information Owen doesn't have. It might make him at least take a harder look at Wes Morgan before they bring the hammer down on Ricky."

"Well, spit it out."

"Krystal Gerrard, the owner at Tanner's, is running an escort service. Small scale, uses a few dancers she chooses, sets them up with 'clients.' Jancee Reynolds was one of her escorts."

"You got any proof on the escort service?"

"My source is one of the dancers, Summer Bradley. She was a friend of Jancee's. She told me and Troy about it. She probably would have told Owen, too, if he'd talked to her. But she wasn't there when he was, and he didn't go back, as far as I know. I'm sure she'd tell him the same, and maybe more—if he's open-minded enough to ask her."

"I think he'd be pretty interested in followin' up on a prostitution ring runnin' in the county," he said, echoing what Coop had said to me the night before.

"But where are you goin' with this? What does it have to do with Ricky Travers not killing Jancee?"

"Jancee went rogue and had a private client that she didn't connect with through Krystal. He paid really well, according to Summer, for Jancee to indulge his special interests."

"Like what?"

"He was into BDSM. He especially liked choking women during sex. It's supposed to—"

"Yeah, yeah, I know what it's supposed to do. Let me fill in the blank here, you think her client was Wes Morgan."

"I do. When hitting on her for a date didn't work, he hired her through Krystal. Then Jancee suggested cutting out the middleman, and he was cool with that. It's not too much of a stretch to think that he arranged to hook up with her after Kent's party. Only when he did, something went very wrong."

"Wes spent the night with his brother, Nash. Did Kent go back on the alibi?"

"No, he still thinks Wes was at the cabin all night."

"Thinks?"

"Kent Morgan is a heavy sleeper—he told me that himself. And he was upstairs, Wes was downstairs that night. It would have been easy for Wes to slip away to hook up with Jancee."

"I'm not buyin' this."

"Okay, why not?"

"What was Jancee doin' after she left the party? Everybody left except Wes, right? Then he stayed around to get yelled at by his brother for bein' a dumbass. What was Jancee doin' all that time? It was a cold night, and she wasn't dressed too warm. You think she was just standing around shiverin' under the trees waitin' for Wes to sneak out?"

"There's a three-car garage out there. It's probably heated," I said. "Think of it like this. Jancee waits in the garage for Wes to come and get her. Then, they get in his truck, start driving down that long track to the road. Wes is in a bad mood. His surprise didn't come off the way he wanted. Kent's pissed at him just when he needs to make a big ask for money. Again. He's been drinking. He's under a lot of stress. Then Jancee says or does something that makes him lose his temper. He lashes out. She gets scared and jumps from the truck and runs away.

"He chases her. She loses her shoes in the field. He catches her. She tries to fight him off. That infuriates him. He chokes her with the strap of her purse. He can't leave the body in a cornfield next to his brother's cabin. He puts her in the truck and he takes her across the county and dumps her."

"You do paint a picture, Nash."

"It fits, Ross. You know it does. Wes is a choker. It would be easy, reflexive even, for him to grab at Jancee's purse strap and strangle her with it."

"Nash, you got some things there worth lookin' at. But if you think that clears Ricky, you're thinking wrong. Krystal Gerrard could be running an escort service. Jancee mighta had private clients. She coulda had a guy into BDSM. That guy might even be Wes. But you got no real proof that links

Wes Morgan to Jancee Reynolds' murder. I don't know if Ricky Travers is guilty or not, but at least there's some solid, provable connections between him and Jancee's death. Sorry, but it doesn't look to me like Wes Morgan has much to worry about."

"Wait, I didn't tell you this part. There's Troy, too. He met with Wes at a bar the night before he got hit. Troy knew about the BDSM stuff and Jancee's private client. He wanted to prove he could follow up on a lead on his own. I think he pushed Wes too hard on the escort service and Jancee. I know that Wes got mad, and they both left early. The very next morning, Troy is hit and almost killed. By Wes, I think."

"Again, where's your proof?"

"I've got Troy's calendar, which shows he had a seven a.m. meeting scheduled at the Polka Dot on Thursday—the morning after he and Wes met at the bar. I think after they both left, Wes had second thoughts. He set up a meeting with Troy on some pretext, but his real plan was to try and take Troy out of commission and shift attention to Ricky Travers. And he did. Now Owen is all in on Ricky, and so far he's given Wes a pass. I think Owen needs to take a serious look at Wes."

"Of course you do."

"And there's something else."

I figured I might as well give him my Monroe theory of the crime, too.

"Nash, you're like one of those choose-your-own-adventure books Allie used to like."

That was painfully close to the truth.

"I know, Ross. But I think one of those theories is right. And I think Detective Fike is on the wrong track."

"You know, it would be real refreshing sometime if you didn't think you were smarter than the cops."

"I don't think I'm smarter than you or Coop. I don't know Owen well enough to tell. We just go at things different ways to get to the same conclusions. And sometimes you catch on to a piece of an investigation that I miss, and sometimes it's vice versa. We each do our part."

"See, the problem is, Nash, you don't *have* a part in police investigations. Yet somehow I always find you there, right in the middle of things."

"I respect your job. Why can't you respect mine?"

"Let me finish. I'm never gonna like that you think bein' a reporter, or a crime book writer, or whatever it is you're doin' these days gives you some kinda business in *my* business. But I'll admit you got a good brain, and what you did for Allie and for me—you got a good heart. I think you should go to Owen with what you just told me. But don't expect he's gonna drop Ricky and arrest Wes. And don't think he's gonna let you mess in things as much as I do."

"I don't 'mess in things.' It's my job to ask questions and to get to the truth—just like yours is. I know Owen won't stop pressing forward on Ricky, but I'd be happy if he'd do some digging into Wes and the whole Tanner's operation."

"Well, good luck with that. Now I gotta go."

"Okay, fine. But can I get you to do one thing for me?"

"What?"

"Could you find out if a gold necklace with a fairy charm was found at the crime scene? Jancee borrowed it from Summer, and she'd like to get it back. I guess it was a gift from her grandmother."

"Yeah, all right. I'll see what I can find out."

"Also, if you hear anything about what they find after they execute the search warrant, could you give me a heads up?"

"You're pushin' my limit, Nash."

"I know. Thanks, I appreciate it. And Ross?"

"Yeah?"

"I miss working with you."

"I told you, Nash, we don't work together."

"I know. But I miss it anyway. Bye."

45

Miguel called me after I had returned Allie's phone and gone up to my office.

"How's Troy? Did you get to see him?"

"No, he's still under sedation. No, no, don't be worried," he added, before I could say anything. "They do that so he will lie quiet. So his brain is settled down to make sure there's no more damage done. He'll be that way for at least a few days. That's what his brother Drew said. He was a medic in Afghanistan so he knows about head injuries."

"Miguel, I didn't even know Troy had a brother—or a sister until this thing started. I didn't really spend any time getting to know him at all. And now—"

"Oh, no, you are not going there and taking me with you. There will be plenty of time to know Troy. Drew said when everything looks good, they will bring him out of sedation."

"How long will that be?"

"I don't know. It depends."

"On what?"

"On everything, *chica*. They are checking him all the time to make sure if any little thing changes, they will know and they will take care of it. We just have to wait."

"That's my worst thing."

"I know."

"Did you ask Troy's mother if we could have his notebook?"

"I did."

"And?"

"She said she doesn't have it here. It's at her hotel, and she's not going to leave Troy just to get something for work."

"Did you tell her we need it to carry on with the stories Troy was working on?"

"Yes, but she said the newspaper was the last thing on her mind. Then she said some not so nice things about you. And she was getting more and more upset. I think we have to wait. Everyone is still being very nervous and upset. Drew said he will pick it up tonight and he could mail it to me, but I said I'll come back to Madison tomorrow to get it."

"Okay. It doesn't sound like we have much choice. Plus, it's possible it might not even have anything we can use. We're just assuming that Troy wrote up his notes from his meeting with Wes."

"And that he asked Wes about Jancee and escorts and breath play with choking," Miguel added.

"Right."

"What is happening with Ricky?"

I gave him a quick rundown.

"They could be executing the warrant right now," he said.

"I know. Cross your fingers they don't find anything that gets Ricky in any deeper than he is. Talk to you when you get back."

I was heating up some chicken vegetable soup my mother had dropped off for me when my intercom buzzed.

"Yes?"

"Leah, it's Dan, can I come up?"

"Sure."

I clicked to unlock the security door at the bottom of my stairs and undid the lock on the door that opens into my apartment. Then I got bowls down and was ladling the soup out when Dan knocked.

"Come in, it's open, Dan!" As he walked into the kitchen, I turned and said, "I was just getting some lunch on, so I thought I'd feed you, too."

"Thanks, that sounds good."

I busied myself getting napkins, offering drinks, pouring drinks, until finally Dan said, "Could you just sit down? You're making me nervous."

"Oh. Sure. Don't be afraid to eat the soup, my mother made it, not me," I said, pulling up a stool to the bar and sitting down across from him.

"Leah, I want to get something off my chest. I know it was you who got Art Lamey to stop telling people I was a suspect in Jancee's murder, and Spencer to quit dogging me in *GO News*. Marilyn told me."

He didn't sound too angry, but Dan is one of those guys who can get quieter, not louder, when they're mad, so I wasn't sure.

"Dan, I'm sorry if you're mad. I know I stepped in where you didn't ask me to go. In fact, where you probably didn't want me to go. I understand how important AA is in your life. I know that you place a lot of value on the 'anonymous' part. I just couldn't stand you taking the heat when Marilyn could so easily end it. I went to her—"

"I know you did, Leah. I know you saw Spencer, too, and threatened to print a story naming Marilyn as the person I was with, and why. She told me everything. I kept hoping that Marilyn would come forward on her own. After talking to her today, I realize she never would have. I could've lived with that, but it was hard knowing I was hurting Coop's campaign. You took that pressure off me. I have to thank you for that."

"No, you don't have to thank me at all, Dan. I'm just happy you're not angry. I realize I overstepped my bounds, but I'd be lying if I said I wouldn't do it over again. I would."

"I know that. But I have to ask. Would you really have run the story about Marilyn? Could you really do that to a person who is suffering as much as she is?"

"No. Even though I don't have much compassion for Marilyn. She's been too nasty to my mother—and to me. The reason I wouldn't have run the story is because I know you would've been disappointed in me."

"Leah," he said in a surprised voice. "I—"

"No, please, let me finish. You're my idea of what a man, what a father, should be. You went out of your way to help me when I was a kid. That meant a lot. And you keep doing that—for me, for Marilyn, for Ricky Travers. You're a special person, Dan."

He stood up then and opened his arms wide.

"Come here a minute. Let me give you a hug."

I did, and it was nice.

When we sat back down across from each other, we both started talking at the same time, and we both started with the same word: "Ricky—"

"No, you go first, Dan."

"I'm really worried about Ricky. His Uncle Jerry called me about half an hour ago. He's pretty shook up. It's bad news, Leah. Ricky's in jail."

"You mean he's at the sheriff's office for questioning, right?"

"No, I mean he's been arrested."

"Damn. Did Jerry tell you why they made the arrest?"

"He didn't even know they'd taken Ricky in for questioning. He thought Ricky was at work, until they showed up at the house with a warrant. They wouldn't tell him anything. Ricky called him from the jail."

"What did Ricky say?"

"That the police found sequins under the bed liner of his truck, so they arrested him for killing Jancee. There has to be more than that, doesn't there? It doesn't really make sense."

But I knew that it did.

"The police have been asking questions and zeroing in on Ricky almost from the beginning. You were just a Lamey and Spencer-inspired distraction. It was fun for GO News to harass you, and Lamey was all for making trouble for Coop's campaign. But when Ricky lied about driving Jancee to the party and Owen Fike found out, that put the focus on him. And he's on video driving back out to Kent Morgan's that night around eleven o'clock."

"I can't believe he killed Jancee."

"I don't want to believe it, but the facts are pretty persuasive. And everyone knew how he felt about Jancee, and that she didn't feel the same about him. That kind of rejection can push a person over the edge."

"No, not Ricky. That kid has dealt with all kinds of crap his whole life—teasing and taunting from kids because of his mother's addiction, because he was poor, because his uncle is a bartender at a strip club, because he's a slow thinker, because he's shy. He was in and out of foster care and put in some really bad situations. He's been hurt a hundred and one times and he is still the nicest, gentlest guy."

"Yeah, well, there's that famous photo of Ricky literally picking up little Dewey Redding by his belt and the back of his shirt and throwing him out of Tanner's bar. That doesn't look too gentle."

"But that was because he thought Dewey was hurting Jancee."

"I could make the case that all those things you said to prove how gentle Ricky is could be used to prove that he was a man who buried his anger and resentment for years. Finally, when the girl he loved taunted him or rejected him one last time, it was too much. All that built-up hurt boiled over and he lashed out and he killed her."

"You don't really think that."

"No, I don't, Dan. At least I don't want to, but with everything else, finding sequins in Ricky's truck is pretty damning. How did they get under the bed liner? Jancee wasn't riding in the back end of the truck. But maybe her body was, after Ricky strangled her. He's in big trouble. It's possible that he should be."

He rubbed his hand over his hair, the same way Coop does when he's upset.

"Leah, I know the kid pretty well. I just can't see it. Jerry called me because he doesn't have a clue how to get Ricky a lawyer. I called Gabe before I came over, but his secretary told me he's out of town. What do you think about Jim Gilroy? I've seen a lot of his ads on television."

"Ads are about the only thing Jim Gilroy is good at. He never met a plea deal he didn't want to accept. And you can be sure they'll be offering one. A deal would wrap things up quickly, show what an effective sheriff Lamey is, and with no family to clamor 'Justice for Jancee' there won't be any bad publicity."

"Well, I guess he could just wait until Gabe gets back, but I hate to think of him sitting there alone and scared for the whole weekend."

"Let me try Miller. He's not a criminal attorney, but he could at least talk to Ricky, walk him through what's going to happen next. And I'll connect with Gabe. I'm sure he'll take Ricky on."

46

"Thanks, Mr. Caldwell, for coming to see me."

Miller Caldwell and I were meeting with Ricky at the Grantland County Jail.

"Not at all, Ricky. But do you understand that having a third party here, and by that I'm referring to Leah, means that what we talk about today isn't covered by attorney-client privilege, because Leah isn't working for the defense? In other words either she, or I, could be required to testify about anything you say to us."

"I know. Uncle Jerry explained it to me after you talked to him," Ricky said. "It doesn't matter. I'm going to tell you the same thing I told Detective Fike. But maybe you'll believe me. He didn't."

"Ricky, I'm curious, why did you want me here so badly?" I asked.

"Because when you talked to me before, I could tell that you understood. You know that I really loved Jancee. Nobody else listens when I say that. And nobody else told me they were sorry for my loss. And it is my loss. And I think you know that. And I'm scared. And I don't want to go to jail forever."

As he spoke, his voice trembled and he struggled for control.

"It's all right, Ricky," Miller said. "It's frightening, I know. But you're at the beginning, not the end, and Gabe Hoffman, who'll be representing you in court on Monday, is very good. You just need to be completely honest from now on."

Miller looked at me and gave a slight nod for me to start the questioning.

"Ricky, let's get the basics out of the way. You're here because you've been lying. Quite a lot. You lied to me and you lied to Detective Fike when you said you didn't drive Jancee to Kent Morgan's. You lied when you said you spent the whole night at home. And you got caught in a lie again today. The police have video that proves you were on the road to Kent Morgan's cabin around eleven o'clock. So, you did go back there to pick up Jancee. What happened after you did? If you didn't kill Jancee, why all the lies?"

"But I didn't lie! I mean, I did lie about driving Jancee, and I lied that I didn't go out to Kent Morgan's. But I didn't see Jancee. I never saw her again after I dropped her off. Please, it's the truth!"

"Ricky, Miller and I want to believe you. We want to help you. But like Miller said, you have to be completely honest."

"I'm not lying now. I told Detective Fike, but he didn't believe me either. What's the use?"

He didn't meet our eyes; instead he looked down and stared at his cuffed hands.

"I know that it can be very frustrating when you feel like no one is really listening to you, Ricky," Miller said. "But you have to trust us. If you don't, then we can't help you, and we might as well leave. Is that what you want?"

Miller's somber voice seemed to get through to Ricky. He looked up, shook his head, and then began speaking again.

"Jancee asked me to take her to the party. She said she'd call me for a ride back to Tanner's if she needed one when she was done. I went home and I did watch Netflix, and I did fall asleep, like I said. She woke me up when she called. But she said she didn't need a ride, she had one. She only called to tell me that she wouldn't be at Tanner's anymore. She was leaving, going to Chicago."

"That must have really upset you," Miller said.

"I couldn't believe it. I knew she was going someday, that's what she always said, but I didn't think it would be so soon. She was saving money for it. And she said just the week before that she didn't have enough. I asked her how could she get the money so fast? She laughed and said it was her fairy godmother. She had this tattoo of a fairy and whenever something good happened, she'd always tap it and say, 'That's my fairy godmother, looking out for me.' I tried to talk her into not moving, not yet. I said I was almost done with my carpentry program, and I'd be making good money. I could go with her and help pay for things. But she said it was time for her to go. I begged her not to, and I started to cry. She didn't like that. She said she only called to tell me goodbye."

"Did she say anything else?"

"She said, 'I'm not who you want me to be, Ricky. It's better this way. Stay sweet.' Then she hung up."

"If she said goodbye and ended things, why would you drive out there to pick her up?" I asked.

"I didn't. I mean I did drive out there, but not right away. After she hung up, I was crying and I just threw my phone down. I hurt so bad. It was like I couldn't breathe. I got up and just started walking round and round the house—living room, dining room, kitchen, kitchen, dining room, living room. Over and over again. I was just hitting my fist into my other hand and crying and yelling like I was crazy. I couldn't stop. Then all of a sudden, I just did. I knew I had to see Jancee one more time. I had to."

"What did you plan to do?"

"Nothing, I don't know. I wasn't thinking, I was just going. I ran out to my truck and I took off. I kept saying over and over in my head, *please be there, please be there, please be there.* My heart was pounding so hard, and I drove faster than I ever have in my life. I didn't even know that I almost hit that lady's car, until Detective Fike showed me the video. It was like I was, I don't know, like hypnotized or something. I couldn't think, I couldn't stop, I just had to go there."

"What happened when you got to Kent's?"

"I drove up the road as fast as I could, but I had to slow down a lot because it was so full of ruts and holes. By the time I got to the cabin, I was calming down a little. I tried to think what I could say to her if she was still there. When I pulled up in front, though, the cabin was dark. I got out and stood there and just stared. And then I really knew."

"Knew what?"

"That I'd never see her again."

"Why didn't you drive to Tanner's to try and find her?"

"Because when I was standing there alone, it was real dark and real quiet and it—this is gonna sound like I'm making it up. But I'm not. And I'm not crazy, either. It really happened."

"Go on, Ricky," Miller said.

"I heard Jancee's voice. She said, *Goodbye, Ricky.* I could hear it so clear, like as if she was standing right next to me. It wasn't in my mind. I heard her. And the way she said it, I knew she was done with me. Crying wouldn't change it, talking wouldn't change it, begging her to stay wouldn't change it. She was gone. I was never going to see her again."

I don't believe in ghosts exactly, but I think that sometimes the people we've loved in life do have ways of reaching out to us after they're gone. Listening to Ricky, his voice hushed but certain, and knowing that Jancee had probably died just a short while before—maybe even right as he was standing there—well, I had to suppress a shiver.

"What did you do next?" Miller asked, interrupting my fantastical thoughts.

"I just went back home. I laid down on the couch, and I guess I fell asleep, because the next thing I knew, Uncle Jerry was shaking me and telling me to go upstairs to bed. I didn't tell him anything about Jancee. I didn't want to talk about it to anybody. It just hurt too bad. Later he told me that Jancee had left. I pretended like it was the first time I heard it. He knew how I felt about her, so he asked me if I was okay about it. I lied. I told him I was fine."

"What about after Jancee's body was found?"

"I knew it was her when I saw the description. I couldn't understand it. I thought she was in Chicago. How could she be dead? That's when I told Uncle Jerry what happened that night and I asked him what I should do. He told me not to say anything, or the police would think I did it. He said they could blame it on me, because all the people at the party where she was were rich. He said police don't go after rich people, they go after people like us."

"Oh, Ricky, that was a bad mistake," I said.

"I know. I knew it wasn't right to lie, but I was scared. And Uncle Jerry, he's my family. He's the one that got me out of my last foster home. He quit his job and came all the way here from out west to get me and take care of me. It was the first time in my life I ever had my own room, my own stuff. It was the first time in my whole twelve years that I knew I wouldn't get moved again. That I would be safe. Do you think Uncle Jerry will get in trouble? Because he didn't tell the police what he knew about me? I don't want that to happen."

"There could be some problems, but I don't think it's likely. At any rate, we can deal with that later. Right now, your problems are front and center," Miller said.

"Do you know why Monroe told Detective Fike that he saw you and Jancee together?" I asked. "In my experience, members of the Granger family stay as far away from the cops as they can."

"Monroe's the one who saw us? Detective Fike didn't say who. He didn't have any reason to be mad at me. I don't know why he'd tell, but I guess it doesn't matter. It's true. I did drive her."

"Ricky, if the police don't have your phone records already, they'll get them soon," Miller said. "They'll be able to track where you were that night. They'll be checking to see whether or not the location information in those records matches the story you're telling now. Namely that you went back home directly and that you didn't go anywhere else after you left Kent Morgan's the second time. Be very sure that you're remembering things correctly."

"I'm saying it exactly like it happened, Mr. Caldwell."

"When Detective Fike told you he had video that proved you had lied about going back to Kent Morgan's cabin, how did you explain it to him? Did you try to lie?" I asked.

"No. I knew it would just make things worse. I told him what I told you about Jancee calling me. He said it would help him believe me if he could look at my phone. But when I gave it to him, he got mad. It didn't show anything about me going back to try and see Jancee, because I threw it down after Jancee hung up and I forgot all about it. I didn't have it with me."

"He probably thinks that shows you were planning to kill Jancee. That you left your phone at home on purpose so no one would know that you went to get Jancee, killed her, and then took her body to the Seetons' property."

"I'm afraid Leah's right, Ricky," Miller said.

"But I didn't lie! I'm not lying now. I was only ten years old when I lived with the Seetons. They were nice to me. But after they quit doing foster care, I got put in another foster home. I never even saw them again. And I never went out to their property. I haven't even thought about it for years."

"Still, you knew about the woods, you knew the area, and from Detective Fike's point of view that means you would have had a pretty good idea of where to drop Jancee's body," I said. I didn't like being so tough on Ricky, but if he was hiding anything else, I wanted to shake it loose.

He hung his head in despair.

"I don't know what to do. I'm telling the truth now, but how do I make you believe me?"

"We're not the ones you need to convince, Ricky. And there's still one damning piece of evidence that you need to explain. How did the sequins that match the ones on the dress Jancee wore that night get under the bed liner in your pickup?"

"I don't know. If they found them in the front of the cab, I could understand, because Jancee was right there in the passenger seat. But she was never in the back of my truck ever, not alive or dead. I'm telling the truth. I'll take a lie detector test if that will make you believe me. I didn't kill Jancee."

47

"Leah, it's great to hear your voice."

I had tried Gabe again as soon as I walked into my apartment after meeting with Ricky and Miller.

"You could hear it more often, Gabe, if you stayed home for a while. We've got a situation here and I sure hope you really are coming back tomorrow."

"I really am. This is about Ricky Travers, right? I gathered that but not much more from the messages you and Miller left. Why was he arrested? And what happened with Dan? When I left, he was Art Lamey's favorite suspect."

"You *have* missed out on a lot. You know the *Times* is online—*Himmel Times,* I mean, not the lesser known New York paper. Though I suppose they might be, too. Dan is officially not a suspect anymore. His alibi came forward. It was Marilyn Karr."

"Well, that's unexpected. But why did the sheriff's office arrest Ricky Travers?"

"I wish I could say that it's because Owen Fike is an idiot and jumped the gun. Sadly, I can't. Ricky gave him plenty of reasons to make the arrest. But I don't think he did it."

I gave him a condensed version of the case against Ricky, and how he had explained himself to me and to Miller.

"So, what do you think? You will take Ricky on, won't you? He's pretty lost and very scared right now."

"It sounds like he should be. Why are you so sure he didn't do it?"

"I know it doesn't look good. And I can *almost* see how he could have done it, if Jancee's death had been accidental. You know, he's a big guy and Jancee was a petite woman. Say Ricky had grabbed her around the shoulders, begged her to stay, and then shoved her away when she said no, and she hit her head or fell down a flight of stairs, or something like that, maybe.

"But I can't wrap my head around the idea that he deliberately strangled the life out of the woman he loved, no matter how she hurt him. And there are two other credible suspects with possibly stronger reasons to kill Jancee."

"Tell me."

I gave him a short but pithy summary of my thoughts on Wes Morgan and Monroe Mepham.

"They both sound promising. Plenty of scope for reasonable doubt, if it gets that far."

"Yes, and I didn't even include the prostitution ring parts. But that's going to take a longer conversation."

"Now I'm really intrigued. I'll need a day to get back and get settled in, but I'll call and leave word with Ricky that he officially has a lawyer. I'll see him on Sunday. Before that, I'll get Miller's assessment on the visit you two had with Ricky."

"Thanks, Gabe. Ricky needs a good lawyer, and he could use a friend, too. Speaking of which, what's up with your friend? No more problems, I hope, that are going to require more trips."

"There's a lot happening, but it's all good. And way more than I can tell you in a phone call. My flight gets in tomorrow at one-thirty. I should be home by three-thirty. Give me a little time to get unpacked and organized, and then come by for drinks and dinner around five-thirty. The stuffed shells I owe you will be on the menu."

"How about the surprise you promised?"

"Yes. That's on the menu, too. I hope you think it's a good one."

The surprise part of the upcoming evening did make me a touch uneasy. Gabe and I had hit a major snag in our developing relationship when he wanted me to move in with him and I didn't want to take that step. That had led to a big fight but ultimately to a better understanding on where each of us was coming from—at least I thought it had. I hoped his surprise wasn't going to change that.

"I'll be there. I'm excited to see you."

"Me, too. I've missed you. Tell me, how's Troy doing? I've been thinking about him."

"So far, so good." I filled him in.

"You know, I think I'd better get back before you think that you can get along without me."

"I agree. What's the use of having a boyfriend who isn't even here to make me dinner when I want it?"

"Is my cooking the only reason you like having me around?"

"Let me think about that. I'm sure there are some others. But your cooking is definitely in the top five."

"I look forward to hearing the other four."

I heard a commotion in the background on Gabe's end, and then someone calling his name.

"I'm sorry. I have to cut you off. I'm needed in the next room. I can't wait to see you tomorrow."

"Have a good flight. I'll see you at five-thirty."

I was looking forward to having his full attention, and to testing out my theories on him.

I had just finished with Gabe when my mother called.

"How's Troy doing, any change? I saw Miguel's car pulling into town when I was on my way to Aldi a little while ago."

I gave her what I knew.

"That sounds hopeful. It's probably a comfort to his mother having both of her other kids there. Especially Drew, because of his medical experience from his time in Afghanistan."

"Am I the only person in the office who didn't know Troy even had a brother—or a sister?"

"Possibly. Though I'm not sure Courtnee knows either."

"Nice, Mom. Are you saying I'm as self-centered as Courtnee?"

"I'd never say that you're self-centered, Leah. But you don't always take the time to get to know people you don't think you have much in common with. There's more to Troy than I think you realize."

Self-awareness and the guilty feeling I'd had ever since Troy's accident kept me from mounting a very vigorous defense.

"I spent time getting to know Troy," I said.

"The last week or so, maybe. Be honest. You dismissed him as a nerdy Eagle Scout who you hired because he can write a decent sentence. Then he faded from your awareness because he's quieter and shyer than Miguel."

No one can zero in on the hard truths I'm trying not to think about better than my mother. Thus, no one can irritate me more.

"Well, he is a nerdy Eagle Scout, and everybody is shyer than Miguel, and I didn't ignore Troy. He just didn't like the feedback I was giving him very well. And he has to learn to take criticism if he's going to make it in a newsroom. You sound like *his* mother, not mine."

"What do you mean?"

"Mary Patterson reamed me out big time at the hospital yesterday. She said Troy was unhappy at the paper because I was too hard on him, that he felt like nothing he did was ever good enough, that as a boss, I'm basically Cruella de Vil. It's one of the reasons I didn't go to the hospital today. I didn't want to upset her all over again when she's got so much on her mind."

"You didn't tell me that. I understand that Troy's mother is in a very terrible place emotionally right now, but that's ridiculous. You did the most important thing. You hired Troy. You gave him a chance to prove himself. You—"

One thing about my mother—she can take me up one side and down the other, but anyone else who tries had better watch out. Her instant switch from my you-need-to-hear-this mom to Carol-for-the-defense mom made me laugh.

"Why are you laughing?"

"Because I love you and your double standards, Mom. When you say it, you're giving me helpful and constructive feedback. When Troy's mother says basically the same thing—though at a much higher emotional pitch—she's ridiculous. I just hope I get the chance to let Troy know that I really do believe that he's got the makings of a good reporter."

"You will, hon. Troy's going to be fine. I know it."

"I'll feel better when he's finally awake."

"I'm making Texas Hash tomorrow. Do you want to come by? That always makes you feel better."

"I would, but Gabe's coming home tomorrow and we're having dinner. And he's going to give me the big reveal about his mystery trips. He also said that he has a surprise for me."

"Oh, good. I miss seeing him around. It feels like he's been gone more than he's been home for the past month or more. The Players are doing *Guys and Dolls* for the spring musical. I want to talk to him about trying out. I think he'd make a great Sky Masterson."

"Well, it would be kind of refreshing to see a male lead in the musical who's actually within ten years of the part he's playing."

"Don't be mean. Can I help it if the only men around who are willing to sing and dance in public are mostly in the 'mature' citizens category?"

"No, that's outside of your control. But you do have some influence over the plays the board picks. Seriously, last year, *Grease*? The "Greased Lightning" number was terrifying. I thought we were going to have to call 911. I still can't believe Dale Darmody didn't have a heart attack."

"Oh, stop it. It wasn't that bad."

I didn't respond.

Finally she said, "You're right. It was pretty bad. But Davina Markham wouldn't let go. She wanted to play Sandy so bad. And she does have the voice for it, and she does contribute a lot to the Himmel Community Players—I don't mean just money, she does a lot of volunteering, too."

"Admit it. You were dying to play Rizzo, too. That's why you cast the deciding vote. And a damn fine Rizzo you made."

"I did, didn't I? But I agree the board needs to face the fact that some of our core members are getting older."

I was sure my mother did not include herself in that category.

"Well, I gotta go, Mom. I've got some work to do."

"Okay— keep me in the loop about Troy if you hear anything this week-end. Oh, I'll save you some Texas Hash. Also, let me know what Gabe's surprise is."

"Yes, will do. Bye."

48

After I talked to my mother, I sat down on the couch with the fireplace going and a Jameson at hand for some serious thinking about what I needed to be doing. However, instead of planning, I immediately and unexpectedly fell asleep. I woke up to the ringing of my phone.

"Yeah, hi, Miguel. What's up?" I asked, finishing the question with a yawn.

"*Chica*, don't tell me you are in bed already! It's only seven o'clock."

"I wasn't. But I did fall asleep on the couch and now the idea of putting my pajamas on is very enticing. Want to come over? I'll make some popcorn and we can watch a movie and exchange notes from the day."

"I would, but I'm on my way to my friend Will's party."

"Who is Will?"

"You know Will. He works part-time in the coffee shop right across the street from the paper. He's studying to be a veterinary assistant."

Miguel said it as though of course I must know every person who works in every business on the street where I live.

"Sorry, no. I don't know Will. But if I ever tried to keep track of your list of friends, my brain would break. I'm glad you're going out tonight, though. You've been working way too hard. Be good, have fun, I'll catch you tomorrow," I said, stifling another yawn.

"No, wait, wait. What is happening with Ricky Travers?"

"I can give you the highlights but it's too long to tell now. They arrested him, Miller and I talked to him today, it doesn't look good for him. But I just don't see it."

"Is it Wes or is it Monroe you think now?"

"I don't know. I keep flipping back and forth. Maybe taking a look at Troy's notebook will help. You're sure his brother will have it for you tomorrow?"

"Yes. But I'm not going over until the afternoon. I think it's hard for them to have outside people always around. Sometimes, it should be just family and close friends."

"I agree. Call me when you get back—or before, if anything changes with Troy."

"I will, but Drew said no news isn't bad news. I think he's a good brother to Troy."

I thought I detected a slightly wistful note in Miguel's voice. Despite his plethora of friends, and his million cousins, he has no brothers or sisters himself. I don't either, now, but at least I did once.

"It sounds like Troy's whole family is good people. Except maybe his mother. No, just kidding. Sort of. Stop thinking about Troy, and the paper, and Ricky and everything else. Go out and play hard, have fun. I'm going to do some writing in the morning. We can do lunch tomorrow before you go to Madison, if you want. I'll fill in all the blank spots about Ricky."

"Yes. Let's meet at the Elite at noon."

Since I couldn't stop yawning, I decided to end my exciting evening by going to bed at seven-thirty. I fell asleep as soon as I hit the sheets, but I woke up within half an hour. I plumped up my pillow, shifted from my back to my side, to my other side, then to my back again. But each time I closed my eyes, thoughts started ping-ponging around in my head.

What if I was wrong about Ricky? It wouldn't be the first time I had backed the wrong person. But Wes was lying about Troy, I knew it. Once we got that notebook, if it detailed the questions and Wes's answers—which I knew it would, that was Troy's way—I'd have something to show Owen. But wait, what if Jancee's private BDSM client was some random dude who hadn't even surfaced yet? No. I could not go there. Things were complicated enough already.

"Oh, this is ridiculous," I said out loud.

I threw off the covers, grabbed my robe, and slid my feet into slippers. Then I went to the kitchen to make popcorn. Some people use a Tibetan singing bowl to calm the mind. Some repeat a mantra. I use the Zen-like simplicity of making perfect stove-top popcorn to stem my racing thoughts.

Of all the life skills my mother has tried to teach me during our long association, perfect popcorn is the one that I have retained and use the most often. Of course, it works as just regular, good-to-eat and watch-a-movie popcorn. But the focus with which I make it comes about as close as I ever will to meditation.

I heated three tablespoons of oil in a pan along with three unpopped kernels of corn. They serve as the advance guard for the kernels to come. When the three kernels popped, I removed the pan from the burner, added one-third cup of popcorn kernels to it, put the cover on, and counted off thirty seconds.

Then I returned the pan to the stove and turned up the flame. When the popping started, I shook the pan gently a few times, until the sound diminished to one or two random pops. I removed the pan from the burner, took the lid off, and dumped the popped corn into a large bowl. Not a single unpopped kernel was left. My mother would be so proud.

Despite Troy's warnings about the ravaging effects of diet sodas on an aging body like mine, I cracked open a can of Diet Coke, poured it over ice, and took it and my popcorn to the window seat. Wrapped up in an afghan, I snuggled in my corner with the bowl of popcorn in my lap and watched the fire. I don't know how long I sat there but when my phone rang, I had eaten almost the entire bowl of popcorn, and I felt much more at ease.

When I saw who the caller was, I was surprised but pleased.

"Linda! I didn't expect to hear from you again for at least a couple of months."

"You wouldn't have, probably, but I just had a brainstorm. I'm driving back to Florida tomorrow and I thought you might like to do something crazy."

"Yeah? Like what?"

"Ride down with me! The *Star Register* just got bought by A-H Media and—"

"Alton-Hoffmeyer bought it? If the *Star Register* was in critical condition before, now it's on life support. And trust me, AssHat Media won't hesitate to pull the plug. They sucked the *Himmel Times* dry, then shut it down. Which is why I was able to buy it for the low, low price of everything I had and then some."

"You're not saying anything I don't know. They already laid off a bunch of staff—"

"Please tell me Hilary was one of them."

Hilary was the boss who had been my nemesis at the *Star Register*, and she had a lot to do with my difficulty finding a job after I left there.

"Sorry, she's still there. But if A-H Media is as bad as you think, maybe she'll finally suffer for her sins."

"Probably not. She's just the kind of employee they'll reward—duplicitous, scheming, amoral, and greedy."

"That sounds about right. Well, the reporters who were fired are putting together a wake for their *Star Register* careers next week. I got an email invitation today and a request to pass it on. So this is me, passing it on to you. I think you should drive down with me. It would be fun to see everyone again, and when's the last time we took a road trip?"

"I would, Linda, but I can't leave right now. I'm in the middle of a book deadline and a murder story at the moment."

"What? Tell me."

I gave her the overview without any details. "But what about you? Did you give up on your Tessa Miles book idea already?"

"I was hoping you wouldn't ask."

"Why, what's going on?

"Nothing, that's the problem. I guess I expected time to stand still in the tiny town of Sherwood for the past fourteen years, but spoiler alert, it didn't. None of the original investigators on the Tessa Miles murder are still there. Harvey's Bar isn't owned by Harvey anymore. And no one who works there now had even heard of Tessa. Some people in Sherwood still remember the murder, but no one had anything new to add."

"What about the case file? Sometimes cops will share that on a cold case."

"I know. I'm the crusty old reporter who taught you that, did you forget? I saw it all right. It was thinner than the file *I* have on Tessa. The one lead I did get from it dead-ended."

"What was that?"

"Remember I said Tessa's house was the last one on the block, only one neighbor was home that night, and he was in bed at ten?"

"I do."

"So he might have gone to bed at ten, but he wasn't asleep, and he wasn't alone. His married girlfriend was there. When she left about one o'clock, her headlights picked up a guy pacing up and down with a cell phone to his ear in Tessa's driveway."

"And she never told the police that?"

"No, because she had lied to her husband about where she was. She was afraid of what he'd do to her if she went to the cops and he found out about the boyfriend. She didn't say anything about it to her boyfriend either. She rationalized that it was okay to keep quiet, because she never saw the face of the guy at Tessa's. He was just a tall man in a Packers jacket, like a million other men that night. It wouldn't help the police any, and it could hurt her a lot."

"So why did she bother to come forward after the fact?"

"It always bothered her that she didn't. Then her husband died and she decided to tell her story to the cops. It wasn't much, and after almost ten years, they didn't get too excited about it."

"Okay, it's not the greatest lead, I agree, but you're a good reporter. You care about the story. You care about Tessa Miles. Don't give up so easily. Track the woman down. You might be able to jog her memory. There could be a detail she didn't think was important that could lead you to something else. You know how this works."

"I do. That's why I did track her down. She's dead. A heart attack last year. When I said the lead dead-ended, I meant that literally."

"Oh, man, I'm sorry, Linda. I know how hard it is to let a story go."

"Yes. It is. But we both know some stories are never going to get written. So, on to the next, I guess."

She might have given up working on the story, but not on me.

"Are you sure you can't drive to Florida with me? Come on, it'll be a great trip down. We can stop where we want, take some side jaunts if we feel like it. We'll get to Miami, have some fun in the sun, get together with old friends. Then you hop on a plane back home with plenty of warm memories to get you through a cold Wisconsin winter. It'll be great, Leah. Connor's going to be there," she finished slyly.

"Okay, I see where this is going. Connor being there isn't a selling point, Linda. It's another reason for me not to go."

"Stop it. You guys were meant to be together. Why else did he follow you to three different newspapers? You two have gone back and forth more than Olivia Pope and the president on that one show."

Linda rarely remembers the correct title of a movie, television show, or book.

"*Scandal* is the title you're searching for. And Fitz and Olivia racked up quite a few dead bodies in the wake of their romance before the end of the series. Connor and I weren't a star-crossed romance, we were a train wreck. I told you when we had dinner, I'm with someone now. I don't do drama anymore. And I can't go. Seriously."

She sighed heavily before giving up.

"Okay, fine. If you change your mind, the wake is November 6 at the Cafe Diablo, seven o'clock. Just think about it, please."

"I'll think about how I can't go. I'm sorry, Linda, it's bad timing. And I'm sorry, too, that the Tessa story is still in your unsolved files. But you've got a book in you. I know you do. You'll find it. Talk to you whenever. Safe travels."

"I'll give your best to Connor. Bye."

49

Such are the powers of making (and eating) perfect popcorn that I slept very well after hanging up with Linda. So well, that I woke up refreshed and ready to go at six a.m. I was showered, dressed, and fed by seven. Feeling very virtuous, I sat down in my office and began to work on pulling together some dangling narrative threads in my manuscript. Which was fortuitous because my first call of the day was from my agent. For once, I was ready for it.

"Yes, Clinton, I'm writing my draft," I said, instead of hello.

"That's what I like to hear, Leah. I have total faith in you. But that's not why I called. PR plans for the re-launch of your second book are shaping up nicely. Also, my mother thinks that *Bury Your Past* is a much better title than *Family Secrets*. She thinks it will really help sales."

"I'm glad we won the mom vote."

"Don't be snarky. Marianna Barnes is very prescient."

"I was being serious, not snarky, about your mom. I've got one of those, too, you know. I hope she's right. What kind of PR are you talking about?"

"*Bury Your Past* is as good a book as your first one, even with no dead nuns or church scandals. But there isn't a very big budget to promote it. So, it'll be a lot of podcasts, some bookstore events in-state, phone interviews, some Zoom book club appearances, that kind of thing. So you'll want to invest in a fast internet connection if you don't already have one, and maybe a good mike. And please take a leave from your second job at the-little-paper-that-could during the re-launch. You're going to need to focus on pushing those book sales."

"Now who's being snarky?"

"*Moi*? Never. I've told you before I'm all about that can-do story. A girl, her paper, and the town who loves her. But, if you want to keep your fight to save local journalism alive, you need money, right? And if you want to make money, you're going to have to sell some books. Also, it won't hurt to show your new publisher that you're a good investment."

"I will, I will."

"And, just to make my heart happy, tell me that right now, at this very moment in time, you really are focusing on finishing your manuscript, not on your newspaper."

"Right now, at this very moment in time, I really am focusing on finishing my manuscript. I will have the draft done by the deadline."

And for the next three hours, I did work exclusively on my draft, so that I didn't have to feel guilty that the rest of my day would have nothing to do with writing my book. At eleven o'clock, Miguel called.

"I'm so sad, I can't meet you for lunch."

"Why, what's up?"

"My aunt needs me to help at the salon for a couple of hours. It's very busy, and the receptionist went home sick. I'm sorry."

"That's okay, I know you're just pretending to be a reporter. Your heart belongs to styling hair."

"Don't make fun. If I could do both I would! I'll go see Troy after I finish, then I'll call you when I get back, okay?"

"All right, talk to you later."

I returned to my writing, and it went well enough that the next time I looked up from my keyboard it was one-thirty. And I was truly hungry. A quick bowl of Cheerios would be enough to hold me over until Gabe's. I had the cereal, but when I opened the fridge—no milk.

I can do cereal for breakfast, lunch, dinner, or snack time, but not without milk. On my way to the Qwik Stop to get some, I glanced down Gabe's street out of force of habit. My heart gave a happy little jump. There was a car in the driveway. Yes! He must have caught an earlier flight.

I turned down the street for a closer look, to make sure it really was his car and didn't belong to the couple next door with whom he shares a driveway. Nope. It was his.

I pulled in and parked behind it. I looked in the rearview mirror and ran my fingers through my hair. My outfit was pretty basic—jeans and a sweater—but Gabe wouldn't care. And I didn't care if dinner wasn't started, and it was too early for drinks. I was excited to see him.

I ran up the walk, rang the bell, and reached out for the latch, but before I could grab it, the door swung inward. I smiled in anticipation. But instead of Gabe, a little face peeked around the edge of the door. As it opened wider, I saw a little boy, maybe five years old or so.

"Hello," he said. "Are you Leah? I'm Dominic. I knew you were coming over."

He said it with the pride young children feel at being in-the-know about grown-up plans.

I squatted down so we were on eye level.

"Hi, Dominic. Yes, I'm Leah. Nice to meet you. I'll bet you're the little boy who lives next door."

He giggled.

"No, silly! I live here with my dad."

50

"Dom, did I hear the doorbell ring?"

Gabe walked in from the kitchen to the hallway, where I stood with my mouth still open in surprise.

He looked equally stunned when he saw me.

"Leah! You're early!"

"I saw your car here when I was driving by. I was anxious to see you. I thought I'd just pop in and surprise you. But you win the surprise contest hands down. This is your son?"

Dominic was looking back and forth between us with interest.

"Yes, it is. Leah, this is Dominic. Dom, this is my friend Leah Nash."

"We've met," I said.

"She's pretty, Dad," Dominic said. "I like her."

I enjoy kids, especially in Dominic's age range—old enough to be good communicators, young enough to retain amazing imaginations. Normally, I would have happily taken his hand and asked him to show me his favorite toys. But finding out that Gabe had a son he had never mentioned was not even close to normal.

"Yes, she is pretty," Gabe said. "I like her, too. You know, Dom, I think Barnacle would really like to play fetch with you out in the backyard for a while."

All three of us glanced over to where Barnacle was snoring softly in the living room doorway, looking more like a rolled-up rug than a dog. However, when Dominic seized on the idea and shouted, "Come on, Barnacle! Let's play fetch," he sprang up and trotted happily after the little boy.

"Wait, Dominic, put your coat on!"

"I will, Dad."

I waited until I heard the back door bang shut before I said, "Gabe! You've got a kid? How did that never come up in the year since I've known you? It's kind of a big thing not to mention."

"I didn't know, Leah."

We sat in the kitchen so that Gabe could look out the back window to watch Dominic and Barnacle in the yard.

"The floor is yours. Please feel free to explain to me how you overlooked mentioning your—how old is he?"

"Five."

"Your five-year-old son. I understood when your half-brother Bram dropped back into your life without any warning. He was an adult, you'd been estranged, it was painful, and I didn't know you that well then. But we've been together for months. I know when your birthday is. I know you're allergic to mangos. I know you failed chemistry in the tenth grade, but I don't know you have a child? How is that even possible?"

"I thought you said I had the floor."

"You're right. I'm sorry. I'll be quiet. You talk."

"It's complicated."

"I'll bet."

I was actually more astonished than angry. I had a dozen questions—make that a couple dozen—but I folded my hands on the table and made a concerted effort to be quiet and let him explain.

"I dated a woman off and on for a year or so when I lived in New York. Lucy Paine. She's an actor. It was nothing serious for either of us. When she told me that she'd met someone and they were getting married, I wished her well and that was that. I didn't hear from her again. Until a couple of months ago. She and her husband had split in a divorce that turned nasty. He had a DNA test done, and it proved he wasn't the father of her son. Lucy was shocked. She called to tell me that I had to be, because I was the only other man she'd been with in the right time frame. I was stunned."

"I can imagine."

"I didn't say anything to you because I had barely taken it in myself. I flew out to New York to see her. And to take a DNA test. I had no reason to doubt her. I just didn't want to spring something else on a little boy who had just had his life upended by his parents' divorce. I wanted to be absolutely certain that I was his father."

"That was the first trip you took a couple of months ago?"

He nodded.

"When the DNA results came in, they were a perfect match. There's no doubt I'm Dom's father. I went back out to spend some time getting to know him. We didn't tell him right away that I was his real father. I wanted him to feel comfortable with me."

I had to ask.

"Gabe, what about Lucy? She's free now. You're free. You have a child together. Have you talked about—"

"Getting together again? God, no, Leah. It's amazing we ever crossed paths in the first place. Lucy is an actor, I'm a lawyer. Our attraction was fun, but it was surface, casual. Neither of us have any interest in making something more of it. But we both want the best for Dominic. That's why I had to go to New York so often—to establish a relationship with him, before we told him that I'm his father."

"How did he take that?"

"He seems totally fine. But I really don't know that much about kids his age. Lucy said her husband wasn't very involved with Dom. He's a director. He spent a lot of time at the theater. His hours didn't match up with a young child's very well. He was sleeping when Dominic was awake, and off to work when Dominic was ready for bed. He wasn't cruel to Dominic, he just wasn't very interested in him, according to Lucy."

"What about Lucy? How did she manage a career and a kid with a husband who sounds pretty selfish?"

"She didn't. She stopped working after Dom was born. But now she wants, and she also needs, to go back to work. That brings us up to the last-minute trip I made this week. A friend of Lucy's from drama school is producing a film. She offered Lucy a part. It's a great role, and it could lead to more. The catch is, it's filming for three months on location in Alaska. She can't take Dom with her, and she doesn't have anyone who can take care of him for that long. She asked me if I would."

"So you went to pack up Dominic and bring him here."

"Yes. Leah, I'm sorry. I should have told you before, but I wasn't sure how to. You got totally freaked out when I asked you to move in with me. And I thought that was going to be a happy thing. I wasn't sure how the news that I have a five-year-old son would hit you. I was going to tell you about Dominic before I ever brought him here. But then Lucy needed me to take him and that threw my plan to break it to you gently out the window. Even today, it didn't go like I planned. I was going to have Dom playing in his room when you got here. You and I would sit down with a glass of wine. And I would tell you all about it, and then I'd bring Dominic out. I couldn't be happier to see you right now, but I couldn't be more nervous about how you're going to react."

"Gabe, I'm not mad at you. I—"

My phone rang just then. Miguel. I sent it to voicemail.

"I'm just stunned is all. You've had weeks to adjust to the idea that you're a dad. I've had, like, five minutes. I'd—"

My phone started in again. I looked down at it.

"It's Miguel again. Sorry, I should take it."

"Hey, Miguel. Are you at the hospital? Has anything happened with Troy?"

"No! I'm at Kent Morgan's cabin, and—"

"What are you doing out there?"

"It's Wes Morgan. He's dead!"

"What? What happened?"

"I don't know yet. They were taking his body away when I got here."

"Who else is out there? Never mind, I'm on my way." I hung up.

"Gabe, I'm sorry, I have to go."

"Right now? But what about dinner, and Dom? What about you and me? We're right in the middle of—"

"I know. I'm sorry. But Wes Morgan is dead. I have to find out what's going on. I'll be back for dinner, but maybe closer to six than five-thirty, is that okay?"

"Yes, sure, I guess."

I leaned over and kissed him before running out the door.

51

The gate on the two-track lane was unlocked and open when I reached it, so I kept driving instead of parking my car and walking the distance to the cabin. When I got there, a marked sheriff's office vehicle was parked in front, but I didn't see Miguel's yellow Mini Cooper.

I knocked on the door and it was opened by a sturdy middle-aged woman with short, dark blonde hair and small, close-set, blue eyes. She wore a badge on her long-sleeved khaki shirt. Marla Jarvis has been with the sheriff's office for more than twenty years.

"Marla, what's going on? Miguel said that Wes Morgan is dead. What happened? Where is everybody?"

"You'll have to get your information from Sheriff Lamey. We have strict orders. No talking to the press."

"Does that include *GO News*?"

She cocked an eyebrow and couldn't stop her thin lips from curving into a smile.

"It especially includes *GO News*. Sheriff likes to work directly with them, or at least with *one* of them."

"Is Lamey at the scene? In fact, where is the scene?"

"Follow that track there," she said, pointing at another rutted road that led deeper into the woods. "It leads to a tree stand. That's where it happened."

"Come on, please, Marla. Can't you give me just a little? Why is Lamey there? Is Ross, too? Or Fike?"

"Listen, Leah, and I'm not kidding. Things are tense at the office. I'm two years away from collecting my twenty-five-years-and-out card, and the pension that goes with it. So—"

"All right, all right, I get it."

She went on as though I hadn't interrupted her.

"Anything I say to you, I never said. And I'm not going to say much. To me, it looks like a hunting accident. Like maybe Wes Morgan was in the tree stand, stumbled, his gun went off and he fell. But that's just my quick and dirty take. I wasn't there very long. But I've seen my share of hunting accidents. The sheriff's there because Kent Morgan is a very important person around here, and important people get special treatment from the sheriff."

"Why aren't you at the scene?"

"I'm babysitting. Mrs. Morgan is inside. She was with her husband when they found his brother. She was pretty upset when we got there. Mr. Morgan wanted her to come back here, but he didn't want her to be alone. The sheriff sent me with her because everybody knows it's a woman's job to take care of emotional witnesses."

Her tone was more resigned than bitter. Marla's had to put up with a lot as a female deputy. She knows which battles to pick. This wasn't one of them.

The door behind her opened. A petite woman with dark brown hair and large brown eyes stepped onto the porch.

"I thought I heard you talking to someone, Deputy Jarvis."

Looking at me, she said, "You're Leah Nash, aren't you? Kent's told me about you. And of course I've seen your photo on the back cover of your books. I'm Sydney Morgan."

The hand she held out was so small and delicate that I gave it only a light squeeze instead of my usual firm shake.

"It's nice to meet you, Mrs. Morgan. I'm sorry about the circumstances."

"Thank you. Please, call me Sydney." Then she turned back to Marla.

"I'm feeling much better, Deputy. It was just the shock of seeing Wes. It was so unexpected. And so gruesome." She shuddered. "You can go now. I know you have more important things to do than babysit me."

Marla hesitated, but Sydney smiled and said, "Truly, I'm fine."

"Well, if you're sure ..."

"I'm not only sure, I insist. Thank you though, for coming back with me."

"You're welcome. You take care now." Marla turned to me.

"I can give you a ride out there, Leah. My SUV can take the road a lot easier than your car."

"No, thanks, Marla. I want to have my car with me. You go on."

"Okay, suit yourself."

As she walked away, I said, "Sydney, could I use your restroom, please?"

Marla looked over her shoulder at me. She knew exactly what I was doing. I ignored her.

"Yes, of course, Leah. Come in."

She led me into the kitchen and then pointed down a short hall leading off it.

"The bathroom is the second door on the right. I was going to offer you tea, but I actually think I could use a drink. Would you like one?"

It was a little early for me, and I was working. On the other hand, most people like to have someone join them when they drink. It makes them feel more comfortable. And I wanted Sydney to be very comfortable with me. A little alcohol in a person as tiny as she was, combined with the high emotion of the day, could make her quite chatty.

"Yes, thank you, that would be nice."

"I can offer you Jameson, Crown Royal, or Maker's Mark. What's your pleasure? I'm having the Jameson. A double."

"We have that in common. Jameson on the rocks is great. But just a single for me."

I went into the bathroom and closed the door loudly so she would know I was inside. Then I very carefully opened it. I tip-toed to the first door on the right and turned the knob. As I expected, it was the downstairs bedroom Kent had said that Wes preferred. What he hadn't mentioned was that it included a sliding glass door that opened onto a small patio. A flag-stone path led from there to the garage. I slid the door open. It didn't make a sound. How very easy for Wes to slip out to a waiting Jancee and then drive her away to her death.

I hurried back to the bathroom where I made sufficient noise flushing the toilet and washing my hands to support the idea that my request for the bathroom had been real and not just an excuse to snoop. When I entered the kitchen, Sydney had already started on her drink.

"Sorry I didn't wait for you. It's been quite a day."

She handed my glass to me, and then added another generous pour to her own.

"Let's take this into the living room."

As we settled down on the leather sofa, she took a long swallow from her glass and gave a soft sigh.

"Kent would be surprised if he saw me. I'm not much of a drinker."

"You had a major shock and a big loss this afternoon. A stiff drink is probably in order."

"To be honest, the loss is really all my husband's. Wes and I weren't close. The only thing we had in common was Kent. That's why I feel guilty for falling apart like I did. I should have been stronger for Kent. But I've never seen a dead person outside of a funeral home before. And then they look so peaceful, and not quite real, don't they? It wasn't like that with Wes."

She took another sip of her drink.

"His one leg, it was bent at such a terrible angle. And his eyes. They were still open. I could see blood on his shirt. I couldn't understand. Why was there blood on the front, when he fell on his back? Of course it was because he'd been shot, but I didn't know that at first. I thought he'd fallen from the tree blind."

"That must have been awful. But how was it that you and Kent found Wes?"

"Kent and I were supposed to come out here this morning. I have an idea for some new window treatments and I needed him to help me measure for them. But he had to change our plans and go to Madison this morning for a business meeting. When he came home I was still a little mad at him for backing out on me. But he had brought me a big bunch of chrysanthemums from the farmers' market, and he was in such a happy mood that I couldn't stay angry. Dinah, our daughter, is at a friend's for an overnight. Kent said we should come out, measure the windows, take a walk, and spend the night.

"So, that's what we did. It's so beautiful out today. When we got near the big oak tree where his tree stand is, I saw something lying on the ground underneath it. I thought at first it was a deer. I whispered to Kent and pointed it out. He looked, and then he motioned for me to stay behind. He started walking toward the spot. Then, suddenly, he began to run, shouting, 'Wes, Wes!' "

She closed her eyes as though picturing the scene.

"When I got there, Kent was kneeling on the ground and tears were running down his face. It was terrible. He was rocking back and forth and he kept saying, 'Why, Wes? Why?' I rushed over to him, but he shook his head and he waved me back. I waited and then after a minute, he stood up. He put his arm around me, and we walked away from the area.

"Then he called 911. I heard him tell the dispatcher that there'd been a hunting accident. That's when I realized why there was blood on Wes's shirt. That's when I fell apart. When the sheriff and everyone got there, Kent insisted that someone take me back to the cabin and stay with me. So, that's what Deputy Jarvis did."

"Sydney, you said that Kent was repeating 'Why, Wes? Why?' Did it seem to you that it was just a sort of cry from the heart? That he was just asking God why such a terrible thing had happened? Or did it seem like—do you think he could have been afraid that Wes—"

I hesitated to say the words, but she said them for me.

"Was Kent afraid that Wes had committed suicide? I don't know. Kent told me last night that they'd had a serious argument yesterday. Wes came to him for money, and for the first time ever, Kent said no. He was very torn about it. He's spent his whole life taking care of Wes. He'll torture himself with guilt if Wes's death wasn't an accident."

"Do you think it's possible that it wasn't?"

"Well, anything is possible, isn't it? But suicide doesn't seem likely to me. Wes wouldn't have given up that easily. He was very good at manipulating Kent."

"Kent mentioned to me that his mother had made him promise to always be there for Wes."

"Yes. As a mother it seems unconscionable to me that she saddled Kent with the burden of Wes. Kent was barely twenty, and she had to know what a self-centered bastard Wes was. It was a lifetime sentence."

"You said that you and Wes weren't close. But it sounds like it was more than that. It almost sounds like you detested him."

I'd hoped for a few alcohol-induced confidences from Sydney, but I hadn't expected anything as starkly honest as she'd been.

"Does it? Well, I'll have to do a better job of acting at the funeral, won't I?"

My surprise must have shown in my face.

"Sorry. I think I've had enough to drink for the moment," she said, putting her glass down.

"I shouldn't have said that. I didn't hate Wes. But I had no reason to like him. He resented it when Kent married a widow with a young child. He thought I was a gold digger, which is quite funny, when you think about it. It's true, marrying Kent gave me and my daughter the kind of money and security that I could never have provided on my own. And I enjoy the lifestyle very much. But I've done my best to make Kent's life happy as well.

"It's Wes who's treated Kent like a cash machine. And he really seemed to enjoy embarrassing him. Look what he did with that dancer he invited here. Kent was humiliated. I didn't care. I thought it was ridiculous. It was different for Kent. He takes a lot of pride in the things he's accomplished. He works hard, and he's proud that people look up to him. Wes could never understand that. He just careened through life making one stupid decision after another, expecting Kent to clean up after him. He acted as though Kent owed *him* something, instead of the other way around."

She sighed heavily.

"You've been a good listener. And apparently I needed one. But I've talked way too much. Please, attribute it to a brush with sudden death and too much whiskey."

"I will," I said. "In my world, sharing a Jameson is a sacred bond."

Her smile was overtaken by a huge yawn.

"Excuse me. It's the Jameson. Alcohol makes me talkative *and* sleepy."

"No worries. I need to go and you should rest. Don't get up, I'll see myself out."

52

"Do you have anything yet?" I asked Miguel.

I had just joined him outside the perimeter of a cordoned-off area in the woods, after leaving Sydney on the sofa with an attack of the Jameson sleeps. It was beginning to get dark and people were wrapping up their work at the scene. Ross was deep in conversation with one of the deputies. I didn't want to compromise him by association with me, so I took care to keep my distance. Lamey was talking to Kent Morgan about fifteen yards away from where Miguel and I stood.

"I can't get anything official. Detective Ross said everything has to come from Sheriff Lamey. But when I asked the sheriff a question, he told me to wait for the official press release. But I know one of the deputies. He's in my fitness class and he told me they think it's a hunting accident. But I can't use it."

"Marla Jarvis told me pretty much the same thing. Wes was in the tree stand, accidentally shot himself and fell. But I talked to Kent's wife Sydney, and she's worried that Kent thinks it was suicide."

"Why would Wes kill himself?"

"He was in financial trouble and Kent told him no on a rescue package. But Sydney isn't buying suicide. She said Wes was good at manipulating Kent and he'd come back for another try."

"What do you think?"

"I'm inclined to agree with her. I'd like to talk to Kent. But I don't want Lamey to realize I'm here. And I can't hang around too long waiting. I ran out on Gabe and I promised I'd be back for dinner."

"That's right, I forgot Gabe is back. You may have a late night," he said with a grin.

"Actually, I'm pretty sure we'll make it an early night tonight."

He gave me a quizzical look, but I ignored it.

"Hey, what about Troy? Obviously you didn't make it over this afternoon, have you heard anything?"

"Yes. I called Troy's brother to say I couldn't come to get the notebook until tomorrow, but I had to leave a voicemail. He called me back and said no change in Troy, and that he put the notebook in the mail. So that I wouldn't have to drive to Madison when things are so busy, and everything is still the same for Troy."

"In the mail? That means the earliest we'll get the notebook is Tuesday. Maybe not until Wednesday, even."

"I know. I'm sorry."

"It's not your fault. It's not Drew's either. He was being thoughtful."

"Does it matter so much now? I mean because Wes is dead."

"If it shows that Troy *did* talk to Wes about BDSM and escorts and Jancee, then yes, it matters a lot. It will give more weight to the idea that it was Wes, not Ricky, who killed Jancee. And that Wes may have tried to kill Troy, too. With Wes dead, it's going to be pretty hard to convince Owen Fike that he should consider him as a suspect. Lamey for sure won't, not with Ricky already jailed."

Out of the corner of my eye, I noticed Lamey clapping Kent on the shoulder.

"Miguel, it looks like the acting sheriff is wrapping things up with Kent. I'm going to circle around from the other side and try to get to Kent without Lamey noticing. See if you can grab Lamey's attention. Tell him you want a photo of him working the scene for the front page. That'll get him. Keep him busy as long as you can."

I slipped behind Miguel and walked rapidly around the taped-off perimeter. I waited discreetly behind a tall pine until I saw Lamey move away and then be accosted by Miguel.

Kent had already begun striding purposefully toward a pickup parked in front of my car. I scurried up to him, crashing so loudly through fallen leaves that he turned to see who was behind him.

"Oh, hello, Leah."

His air of easy confidence was gone. His shoulders slumped, the front of his jacket was stained, quite likely with his own brother's blood. Even his bright blond hair looked dull and mussed. He seemed utterly weary and defeated. There are moments in reporting that don't feel very good—asking bereaved family members questions on the heels of a tragedy is one of them.

"Kent, I'm so sorry about Wes. This must be devastating for you."

He nodded, and then, as people often do in the first grip of grief, he began talking as though he couldn't stop.

"I don't understand. Sheriff Lamey said Wes may have gotten dizzy up on the platform. But Wes walks on scaffolding much higher than that all the time. He doesn't—didn't—look that graceful, but he was very light on his feet—like a cat. He never missed a step. It's such a stupid way for him to die."

"What happened?"

"I don't know. I don't even know what he was doing here. The only thing I can think of is that there's a coyote that's been running the woods. This close to deer season, Wes was worried that he'd scare the deer off. Maybe he came out and climbed the stand to get a good shot at it when it came around. I guess he could've—he must've—stumbled, lost his footing, and the gun went off. Or maybe it jammed and misfired. I hope to God that's what happened. Otherwise, it was deliberate."

"Do you really think that?"

"I told you yesterday Wes was having money problems. He came to see me. I found out it was much worse than I'd expected. He's been cheating on his taxes. He got caught. His lawyer said the best he could hope for was a huge payout in penalties, plus fees and interest. Worst case was that and prison as well. He needed money. Quite a lot of it."

He stopped and shook his head.

"I was shocked. He'd made bad business decisions before, but this was actually criminal. And he gave the news to me like it was a bill that I owed and he was collecting. I snapped. I told him I was done. He had to find his own way out of his mess for once in his life. And I just left.

"I wanted to teach him a lesson, and I did. I taught him he had nowhere to turn. I taught him his own brother, who had plenty of money, wouldn't lift a finger to help him. But I would have. I just wanted him to stew for a while, to think about what he'd done, to take some responsibility for once in his life. I wouldn't have let him go to jail. But what if he believed that I would?"

"Kent, don't do that to yourself. Especially before you even know what happened. Let the sheriff's office and the medical examiner do their work and see what they find."

"That's just it. I'm afraid of what they'll find, Leah. I'm afraid Wes killed himself, and I pushed him to do it."

He could barely get the words out, and nothing I could say was going to comfort him.

When I left Kent's property, he was sitting in his pickup truck, staring straight ahead.

It's a terrible thing to lose a sibling. I know that first-hand, and for that, my heart hurt for him. But I didn't feel bad that Wes was dead—except for the fact that now it was going to be even harder to prove that Wes, not Ricky, had killed Jancee.

53

All the way back to Himmel I thought about how to build a case for Wes as Jancee's killer that Owen would seriously consider. It was going to be tough. Especially because there was now zero opportunity that clever questions and good interview techniques could produce a *Law & Order* moment that would cause Wes to crumble and confess.

Because I was distracted, I drove right past Gabe's street and my car followed my usual route toward home. While I was waiting at the stoplight, a display window at Buy The Book caught my eye. It was then I realized that I'd been on automatic pilot and I was headed in the wrong direction. But on second thought, I decided I wasn't. I parked in front of the bookstore and sprinted to the door just as Marcus Scanlon, the owner, was putting up the closed sign. He took pity on me. I ran in, picked up what I wanted, and drove over to Gabe's.

This time when I knocked, I was prepared for the small boy with big, dark eyes who opened the door.

"Hi, Leah. It's me, Dominic. I'm so hungry! Dad said we can't eat without you."

"Yes, I remember you, Dominic. That was kind of harsh of your dad. Hungry little boys should always be fed, even when dinner guests are late."

"Well, come in," he said, taking my hand and pulling me inside. "It smells good, doesn't it?"

"It does. Here, Dominic. I brought you something."

He took the bookstore bag solemnly from me and said, "Why did you bring me this?"

"Well, it's something I really like. I thought you might be the kind of boy who would like it too."

He pulled the book out of the bag and his eyes lit up.

"My teacher read this to us. It's so funny! I love *The Cat in the Hat.* Thank you!"

"You're very welcome."

Gabe had come into the hallway and had watched our exchange silently. Now he clapped his hands and said, "Did I hear someone was hungry? Come to the kitchen and I'll feed both of you."

Dinner was a bit awkward. We obviously couldn't continue the discussion that had been interrupted when I got Miguel's call until Dominic went to bed. But it was hard to come up with casual conversation when something so enormous was literally between us.

So, Gabe and I both encouraged Dominic to talk about school, and his friends in New York, and his favorite movies, and he seemed to enjoy being the center of attention.

"That was delicious," I said to Gabe as we finished.

"You ate a lot, Leah."

"Dominic, it's not polite to comment on how much a guest eats."

"But she did, Dad. Didn't you, Leah?"

"I certainly did. And I enjoyed every bit of it. And you, mister, have a big blob of tomato sauce on the end of your nose."

I grabbed a napkin and wiped it off, wiggling his nose gently as I did. He smiled and took the napkin from me and scrubbed it all over his face.

"There! Now I'm clean."

"Dominic, why don't you keep up that good work and go wash your face and brush your teeth and get ready for bed."

"I'm not tired, Dad. It's way too early. Mom lets me stay up 'til midnight o'clock."

"Midnight o'clock you say? Well, now you're in Wisconsin, Dom, and the time is different. Midnight o'clock is actually eight o'clock here. But I didn't say you had to go to bed yet. Just wash, brush your teeth, and get your pajamas on. We'll clean up here and then meet you in the living room. And do a good job on those teeth. I'll be checking, okay?"

"All right," he said, pushing away from the table and moving toward the door. He turned back before he got there and asked, "Dad, can Barnacle use my toothbrush, too?"

"No. Definitely not. Besides, dogs don't brush their teeth."

"That's not right, Dad. I saw a show all about dogs, and they were brushing their teeth."

"Oh, no, you're not going to trick me into believing that. How could dogs brush their teeth? They don't have any hands."

Gabe got up then and chased Dominic, making him laugh until he got the hiccups and went in to brush his teeth. When Gabe came back I was loading the dishwasher.

"Hey, I'll do that. You're the guest."

"And you're the chef. Technically, your work is done."

"Not quite all my work," he said as he put his arms around me and kissed me.

"Oh, that's work, is it?"

"My favorite kind," he said.

But both of us knew that we were trying too hard, and our usual banter was strained.

After we finished in the kitchen and Gabe had inspected Dominic's bedtime efforts, the three of us settled on the couch. Dominic asked me to read his new book to him, but as soon as I started his eyelids began to droop. He didn't even make it until Thing One and Thing Two showed up. He protested mildly that he wasn't tired but waved me a sleepy good night as Gabe carried him to bed.

"Drink? I have Jameson on hand, or wine if you'd rather," Gabe said when he came back into the room.

"No, I don't think so," I said. "I really should be getting home."

"What? Why? I thought you wanted to talk about things. And we have a lot to talk about besides Dominic."

"I do want to. But it's been a pretty intense day. And not just because Wes Morgan died. I think I need to sit with the idea that you're somebody's dad for a little while longer."

"Leah, are you angry? I can see why you would be. I should have told you sooner, but I was trying to figure things out myself."

"No, I told you before, I'm not mad. More ... unsettled, I guess is the word. You've been getting used to the idea for a while. I only just found out. Do you think you could come over tomorrow afternoon and then we could talk?"

"I'm going to meet with Ricky at ten-thirty. Patty said she'd come over and stay with Dom. I guess I could ask her to stay longer." Patty Delwyn is Miller's long-time secretary and most ardent fan. She's pretty fond of Gabe, too.

"That sounds fine."

"All right. I'll pick up something for lunch and we can talk things through."

He walked me to the door. I kissed him good night and he hugged me just a little harder and longer than usual. As I buckled my seatbelt, there was a tap on the driver's side window. I rolled it down and Gabe leaned in.

"We're okay, aren't we, Leah?"

"Yes, Gabe. We're fine. I'm just tired. I'll see you tomorrow."

I kissed his cheek and he stepped back. I could see him in my rear-view mirror, still standing in the driveway, watching as I pulled away down the street.

54

I wasn't lying when I told Gabe I was tired, but the weariness was more emotional than physical. The whole Gabe's-a-father thing really threw me. Instead of going straight home, I drove over to Coop's. But when I got there, the house was dark.

Where are you?
Hailwell. Birthday party for Kristin's dad. Why?
Nothing. Just wanted to talk. I'll catch you later.
Everything all right?
Yeah, all good. Night.

I almost texted him back to tell him Wes Morgan was dead but decided it could wait. Besides, he might know already. As an attorney in the prosecutor's office, Kristin would be in the loop.

When I left Coop's I turned to go home but changed my mind. This time I was in luck. There was a light on in the living room of Father Lindstrom's apartment. When I rang his bell, he opened the door with such a pleased smile that I instantly felt happier.

"Leah, come in. What a nice surprise. I was just making a cup of tea. Would you like some?"

"Yes, I think I would. It's been quite a day."

I followed him into the kitchen where the tea kettle was just beginning to whistle.

"I'm having chamomile tea. Would you prefer something else?"

"Oh, you know me, Father. I like a walk on the wild side now and then. Chamomile it is."

"Now, what's on your mind?" he asked as he handed me my tea in a St. Francis mug.

He sat down across from me at the kitchen table with his Packers mug, which he uses as a good luck talisman for his team during football season.

"Now you're making me feel bad. Like I only come around when I need something."

"Nonsense. I always enjoy your company, no matter why you come. So, why has it been quite a day?"

He'd already heard about Wes. Then I talked to him about the hard time I was having trying to get to the truth of why Jancee had been killed and by whom. I told him about Ricky and my fear that I might not be able to help him, and my nagging worry that Coop might not win the election. In short, I talked about everything but what had drawn me to his warm kitchen and his chamomile tea that night. He wasn't fooled. He never is.

"Leah, you've taken on another challenge. The death of the young dancer is tragic. You certainly have many threads to follow, and there are many uncertainties. But that's the nature of your work. It's the same situation you come to in any investigation you do, isn't it?"

I nodded.

"Advice on how to research a story or investigate a crime isn't my province. So, I assume what's troubling you is personal rather than professional. If you'd like to talk about it, then we will. If you'd rather not, there are a number of other things we can discuss. I just finished binge watching the *Veronica Mars* series. It's very good. Have you seen it? The lead character puts me a little in mind of you."

I'm always surprised by Father Lindstrom's wide-ranging tastes in TV shows and movies.

"No, Father, I'll check it out. But I guess I'd rather talk to you right now about something personal on my mind."

I proceeded to tell him about the unexpected appearance of a son in Gabe's life.

"The thing is, I am one thousand percent behind Gabe connecting with his son, spending time with him, loving him, doing everything a father should do. And Dominic is a cute, smart little boy. I like him. I'm sure I'll have fun with him. But—argh!—I hate to say this out loud. Especially to you, because it shows what a selfish, self-centered person I am. Though I guess after all these years, you already know."

"You're too harsh on yourself, Leah. Finish what you started. But what?"

"But I don't know if I'm ready to have a kid dropped into the middle of my life. It means not being able to do things on the spur-of-the-moment. Having to think about babysitters and doing kid-centered things like watching *Shrek* a thousand times and playing Candyland and building Legos things for hours. I don't want to plan healthy snacks, and make sure he brushes his teeth. I like doing what I want, when I want, and not worrying about anybody else."

"Aren't you getting a little ahead of yourself? You just met Gabe's son. From what you said, the boy's mother is away for a few months, not forever. I'm sure all the parenting responsibilities won't fall on Gabe indefinitely— or on you by extension. He already has a mother."

"I know that, but you have to admit things are going to change. I'll still have to step up to some kind of quasi-parenting role. Gabe and I will have less time together. He'll be different. He has to be. He's a father. He's going to change. I'm going to change. Things are going to change just when I finally feel like I'm in a pretty good spot, emotionally speaking."

"And that frightens you?"

"Maybe, a little. All right, maybe quite a lot. I get that things don't stay the same. But I guess I like to be the one initiating the changes. I don't want them thrust upon me. Most of the changes that I haven't had control over haven't worked out that great for me. I guess that's why I fight them."

"Has that ever stopped them from coming?"

"No, not really."

"There is a quote attributed to Thoreau that you might find useful to think about. *Things do not change; we change.*"

"What does that even mean? That events happen and whether they turn out good or bad depends on whether we adapt to them?"

He looked at me, his eyes unblinking behind the lenses of his glasses, but he didn't say anything.

"Are you saying that change is supposed to happen to help *me* change? That I'd be a better person if I just let things happen?"

"Leah, you're a fine person just the way you are. Your instinct is to fight change to keep yourself safe. Only you can tell when—or even if—it's time to embrace change instead of take arms against it."

I stared at him, once again surprised by the uncanny ability of this elderly, childless, celibate man to see so clearly into the worries and fears that roil in my murky subconscious.

Then I kissed him on the top of his head, thanked him for the tea, and went home to bed.

55

"Well?"

"Well what, Miguel?" I had been sitting on my window seat with a cup of coffee, staring blankly at the street below when he called.

"Well, how is Gabe? Are you home or at his house? I waited until eleven o'clock to call you in case you had a late night of romance."

"I didn't have a late night. There was no romance. And Gabe has a five-year-old son."

"What? Do you mean he's fostering one? No! He didn't adopt a son, did he? Without telling anybody?"

"No, he's not fostering and he didn't adopt. He got Dominic the old-fashioned way. But he didn't know it until a couple of months ago. I just found out yesterday."

I quickly gave him the facts to stem the tide of questions.

"This is so *fabuloso!* A family! Gabe is a father and you—"

"No."

"No?"

"Don't say it. Dominic has a mother, and it's not me."

"I wasn't going to say that, but the three of you will have so much fun together. You and Gabe and Dominic, you can—"

"Miguel, I'm not quite as excited about this as Gabe is—or you, apparently. I'm happy that Gabe's happy, but I'm kind of feeling like I got caught up in a whirlwind and I don't know where I'm going to land. I'm still processing. Let's leave it for now."

Miguel is nothing if not sensitive to mood.

"Okay, *chica*. What did Kent say to you when you caught up with him yesterday?"

When I finished telling him, he said, "Do you think that Kent is right, that Wes killed himself?"

"It seems unlikely to me. And there are easier ways to kill yourself than with a rifle to the chest."

"That is true. And for us, it doesn't really matter, does it? Either way he's dead, right?"

"That's refreshingly callous of you, my uber-nice friend. But you're right. The manner of death—accidental or suicide—doesn't matter that much to us, though it does to Kent. When will the autopsy be done?"

"Today, the sheriff said."

"Sunday? Wow. Well, I guess important people—or brothers of important people—get special treatment. I wonder if Lamey knows that Kent and his wife donated to Coop's campaign, and that all his toadying is for naught? It would be fun to tell him, but I don't think Coop would like that. All right, I better go. Gabe will be here in a minute."

"Is it a secret? That Gabe has a son?"

"No, it's not. Fly, be free, to spill all the tea you want about that."

"So, where does that leave us?" Gabe asked.

We'd spent almost an hour trying to figure things out and struggling to see each other's point of view.

"About where we were when we started, I guess. I understand that you want to be there for Dominic, and that you have a lot of lost time to make up for. I'd be disappointed if you felt any other way."

"And I know you're leery about the way it's going to change things."

I noted that he had said "know" instead of understand.

"You wanted me to be honest, right? I'm aware my feelings and fears don't cast me in the best light, but they're real."

"I have some fears and feelings, too, Leah."

"Okay, tell me."

"I've seen you with other people's kids. You're good with them. You were great with Dominic yesterday. He thinks you're great, too, by the way. So what I'm afraid of is that you're using this to pull away from our relationship."

"Gabe, no. I'm not doing that. I don't know how many other ways to explain it, but let me try once more. I love being with you. You're funny, and smart, and kind. I trust you. I rely on you, even—and I don't on very many people. I don't want to lose—"

"Leah, you won't lose me."

"Actually, I was going to say I don't want to lose *us*. And adding Dominic into the mix—which you need to do, and I want you to do—it complicates things. You can't deny that."

"Complications and change are what life is about. Why does that scare you so much?"

"Because I'm emotionally stunted? I don't know why, Gabe. It just does. So, I think we should—"

He leaned forward and looked intently at me, his eyebrows drawn together in a worried frown.

"We should what? Take a break? Break up?"

"No! I was going to say we should just do our best and see what happens. With the caveat that my best isn't all that good sometimes."

He blew out his breath audibly and then smiled.

"I can do that. We can do that. And I promise not to push you too hard —which I know I can do sometimes."

"All right, then, I think we're good."

"Not just yet. Come here, please."

I got up and walked to the stool where he sat. He turned and pulled me half onto his lap, and then gave me a very attentive kiss. Which led to several more. I pulled him to his feet, turned on some music, and we went to bed.

"It doesn't get much better than this," he said as we lay in bed, listening to an afternoon rainstorm hit the windows.

"Don't get too comfortable," I said, lifting my head from his shoulder to look at the clock. "It's two o'clock. How long is Patty able to watch Dom?"

He shot straight up and reached for his clothes.

"I told her I'd be back by two-thirty. She has her granddaughter's recital to go to. I didn't tell you about my visit with Ricky yet."

"Welcome to parenting, I guess. Talk fast."

"He gave me the same answers he did when you and Miller saw him. He's a pretty scared kid, and I didn't sugarcoat it. He needs to be. I think I can get him out on bail. Jancee didn't have a family who would oppose it, and Ricky's willing to submit to GPS monitoring, or even strict in-house arrest. The issue will be bail. His uncle is ready to mortgage his house, and it will probably take that, because the judge is sure to set it high."

"I hope Jerry can manage it. Getting Ricky out of there would be a huge boost to his state of mind. And there's no way he's a flight risk. Where would he go?"

"I agree. Meanwhile, if you can get Owen Fike to take your Wes theory seriously, that could change the whole picture. Even if he won't, I can use it to build an alternate theory of the crime for Ricky's defense. Those sequins in his truck were the find that resulted in Ricky's arrest. But Wes could be the one who put them there. He had easy access to Ricky's truck. And from what you say about the layout at Kent's cabin, Wes also had easy access to hooking up with Jancee that night."

"Yes, but if that doesn't work out, don't forget about Monroe. He still might figure in this."

He smiled.

"Always have a backup, don't you?"

"I try. And I had another thought."

"I'm not surprised."

"I might have more power to persuade Owen—and definitely to get to Lamey—if I could get Kent to see the possibility that Wes killed Jancee."

"That seems like a pretty big stretch, even for you. Kent did just lose his only brother."

"I know, and he's feeling guilty about it. But if Wes killed Jancee, I think that could ease Kent's guilt quite a lot. Obviously, I'll wait until after the funeral, but I'm going to put some polish on the theory and try to approach Kent."

"Well, if anyone can do it, you can. I've got a good feeling about things all of a sudden. Ricky, Dominic, you and me. We'll make it work, Leah. All of it."

Several things happened on Monday.

A press release from the sheriff's office pronounced the investigation into the death of Wes Morgan closed. The manner of death was accidental, and the cause of death was a gunshot wound to the chest.

Bail was set and Ricky Travers was released with a GPS ankle monitor and instructions from Gabe to lie low and not to talk to anyone from the sheriff's office or *GO News* without Gabe present.

But the most important thing that occurred was that Troy regained consciousness.

"He is very confused still," Miguel said, reporting from the hospital in Madison. "But he woke up, and he knew his name and he recognized his family, too. But he doesn't remember anything about the hit and run, and he doesn't even know why he was on the road."

"But that's normal, right?"

"Yes, yes. They did some tests with him, and his mother told me the doctor is very pleased, and it looks good."

Relief swept through me with a force that almost made my knees buckle. I must have been holding even more anxiety in check than I realized.

"That's great, Miguel. I can't wait for the chance to see him. I'll spread the word here. Oh, by the way, you did an excellent job spilling the tea about Gabe's son. So far today Allie and my mother have offered their services as babysitters. Courtnee warned me that Gabe will probably dump me, because he'll want someone who's nice and can cook now that he has a kid. And Miss Fillhart at the library asked if I wanted to sign him up for after-school story hour."

"What did Coop say?"

"You know Coop, not much. But he did offer to hook Dominic up with a ride in a police car. That kind of pull may outweigh my lack of niceness and cooking skills and keep me in the running as Gabe's girlfriend."

"I think maybe Gabe is more the one who has to worry than you. Am I right, *chica*?"

"It's a big change and Gabe and I both know it. We'll see what happens. Right now, I'm happy, and Gabe is happy, and I hope Dominic is, too. That's all I can say."

56

Wes's funeral was held at the Whitman Funeral Chapel in Omico. I arrived just before it started and slipped into a folding chair in the last row. Next to, as it happened, Wes's office manager, Sandy. There wasn't time for more than a quick hello before the service started.

It was a short and simple ceremony with some readings from the Bible, a few of the usual funeral songs, and then a time for people to share memories of Wes. The service was sparsely attended. The sheen of success the well-attired men and bejeweled women possessed made me think that most of the attendees were Kent's friends, who had come out of respect and friendship for him, not for Wes.

Only two people felt moved to stand and say something about Wes when the minister offered the opportunity. One man talked about Packers trivia night, and how Wes liked to cheat. In a similar vein, the other man who spoke appeared slightly intoxicated and told a rambling story about Wes stealing his girlfriend in high school. I made a mental note to request that the speakers at my funeral be carefully vetted, so there'd be no impromptu, unflattering revelations.

On the way out, Sandy walked beside me.

"Are you going to the cemetery for the graveside service?"

"No," I said.

"I don't want to go either. Those things give me the willies. I came to the funeral with Brian, he was the site manager for Wes. He wants to go to the cemetery. Do you think you could give me a ride back to the office?"

"Sure, no problem."

"I feel sadder than I expected," she said, once we got in the car. "Wes had so many chances and he just pissed them all away. He was married, you know, but divorced before I ever came to work for him. Had a kid, too. I think she's in high school. How bad would it feel to have your own kid not care enough to come to your funeral?"

"Pretty bad. I guess it's a good thing he's dead, or he might be really depressed."

She looked at me sideways. She started to giggle, and then to laugh, and I did, too. Not because it was funny that Wes had died, or hilarious that no one cared. We laughed to reassure ourselves, to assert our own "aliveness." It was a way of whistling past the graveyard, knocking on wood, being grateful that this time around, it wasn't our turn, but knowing that one day it would be.

"What's going to happen to Wes's business?" I asked when we had sobered up.

"I knew it was in bad shape, but I guess it's worse than I even thought. His brother is the executor of his estate—not that there's much of one, I guess. Kent's going to have the lawyer file for bankruptcy. He asked me to organize the files and label and box them up. So, I'll get another week's pay out of it, I guess. Hey, I heard about Ricky Travers being arrested for killing that dancer. That's a shocker. What's going on with that?"

"Ricky was a friend of hers, and he was with her the night she died. They found some other evidence that pointed to him, and so now he's charged with murder."

"I would never have thought Ricky had it in him. I guess you never know."

"What about Wes, do you think he had it in him? It turns out he knew the dancer pretty well."

"Wes? Nah. He yelled at the guys a lot, and he liked to poke the bear, but I never saw him get violent or anything."

"What do you mean, 'poke the bear?' "

"Oh, you know, tease people in their sore spot. He could say some real mean things, then laugh like that made it okay. He was always riding one of the guys, Darryl, who's kind of overweight. You could tell it made Darryl feel bad, but Wes never let up. He sure didn't like it, though, if you teased him like I did a couple weeks ago."

"Yeah? What happened?"

"I was in early and I didn't think anyone else was there. I went to get something in Wes's office, and there he was lying flat on his back on the floor. He had his mouth open, he was snoring to beat the band, and he was cuddling an empty bottle next to him like it was a baby. I took a picture with my phone before I shook him awake. I showed it to him, and told him I was gonna put it on the bulletin board in the break room with the title, *Our Fearless Leader*. I was just kidding, but he got so mad! Grabbed the phone right out of my hand and deleted the picture. I think if he could've shot me, he would've. Oh!"

She put her hand to her mouth as she realized it wasn't the best choice of words given the circumstances. She was saved from stammering out an unnecessary apology when her phone rang.

"Hello? Yes. All right. I'll pick you up at Hayley's at five. Bye, hon."

"Your daughter?"

"Yes. She's ten going on thirty. I'm not looking forward to the teen years. You don't have kids, do you?"

"No, I don't."

"I love mine to pieces, but a word of advice: don't have one until you're sure that there's nothing in the whole world that you want more. Because trust me, after they're born, you won't have time for anything else ever. Well, I'm hoping that when she actually *is* thirty, I might."

I pulled up to the door and Sandy hopped out. She leaned back in before she shut the door. "Thanks, Leah, I appreciate it. Hope you get that next book out soon, I'm dying to read it."

"You sound like my agent. I'm working on it, Sandy. Nice seeing you again."

"Same here."

Sandy's description of the all-consuming responsibility of having a child was timely as well as a little disturbing. At present, I had quite a few things that I enjoyed doing, and I definitely did not feel an all-consuming desire to give them up in exchange for unplanned parenthood.

My phone rang and I punched the button on my steering wheel to pick it up, but nothing happened. Then I realized the sound was coming from the floor on the passenger side. It wasn't my phone I'd heard. It was Sandy's. It must have fallen out of her pocket or purse. I turned the car around and drove the few blocks back to return it to her.

She looked up in surprise from the boxes that surrounded her as I came through the door.

"Leah, what are you doing here?" She stood in the middle of the outer office, surrounded by boxes.

"You forgot your phone," I said, holding it out to her, then looking around.

"Oh, thank you! I'd be lost without it."

"Man, Sandy, you said you'd have another week's pay coming for packing up the office. From the looks of things, you might have another month."

"Yeah, it's kind of overwhelming right now. And I can't just toss things anywhere. I have to separate the business stuff from the personal stuff and keep everything in order. So I have to look at everything and at least skim it before I file it away. I got most of the stuff out of Wes's office and carried it here. This box is all junk I pulled from his shelves and his filing cabinet. You can't believe all the Packers stuff. Key chains, bobble heads, football programs, autographed pictures. I called Kent to see if he wanted any of it. I thought it might be sentimental to him. You know, because it meant so much to Wes. But he said no. He didn't even want that picture."

She pointed to the one on the wall I'd noticed the first time I came. The one with Kent and Wes, two young guys together in their matching Packers jackets, grinning their heads off with no idea how things would end for one of them.

"Yeah. Wes told me his 'game of the century' story the first time I was here. Maybe it's just too hard for Kent to see how they were then, and how things are now. You could always keep it and ask again in a few months before you throw it out."

"That's a good idea. You don't know anybody that would like any of the Packers stuff, do you?"

An image of Father Lindstrom's Packers mug came to mind.

"You know, maybe I do."

"Great, just take the whole box with you. Toss anything you don't want. It'll be one less thing for me to trip over in here."

"All right, I will, thanks."

57

As I drove by the *GO News* building, I glanced over as I always do when passing by, in the hope that by focusing the strength of all my mental powers I can cause it to burst into a ball of smoke and sulfur. It didn't, but it would have been a particularly opportune time if it had. Walking out of the back door was a tall man wearing sunglasses and a baseball cap that covered most of his curly brown hair. However, there was nothing he could do to hide his retro mustache or his swagger. Monroe Mepham.

I turned at the corner, but before I even got into the parking lot he was climbing into a dark green truck and squealing the tires as he sped away. I made a quick call.

"*GO News*, how can I help you?"

"Is Monroe still there? This is his wife Tabitha," I said.

"No, you just missed him."

"Okay, thanks."

All right, I'd verified that my eyes had not deceived me. That had been Monroe. I wondered if he really had been in Kentucky when I talked to Cole and had just now returned. Or had he been around all the time, lying low, waiting for the right time to resurface. If so, was it Wes's death or Ricky's arrest that made now the right time?

I had told Coop that I didn't feel like I was missing pieces of the story I was tracking. Instead, I felt like I had too many. I couldn't tell which ones mattered, and which ones didn't. Was Monroe a crucial piece that could provide the frame I needed to fill in all the rest of the puzzle? Or was he just an extra, unnecessary distraction?

I put those thoughts aside. I had a Zoom meeting with Clinton and my publicist at Clifford &Warren Publishing at four o'clock. The subject was increasing my engagement on social media to boost sales of my second book. Since I had done almost nothing in that area with my former publisher, I needed to prep and pay attention.

<hr />

After my meeting, I went to my mother's for dinner. I knew that along with the salmon, I, too, would be in for a grilling, in my case about Gabe and Dominic. It was late when I got home, but I wasn't ready for bed.

I poured a short Jameson over ice, turned on the fireplace, and sat down on the window seat. I tried clearing my mind. I focused on breathing. Any thoughts that arose in my mind, I simply observed, but did not attach. I viewed them as though they were clouds floating by in the sky.

That lasted about thirty seconds. Then I gave in and wrestled one of the ideas drifting by to the ground where I could really dig into it.

Maybe it really was Monroe after all.

I spent some time seriously trying to put flesh on the bones of that idea.

Monroe and Jancee had a thing once. He could have persuaded her to meet him for a last-time hook-up when she finished at Kent's. One final fling with Monroe might have appealed to her. And then Monroe tried once more to charm her out of her money, or to play on her sympathy. When neither worked, he threatened her. When that didn't work, he killed her, and took her money.

Then he figured out—or maybe his brother-in-law Cole helped him figure out—how to make sure suspicion didn't fall on him. First, he gave *GO News* the photos of Dan and Dewey what's-his-name fighting over Jancee's honor. That provided a distraction. But Owen Fike was too smart to fall for Lamey's politically motivated interest in Dan as a suspect.

Monroe settled on Ricky as the real target—or, again, Cole helped him figure that out. Everyone knew Ricky was crazy about Jancee, and she didn't treat him very well. That made a nice set-up for a jealous anger motive. Monroe told Owen about seeing Ricky and Jancee together in Ricky's truck. Who knew if he really had or not? Ricky provided some bonus help by lying at every turn because he was so scared. Could Monroe have also provided the information that Ricky had once lived on the property where Jancee's body was found? I could check that out with Ross.

The video of Ricky's wild drive to Kent's that night fell into Owen's lap, and proved that for Monroe, anyway, it really was better to be born lucky than smart. His *pièce de résistance* was putting the sequins in the back of Ricky's truck. He could have done that anytime—when Ricky's truck was in the parking lot at Morgan Construction, or at Tanner's, or in his uncle's driveway. The sequins provided the key piece of physical evidence that clinched Ricky's guilt in Owen's eyes. If the video hadn't come to light, a timely anonymous phone call could have directed Owen Fike's attention to the need to examine Ricky's truck. I took the last swallow of my Jameson. I looked at my theory this way and that, let it hang out in my mind for a while. It was possible, but what were the holes?

I was a little too tired and too Jamesoned to think it through again. Still, it might hang together with a little more effort.

Then again, it might not.

58

Coop called me at nine the next morning.

"I've got an interview with Andrea Novak this morning for a *GO News* profile. Any advice?"

"Yes. Don't do it. She is not your friend, Coop. Why did you agree to an interview?"

"I couldn't tell her no. She's doing one on all the candidates up and down the ballot, not just Art and me. It would look pretty bad if I didn't agree."

"I suppose. Don't let her trick you into saying anything she can turn against you. Be your strong, silent self. Not all reporters are as nice as I am."

"Noted. What are you up to today?"

"I had a brainstorm last night. I'm going to think about it some more. I'd like to run it by you before I get Gabe's hopes up for Ricky's defense. It sort of hangs together. But I know there are some holes. And I know how much you like finding the flaws in my theories."

"Just trying to make them better. When do you want to talk? How about a beer at McClain's around eight?"

"Sure. I should be doing my 'real job' today, anyway, I guess. I'll do some writing this morning and then later I'll see if I can put a little polish on my ideas before I spring them on you. Good luck with Andrea."

I met Gabe for lunch at noon. I mentioned that I was working on an idea that might help Ricky. Normally, he would have asked for more detail. But this time his mind was more on Dominic than defense work. The woman he had hired to take care of Dom after school had just informed him that Friday would be her last day because she'd been offered a full-time job.

"She came with great recommendations, and Dominic really likes her. Now I don't know what to do."

"Maybe you should try a daycare center. He'd have other kids to play with. You could call Jennifer Pilarski. Her kids go to one she really likes."

"Thanks, that's a good idea. I was trying to keep things sort of like his old routine. With Lucy not having an outside job, Dom's used to going home after school. But a daycare center might actually provide more stability to his routine than part-time babysitters. Besides, I'm sure he'll be going to one in New York when Lucy takes him home. I guess it won't hurt him to get used to the idea while he's here. How about coming over for pizza tonight with us? He's got a new dinosaur book he wants to show you."

"Sure, that sounds nice."

"Maybe we can talk about your idea for Ricky after Dominic goes to bed."

"I have to leave about then. I'm meeting Coop for a beer at McClain's. You want to co—"

I realized before I finished that of course he couldn't come.

"Sorry, that was dumb. Of course you can't come. What's your morning like tomorrow? I could come by the office."

His face brightened. "Ten o'clock would be great."

"All right, but I'll see you tonight at six for pizza and dinosaurs."

When I got home, I noticed the box of Packers goodies Sandy had given me still sitting on the bar. I carried it over to the couch and began going through it. I found some vintage stuff that I knew Father Lindstrom would like—a monthly football magazine in mint condition with a photo of Bart

Starr on the cover, a Green Bay Packers mug imprinted with a football schedule from the nineties, and a key chain with a helmet ornament proclaiming *Go Packers!*

Near the bottom of the box was a football program from the January 2004 Packers/Seahawks game. That was the one featured in the Wes and Kent photo that Kent didn't want. Father Lindstrom might enjoy the official program from the game. Wes had said it was "legendary." I tossed it in the keep pile.

The last thing I took out was an accordion file folder. It looked like newspaper clippings in all of the sections. I pulled one out, expecting it to be a feature about a favorite player or an especially great game Wes wanted to remember.

It wasn't.

After I read the first article, I began pulling out the rest. All of them, and there were at least twenty, some from a small weekly paper, some from the *Green Bay Gazette*, covered the unfolding story of a young woman who had been strangled in the small town of Sherwood sixteen years ago. Her name was Tessa Miles. Several of the bylines belonged to my friend Linda Linkul.

I read all the clips that Wes had so meticulously saved, my thoughts racing.

When I finished, I called Linda. After we hung up, I went through all my notes to confirm that I was on the right track. Then I made one last call.

"Hi, Leah. Don't ask me to take back that box of Packers junk I gave you, because the office looks even more like a disaster area today than it did yesterday."

"No, Sandy, it's something else I want to ask you."

"Okay, what?"

"You said that Wes was hungover, sleeping on the floor when you came in to work a couple of Tuesdays ago. Do you remember which Tuesday that was?"

"The twelfth. Why?"

"Did you have the impression that he'd been there all night?"

"Well, yeah. He was wearing the same clothes he had on the day before. Why? Is it important?"

"Maybe. I'm not sure yet. Thanks. Good luck with the cleanup."

The "little Podunk town" where Wes and Kent had stopped the night of the Packers/Seahawks game, the one Wes had told me was "wall-to-wall green and gold" that night, where everyone was laughing and buying the two Morgan brothers drinks—it was Sherwood. They'd been at Harvey's Wonder Bar, where Tessa Miles was working.

Wes was the tall blond customer Tessa Miles had taken home from Harvey's Wonder Bar in Sherwood. He had sex with her, and he choked her, and he had killed her. Just as he had Jancee.

I stood still, closed my eyes, and imagined that night in Harvey's Wonder Bar sixteen years ago.

Wes and Kent stopping in Sherwood for a beer on their way home from the game. Everyone there is friendly, drinking, laughing, flirting, caught up in the victory celebration. Tessa is, too. She enjoys the excitement and she enjoys Wes's attention.

He asks and she agrees to take him home with her. Maybe she doesn't mind or she even enjoys BDSM. But things go wrong. Wes is less experienced then. He isn't skilled at taking "breath play" to the edge, but not over. He doesn't mean to kill her —but he does.

What is Kent doing while this is happening? Waiting at the bar for Wes's call to pick him up?

When Wes realizes that Tessa is dead, he panics. He runs out of the house. He calls Kent to come for him. Wes is the tall blond man on his cell phone, pacing in Tessa's driveway as Linda's witness leaves her lover's house.

Does Wes tell Kent what he has done? Or does Kent find out when the story about the murdered waitress in Sherwood runs in the paper? Wes says it was an accident. She wanted it. I didn't mean to hurt her. Please, help me.

"I promised my mother that I would always look out for Wes."

That's what Kent had told me. He had kept that promise through all the years, and all the mistakes, and all the trouble Wes had gotten himself into. He had even kept it when Wes killed again. Wes didn't spend the night at the cabin. He had killed Jancee, and then he had gone to his office and drunk himself into a stupor. Kent had lied.

But now it was Ricky's life, Ricky's freedom that was in danger. And Wes was gone. It was time for Kent to stop protecting his baby brother.

59

It was just after five when I parked my car at the locked entrance and began walking the track to Kent's cabin. The afternoon light was leaving. The branches of the tall, bare trees began clacking in the wind as I hurried down the path.

A truck was parked in front of the cabin, not Kent's white Escalade. I hoped no one else was there. When I'd called and he told me to meet him, he hadn't mentioned anyone else being at the cabin.

He opened the door almost immediately in response to my knock. He had dark circles under his eyes, and held a whiskey glass in his hand.

"Kent, hi. I don't see your Escalade. Is someone else here?"

"No, it's around back. I use the truck for hauling things. I was working on a new tree stand today. I can't go back to the old one."

"Sure, of course not."

"Where's your car?" he asked. Then he realized what had happened. "I'm so sorry, Leah. I meant to unlock the gate for you. I'm not functioning very well, I guess. You should have called me to come down."

"No, no, that's fine. It's not that far. I'm sorry to bother you so soon after the funeral. I wouldn't have if it wasn't important."

"So you said on the phone."

He seemed to realize then that I was still standing out in the cold.

"Please, come in, come in."

I followed him through the door. He pointed toward the sofa.

"Can I get you something to drink?"

"No, I'm fine, thanks."

When we were both seated, I said, "I don't know how to ease into this, Kent. So, I'll just start. I know that Wes killed a waitress in Sherwood sixteen years ago—the night of the big Packers game against the Seahawks. And I know you covered for him."

His expression shifted from one of patient listening to shock and denial.

"Please, don't deny it. Just let me tell you what I know, and how I know, and why it's so important that you realize it's time to stop protecting Wes."

I laid out for him everything I had put together—the game, the bar, Tessa, Wes's call for help that night. His part in covering it up. And Jancee.

He had put his glass on the table next to him, and all the while I talked he sat with his chest bent over, his elbows resting on his knees, his head looking down, cradled in his hands. When I finished he was quiet. Then he sat up straight, took a long swallow of his drink, and began to speak.

"I didn't want him to leave the bar with her, but what was I going to do? They were both adults. I waited for a while at the bar. Wes was supposed to call me to pick him up. The longer I waited the madder I got. Finally I decided to let him find his own way home. I left. But when he called, I turned around and went back after him.

"He was a little drunk when I picked him up at the girl's house. He didn't say much and neither did I. I was still angry at him. Then a couple of days later, I read the story about the waitress, and I saw her picture in the paper. I couldn't believe it. But I knew Wes was the one. I confronted him. He told me he didn't mean to hurt her. They were doing some kind of sexual fantasy role-playing. It was fine, she was into it, he said. But then it wasn't fine.

"He had choked her too hard. He didn't stop soon enough. He begged me not to tell. He was only twenty-one. He wasn't even out of college. His whole life would have been ruined for something he didn't mean to do."

"Tessa's life was more than ruined, Kent. It was taken from her."

"You think I don't know that? That I haven't agonized over it? But Wes was my brother. And my mother asked me, literally on her deathbed, to take care of him. But I've lived with a terrible guilt ever since."

He shook his head.

"It's why I've kept bailing him out all these years. What I had done, the lie I had told for him, it would all be a waste unless I could help him do something with his life. I let everybody think that I was the generous, forgiving brother, always there for Wes. Even my wife thinks that. But I was really always there for myself, trying to make myself believe that I could be forgiven for what I had done, if I could make Wes a better man."

"You did it again when he killed Jancee. You covered for him again. When did you know he was the one who killed her?"

He didn't look at me while he spoke this time.

"I suspected right after her body was found. I asked him, but he swore he didn't do it. He said it must have been whoever picked her up from the cabin. I couldn't see any reason why he would have done it. I knew that he still enjoyed different ..."

He hesitated.

"Different forms of sexual play. But he was older, more experienced. There had never been a recurrence of the accident with Tessa. When he told me that after we argued he'd gone back to his office and got drunk and fell asleep, I believed him."

"Did you, really? Or did you just ignore everything but your need to take care of Wes?"

He went on as though I hadn't said anything.

"I didn't want all of the others at the poker game to be dragged into the middle of things because of Wes. So I agreed when Wes said we should all keep quiet. But then Lewis Webber called and told me that you knew Jancee had been here, and that he was going to the police. That's when Wes asked me to say he'd spent the night here, so he'd have an alibi. I agreed, because I believed him when he said he didn't do it."

"Did you know that Jancee worked on the side as an escort and that Wes was a private client of hers who enjoyed choking her?"

"I knew he paid different women at times. I didn't know specifically about Jancee Reynolds. I suppose you know everything then. And it won't be long until it's public. Have you already spoken to the police?"

"No, I haven't spoken to anyone about it. I only figured it out just before I came here. But I don't know everything, Kent. I don't know how you could let Ricky Travers be arrested for something you knew Wes had done."

"But I told you, I didn't know that! I believed him. I was glad when the evidence began to come out about Ricky Travers. It seemed to prove that Wes was telling me the truth. I held on to that belief until today."

"What happened?"

"Sandy, Wes's office manager, called and said that there was a drawer in Wes's desk that was locked and she didn't have the key. I told her I'd take care of it. Frankly, I was afraid Wes might have kept pornography locked up there and I didn't want Sandy to see it. I stopped by the office this afternoon, but what I found was worse than pornography."

"What was it?"

He left the room without answering me but was back in a minute and held something out to me in the palm of his hand. It was a small plastic case of red sequins. I looked up and Kent met my eyes.

"Sequins seem to have played a big role in this, haven't they? The sequins on Jancee's dress, the one you found on Troy's hair, the three in the back of Ricky Travers' pickup, and this box in my brother's locked drawer."

"Wes planted them in Ricky's truck."

He nodded.

"When I saw them, I knew. Wes had killed Jancee and then tried to set up Ricky Travers for her murder. And there were other things that fell into place then."

"Like what?"

"After everyone left that night, I noticed a light on in the garage. When I checked, the small lamp I have on the work bench was on, and a stool was pulled out facing the window. I didn't remember turning the light on. I rarely use it. And it was odd that the stool was pulled out that way. But I dismissed it, like you do when something doesn't make sense, but it doesn't seem important."

"Jancee did it, waiting for Wes to come out and take her wherever they had planned to go after the party," I said.

"Yes, I think so. I paid Jancee and sent her away early. I assumed she had her own car parked in the back. But Wes must have been her ride. He spoke to her after I did. I thought he was apologizing for me cutting her time short. He must have been telling her to wait for him in the garage where it was warm. When I found the sequins, things came into focus. I realized what Wes had done. That he had been working to focus attention on Ricky, so that it wasn't on him. Those sequins proved it to me. You cannot imagine the feeling when that realization hit me."

We were both silent for a moment. Then he said, "Well, what happens now?"

"I think you know, Kent. It's time to tell the truth. I'd like you to come with me to see Detective Fike. I have the clippings about Tessa and all my notes in my car. I'll lay out the story for him, and with you to back it up, I think Ricky will be all right. Though you may not be."

"I understand that. I should have done this a long time ago. I'll get my coat."

It occurred to me to mention that he might want to get his lawyer, too. I thought better of it. A lawyer would definitely advise him not to be as candid with the police as he had been with me. If he was too distraught to think of that himself, why should I tell him?

60

I shivered as we walked the few steps to his pickup. He turned on the engine, then set the heater on full blast while we settled in. I reached around to pull my seatbelt down. An insistent beeping began as I felt for, but couldn't find, the latch to click the belt into place.

"Sorry," I said, "I can't seem to find the bottom thingy to buckle it up."

"It gets lost down in the seat sometimes. Here, let me turn on the overhead light so you can see." As he did, he added, "I know you're cold, but I need to open the windows for a minute, the windshield is fogging up."

"That's okay," I said. I pushed my hand deep into the crevice between the back of the car seat and the cushion on which I sat.

"Finally," I said as I grasped the end of the seatbelt and tugged it out. Something else came along with it. I gasped when I saw what it was—a delicate gold necklace. A fairy charm embedded with a tiny diamond winked and sparkled in the light as it twirled from the chain I held in my hand.

Summer's necklace. The one Jancee had worn the night she died.

Kent looked up from fiddling with the heating controls. He smiled.

"You found it! My daughter's favorite necklace. She was heartbroken when she lost it. She'll be so happy to get it back."

"It's very pretty."

I forced myself to smile as I handed it to him. My thoughts were rapidly reassembling themselves into a very different conclusion.

Kent. Not Wes.

I had the wrong brother. Kent had killed Jancee and Tessa, not Wes. He wasn't going to the sheriff's office with me. He was going to kill me.

If it were just Jancee, he could have taken the lifeline I threw him by suspecting Wes and finessed things. He could have used my flawed theory and a good lawyer to keep himself from any real consequences. But by bringing Tessa into the mix, I had made that impossible. With Tessa there were fingerprints, DNA. They wouldn't match Wes, but they'd show a familial link, and that would lead directly to Kent. And of course I had stupidly told him that I hadn't told anyone else yet what I'd figured out, that I hadn't given any information to the police, and that all my files were in my car just waiting for him to destroy.

I wriggled around on the seat as though getting comfortable to cover the fact that I was reaching into my pocket for my phone. When my fingers wrapped around it, I pressed the side and volume button and thought, *Thank you, Miguel, for insisting on setting up emergency SOS on my phone.*

I continued to hold the buttons in a tight grip, as though the harder I pushed them the faster the automatic call to 911 would go through.

Then, a *whoop, whoop* noise shrieked out from my pocket. Shit! I forgot about the warning that comes on to give you a chance to cancel an accidental call. I yanked the phone out of my pocket.

"What's that? What are you doing?"

Kent's voice was no longer pleasant.

"Just a text coming in," I babbled.

"Give me that phone."

He moved to grab it.

I flipped around and curled my body over my hand to protect it from him. He grabbed my hair and yanked my head back so hard I yelled and dropped the phone. He dove for it, but I reached it first and hurled it out the window.

He pulled his hand back and struck me hard across the cheek. Tears sprang to my eyes.

"I texted 911. As long as it's on, they'll know exactly where I am."

I hoped like hell Kent was too tech-deficient to know that my phone didn't have to be on. Along with the text, the phone had sent my exact location to emergency services. As long as I stayed in this general area, they'd find me. But I needed Kent to run after my phone to turn it off in order to give me the chance to break free.

He hit me again, this time with a closed fist. My head jerked back and I moaned. I covered my nose with my hands to stem the blood that spurted from it. He pulled a flashlight from under his seat and leaped from the truck, running toward where I had thrown the phone.

But I wasn't hurt as badly as I had made it seem. As soon as he took off, I slipped out of the truck and took off down the track toward my car.

It was full-on dark with only a half-moon to light the way. The trail was full of holes and protruding roots that caused me to stumble and slip as I sprinted forward. Behind me I heard Kent let out an outraged roar as he discovered I was gone. I turned my head to look.

Bad idea.

I veered off the track, tripped, and fell. I was back on my feet in nanoseconds, like James Brown rising from the splits. I dashed forward again but I had lost valuable time. Kent's footfalls were crashing down the path behind me.

Jancee flashed into my mind. She must have run like this. Her heart had beat as fast as mine. Her breath had come in gasps like mine. Her will to escape had been as strong as mine. But she hadn't made it. She had been choked until her heart stopped beating and her lungs stopped breathing.

My own heart faltered for a second.

But I wasn't Jancee, running first in impossibly high heels, and then barefoot over rocky ground. I could do this. No one had come to help Jancee, but the police were on their way to me. *Unless when I tried to silence the phone, I'd cancelled the call.*

The gate was in front of me. My car just on the other side.

Kent's labored breathing came closer and closer. In seconds he'd be on me.

I pumped my arms and moved my legs so fast my feet barely touched the ground. My hands reached out for the gate. I vaulted onto it. With my right foot on the lowest rung, I swung my left leg up. As it reached the top, Kent seized my hair and pulled me back.

I twisted and elbowed him in the ribs. He grunted and fell and took me with him. I kneed him in the groin. It didn't have much power in it, but it was enough to slow him down.

I scrambled up and ran for the woods.

The ground was soft with decades of decayed vegetation that slowed my stride. I plunged deeper into the forest, but I couldn't catch my breath. I had to rest for a minute. Ahead of me was a huge fallen tree. At its base, a tangle of roots and dirt formed a large rounded shield. I ducked behind it to hide. Everything was quiet. I fought to slow my ragged breathing.

Where was Kent? I inched my head up and peered into the darkness. Suddenly, a beam of light pierced the woods and I saw him. He was standing just off the trail. He held a flashlight in one hand. In the other was a gun.

I shrank back, my heart thumping. I couldn't run anymore. But I had to run. I couldn't sit there waiting for him to kill me.

"I know these woods. I'll find you!"

I closed my eyes for a second. I could hear him moving deliberately through the trees. If I waited here, he would find me. If I ran, he would shoot me.

"I can hear you breathing. You're going to die, Leah. I'm going to put you where I should have put Jancee. In the bottom of a deep, cold gravel pit where no one will ever think to look for you."

An owl hooted overhead, startling us both. Kent swung his flashlight wildly upward and cursed the bird, but beneath his shout I heard something else. A very faint siren. Help was coming. I just had to stay alive for another minute. Anyone can hang on for just one minute more, right?

Kent began to walk forward again, moving the beam of his flashlight in wide sweeping arcs. I crouched down and grabbed up a fistful of dirt and gravel, the only weapon at hand. I stayed low, marking his progress by the light coming closer and closer. He would see the tree. He would know where I was hiding. But I would be ready.

He was within feet of me now. My right hand tensed. Every fiber of my being shouted Run! Run!

I willed myself to stay very still.

Suddenly, he was there!

"I see you. Come out."

He spoke with the snarl of a wild animal.

I continued crouching behind my shield of roots and dirt. He came closer. So close I could smell him—the acrid odor of sweat, and fear, and fury. He had reached the tree. He pointed the light right at me, waving his gun. I stood up. With a rapid motion I turned and flung the dirt and gravel with all the force I could muster directly into his face. As he flinched, I ran.

A bullet whizzed past my ear. I slammed to the ground and stayed there.

Sirens split the air. High beam headlights flooded the woods with light. I turned my head to watch. Cops piled out of cars, guns drawn, shouting, ordering Kent to drop his gun. Still I waited and I watched. I couldn't make myself stand until I saw him on his knees, hands clasped behind his head, a deputy pulling him roughly to his feet.

"Where is she? Where's Leah?"

That was Ross. He must be really worried about me, one part of my brain said. He called me Leah instead of Nash. I tried to answer, but nothing came out.

I pulled myself slowly to my feet and croaked, "Here. I'm over here."

"What the hell do ya think you're doin', Nash? How many damn times do I have to tell you? Stay in your own lane!"

I didn't take the reprimand to heart. Ross had delivered it immediately after enveloping me in a bear hug as I stumbled out of the woods.

"Take it easy. I called you, didn't I?" I asked with a weak smile.

"If you'd tell me what you're up to now and then, you wouldn't have to reach me by 911. Come on, lemme get you a blanket. You're shiverin' like a scared puppy."

I had no rejoinder to that, because I felt very much like a scared puppy just then.

The surge of adrenaline that had flooded my body over the last twenty minutes had abated and left me with the jitters. I gladly wrapped myself in the blanket Ross handed me and was about to step into the warmth of his SUV when two more vehicles pulled up. Coop leaped out of one as Miguel sprang from the other.

"Leah!" Coop shouted as he ran toward me.

"You're hurt," he said. He took my face in his hands and turned it gently, checking for the source of the blood that had dried on my face and my jacket.

Miguel was right behind him.

"What is happening?"

"No, no, she's all right," Ross said. "Just a bloody nose and some bruises, I imagine. I'm gonna take her in and get a statement. Try to find out why the hell Kent Morgan was chasin' her through the woods with a gun."

"A gun! You were shot, *chica*?"

"No, I'm fine. Thanks to you."

"Thanks to him?" Ross asked with pretend outrage. "I was the one who saved you."

"You came in the nick of time, Ross, but it was Miguel setting up the emergency thing on my phone that got you here."

"I told you, *chica*. I told you, you needed to set it up. But what did you say?"

"I said, 'I don't have time to fuss with it.' "

"And what did I say?"

"You said, 'Then I'll do it because if anyone is going to need an emergency SOS, it's you, *chica*.' Are you going to hold that over my head forever? Or is it enough for me to say that you were so, so right, and that you have my undying gratitude? I can go either way," I said.

He smiled. "It's enough."

"But why are you guys here?" I asked, looking at Coop and him.

"Because we're your emergency contacts. When you set the SOS up, you can make it so emergency contacts get a text that says you called 911, and where you are. We both got a text, and so here we are," Miguel said.

"Well, I'm just glad that you didn't include my mother on that. Oh! What time is it?"

"Almost six-thirty," Ross said. "Why? Ya gotta date? Cause I think you're gonna be kinda busy for the next few hours."

Ross and Owen Fike took my statement. Kent was in an interview room, waiting for his lawyer to arrive. Fortunately for all concerned, Lamey was speaking at a meeting of the Himmel Women's Club. By the time he was finished, I'd be gone. I didn't want to be there while they explained the arrest of Grantland County's most prominent citizen and my involvement in it.

I found Coop waiting for me when I finished around eight-thirty.

"Hey, you didn't have to wait. I can drive myself home."

"In what? Your car is still out at Kent Morgan's."

"Oh, yeah. I forgot. Do you want to take me out there to get it now?"

He looked at me for a second, surprised, then he shook his head and laughed.

"What?"

"You're something else, Leah."

"Something good, or something bad?"

"Mostly good. I'll take you to get your car tomorrow. Right now, Miguel and Gabe are waiting at your place. Miguel called your mother, too. We all want to hear how you got from Wes, to Monroe, back to Wes, and then made a hard right and came up with Kent."

61

We—Miguel, Gabe, Coop, and my mom—sat in my living room each with our drink of choice in hand. They'd all waited patiently while I showered and changed and ate a bowl of cereal.

"Okay, I'm ready for you. Ask me anything. With the caveat that what I'm telling you is part what I know for sure, and part what I finally pieced together, but I think it's mostly right."

They erupted with questions.

"How did you know Kent killed Jancee Reynolds?"

"Why did he murder Jancee?"

"What were you thinking going to confront a killer?"

"Why didn't you take me, *chica*?"

"Slow down, I can only do one at a time. Kent killed Jancee because he, not Wes, was her BDSM client. She tried to blackmail him to get the money she needed to leave Tanner's. But he knew he had to kill her, because he already had one extortionist bleeding him dry."

"Who?"

"His brother."

"Why was Wes blackmailing Kent? For what?"

"Because Kent killed Tessa Miles."

"Wait, who is Tessa Miles?"

"A waitress Kent strangled sixteen years ago. Wes helped him cover it up. Kent didn't clean up after Wes's screw-ups and failures because he was a kindhearted brother. He did it because Wes could prove Kent was a killer."

"No, no, no, *chica*. Go back. First Jancee, then Tessa Miles."

"When Jancee came dancing out to entertain the poker boys that night, she recognized Kent as her BDSM client right away. She could see the way he lived, how luxurious his 'cabin' was. She was a smart girl, and she realized that he might be willing to pay her a lot of money in order to keep his secret life secret. She approached Kent as though she were flirting, but she was telling him that they needed to talk. He knew what she meant, and he agreed. He paid her to 'leave' early, but he sent her to the garage to wait while he got rid of everyone else. He probably said he'd drive her home and they could talk along the way. But he already planned to kill her and dump her body in the gravel pit just over the county line road."

"He told you that?" my mother asked.

"More or less. He told me that's what he was going to do with me, and that it was what he should've done with Jancee."

She gasped.

"It's all right, Mom. He didn't, right? And he didn't dump Jancee's body there either because he couldn't. While he was driving her away from the cabin, something he did or said must have spooked her. She managed to get out of the truck and run, but he caught her and he killed her right in the field next to his cabin. He couldn't leave her there, he had to get her as far away from his place as possible. He tried to get her body to the abandoned gravel pit, but he couldn't."

"Why not?" my mother asked.

"Because there was a fatality on Rogers Road that night. It was very bad," Miguel answered. "It's why the sheriff's office didn't follow up on my friend Judy's video. The one with Ricky driving so crazy to Kent's cabin. Rogers Road is the only way to that gravel pit. Kent couldn't get there because of all the police. But also, he couldn't keep driving around with the body in his truck. So he took it to the nearest place he knew where nobody was, and that was the Seetons' property."

"Got it in one, Miguel," I said. "I bet if anyone checks, the Seetons are clients of Kent's. He'd know that they were away for the winter."

"Did Wes know about Kent and Jancee? About their arrangement, I mean."

"Not at first. Kent certainly wouldn't have confided in Wes. That would have given Wes something else to hold over his brother's head. And Jancee couldn't have told Wes, because I'm sure Kent didn't give her his real name. Actually, I think Troy is the way Wes found out. When Troy went to see Wes on his own, I think he asked him about the escort service Krystal Gerrard was running at Tanner's, and maybe even if he was Jancee's BDSM client. I think Wes made the connection to Kent and his past and called his brother to warn him—and to subtly, or maybe not so subtly, threaten him with his new cache of blackmail information."

"So then was it Kent, not Wes, who Troy was going to meet?" Miguel asked.

"I think it's pretty likely. And it could be that the truck Kent so kindly gave me a ride in tonight is what he used to take out Troy. Anyway, after his chat with Troy, Wes probably thought he was in a pretty good place. He could demand whatever he wanted from Kent, and Kent would have to give it to him. But Wes didn't realize that Kent had reached his limit, and he'd decided Wes had to go. I think the story Kent put out that Wes asked for a loan and that he'd finally said no was a lie. Wes probably did ask for some serious money. But Kent didn't say no, he told Wes to meet him at the property and they'd talk it over."

"Only he killed him instead, and made it look like a hunting accident. His own brother. What a terrible man," my mother said. "Leah, do you think Kent purposely tried to set up Ricky Travers to take the blame for Jancee's death?"

"I don't think that was his original idea. He was probably going to have Wes come into focus as Jancee's killer, and then get rid of him before he was arrested, so there was no chance he'd confess. That way both his problems, Jancee and Wes, were solved. It would look like Wes killed Jancee and then killed himself out of guilt or remorse.

"But when Ricky's lies and his bad luck focused Owen Fike's attention on him, it didn't matter that much to Kent. If Ricky took the fall instead of Wes, that was all right with Kent. But he still needed to get rid of his brother. Wes was getting worse. He drank too much, he talked too much, and he knew way too much. Kent would never be safe until Wes was dead. I think he decided to foster the idea that Ricky was guilty, and at the same time get Wes out of the way."

"Okay, now tell us who Tessa Miles is, and why Kent killed her," Coop said.

I took them through my friend Linda's quest to find justice for Tessa Miles, to the point where her dead end became my open door into solving Jancee's murder.

"Once I had Wes and Kent connected to Harvey's Bar on the night Tessa was killed, I started to see the whole picture. That's when I realized that Tessa's murder was linked to Jancee's. Before, I had wavered on whether Wes or Monroe had killed Jancee. But the Tessa information made me decide it must be Wes. I was absolutely sure after I remembered something that hadn't registered the first time I heard it."

"What was that, Leah?" Coop asked.

"After his funeral, Wes's office manager mentioned that when she came in early one Tuesday morning, Wes was sleeping off a hangover in his office. I checked the date with her. It was the morning after the party at Kent's house. It finally clicked—though again, I had the wrong brother. I thought it meant that Kent had covered for Wes because Wes had killed Jancee. Just like he'd covered for him years earlier when Wes had killed Tessa. That's when I went to see Kent, to tell him it was way past time to get Ricky out of jail for a crime Wes had committed. My theory was right, except that I had the wrong brother.

"And when I gave it to Kent, he told me exactly how Tessa's murder had gone down. It was almost too late when I finally realized the truth. That everything Kent had told me about Tessa's murder was true, except that he was the one who had committed it, not Wes."

"When did you know you got it wrong?" Gabe asked.

"When we were in the truck and I found the necklace Jancee wore the night she died. The only possible way it could have gotten there was that Jancee had been in the passenger seat of Kent's truck that night. Everything shifted then. I realized Kent was the killer, and that he was going to kill me. But I should have figured it out sooner."

"How?"

"Kent overplayed his hand. When I was talking to him at the cabin, he showed me a box of red sequins that he *said* he found in a locked drawer in Wes's office. He told me that when he saw it he realized that Wes had set Ricky up by planting the sequins. That he knew then that his brother was Jancee's real killer, not Ricky. But the cops haven't release anything about the sequins yet. The only way Kent could know about them is if he put them there himself."

"I'll say it again. What a terrible man! And what a dangerous one. I don't understand why you would go out by yourself to confront a murderer," my mother said again.

"Mom. I didn't think Kent was the killer, remember? I thought Wes was, and he was dead." A huge, unexpected yawn escaped me as I finished, followed quickly by another.

"Oh, hon, I'm sorry. Of course you're exhausted. We can talk more tomorrow. Come on, everyone, let's clear out and let Leah get to bed."

"Yes, you go to sleep, *chica*. I'll put a story up on the website. I just checked. *GO News* doesn't have anything yet. I'll follow up tomorrow."

I didn't object. There were hugs all around, and everyone left but Gabe.

"I'm sorry, Gabe. I really did want to have dinner with you and Dominic."

"More than you wanted to spend the evening being chased through the woods by a killer? I'm not sure I think that's much of a compliment."

He smiled, but I could tell something was upsetting him.

"You were awfully quiet this evening. That's not like you. What's going on?"

"No, there's nothing."

"Yes, there is. You're mad about something, aren't you? What is it?"

"I'm not mad, really. How could I be when I think about how this night might have ended? I'll admit, though, that it feels strange to know that you have Coop and Miguel as people to get an automatic text if you're in trouble, but not me. Shouldn't I be on that list?"

"Gabe. Miguel set that up, I didn't. He probably just didn't—"

"Just didn't think that you'd consider me as one of your close contacts, maybe your closest?"

"Come on. Don't be like that."

He sighed.

"You're right. I'm sorry. It's petty and childish. My only excuse is that it scared the hell out of me when Miguel told me Kent had chased you through the woods with a gun. And I feel terrible that I wasn't there for you. Forget everything I said before. Seriously."

He put his hand under my chin and tilted my face up before he kissed me lightly.

"You do keep a man on his toes, Ms. Nash."

"Would you like to stay a while longer? We can stare at the fire and not talk. Fair warning, I'll probably fall asleep on your shoulder."

"That sounds perfect, but I can't. Allie Ross is babysitting Dominic and it's after ten o'clock. Charlie will have my head if she's out much later on a school night. Would you like to come home with me?"

"Ah, no. I don't think Dominic's ready for that yet. And I'm pretty tired and a little sore. My own bed sounds good to me. Okay?"

"Sure, another night."

"Yes, another night."

He kissed me again before he left, but neither of us felt quite right about the ending.

62

"*Chica*! *Chica*! *Chica*! Wake up! We've got big news! Lots of news!"

My eyes flew open. Miguel was standing in my bedroom, his face inches from mine. His excitement charged the air around us. I bolted upright in bed.

"What? What is it? Is it Troy? Did something happen?"

"No. Yes! Part of it. First, the small news. Troy's notebook came in the mail yesterday. But when you almost got killed, I forgot about it."

"And?"

"And yes, he did talk to Wes about Jancee and escorts and BDSM."

"Did he have a meeting with Wes the morning he got hit?"

"Not with Wes. You were right. Kent called him. He asked Troy to meet at the Polka Dot Diner to talk off the record. Kent said he had learned something about Wes that worried him. And now Troy is all the way awake and he can tell us about it."

"That's great news, well worth waking me up for."

"But it's not the greatest. Guess what else came in the mail?"

He began waving a sheaf of papers in front of my face.

"This, this, this!"

"Okay, what is 'this?' "

"Here, read it!"

But as I reached out my hand, he snatched the papers back.

"No, it will take too long. I'll just tell you."

"Did you win the lottery or something? What is up with you? Will you chill for a minute?" I asked, laughing.

"It's the annual report for Girlzelles, LLC. For Tanner's!"

"I almost forgot all about that. Why are you so fired up?"

"Because, *chica*, one of the owners is Sheriff Lamey, and the other is Bruce Dengler, his friend that he wouldn't investigate. Now we have them both!"

"Say that again. Slowly."

"Sheriff Lamey and Bruce Dengler are the owners/members of the LLC that owns Tanner's. Joyce and Nadine at Tanner's were right. Krystal doesn't own it."

"Wait a second. The acting sheriff, the chief law enforcement officer of the county, owns a strip club? A strip club that's also involved in drug sales and escorts? Miguel! Coop is so going to be the next sheriff! There is no way Lamey recovers from this. It's not going to be too nice to be in Bruce Dengler's shoes either."

I had thrown off my covers and was grabbing my clothes as I talked.

"Okay, tell Maggie I'll be down in two minutes to work on this with you. We can get a front-page story together for today's print edition. We'll have enough news for a dozen front pages."

I paused long enough to rub my hand in his perfect hair while we both laughed like loons. Then I pulled his head down and kissed the top of it.

"You are the best ever!"

I ran into the bathroom and paid no attention to the sharp reminders my body gave me of the night before as I jumped in the shower.

The news that Acting Sheriff Arthur Lamey was the owner of a strip club began the collapse of his campaign for sheriff. We discovered that he had bought the club several years earlier with Bruce Dengler. They had kept Krystal on as manager and paid her a little more to front for them. She had acted as both the organizer and the registered agent for the LLC, which allowed Lamey and Dengler to hide their ownership from public view. Except from those persistent enough to dig into the annual report, which revealed that they were both the owners/members of Girlzelles.

That was just the first domino to fall. Miguel, Maggie, and I all worked on the reporting. By the time we were done, we had dancers, past and present, on the record about Krystal's extracurricular escort business. They were also cooperating with the prosecuting attorney. Lamey and Dengler claimed they knew nothing, that Krystal Gerrard had taken advantage of them and operated all on her own. However, Krystal had flipped on both of them, claiming that they not only knew about her escort service, they took a cut of the business. And she had records to prove it. Then Dengler cut a separate deal with the prosecutor to turn on his friend and partner Art Lamey.

On the Granger side of things, Monroe had confessed both to selling drugs and serving as driver and security for the escort service, solely on his own with no Ride EZ involvement. I suspected he had been told to sacrifice himself for the greater good of the Grangers as a whole, or else. Tanner's and Lamey and Dengler went down in a glorious mess of accusations, counteraccusations, and rats jumping from a sinking ship.

Meanwhile, Kent Morgan was denied bail both because of the heinous nature of his crimes and because his financial resources made him a flight risk. His wife Sydney had filed for divorce and left town with her daughter. His business was in the process of being sold, and, no doubt, renamed and rebranded.

The best news was that Troy continued to improve. He was released from the hospital and allowed to go home under the watchful eye of his mother, who had moved in for the duration of his recovery. I avoided visiting him if I saw her car in the driveway. She had dropped her overt hostility at Troy's insistence, but she still didn't like me.

When I stopped in one afternoon to check on him, he was in exceptionally good spirits.

"My doctor said I can go back to work in another couple of weeks. If you want me, that is."

"Troy, that's amazing. Of course we want you. Why would you even ask?"

"Because I did a bunch of dumb things. Missing all the early stuff when Jancee's body was found. Pushing Wes Morgan on the escorts and Jancee. Going out to meet with Kent without telling anybody. I almost got myself killed. It's weird I can't remember anything past leaving the office to go to Stan's Bar that night. If it wasn't for my notes being pretty clear, I wouldn't even know I'd been there."

"They're extremely clear, because that's what you do. You're precise, you're organized, you're smart. So, you don't always get things right. Nobody does. You might have made different decisions if I'd been a better listener, a better explainer. Troy, I know I can get a little—or a lot—cranky sometimes. Call me out on it. Miguel does. Or own it if you deserve it. But don't doubt yourself because of me. You were key to breaking this story. You gave us Lewis, the first crack in Kent's wall. That was pivotal. Yes, I want you back."

"Okay. You won't be sorry. Count on it."

"I will."

Coop won the election handily.

His victory party, planned by Miguel and hosted at McClain's, was a great night. I looked around the room at so many people I knew—and even more that I didn't—laughing, talking, drinking—there was even a little dancing going on. My mom and Paul were there, Maggie, Miguel, Courtnee, Ross, and a bunch of guys from the sheriff's office, including Owen Fike. Dale Darmody, Rudy Davis, and Erin Harper from the Himmel Police Department. But no Rob Porter, who was the HPD captain, Coop's former friend, and then his chief reason for leaving.

I saw Father Lindstrom talking to Ricky and his uncle. The only person I really cared about who wasn't there was Gabe. He'd come for the early part of the night but had to leave before we knew for sure that Coop had won by a landslide. Dominic's babysitter could only stay until ten.

I spotted Coop sitting on a stool near the end of the bar by himself. I grabbed the seat next to him.

"Well, you did it. And you're going to be a great sheriff."

"Thanks. I didn't do it alone, though."

"Oh, I know. Your dad was great. Look at him over there."

I pointed to a table where Dan Cooper sat talking to a group of people.

"He's so proud of you, he hasn't stopped smiling all night."

"I wasn't talking about my dad. Or Kristin, or your mom, or any of the other people who helped me get elected. I'm grateful to all of them. But I was talking about you. When Spencer was going after Dad, you're the one who put an end to it. Art Lamey was running ahead until you broke the story on Tanner's. And the follow-ups that came after about the escorts, the double set of books, the drug sales. You made it really easy for people to choose."

"That's me, the kingmaker. Or at least the sheriff-maker."

"No. That's you, the friend everyone wishes they had. I'm glad you're mine."

I was really touched, but I'm not always at my quickest when a heartfelt answer is called for. I paused for half a beat, and before I spoke, Sherry came up on his other side.

"Hi there, Coop. I thought you could use one of these. On the house," she said.

She slid a beer in front of him, managing, as usual, to practically lay in his lap as she did.

"Thank you," he said.

"No problem. I'm a big supporter of the sheriff's office. Especially now." She batted her eyelashes at him.

"Hello, Sherry," I said.

"Oh. Hi. I didn't see you there. Where's your boyfriend? Did you lose another one?"

I shook my head but didn't answer. Sherry and I have had this mean girl thing going since high school, but I didn't have the energy to participate at the moment.

"Coop, I have to go. I promised Gabe I'd come by with a report on the party and a piece of victory cake."

"Sure, tell him I'm sorry he couldn't stay."

"I will. See you later, Sheriff."

On impulse, and okay, maybe to irritate Sherry, I leaned down as I left to kiss him on the cheek. At the same moment he turned his head to answer something she said, so our lips touched instead. We both pulled away, startled.

"Hey, I didn't mean to do that," I said, laughing. "I'm sorry!"

"I'm —"

He didn't get to finish, because suddenly the crowd started chanting his name. His girlfriend Kristin came and pulled him away to the makeshift stage to give his victory speech. I waved to them both as I left.

On the way to Gabe's I thought about how the night could have ended if Coop hadn't won. He wouldn't have stayed, and I was pretty used to having him around. And Gabe was right, I don't like change. Although I was in the middle of a pretty big one right then.

The more time I spent with Dominic, the more I enjoyed him. Gabe was already crazy about him. It was fun to see them together. He had fully embraced the whole dad thing, and for Dom's sake I was glad. I admit to missing the ability to be more spontaneous than you can be with a child in the picture, but it wasn't that bad. And it wasn't like Dominic didn't have a mother. He wasn't going to be with Gabe full time. When Lucy was done filming, she'd be picking him up and then they'd work out a more regular custody arrangement.

As I turned into Gabe's driveway my phone pinged with a two-word text from Coop.

"I'm not."

DANGEROUS WATERS: Leah Nash #8

True-crime writer Leah Nash is reluctantly drawn into a modern family drama with a very old story to tell.

Bryan Crawford's murder is the perfect crime: no witness, no weapon, no indication that his death is anything other than the result of diabetes complications.

That's what the medical examiner says.
That's what the autopsy proves.
And that's what the killer is counting on.

But when new evidence surfaces, crime writer Leah Nash is pulled into the investigation, and all bets are off.

Leah quickly zeroes in on the dysfunctional dynamics of the Crawford family. Beneath the happy fable they tell the world lies a dark tale of jealousy, greed, and revenge.

Bryan's wife, daughter, sister, and stepson each have secrets to hide. Every one of them have reasons to want Bryan dead. And they are all going to great lengths to keep Leah from the truth.

Then Leah makes a shocking discovery, and is propelled into a confrontation with the killer. It's a fight she must win to save someone she loves. But time is running out. As raging flood waters surge forward, Leah acts...and the consequences will change her life forever.

Get your copy today at
severnriverbooks.com/series/leah-nash-mysteries

ACKNOWLEDGMENTS

Thanks are due to friends and family who patiently listened to the hundred and one iterations of the plot before I finally landed on the idea that I went with. Your reactions and suggestions helped immensely. Special thanks to my BSN daughter, Brenna, who helped me out with some medical terminology and reviewed copy to ensure it had at least a nodding acquaintance with real life in an ER.

As always, I'm grateful to my husband Gary Rayburn, for reading—and rereading—drafts, making suggestions (some of which I actually take), and for being an endless font of encouragement. And finally, thank you to all the readers who are following along on Leah's journey, and whose reactions, questions, and observations I love to read, and often use to help me make the books better.

ABOUT THE AUTHOR

Susan Hunter is a charter member of Introverts International (which meets the 12th of Never at an undisclosed location). She has worked as a reporter and managing editor, during which time she received a first place UPI award for investigative reporting and a Michigan Press Association first place award for enterprise/feature reporting.

Susan has also taught composition at the college level, written advertising copy, newsletters, press releases, speeches, web copy, academic papers and memos. Lots and lots of memos. She lives in rural Michigan with her husband Gary, who is a man of action, not words.

During certain times of the day, she can also be found wandering the mean-streets of small-town Himmel, Wisconsin, looking for clues, stopping for a meal at the Elite Cafe, dropping off a story lead at the *Himmel Times Weekly*, or meeting friends for a drink at McClain's Bar and Grill.

**Sign up for Susan Hunter's reader list at
severnriverbooks.com/authors/susan-hunter**